Bitter Gourd

鮑瓜

Bitter Gourd

Fang I-chih
and the Impetus for Intellectual Change

WILLARD J. PETERSON

New Haven and London
Yale University Press
1979

Designed by Thos. Whitridge
and set in Monotype Bembo type.
Printed in the United States of America by
The Alpine Press, South Braintree, Mass.

Published in Great Britain, Europe, Africa, and Asia (except Japan)
by Yale University Press, Ltd., London. Distributed in Latin America
by Kaiman & Polon, Inc., New York City; in Australia and New Zealand
by Book & Film Services, Artarmon, N. S. W., Australia; and in Japan by
Harper & Row, Publishers, Tokyo Office.

Library of Congress Cataloging in Publication Data

Fang, I-chih, 1611–1671.
  Bitter gourd.

  Translation of Ch'i chieh which is a part of Chi ku
t'ang wen chi.
  Bibliography: p.
  Includes index.
  1. Fang, I-chih, 1611–1671, in fiction, drama, poetry,
etc. 2. China—History—Ming dynasty, 1368–1644—
Fiction. I. Peterson, Willard J. II. Title.
PL2698. F33C5213 1978   895.1'3'4'   78–18491
ISBN 0–300–02208–5

for Toby

Am I a bitter gourd,
fit to hang up
but not to eat?

Confucius, *Analects*, 17.6

Contents

Preface

Sometimes as historians we are persuaded of the inevitability of all that happened in the past, that it could have been no other way. We also sometimes recognize that what we call history includes not merely the effects of some "inexorable forces," but also the sum of a set of individual actions. Deluded or not, men in the past have often enough acted as if their conduct and ideas of today affected their tomorrows. We probably all agree that their range of choice was bounded by certain temporal, cultural, social, political, economic, familial, and personal constraints, and we may agree that individuals are able to say yes or no or maybe, and are able to do some bits of action and think some particular thoughts which were not predictable. In the realm of Chinese intellectual history, historians have been most interested in phenomena involving change and difference, and we have been generally unconvincing in accounting for those phenomena. My intention in the chapters that follow is to explore the roots of intellectual change at one historical moment by portraying the texture of a brief period in the life of one man who was an important player in the drama of Chinese thought.

Over the years I have incurred an enormous obligation to numerous teachers, colleagues, and students. It would be out of place here to try to name them all. I must, however, name the colleagues who patiently read one draft or another and offered suggestions and corrections which improved the manuscript which became this book. My thanks, and unknowingly the readers', too, go to William S. Atwell, D. C. Lau, James T. C. Liu, F. W. Mote, Christian Murck, Larry Schulz, T'ang Hai-t'ao, L. S. Yang, and Ying-shih Yü. After their kindness, none of them should be blamed for the shortcomings which remain; I am responsible for all of the errors and infelicities. I am further indebted to Professor L.S. Yang for kindly consenting to write the *p'ao-kua* which appears as the frontispiece. I gratefully acknowledge the support provided at the inception of this project by a grant from the American Council of Learned Societies, and the support provided for the physical production of the typescript by the Princeton University Committee on Research in the Humanities and Social Sciences.

I write these words this evening under the influence of the fragrant path planted by the person who has most helped me to learn.

W. J. P.
16 Alexander
27 August 1977

Editorial Conventions

· The romanization of Chinese words is according to the so-called Wade-Giles system, modified by the omission of unnecessary diacritical marks, and by the use of *yi* instead of *i* in some instances.

· I follow the convenient but not strictly correct form of referring to Ming and Ch'ing emperors by the titles of their reigns rather than by their posthumous titles.

· Years are given according to the Western, continuous series (e.g., 1637) for the Chinese years with which they largely correspond (e.g., Ch'ung-chen 10, *ting-ch'ou*). Months are given as the Chinese recorded them (e.g., third month, fourth month). For example, Fang Chung-lü's year of birth is given as 1638; he was born in the twelfth month of Ch'ung-chen 11, which corresponds to 1638, but was January 1639 by the Western calendar.

· In giving a man's age, the Chinese convention has been followed of saying he is in his twenty-seventh calendar year (*sui*), rather than the Western convention of saying he is "twenty-six years old" after he has passed the twenty-sixth anniversary of his birth. Thus, Fang I-chih was born in 1611 and was in his twenty-seventh year in 1637.

· Place names are usually given according to Ming denominations, except when an englished form seems established (e.g., Peking, Canton). Twentieth-century names are supplied when they seem to be helpful to the reader.

· The following equivalents are used to indicate administrative units in Ming times: *hsien* and *chou* are districts (although strictly speaking *chou* might be distinguished as subprefectures); *fu* are prefectures; *sheng* are provinces; and the two *chih-li* regions are the Northern and Southern Metropolitan Areas.

· For the translation of titles of offices in Ming, I have followed where possible the renderings given in C. O. Hucker, "An Index of Terms and Titles in 'Governmental Organization in the Ming Dynasty,'" *Harvard Journal of Asiatic Studies* 23 (1960–61), 127–51, which may be consulted for the characters to accompany the transliterations given here after the translations of the titles.

· Weights and measures are not translated. Approximate equivalents are

> *li* 里 = 1/3 mile
> *mou* 畝 = 1/7 acre
> *shih* 石 = 133 pounds
> *chin* 斤 = 1 1/3 pounds

· Two units of weight which were also units of money have been translated:

> 1 tael = 1 *liang* 兩 (weight of silver) = 1/16 *chin*
> 0.1 tael = 0.1 *liang* (of silver) = 1 *ch'ien* 錢 (weight of silver)
> 1 cash = 1 *ch'ien* 錢 (unit of money, a coin mostly of copper and usually weighing about 0.1 *liang*) = 0.001 tael (of silver)

· Examination degrees have not been translated. The three most commonly mentioned ones are *sheng-yuan* 生員 (officially recognized student), *chü-jen* 舉人 (a man who has been "recommended" by virtue of having passed the provincial examination), and *chin-shih* 進士 (a literatus who has been "presented" at court by virtue of passing the metropolitan and palace examinations).

· Finally, when I indicate that such-and-such a passage "quotes" from or alludes to this or that source, I do not mean that the author of the passage *necessarily* had in mind the source I have cited in the annotation.

China in Late Ming

□ Prefectural city of higher
○ District city [hsien or chou]

□ Peking

PEI CHIHLI

SHANTUNG

SHANSI

□ Chi-nan

SHENSI

Yellow River

HONAN

NAN CHIHLI

□ Yang-chou

Nanking □

Soochow

T'ung-ch'eng ○

Lake T'ai

Sung chian

An-ch'ing

Hang-chou

SZECHWAN

Yangtze

Wu-ch'ang

○ Hsin-an (She)

Shao-hsing

□ Ch'eng-tu

□ Chiu-chiang

CHEKIANG

○ Chia-ting

Nan-ch'ang

Lake Po-yang

KIANGSI

HU-KUANG

Chi-an ○

Hsin-ch'eng ○

Fu-ning ○

○ Wu-kang

T'ai-ho ○

FUKIEN

KWEICHOW

○ Wan-an

Foochow

YUNNAN

Kan-chou

□ Kuei-lin

○ P'ing-lo

KWANGTUNG

Wu-chou □

□ Canton

KWANGSI

Chao-ch'ing □

Macao

Grand Canal

500 Kilometers

1 The First Generation of Ch'ing Thought and Fang I-chih

Historians for more than two centuries have recognized that an important shift in intellectual orientation was accomplished in the seventeenth century. The end-points of the change have been characterized in numerous ways, often in terms of pairs of labels. Thus, in Ming thought the emphasis is depicted as having been on enlightenment, on thinking, on the transcendent, on introspection, while, in contrast, Ch'ing thinkers stressed preparation, learning, the here-and-now, and knowledge gained from books. Abstract ideas, such as principle, mind, and human nature, gave way as the primary objects of intellectual inquiry to concrete, particular things and events. Or, if in the last century of Ming the dominant fashion was for men to look within their minds to discover guides to action, in the first century of Ch'ing men searched for evidence outside their minds, whether in books or the world at large; intuitionalism was displaced by evidential studies. More narrowly, in the late eighteenth century, the shift was conceived by some historians as the rise of "Han learning" (*Han hsueh*) at the expense of teachings pervaded by questions, and answers, brought to the fore in Sung (i.e., the so-called *Sung hsueh*). The intellectual scene in the seventeenth century was more diverse than is implied by any of the attempts to reduce even dominant outlooks to a few words, and the suitability of any particular words is arguable. Moreover, some strands of thought continued on through the century relatively unaffected by contemporary developments. Nevertheless, what seems unarguable is the assertion that a reorientation in the tenor of the thought was effected between 1600 and 1700, or, extending the compass of "seventeenth century," from the Wan-li (1573–1619) through the K'ang-hsi reign (1662–1722).

The shift was not accomplished in a moment. Some historians have emphasized the role of the Manchu conquest of China as a major factor in the reorientation, and thus minimize the importance of antecedents in order to focus on what took place after the dynastic changeover in 1644. There is no doubt that the events symbolized in that date influenced each person who lived through them, and any discussion of seventeenth-century history at least implicitly refers forward or backward to 1644, but if the shift was already underway before then, the Manchus were not a direct cause. Other historians have emphasized late sixteenth-century antecedents, and even Sung precedents can be found for much of what was "new" in early Ch'ing. My contention is that, precedents notwithstanding, it is to the 1630s, before there was a recognition that the Ming dynasty was in irreversible decline, that we should look for the point of departure of the new orientation in thought.

On the plane of intellectual trends, or the internal history of a particular sphere of culture, in which the development of ideas is accorded a dynamic of its own, the discussion by historians in the latter half of the twentieth century is mostly agreed that the shift is best regarded as a logical if not inevitable outgrowth of problems and concerns raised in the sixteenth century. To a large degree, the same "language" was still being spoken. This view, however, may be so true that it is tautological. An alternative approach is to bear in mind the perceptions of men in the seventeenth and eighteenth centuries who had leading roles in effecting and establishing the change in outlook. Although most of them had a strong historical consciousness, they could not understand the books they were writing in terms of the pattern of change in the "history of ideas" which we of three centuries later perceive. Some of them were not unmindful of making history by what they were doing and saying, but they could have no certainty, only hopes, of how later men would regard them. Moreover, the few men who are generally credited with being the founders of Ch'ing thought believed they were on a different course from men of preceding generations and, indeed, from most of their contemporaries. It is my contention that the lives and ideas of these men were not merely a function of "historical forces," but were a result of choices they made about how they would act and think. Each was able, within ill-defined limits, to choose what sort of a man he would be.

A Matter of Choice

Part of the impetus for evolving a "new" kind of scholarship in the seventeenth century came from a need to construct an alternative to government service, which for centuries had been an assumed responsibility of the educated man, but which also had been in tension with notions of maintaining one's integrity. One justification for remaining out of government service was on the grounds that a man did so against his will because conditions were temporarily such that anyone with scruples could not serve. Confucius had said, "When the Way prevails under Heaven, then show yourself; when it does not prevail, then hide,"[1] and it was later held that he did not serve importantly or for any length of time because he was not offered a suitable opportunity to implement the Way.[2] Yet Confucius wanted to exercise his capacities in government. He was waiting for a suitable offer for his "lovely jewel" (*Analects*, 9.12) and distinguished his motives

1. *Lun yü*, 8.13; Arthur Waley, trans., *Analects of Confucius*, 135
2. *Mencius*, 5B7.

from those of the escapists who would ". . . shun this whole generation of men" (18.6). Confucius would be a man among men, so much so that one of his disciples had to remind him that serving in government could not transcend all other considerations. "Pi Hsi summoned the Master, and he would have liked to go. But Tzu-lu said, I remember your once saying, 'Into the house of one who is in his own person doing what is evil, the gentleman will not enter.' Pi Hsi is holding Chung-mou in revolt. How can you think of going to him? The Master said, . . . Am I indeed to be forever like the bitter gourd that is only fit to hang up, but not to eat?"[3] Yet Tzu-lu himself also underscored the obligation to serve when he commented about the life of a recluse: "Not to take office is to be without righteousness. . . . A gentleman's taking office is to put righteousness into practice. That the Way does not prevail, he knows well enough beforehand" (18.7). The dilemma, then, remains. One must take office to help implement the Way, but not, by holding office, sacrifice his commitment to the Way. A difficult judgment was entailed in determining the shifting boundary between the responsibility to assume office and the need to withdraw if one could not be morally effective.

In later imperial times, that is, from the eleventh to the twentieth century, because civil service examinations usually were the primary means not only of gaining appointment to office but also of achieving higher social status, we should distinguish attaining a higher degree from holding an official position. When I use the term *withdrawal* to describe someone's conduct, I mean he fits into one of three categories: he has not taken any examinations (and such cases were rare among the highly educated in most periods); he has, or has sought, a degree but never served in office; or he accepted appointment, but not for a significant portion of his adult career. These categories sometimes are ambiguous when applied to a particular case, for they must depend on the historian's assessment of a man's motives and circumstances. The application of the term *withdrawal from government* is warranted in such cases when a *choice* seems to have been exercised, and not when, because of real illness or political misfortune, a man is compelled to remain out of office.

The character of the Confucian (*ju*) alternative pursued in lieu of government service did not remain the same. In the Sung dynasty, there was a tendency among a relatively small segment of the educated elite away from *wanting* to assume administrative responsibilities and toward choosing instead to concentrate on improving one's moral self and teaching others about the Way. An important justification for the decision not to accept a government appointment was found in the claim that one could better serve the commonweal by promoting morality, but the choice was seldom unproblematic and usually criticized. In the eleventh century Chang Tsai (1020–77), who achieved a lasting reputation as a moral thinker, disapprovingly observed that in the government there were men

---

3. *Lun yü*, 17.6; Waley, trans., *Analects*, 211. Cf. *Lun yü*, 17.4.

who regarded the art of governing (*cheng shu* 政術) and ethical teachings (*tao hsueh* 道學) as two separate endeavors.[4] In spite of such disapproval, the possibility of separating the two remained. Chu Hsi (1130–1200) stands for a number of lesser men who took seriously the aim of moral rectification which was a major part of the growing appeal of the ideas formulated by Ch'eng I (1033–1107) and some of his contemporaries at the end of the eleventh century. Though Chu Hsi served in various minor and local offices, he persistently refused to accept a post in the capital, except for one brief period at the end of his life. His political enemies accused him of not sincerely wanting to serve his government, while Chu Hsi explained his disinclination by citing the debasing character of current court politics.[5] An entire chapter of *Reflections on Things at Hand* (*Chin ssu lu*), the widely used anthology compiled under Chu Hsi's direction, was given over to the question of whether to serve in the government. The stress in the excerpts in the chapter was on realizing that righteousness must not be sacrificed for or to office holding—with the implication that it all too commonly was—but still recognizing the desirability of government service.[6] Although personal predilections and circumstances were factors in each individual's choice of whether to serve, a propensity to withdraw to devote oneself to moral growth and cultivation (*hsiu shen*) was built into the Neo-Confucianism (*Tao-hsueh*) that these men taught their followers. Commitment to government service and even to solving political problems was weakened[7] as fathoming principle and regulating one's mental state, philosophical speculation and contemplative introspection took precedence.

Cultivation of one's moral self continued to appeal to high-minded men confronted in the thirteenth and fourteenth centuries with the Mongol domination of China. Yet at the same time another justification for remaining out of government was gaining force. The task of preserving and contributing to "our culture" (*wen*) was evaluated as a means of serving the wider community at a time when government positions were unattractive if not unattainable. Aside from considerations of escapism and loyalty to the fallen Sung dynasty,[8] both of which played no negligible part in men's motives during the Yuan, being a

4. Chang Tsai, *Chang Heng-ch'ü wen-chi*, 11.159. Cf. James T. C. Liu, "How Did a Neo-Confucian School Become the State Orthodoxy?" *Philosophy East and West* 23 (1973), 485. Ch'ien Mu, *Chung-kuo chin san-pai nien hsueh-shu shih*, 5, suggested the implementation of Wang An-shih's "New Laws" was crucial in turning high-minded men away from government service in the eleventh and twelfth centuries.

5. Cf. Conrad Schirokauer, "Chu Hsi's Political Career: A Study in Ambivalence," in A. F. Wright and D. C. Twitchett, eds., *Confucian Personalities*, especially 165, 169–70, 175–76, 183, 186–87.

6. W. T. Chan, trans., *Reflections on Things at Hand*, chapter 7.

7. Ch'ien Mu, *Sung Ming li-hsueh kai-shu*, 24.

8. Cf. F. W. Mote, "Confucian Eremitism in the Yüan Period," in A. F. Wright, ed., *The Confucian Persuasion*.

"man of culture" (*wen jen*) was taken as a course imbued with moral and political connotations.[9]

In the fifteenth and sixteenth centuries, a significant proportion of the historically prominent Neo-Confucian (*Tao-hsueh*) thinkers and philosophers resisted serving in the government. A sample of every fifth biographical entry in Huang Tsung-hsi's *A Source Book of Ming Confucians* shows that nearly a third of the men did not take examinations, did not serve, or lived most of their adult lives in some form of private retirement. Many of these men self-consciously and even ostentatiously refused to accept office while seeking to *live* their commitment to a rigorously moral life, in the pattern set in the Sung.

Wu Yü-pi (1391–1469) is an outstanding example. From the age of nineteen he declined to participate in the civil service examinations, and devoted himself instead to the five classics and writings of the Sung Neo-Confucians. Earning a poor livelihood by farming, he worked the plow himself, and the students who came to him in large numbers also had to help in the agricultural work. His fame as an earnestly moral, devoted Confucian spread, but he refused all attempts to appoint him to office until at the beginning of the T'ien-shun reign (1457–64) he was more or less coerced to go to the capital in an attempt to add lustre to the court of the restored emperor. Wu remained in the capital for only two months and tried to resist all attempts to honor him. The emperor finally relented and allowed Wu to return home on a plea of illness.[10]

Why did Wu Yü-pi decline office? There is no easy answer. Possibly, as some who wanted to impugn his motives contended, in the hopes that he would be able to imitate Yi Yin or Fu Yueh, who were invited out of rustic retirement to provide crucial aid to their monarchs.[11] Possibly out of loyalty to the deposed Chien-wen emperor in 1402, although Wu's father transferred his loyalty to the Yung-lo emperor by serving as a Hanlin compiler after having been a tutor in the Imperial Academy in the preceding reign.[12] Or possibly out of a realistic assessment of the contemporary hazards of holding office.[13] Much later Wu was depicted as acting out of a determination to devote himself to living a moral life. In various ways he showed that he was rejecting the "world": he did not immediately go to the wife arranged for him when he was twenty-one, he wore humble clothes unworthy of his dignity as son of a Hanlin official, he did physical work.[14] Summoned to the court for an interview with the emperor, he later refused to draw on the prerogatives to which he was entitled after his brief sojourn in the cap-

9. See chapter 2 for a fuller examination of the ideal of "man of culture."

10. Huang Tsung-hsi, *Ming ju hsueh an*, 1.1–2. Also, *Ming shih*, 282.7240. Cf. Hellmut Wilhelm, "On Ming Orthodoxy," *Monumenta Serica* 29 (1970–71).

11. Huang Tsung-hsi, *Ming ju hsueh an*, 1.2.

12. *Ming shih*, 282.7240 Wu Yü-pi made his decision to abandon preparing for the examinations in the seventh year of Yung-lo, when he was visiting his father in Nanking.

13. Wilhelm, "On Ming Orthodoxy," 11.

14. Huang Tsung-hsi, *Ming ju hsueh an*, 1.1.

ital even when the local magistrate tried to subvert him with a trumped-up legal case.[15] When Wu returned south after the emperor had let him go, he was asked why he had refused to accept appointment. Supposedly, he only said, "I merely want to preserve my nature and destiny." (*Yü pao hsing-ming erh i.*) The narrow construction put on these words is that he realized that Shih Heng (d. 1460), the powerful advisor who had instigated Wu's being summoned to Peking, would soon fall from the emperor's favor, and Wu did not want to be involved;[16] but that interpretation would impute a selfish motive to Wu. If we read his words as being generally applicable to his entire life (he was over sixty-five at the time he made the statement), then we see he may have been preserving his nature and destiny all the while he tried as a humble commoner to live the principles he read about in the classics and Sung philosophers.[17] As has been observed, Wu Yü-pi ". . . was convinced that by teaching and moral endeavors alone he would fulfill the vocation of a Confucianist."[18] It is clear that Wu believed becoming an official would conflict with his aims, and his example remained influential.

Of Wu Yü-pi's many followers, some of the less well known ones passed their lives as commoners, living much as he had,[19] while others went on to be *chin-shih* and high officials. Wu's example probably influenced one of his students who established a reputation as a thinker in his own right, Hu Chü-jen (1434–84). Hu gave up all ambitions of passing the examinations after he had studied with Wu. He went on to become a famous teacher and moral exemplar who sought in daily life to observe scrupulously the details of the rites and implement the moral precepts taught by his Sung masters.[20] Another well-known fifteenth-century thinker, Ch'en Hsien-chang (1428–1500), was less clearly influenced by Wu Yü-pi and more ambivalent about accepting an appointment. After two failures in the metropolitan examination, Ch'en traveled to Kiangsi to study under Wu Yü-pi. He then "returned home and gave up any ideas about passing the examinations."[21] Years later Ch'en accepted a minor appointment in Peking and failed a final time in the examination before returning to Kwangtung with the resolve to forget about passing.[22] When asked about the difference between Wu Yü-pi's and his own experiences

15. Ibid., 1.2. The veracity of this story is doubted in Goodrich and Fang, *Dictionary of Ming Biography*, under Wu Yü-pi.

16. Ibid., 1.2. Shih Heng died in prison.

17. Wu Yü-pi's diary, which I have not seen, would afford a more subtle interpretation.

18. Wilhelm, "On Ming Orthodoxy," 12.

19. For example, Hsieh Fu 謝復 (d. 1505), Cheng K'ang 鄭伉, and Hu Chiu-shao 胡九詔 studied with Wu Yü-pi and did not take office. Huang Tsung-hsi, *Ming ju hsueh an*, 2.14.

20. Huang Tsung-hsi, 2.7–8. Cf. Jung Chao-tsu, *Ming tai ssu-hsiang shih*, 23–33, and Goodrich and Fang, *Dictionary of Ming Biography*, under Hu Chü-jen.

21. Huang Tsung-hsi, *Ming ju hsueh an*, 5.29.

22. Jen Yu-wen, "Ch'en Hsien-chang's Philosophy of the Natural," in W. T. deBary et al., *Self and Society in Ming Thought*, 60; and Huang Tsung-hsi, 29.

in going to the capital, Ch'en Hsien-chang wrote that Wu had wanted the chance to offer philosophical enlightenment to the emperor, but when frustrated he left, and as a *commoner* had not accepted an appointment to office. On the other hand, when someone has already been an Imperial Academy student and memorialized that above all he wants to serve in government (i.e., Ch'en himself), ". . . he therefore does not dare [later] to decline appointment spuriously in order to fish for a hollow fame. Some accept office and some do not, according to what is fitting for each individual."[23] Thus Ch'en Hsien-chang was acknowledging that as he had accepted a greater involvement in the bureaucracy, he had less right to refuse further participation than a commoner; he was acknowledging that some might refuse office on the grounds that such an action would prove their aloofness from the muddy world, although he denied that he was doing so; and he was defending the prerogative to be able to choose whether to serve, without saying it was necessarily "better" not to accept office. Ch'en was pressured in 1482 to go to an audience with the emperor in Peking, but he avoided accepting a position with pleas of illness and never responded to subsequent calls.[24] It is said that many of Ch'en Hsien-chang's followers chose "poverty and independence, disavowing wealth and high station."[25] By the beginning of the sixteenth century, then, there was a well precedented tradition, although certainly appealing only to a minority, of pursuing the study and practice of Neo-Confucian values while avoiding service in the government. Left aside here is the question of how "Confucian" these men were. Hu Chü-jen had already criticized Ch'en Hsien-chang for being too influenced by Ch'an Buddhism, although Ch'en thought he was an adherent of Neo-Confucianism (*Tao-hsueh*).

The most influential thinker and teacher at the beginning of the sixteenth century was Wang Yang-ming (1472–1529). By his example and his teachings he stood against this minority trend. He pursued an official career with great success, especially in military affairs.[26] Even though he suffered periods of banishment and disgrace, Wang's apparent commitment to government service was a neat validation of his insistence on the unity of *moral* knowledge and *social* action. The thrust of his teachings can be taken as an attempt to bridge the developing sense that involvement in the affairs of state could be in inevitable conflict with moral integrity. Many of Wang's followers passed examinations and had long careers in office,[27] but some of the most prominent ones exhibited an ambivalence about serving. One of his outstanding disciples, Wang Chi (1498–

23. Ch'en Hsien-chang, quoted in Huang Tsung-hsi, *Ming ju hsueh an*, 5.29 and 31.

24. Jen Yu-wen, "Ch'en's Philosophy," 62.

25. Huang Tsung-hsi, 5.28. Not many names are cited, but Chang Hsu 張詡 and Li K'ung-hsiu 李孔修 are two obvious examples.

26. Cf. Wing-tsit Chan, "Wang Yang-ming: A Biography," *Philosophy East and West* 22 (1972), 66–72, and Goodrich and Fang, *Dictionary of Ming Biography*, under Wang Shou-jen.

27. Huang Tsung-hsi, 11.94–95.

1583), had failed in the 1523 metropolitan examination and did not want to go to Peking for the 1526 session. Persuaded by Wang Yang-ming to take the examination, Wang Chi passed, as did his fellow student Ch'ien Te-hung (1496–1574). As they waited for the palace examination, which would confirm them as *chin-shih*, Wang and Ch'ien concluded that the men currently responsible for the conduct of government affairs were not sufficiently involved with moral learning. "How is this a time for you or me to serve?" Wang said to Ch'ien, and without participating in the palace examination they both left to return to studying and teaching.[28] Later, in 1532, after they had mourned Wang Yang-ming's death, both Wang Chi and Ch'ien Te-hung went to the capital and became *chin-shih*. Ch'ien continued with an official career. Wang served two short terms as a secretary in Nanking and then retired to spend the last forty years of his life lecturing on moral teachings.[29]

In Ming times men who thought themselves Confucian were aware of confronting a choice. On the one hand, there were those who, continuing to profess their veneration of the teachings of Confucius and the classics, held that the highest duty and aim was to serve in office. On the other hand, there were those who, instead of giving or implying the traditional apology, "I would serve in government if conditions were suitable," determined they would not serve short of physical coercion. It was more than prudence that was leading men to forgo government service, and they were not simply finding satisfaction in promoting morality as a consolation for failing to attain an appointment. The relative devaluation of holding office left more scope for the particular Neo-Confucian (*Tao-hsueh*) form of withdrawing to devote oneself to moral self-improvement; withdrawal was the course to be followed by men with a heightened sense of morality.[30] But as it came to involve an asceticism, even self-abnegation, in abstaining from the concerns of the world, such withdrawal was subject to criticism as a selfish pursuit influenced by Ch'an Buddhism.

In opposition to the tendency to condone withdrawal, the leaders at the Tung-lin Academy aimed at bridging the gap they sensed between personal morality and political conduct by recovering the authentic meaning of Neo-Confucian teachings and opposing the supposed breakdown in morality represented both by some of the men associated with the T'ai-chou school and by the political climate at the capital.[31] In contrast to the Ming thinkers who avoided involvement in politics, Ku Hsien-ch'eng (1550–1612), one of the prime

28. Ibid., 12.101.

29. Ibid. Cf. Goodrich and Fang, under Ch'ien Te-hung and Wang Chi.

30. Cf. Wilhelm, "On Ming Orthodoxy," 5–6. Wilhelm seems too negative in his formulation of Ming Confucianists' willingness ". . . to bear what at other times was considered a harsh vicissitude with few signs of frustration. . . ." It is my contention that they were not frustrated, but were choosing to remain out of office.

31. This point, or something close to it, has been made by several authors, e.g., Ch'ien Mu, *Chung-kuo chin san-pai nien hsueh-shu shih*, 18, and Heinrich Busch, "The Tung-lin shu-yüan and Its Political and Philosophical Significance," *Monumenta Serica* 14 (1949–55), 47–49, 75.

forces behind the Tung-lin movement, attempted to have a direct influence on contemporary court affairs from outside the government after he was forced to retire in 1594.[32] He saw the need to reintegrate the responsibilities of the official and the man in retirement.

> The superior man does not approve of officials at court whose minds are not set on their emperor, officials in the provinces whose minds are not set on the commoners, nor those [literati who, dwelling in retirement] in the countryside, meet in small groups to discuss human nature and fate and work at improving their virtue and righteousness, but whose minds are not set on implementing the Way in the ordinary world, even though they may have other admirable qualities.[33]

Ku's younger brother lamented to him that those ostensibly devoted to "moral teachings" paid no heed to the calamitous times, and that their teachings to officials and degree holders amounted to the phrase "The wise man protects himself," and to commoners the phrase "Live off one lord after another."[34] Although some of the men prominently associated with the Tung-lin Academy were disinterested in politics,[35] its contemporary impact and its historical importance were the result of an attempt to turn morality into politics. The catastrophe visited on the Tung-lin movement in 1625 again reminded some of the applicability of the phrase "The wise man protects himself" for any man who would be resolutely moral. The problem in the 1630s still was to maintain a moral, socially effective course and to avoid crossing the ill-defined boundary of Confucianism into the territory of the Taoists and Buddhists.

The First Generation

During the 1630s, a handful of men who are accorded a leading place in the development of the "new outlook" were in their twenties and facing these problems in making decisions that would affect the course of their thought and lives. The most prominent, then and since, were Huang Tsung-hsi (1610–95) and Fang I-chih (1611–71); Ku Yen-wu (1613–82) was less well known in the 1630s but subsequently achieved an enduring reputation surpassing that of the other two. Because the next set of important figures in the intellectual shift was composed of men born in the 1630s,[36] Huang, Fang, and Ku constitute the

32. Busch, 26–27.

33. Quoted as what Ku Hsien-ch'eng "often" said, in Huang Tsung-hsi, *Ming ju hsueh an*, 58.615. Also translated in Busch, 47–48.

34. Recorded in Huang Tsung-hsi, *Ming ju hsueh an*, 60.655. The first phrase is derived from *Songs*, "Ta ya, Cheng min 烝民," the second from *Mencius*, 3B4.

35. Busch, 48.

36. E.g., Chu I-tsun (1629–1709), Yen Jo-chü (1636–1704), Hu Wei (1633–1714), Wan Ssu-t'ung (1638–1702). Wang Fu-chih (1619–92) falls between these two "generations," but he cannot easily be assigned a formative role in seventeenth-century developments as he was largely unpublished until the nineteenth century and generated no "school" of followers.

"first generation"[37] of what came to be known loosely as "Ch'ing thought"; that is, they can be regarded as the immediate progenitors of the modes of scholarship which reflected a new orientation. A few other men might be included among the first generation, but they are of less historical importance: Ch'en Tzu-lung (1608–47), whose untimely death precluded his bringing to fruition the promise of the literary and scholarly contributions of his early years; Lu Shih-i (1611–72), whose encyclopedic interests touched fields later developed by more specialized men; Chang Erh-ch'i (1612–78), one of his time's foremost commentators on ancient texts, classical and otherwise.

Huang, Fang, and Ku had more in common than being born at about the same time. Sons in well-off, landowning families in the prosperous southeast, they all had high expectations as they grew up. In the 1620s they not only knew men who suffered during the 1625/26 suppression of Tung-lin partisans, but they also became involved in the activities of the Tung-lin movement's ostensible heir, the Fu she. As young men they were aware of the threat to social order posed by widespread peasant uprisings, particularly in the northwest, and the growing Manchu military menace in the northeast, but they do not seem to have been infected by an "end of our dynasty" pessimism. They perhaps knew each other, and they certainly had overlapping circles of friends and acquaintances. They partook to some extent of a Nanking-Soochow experience by visiting or residing in those two centers of culture during the 1630s. During that decade, or the first dozen years of the Ch'ung-chen reign, which was inaugurated in 1628 and ended with the Ming dynasty, Huang and Ku and Fang were turning their interests to the scholarship that brought them prominence.

Huang Tsung-hsi's importance in Ch'ing intellectual developments was due to his historical studies. He made contributions in other fields, but his in-

---

37. I intend "generation" to be taken in the rather rudimentary sense conveyed in Wilhelm Dilthey's assertion that it is a term applied to a relationship ". . . between those who in one way or another grew up together, who had a common childhood, a common adolescence, and whose years of greatest manly vigor partially overlap. . . . Those who received the same guiding influences in their formative years jointly constitute a generation." From *Über das Studium*, translated by H. C. Raley in Julián Marías, *Generations: A Historical Method* (University, Alabama: University of Alabama Press, 1970), 55. Also see Karl Mannheim's posthumously published "The Problem of Generations," *Essays on the Sociology of Knowledge*, 276–320. I agree with Mannheim's characterization of Dilthey's approach to the question of generations as "romantic-historical," in contrast to the "positivist" approach and to Mannheim's own, presumably sociological approach. Mannheim made a useful distinction between an "actual generation" and a "generation unit," that is, a portion, even a small one, of an "actual generation." No one should infer that the experiences and attitudes of Huang, Fang, and Ku stand for those of all men, or even all literati, born about 1610; they represent a small "generation unit" which became more prominent on the intellectual scene than any other. A final point that ought to be made here is that Mannheim was concerned with clarifying the concept of generation as a causal factor in historical, especially intellectual change; I am using the term simply as a convenient descriptive device and I accord it no explanatory power.

fluence on the compilers of the *History of the Ming (Ming shih)* and his still widely cited, monumental compendium of selections from the writings of Ming thinkers, *A Source Book of Ming Confucians (Ming ju hsueh an)*, together were enough to secure him a place as a major figure. Huang was involved in the efforts to restore the Ming house after the fall of Peking in 1644, and served in minor capacities at the Southern Ming court. In 1649 he returned home to Chekiang and devoted his efforts for the remainder of his long life to writing.[38] His major work was undertaken in his last forty-five years, but in his twenties he was already turning to what became his particular mode of scholarly endeavor.

Ku Yen-wu's contributions are more broad than Huang's and more concerned with textual problems, but they also have a strong historical orientation. His published works in geography, phonology, epigraphy and hermeneutics, as well as his most famous book, the *Record of Knowledge Gained Day by Day (Jih chih lu)*, which is a collection of notes on nearly every aspect of the cultural tradition, all can be taken as part of Ku's effort to shed critical light on the past in order to further understanding of the present. Like Huang, Ku was at least marginally involved in the resistance to the Ch'ing conquest, though he never served as an official in Southern Ming. By the early 1650s he was becoming reconciled to the permanence of Manchu rule, and he devoted the remaining twenty-five years of his life to a career of travel and scholarship.[39] Although we cannot be certain, since Ku apparently destroyed all of his writings from before 1644, there seems no reason to doubt his later assertions that he turned his scholarly attention to historical materials in 1639.[40]

Fang I-chih is less securely established in the histories written over the last two hundred years as a leading figure in the rising fashion of scholarship in the seventeenth century, although he was authoritatively cited in the 1770s as the outstanding early practitioner of the type of scholarship which Ku Yen-wu exemplified.[41] By 1640 Fang had begun to draft the manuscript which became the *Comprehensive Refinement (T'ung ya)*. The book focuses on the etymology, orthography, pronunciation, and meanings of words and phrases drawn from a wide range of human concerns, including medicine, astronomy, geography, and political institutions. His *Notes on Principles of Things (Wu li hsiao chih)*, in contrast, focuses on physical objects and processes, instead of language, but both books usually treat the historical dimensions of a given topic. Fang also was

38. Ch'üan Tsu-wang, "Li-chou hsien-sheng shen-tao-pei wen," in *Li-chou i-chu hui k'an*, vol. 1, 4b–5a. Ch'üan's view is followed in Hsieh Kuo-chen, *Huang Li-chou hsueh-p'u*, 7, and Hummel, *Eminent Chinese of the Ch'ing Period*, 352.

39. Cf. Willard J. Peterson, "The Life of Ku Yen-wu," Part II, *Harvard Journal of Asiatic Studies* 29 (1969), 201.

40. Ibid., Part I, *Harvard Journal of Asiatic Studies* 28 (1968), 131. Other biographers of Ku Yen-wu have noted his turn to scholarship in the late 1630s and emphasized his desire to pursue studies that were applicable to current problems in society. Cf. Hsieh Kuo-chen, *Ku T'ing-lin hsueh-p'u*, 21, and Yang T'ing-fu, *Ming mo san ta ssu-hsiang-chia*, 67–68.

41. *Ssu-k'u ch'üan-shu tsung-mu t'i-yao* (Shanghai: Shang-wu, 1934), 2501.

involved with the Southern Ming government after 1644, but unlike Huang and Ku, he did not thereafter retire to a life of scholarship. Fang became a Buddhist monk in 1650, and in the last years of his life did not pursue the scholarly endeavors he had embarked upon in the late 1630s. He thus was less influential on his own and succeeding generations.

There are three interrelated facets which link the otherwise separable scholarly products of Huang, Ku, and Fang. They were all concerned with evidencing assertions. They all tended to approach their subject matter historically, in a manner which implies that understanding comes only through grasping the developmental, dynamic character of moral thought, politics, geography, language, or whatever. They all, by emphasizing the plethora of phenomena, their complexity and multiplicity, manifest a disinclination or even resistance to the dominant view that there is an underlying, overarching, or unchanging unity that could and should be revealed to men's minds.

The three have something else in common. It is obvious that, if in fact they were the innovators in intellectual endeavors that the consensus of historians makes them out to be, they were discontent with prevailing modes of thought. Ku Yen-wu and Fang I-chih were "masterless."[42] They both acknowledged intellectual debts to elder members of their families, they both had teachers, and of course they both drew from the writings of earlier times, but they did not portray themselves as continuing the teachings of a particular mentor, even one at some remove in time. Their discontent was manifesting itself by the 1630s, and their perceptions of the contemporary situation helped shape the particular configuration of what they developed "anew." Using the example of Fang I-chih, I seek here to illustrate that willing choice was crucial in the evolution of the new intellectual orientation which was to become Ch'ing thought.

Fang I-chih

From our historical perspective three centuries later, what sort of a man was Fang I-chih? He has been put to a variety of uses by historians. Fang was cited in the 1920s for his contributions to Ch'ing scholarship and especially for his use of roman letters to represent the pronunciation of Chinese words. Later he was studied as a representative of the early Chinese interest in Western scientific knowledge. In the 1950s and 1960s Marxist historians interpreted Fang as a protomaterialist and even a dialectical thinker. He has been praised for his scientific knowledge. Most recently, he has been presented as an example of Chinese loyalism for his adamant refusal to serve the Manchu emperors of the Ch'ing dynasty.[43] Without arguing about the validity of any of these inter-

42. Huang Tsung-hsi, who regarded Liu Tsung-chou as his "master," clearly had a greater esteem for, and commitment to, Neo-Confucianism (*Tao-hsueh*) than did Ku or Fang.

43. See Bibliography, under Lo Ch'ang-p'ei, Liang Ch'i-ch'ao, Fang Hung, Willard J. Peterson, Hou Wai-lu, Sakade Yoshinobu, Joseph Needham, Yü Ying-shih.

pretations of Fang, I propose that we view him as one of the literati, a word introduced into the English language in the seventeenth century by way of Jesuit reports from China that referred to a segment of society for which there was no close European counterpart—the *shih*.[44] Fang was manifesting the concerns of other literati, and contributing to that body of thought which they held, at least ideally, in common.

Our understanding of Fang's life will be furthered if three periods are distinguished: from his birth in 1611 to 1639, when he was in his twenty-ninth year; from 1640 to 1657; and his last fourteen years, until his death in 1671.

In the first period, when Fang was growing up physically, socially, and intellectually, he was an advantaged young man. He had been born into a wealthy family whose members had been officials and landowners for two generations. For three generations the Fang family had maintained a reputation for moral rectitude. Fang I-chih was intelligent, gregarious, and facile in all of the refined arts. He was widely traveled and well connected. He was highly regarded by his elders, and a leader of his peers in the metropolis of Nanking.[45] Fang came to realize that what he might be lacking was a suitable outlet for his talents and ambitions. Thus, his years through the 1630s were a time of searching, of trying on various roles, being successful at all of them, and satisfied with none.

The first period of Fang's life ended with his passing the provincial examination at Nanking in the autumn of 1639 and going north to Peking, where his father had just been imprisoned for losing a battle to a rebel army while he was governor of Hu-kuang province. With that inauspicious beginning, the second period continued as a series of trials for Fang; he was struggling to be a scholar in the midst of a political environment that was in turmoil. At the same time that he tried to distance himself from involvement in the collapsing Southern Ming courts, first in Nanking, then in Foochow, and finally (for Fang) in Kwangtung and Kwangsi, he also kept close enough to be offered official opportunities in the refugee governments. Although he fled, and lived in remote mountain villages in the South, from 1645 to 1650 Fang repeatedly found himself in places where his life was at risk. Yet he maintained his involvement in scholarship, and in 1650 sent a box of manuscripts back to his family in T'ung-ch'eng. Events bore in on him, as the Ch'ing conquest of the South was resumed. Like a number of other men who wanted to remain loyal to the Ming dynasty, he shaved his head in the style of a Buddhist monk in the winter of 1650 rather than submit to the Manchu hair style and the Ch'ing general who captured him. He was an ambivalent monk. He took one of the foremost Buddhists of the day as his master in Nanking, and took up residence at a temple in northeastern Kiangsi by the winter of 1654, but he also completed an eclectic book entitled *Tung hsi chün* in 1652 and went into the ritually correct three years of mourning after his father's death in 1655. The end of the mourning period is

44. See *Oxford English Dictionary*, under *literati*.
45. All of these statements are based on evidence presented in later chapters.

also the end of the second period of Fang's life. At that point he could have discarded his monk's garb and lived in quiet retirement, pursuing his former scholarly interests, as his father had done for ten years, and as Huang Tsung-hsi and Wang Fu-chih essentially did from 1650 on. Instead, Fang unequivocally acted as a monk.

In 1658 he returned to northeastern Kiangsi, near Hsin-ch'eng, and worked at reviving several Buddhist establishments there. He also wrote a critique of the *Chuang tzu* from a Buddhist point of view. In 1664 he assumed the position of abbot at the famous Ch'ing-yuan temple complex near Chi-an in central Kiangsi. He mostly remained there until the summer of 1671. At about that time, a legal proceeding was initiated against him in Kwangsi, perhaps because he had been accused of anti-Ch'ing activities. Whatever the cause of the pressure on him, he apparently killed himself while going south up the Kan River in Kiangsi in the autumn of 1671.[46]

Our focus is on the end of the first period and the beginning of the second, on how, and why, Fang made the transition from being a young man who was conscious of a kind of intellectual malaise which affected him and his contemporaries to being a man who would involve himself with a "new" form of scholarship which was intended to be of social use and not for some private good. Fang wrote of himself in 1639, ". . . I am moved and want to do something. I feel for the age and want to help the times."[47] In articulating his sense of dilemma in the 1630s, he assumed he could choose a course through which he might exercise his sense of social responsibility.

In 1637 Fang I-chih wrote a piece of prose entitled "Seven Solutions" (*Ch'i chieh* 七解) that laid bare the alternative routes open to an earnest young man of his day. The piece has autobiographical implications; as Fang commented in the winter of 1638/39, "Thus, I wrote the 'Seven Solutions' as an allegory on myself." (*Ku tso 'Ch'i chieh' i tzu k'uang* 故作七解以自況)[48] Yet it was not a confessional document and does not enable us to gain easy access to the inside of his mind and motivations. Rather, it was a public piece, intended to strike responsive chords in the hearts of his peers. Fang noted a friend's reaction: "Ch'en Tzu-lung, after reading my 'Seven Solutions' as well as my response to Li Wen's poems and letters,[49] gave much thought to them and sent me a letter saying, 'Recently the intense resentment in what you have been writing goes beyond what is proper. It is inauspicious when someone is like that without good cause.' "[50] Even Fang's boyhood friend, Chou Ch'i, who wrote a laudatory

46. See chapter 8 for the evidence in support of the statements in the preceding two paragraphs.

47. Fang I-chih, "Sung Li Shu-chang hsu," *Fu-shan wen-chi*, 3.32a–b; also in *Fang shih ch'i tai i shu* (hereafter cited as *Ch'i tai i shu*), 2.17b–18a.

48. Fang I-chih, "Sung Li Shu-chang hsu," *Ch'i tai i shu*, 2.19a; also in *Fu-shan wen-chi*, 3.33b.

49. Fang probably was referring here to his "Sung Li Shu-chang hsu."

50. Fang I-chih, "Hsi yü hsin pi," 20a.

postface for the "Seven Solutions," gave Fang "a severe warning" about the ideas he was expressing. Fang mused, "I do not know why they [i.e., Ch'en and Chou] say that. However, it is a matter I ought to look into carefully. It could be that one should submerge his soaring, overbearing spirit."[51] His friends may have given Fang pause, but he did not renounce his ideas or destroy his writing. To this extent, at least, Fang meant what he had said. He had already defended himself. "To like to be depressed and hateful without good cause," Fang had written to Li Wen, "is not what a true gentleman would like."[52] What was too acerbic for Ch'en and Chou is all the more interesting for us.

The "Seven Solutions" relates how a young man, whom Fang called Pao-shu Tzu 抱蜀子, sought ways of escaping from the depression he felt when frustrated in the desire for a suitable outlet for his talents and ambitions. As Fang explained in a prefatory note, the seven solutions of the title "concern seven strangers trying to provide a solution for someone's depression, but his depression could not be resolved."[53] Pao-shu Tzu is saved, though not by the seven men who offer him advice. In the retorts he put in the mouth of Pao-shu Tzu, Fang I-chih evaluated the range of career alternatives, including some which are distinctly not Confucian, that he felt his peers might follow. The rejection of conventional modes of conduct and the realization of a better way represent in fictional form the discontents that Fang I-chih, and Huang Tsung-hsi and Ku Yen-wu, each in their separate styles, experienced, and the solution they found for themselves in a mode of life dedicated to the particular scholarly endeavors which came to characterize Ch'ing scholarship.

As a literary piece, the "Seven Solutions" adumbrates four of the characteristics of the new orientation in thought. It is difficult, draws on a wide range of sources, is original while being rooted in the past, and aims to have an effect on our minds and conduct. A friend of Fang I-chih pointed to the first two of these qualities, though from a different perspective, when in a postface he praised the achievement in the "Seven Solutions."

> Such talent as this is extraordinary. Nevertheless, were it not that Fang I-chih's broad learning is what it is, we would not perceive his talent. Galloping through [allusions to] the *Tso Commentary, Discourses of the States, Records of the Grand Historian*, and the *Han Histories*, weaving in [allusions to] "On Encountering Sorrow" [by Ch'ü Yuan] and the [two] "Ya" [sections of the *Songs*], and enslaving [the great prose style of] Chin and Wei times, of Han Yü (768–824) and Su Shih (1037–1101) in this piece, he has also put forth his own ideas. How can what men of the world call ancient style prose measure up to this? . . . When men do not have such talent, do not have such learning, and also are unwilling to make an effort of this difficulty, is it any wonder that they propound what is simple, easy, shallow, familiar, and even Buddhist?[54]

51. Ibid.
52. Fang I-chih, "Sung Li Shu-chang hsu," *Ch'i tai i shu*, 2.17a; *Fu-shan wen-chi*, 3.32b.
53. Fang I-chih, prefatory note to "Ch'i chieh."
54. Chou Ch'i, postface to "Ch'i chieh," in *Fu-shan wen-chi*, 2.29a.

In composing the "Seven Solutions," Fang intentionally sought to challenge the wits of his readers by making extensive use of unusual words and phrases, compacted sentences, and a wealth of allusions, some quite obscure. In my translation I have attempted to retain some impression of the difficult, sometimes stilted, quality of the writing.

Fang himself claimed the other two qualities. He was aware of a tradition of using "seven" as a symbol for "lesser yang," which suggests movement toward greater light and greater understanding. A possible source of Fang's title, "Seven Solutions," is in the early Taoist text, the *Classic of the Great Peace* (*T'ai p'ing ching*). It has a section called "The Method for Resolving Delusions with regard to Seven Modes of Conduct" (Ch'i shih chieh mi fa 七事解迷法),[55] which argued that virtue (*te*), benevolence (*jen*), righteousness (*i*), ritual (*li*), literary endeavors (*wen*), laws (*fa*), and military means (*wu*) all must be pursued, but all also must be subordinate to the Way as the basis for public order and personal content. If the point of the section is taken generally to be that men should not mistakenly follow partial ways, as advocated by various schools of thought, then Fang's "Seven Solutions" has a parallel point, as we shall see. I have, however, no evidence that Fang knew of this piece of text. He almost certainly knew of such pieces as "Seven Remonstrances" (Ch'i chien 七諫), often attributed to Tung-fang Shuo,[56] "Seven Stimuli" (Ch'i fa 七發) by Mei Ch'eng,[57] "Seven Disputations" (Ch'i pien 七辯) by Chang Heng, "Seven Arousals" (Ch'i chi 七激) by Ts'ui Yin, "Seven Fates" (Ch'i ming 七命) by Chang Hsieh, and "Seven Beginnings" (Ch'i ch'i 七啓) by Ts'ao Chih. Yet Fang was disparaging of attempts to merely follow these early efforts. In his preface he declared he was not working old veins.

> From Wang Ts'an's ["Seven Griefs" (Ch'i ai 七哀) of the third century] on, pieces with seven in the title have all been cast as persuasions of eminent men through the use of extravagant, grandiose language. Yet even the most stupid person should realize those imitative pieces could not move anyone's mind. They try to cover over their shortcomings with harmonious sounds and allusive elegance, but if someone were to read them aloud, there would be nothing in them to arouse or stimulate him. For this reason, changing the established methods for writing biographical accounts and ancient style prose, I have on my own founded another model so as to resolve [one's depression] for oneself.[58]

What follows here is a historical discussion of aspects of Fang I-chih's life and ideas into the 1640s, when he began to devote his energies to producing the *Comprehensive Refinement* and *Notes on Principles of Things*. The several aspects

55. *T'ai p'ing ching ho-chiao*, 729–30.

56. Translated in David Hawkes, *Ch'u Tz'u: The Songs of the South*, 121–34.

57. Translated in David R. Knechtges and Jerry Swanson, "Seven Stimuli for the Prince: The *Ch'i-fa* of Mei Ch'eng," *Monumenta Serica* 29 (1970–71), 99–116.

58. That is, instead of the usual model of having the author or speaker change a superior's mood or mind.

are illustrated, and in part defined, by the "Seven Solutions." It is translated in its entirety, but presented in sections which set the tone for the ensuing essay.

We are concerned here with the questions of why Fang I-chih chose to be a scholar (*hsueh-che*), what values were being satisfied, and what aims were implicit. By understanding Fang's motives, we enhance our capacity to answer a larger question: Why did "evidential studies" begin to move toward the center of intellectual concerns in the seventeenth century? My purpose is to suggest, rather than prove, that perceptions of the social and political environment helped shape the particular characteristics of the "new" mode of scholarly endeavor as it evolved from the 1630s.

2 A Young Man

Pao-shu Tzu's Talents, Ambitions, and Frustrations

As a young boy Pao-shu Tzu was of surpassing demeanor and grand ambition. In his ninth year he was able to compose poetry and prose. By
twelve he was reciting the six classics.[1] As he grew older he became increasingly broad in his learning and widely read in historical literature.
Bearing a pack,[2] he went seeking teachers. Letting down a screen in the
mountains to study in seclusion, he learned about Yin and Yang, Images
and Numbers, the signs of the stars, and observing the atmosphere for por-
tents.[3] He fathomed the fundamentals of music and investigated the important points of martial techniques. Yet he did not fulfill his desire to be like
the learned men of antiquity, so that when the times were suitable he could
help the whole empire thrive. His disposition was to take the overview and
he found it easy to grasp general ideas; rote learning, on the other hand,
not only was difficult for him, after a while he began to forget [what he had
memorized]. Privately he was extremely regretful. He regretted that his
abilities and intelligence did not come up to that of the men of antiquity,
and, what was more, that his body was weak and sickly. Moreover, he was
good in calligraphy, adopting the style of the two Wangs;[4] he was fond of
playing go (wei-ch'i) and flourishing a sword; he knew something about
performing on the zither (ch'in), Soochow singing, and other extraneous
amusements. Whatever he saw, he immediately wanted to do. He lived in

---

1. The Five Classics were the *Changes*, the *Songs*, the *Documents*, the *Rites*, and the *Spring and Autumn Annals*. The sixth classic, *Music*, was not extant as a text but nevertheless represented a branch of learning along with the other five.

2. A *chi* (or *chieh*) 笈 by Fang I-chih's time was a container for books, and the phrase
"bearing a pack" a metaphor for going away from home to study with a teacher.

3. *Hsiang-shu* 象數, taken narrowly, refers to the technique of consulting the *Changes*.
T'ien-kuan 天官 refers to the constellations and planets, knowledge of which was one of
the charges of the Grand Historian in Han times (cf. "T'ai-shih-kung tzu hsu," *Shih chi*,
130.3293). *Wang ch'i* 望氣 refers to observing the movement of the *ch'i*, or air, as a way of
discerning what was to come. Taken together, the four terms refer to knowledge of natural
phenomena as well as to the arts of prognostication.

4. The two Wangs were Wang Hsi-chih 王羲之 (303–79) and his seventh son, Wang
Hsien-chih 王獻之 (344–86).

one room and would restlessly stir about in it. Sometimes singing with accompaniment, sometimes drumming,[5] *he achieved a certain contentment. Why should he have been restless or uneasy?*[6]

When he was twenty, he thought to himself that by this age Ssu-ma Ch'ien was traveling in the world.[7] *What is the point of dwelling in a narrow lane and growing old at home before one's window? Again taking his books, he journeyed in the areas around the Yangtze and Huai rivers as well as in southern Kiangsu and Chekiang. In his childhood he had followed his father in traversing planked routes in the mountains, in viewing Mt. O-mei in Szechwan, in going down through the Three Gorges on the upper Yangtze in Szechwan and Hupei, and in crossing the Wu-i and T'ai-mu mountains in Fukien. On his way north to the capital he had ridden before the cities of Shantung. In his earlier travels he had given thought to the famous mountains and great rivers; there had been something about them that stirred his emotions. While journeying in the East it welled up in him that his previous [travel] was no longer the satisfying experience it had appeared to be. When he lived in his home village, he thought that in the world there certainly were men like those in antiquity, or even men who surpassed those of antiquity. Now that he had seen some of the men of his day, they were leaving him as unmoved as the mountains and rivers. Only a few men had truly understood him as a friend; he realized that the abilities and intelligence of those who are unswervingly dedicated to what is right and who achieve a laudable reputation are generally equivalent. With this realization, he returned home. He intended to retire to the mountains and summon his strength to write a book which would bring together knowledge about ancient and modern times as well as what is above in the heaven and below on earth.*

But a crisis occurred in his home district, followed by bandit gangs going back and forth across the district. Because murders and robberies and the pillaging by troops never ceased, he drifted to Nanking. How could he do otherwise!

His family for generations had been devoted to moral good, but to do

---

5. 或歌或哭, quoted from *Songs*, "Ta ya 大雅, Hsing wei 行葦." (Cf. Legge, trans., III.2.2.2: "With singing to lutes, and with drums.")

6. On *yen-ju* 晏如, *chi-chi* 汲汲, and *ch'i-ch'i* 戚戚, see "Yang Hsiung 揚雄 chuan," *Han shu*, 87A.3514. When young, Yang Hsiung was devoted to his studies. His wants were few, and ". . . he was not restless (*chi-chi*) about wealth and high standing, he was not uneasy (*ch'i-ch'i*) about being poor and humble." Although his family had little money or grain in store, he was content (*yen-ju*). Also see *Lun yü*, 7.36. (Cf. Waley, trans., *Analects of Confucius*: "A true gentleman is calm and at ease; the Small Man is fretful and ill at ease.")

7. 龍門, the name of the place in Shensi where Ssu-ma Ch'ien was born, is a way of referring to him. Ssu-ma Ch'ien began a period of extensive travels when he was twenty. See "T'ai-shih-kung tzu hsu," *Shih chi*, 130.3293. (Cf. Burton Watson, *Ssu-ma Ch'ien, Grand Historian of China*, 48.)

good now was impossible. His family for generations had been devoted to study, but those who did not study despised them for it. Although he lived away from home and busily went about his work, ridicule and abuse came his way day after day. If any of what he wrote was critical of contemporary affairs, he burned the manuscripts. Did he dare let men of the present age see them? The times were not suitable. How could he associate with his peers while seeking the acceptance of his superiors by being obsequious and accommodating?[8] On the other hand, his family was now poor and he was unable to show his liking for his guests. When guests arrived, they merited more than a simple meal of three dishes as was given to old men.[9] Yet those who truly liked him did not find fault with the meagerness of the reception.[10]

He never dared to show his esteem for the learning of antiquity by discussing the kings of earlier times. How much less could he use this learning to exhort others? When his thoughts touched upon his ambitions, he would begin to whistle and sing.[11] And as he whistled and sang, he lamented that no one understood him.

31b

Fang I-chih's description of the young Pao-shu Tzu was obviously drawn from his own experiences. Because it was ostensibly fictional, Fang was released from the constraints of humility, but anyone who knew him easily understood whom the character Pao-shu Tzu represented.

8. Reading 弟 as 梯; 突梯滑稽 quoted from "Pu chü 卜居," *Ch'u tz'u*, 6.88. (Cf. David Hawkes, trans., *Ch'u Tz'u: The Songs of the South*, 89: "Is it better to be honest and incorruptible and to keep oneself pure, or to be *accommodating and slippery*, to be compliant as lard or leather?")

9. On 浮, see "Fang chi 坊記," *Li chi*. (Cf. S. Couvreur, trans., *Li Ki*, II, 404: The gentleman "aime mieux recevoir un traitement qui soit au-dessous de son mérite. . . .") On 叟 and 三豆, see "Hsiang yin chiu i 鄉飲酒義," *Li chi*. At village celebrations for the elderly, those age sixty were given three dishes, or types, of food, and older men received correspondingly more. (Cf. Couvreur, vol. 2, 659; also, cf. vol. 1, 543, for the correspondence between number of dishes and official rank.)

10. In this paragraph, Fang I-chih has anticipated two points which were made more explicit later in the "Seven Solutions." First, he raised the possibility that a willingness to attach oneself as a "guest," or retainer, in the entourage of a person of influence might discredit one in the eyes of his peers. Second, Fang noticed that if one himself were to assume the position of host and accept dependent "guests," there would be some potential guests who, seeking to derive personal benefit by establishing a relationship, would stay away if the host did not have sufficient money to lavish on them. See below, "Seven Solutions," p. 84ff.

11. On 嘯歌, see *Songs*, "Hsiao ya, Po hua." (Cf. Legge, 2.8.5.3: "I whistle and sing with wounded heart,/Thinking of that great man.") Also see *Songs*, "Shao nan, Chiang yu ssu." (Cf. Legge, 1.2.11.3: "She would not come near to us;/But she blew that feeling away, and sang.")

Fang I-chih Grows Up

Fang I-chih was born in T'ung-ch'eng, Anhwei, in 1611, and passed his early years in a family setting that afforded him all the advantages of wealth, security, and education. An "uncommonly gifted boy,"[1] he conformed to his family's expectations by pursuing a solid foundation in the classics. His friend Chou Ch'i said that "from the time he was a boy, he was able to write 'ancient style' essays, poetry, and rhyme-prose."[2] Fang himself recalled, "When I was a child, my grandfather enjoined me to recite the classics and carefully read the histories, but not to mumble examination essays. By fifteen I was largely able to recite from memory the thirteen classics and to allude to histories such as the *Han History*."[3] His grandfather, Fang Ta-chen (1558–1631), as the eldest of three brothers and already at the time of I-chih's birth pursuing his official career in a succession of censorial posts, was by right the person to give direction to the boy's studies. I-chih's father, K'ung-chao (1591–1655), was still a young man engaged in preparing for the civil service examinations until his final success in 1616.[4] His interests would only have reenforced the direction of his first son's early education toward the classics and histories.

Fang I-chih's mother, née Wu Ling-i,[5] died when he was twelve.[6] His father's elder second sister, Wei-i,[7] widowed at seventeen,[8] had returned to the Fang household after mourning her husband.[9] She had been on very good terms with her sister-in-law (I-chih's mother), sharing all of the household tasks with her as well as an interest in literature and history.[10] She must have been an unusual person. According to her nephew, who wrote a postface for a collection of her writings, "She had the ambition of being a 'true man,' and always regretted that she was not male so that she could have a career in the world at large."[11] She had been a strict teacher for her young nephew,[12] and after I-chih's mother died, his aunt looked after him as if he were her own son for eight years.[13] I-chih recalled that he had been too young to serve his mother properly prior to her death and that although he had been as a son to his aunt,

1. Chou Liang-kung, *Tu hua lu* (Tu hua chai ts'ung) 2.8a. I have followed the translation of Chou's appraisal in Siren, *A History of Later Chinese Painting*, 125.
2. Chou Ch'i, preface, 1a, in *Fu-shan wen-chi*, 2. The preface was dated 1639.
3. Fang I-chih, "Yu chi Erh-kung shu," in "Chi-ku t'ang wen-chi," *Ch'i tai i shu*, 2.29a.
4. "Ming shih pen chuan," in *Ch'i tai i shu*.
5. *T'ung-ch'eng Fang shih shih chi*, 1.9a.
6. Fang I-chih, "Hsi yü hsin pi" *Ch'i tai i shu*, 4a.
7. *T'ung-ch'eng Fang shih shih chi*, 1.9a.
8. "Hsi yü hsin pi," 3b.
9. Fang I-chih, "Ch'ing-fen ko chi pa 清芬閣集跋," *Fu-shan wen-chi*, 2.8a. (Also in *Ch'i tai i shu*, 2.6a.) Written in 1629.
10. Fang I-chih, *Fu-shan wen-chi*, 2.8a; *Fang shih shih chi*, 1.9a.
11. Fang I-chih, *Fu-shan wen-chi*, 2.8a.
12. *Fang shih shih chi*, 1.9a.
13. Fang I-chih, *Fu-shan wen-chi*, 2.8a.

he had not dared to treat her as if she were his mother.[14] Nevertheless, at the time of his mother's death there had been an easy transition to the familiar figure of his aunt, and we may infer that Fang I-chih's early years were without severe trauma. The family was financially and socially secure, with both his grandfather and father holding official appointments until 1625.

Fang traveled extensively as a child. When his father received his first appointment to the post of *chou* magistrate, I-chih went with him to Chia-ting in Szechwan.[15] In 1619, when he was only nine, Fang was taken up a peak by a boatman to the celebrated Yellow Crane Tower (Huang ho lou 黃鶴樓) in Wu-ch'ang, near Han-yang.[16] At the time, the boy was passing down the Yangtze with his father, who was on his way to a new appointment as *chou* magistrate in Fu-ning, Fukien.[17] When Fang K'ung-chao was promoted to be Vice Director of the Bureau of Operations (*Chih-fang-ssu yuan wai-lang*) in the Peking Ministry of War in 1622,[18] his son was with him in the capital.[19] In a poem written years later Fang I-chih recalled the palace gates and great houses, the clamor and pageantry which had struck him when he was thirteen and fourteen.[20] At this time, his grandfather Fang Ta-chen was serving as a Regional Inspector (*hsün-an*) for the metropolitan area, a post which was a continuation of his off and on service in the censorate over a twenty-year period.[21] He was quickly promoted to be an Assistant Minister (*ch'eng*) and then Vice Minister (*shao-ch'ing*) of the Grand Court of Revision (*Ta-li ssu*).[22] K'ung-chao was also being promoted, in 1624 to Director (*lang-chung*) of the Bureau of Personnel (*Wu-hsuan ssu*) and then of the Bureau of Operations in the Ministry of War,[23] and in 1625 to Defense Intendant (*ping-pei*) at Kan-chou, Kiangsi.[24] K'ung-chao had not taken up the latter post when he was dismissed from office for balking at Wei Chung-hsien's proposal to invest his brother as an earl and for opposing Ts'ui Ch'eng-hsiu, who was becoming the principal ally of Wei.[25] Because of

14. Ibid., 2.8b.

15. Fang I-chih, *Wu li hsiao chih*, 12.21b. In ibid., 1.7b, Fang recorded that his father was still in Szechwan in 1618.

16. Fang I-chih, "I teng Huang ho lou 憶登黃鶴樓," *T'ung-ch'eng Fang shih shih chi*, 24.19b.

17. *Ch'ung-chen ch'ang pien* (Shanghai, 1917), 2.1b. Cf. Fang I-chih, *Wu li hsiao chih*, 1.4a, where K'ung-chao is quoted as saying he was in Fu-ning in 1619.

18. *Ming shih*, 260.6744.

19. Fang I-chih, *Wu li hsiao chih*, 2.4b, 8.37b.

20. Fang I-chih, "Yung huai 詠懷," *T'ung-ch'eng Fang shih shih chi*, 22.19a.

21. Ch'en Chi-sheng 陳濟生, "Fang Ta-li chuan," in *Ch'i tai i shu*, 1a. A *chin-shih* in 1584, Fang Ta-chen was appointed as a Prefectural Judge (*t'ui-kuan*) and was shifted to the censorate in 1602, but resigned on a plea of illness. Reappointed as a salt control censor in 1607, Fang requested to be relieved the next year. In 1612 he was assigned as a Regional Inspector for the censorate, but again resigned on a plea of illness. Thus, in his return in 1622 to the post of Regional Inspector, Fang Ta-chen was still at the same rank (7a) as when he started his career.

22. "Fang Ta-li chuan," 1a–b.

23. *Ch'ung-chen ch'ang pien*, 2.1b.

24. Ibid.

25. Hsu Tzu, *Hsiao t'ien chi-chuan*, 610, and *Ming shih*, 260.6744.

Wei's domination, Fang Ta-chen requested leave rather than take up an appointment of Chief Minister at the Nanking Court of Imperial Entertainments (*Kuang lu ssu ch'ing*),[26] and he returned to T'ung-ch'eng with his son and grandson.

While still young Fang I-chih branched out in his studies from the standard fare of classics and histories to more abstruse subjects.[27] He also began in a superficial way to acquire what later developed into a more than rudimentary knowledge in the field of medicine, a concern which had over three generations been traditional in his family.[28] His tutor, Wang Hsuan, whose *tzu* was Hsu-chou 虛舟,[29] was a specialist in the "River Diagram" (*Ho t'u* 河圖) and "Lo Writing" (*Lo shu* 洛書) and, more generally, in the numerological discipline of Numbers and Images (*hsiang shu* 象數) associated principally with the *Book of Changes*. He completed a manuscript entitled "From Whence the Principles of Things" (*Wu li so* 物理所), which Fang I-chih later drew upon in his own writings.[30] As a student, however, Fang did not make as much use of his tutor's knowledge as he later wished. As he lamented in 1643, "I was taught something about the 'River Diagram' and 'Lo Writing' when I was young by Wang Hsu-chou. . . . I particularly regret the waste of having practiced elegant writing, as well as the fact that I roamed about and yearned to be broad."[31] As later was observed of the young Fang I-chih, "[His interest in] the heavens, man, rites, music, law, mathematics, phonetics, letters, calligraphy, painting, medicine, even playing the zither, flourishing a sword, and techniques of combat, all splintered any purposefulness he may have had."[32]

There is no doubt that Fang I-chih by his late teens was enjoying a rather dilettantish way of life. From the age of ten he had been fond of practicing with swords, and at one point in a drunken disorder had wounded someone.[33] He referred repeatedly to his deep involvement when he was young in writing poetry,[34] and in 1628 together with a few friends he formed a literary society which they called the Tse she 澤社.[35] Joining with him was Chou Ch'i, whose *tzu* was Nung-fu 農父. Fang recalled that, "From the time I was binding my

26. "Fang Ta-li chuan," 1b.

27. Fang I-chih, "Yu chi Erh-kung shu," in "Chi-ku t'ang wen-chi," *Ch'i tai i shu*, 2.29a.

28. Fang I-chih, "I-hsueh hsu 醫學序," *Fu-shan wen-chi*, 3.41a.

29. Fang I-chih, *Fu-shan wen-chi*, 5.1b; 8.11a. Cf. *Ch'i tai i shu*, 2.29a.

30. Fang Chung-t'ung, "Wu li hsiao chih pien-lu yuan-ch'i."

31. Fang I-chih, "Chou i shih lun hou-pa 周易時論後跋," *Fu-shan wen-chi*, 5.29b. Cf. "Yu chi Erh-kung shu," in "Chi-ku t'ang wen-chi, 2.29a.

32. Ma Ch'i-ch'ang, *T'ung-ch'eng ch'i chiu chuan*, 6.17a. Some of these interests may have been only rudimentary before he was twenty, but they represent the scope of what Fang meant by "broad."

33. Fang I-chih, "Yung huai," *T'ung-ch'eng Fang shih shih chi*, 22.19b.

34. E.g., "Chi-ku t'ang wen-chi," 2.29a: "By nature I was fond of writing poetry and songs." Ibid., 2.29b: "In my youth I was given over to writing petty literary pieces." *Fu-shan wen-chi*, 8.18b: "When young I liked elegant writing."

35. Fang I-chih, *T'ung ya*, shou 2.5b.

hair [i.e., young adulthood], I associated with Nung-fu. Given over to literary pursuits, we sang together in the Tse she. Our ambition was to be Confucians (*ju*)."[36] Another member of the Tse she was Fang's brother-in-law, Sun Lin (1611–46),[37] married to Fang I-chih's younger sister. In part because he was orphaned when young, Sun remained closely involved with the Fang family.[38] Fang, Sun, and Chou would meet to drink, compose poems, and sing into the night the songs of lamentation of which they were particularly fond. They would drunkenly wander in the hills around T'ung-ch'eng. "Sometimes we would start singing in the marketplace as if there were no one around. Everyone thought we were madmen (*k'uang sheng* 狂生), but we said to each other that the rest of the world was mad."[39] Fang acknowledged that his paternal uncle, Fang Wen, and his maternal uncle, Wu Tao-ning, who were both about the same age as the three friends, did not understand why they acted that way, and Fang's father repeatedly warned against such conduct, but they could not stop.[40] Yet Fang I-chih even found it necessary to counsel Sun against being too easy-going.[41]

The three friends were not wholly frivolous. They talked about current affairs and military matters,[42] as well as discussing the difficulties they had come across in reading the classics and histories and also with regard to medicine and principles of things (*wu li* 物理).[43] At about this time Fang tried his hand at drafting imperial rescripts addressed to important contemporary problems, such as recruiting men of worth to aid in government and plans for restoring order in an increasingly troubled empire.[44]

After remaining out of office for three years, Fang K'ung-chao in 1628 accepted reappointment as a Director of the Bureau of Operations in Peking,[45] for with the accession of the Ch'ung-chen emperor and the death of Wei Chung-hsien in 1627, there were widespread hopes that the government had recovered its stability. With his father gone from T'ung-ch'eng, I-chih by 1630, when he was twenty, had begun a period of "roaming about" on his own, determined to follow the famous precedent of Ssu-ma Ch'ien, who at twenty traveled to see the world.[46]

36. Fang I-chih, *Fu-shan wen-chi*, 5.23a.
37. Ma Ch'i-ch'ang, *T'ung-ch'eng ch'i chiu chuan*, 6.6b, says Sun was thirty-six when he died in 1646. Cf. *Ming shih*, 277.7103.
38. Ma Ch'i-ch'ang, 6.5a.
39. Fang I-chih, "Sun Wu-kung chi hsu 孫武公集序," *Fu-shan wen-chi*, 2.27a.
40. Ibid.
41. Ma Ch'i-ch'ang, *T'ung-ch'eng ch'i chiu chuan*, 6.5a.
42. Fang I-chih, *Fu-shan wen-chi*, 5.23a.
43. Fang I-chih, *T'ung-ya*, shou 2.5b.
44. Fang I-chih, "Chi-ku t'ang ch'u chi," *Fu-shan wen-chi*, 1.1a–5b.
45. "Fang Chen-shu mu-chih-ming," in *Ch'i tai i shu*, 1b.
46. Fang I-chih, "Sun Wu-kung chi hsu," *Fu-shan wen-chi*, 2.27a.

Man of Culture

Fang I-chih's sojourns away from T'ung-ch'eng were most important to his social development. Basing himself in Nanking, Fang first rented a place on the south side of the city, but then moved to the west side to a house with an attractive garden. The house was so small, barely sufficient for his books and bed, that he named it "Room for My Knees"(Hsi yü 膝寓). His neighbor was his brother-in-law, Sun Lin, and their close friend from T'ung-ch'eng, Chou Ch'i, lived one or two lanes away.[47]

Hundreds of men went to Nanking to try to pass the triennial provincial examinations for the Southern Metropolitan Area (Nan Chih-li), the region which in Ch'ing times became Kiangsu and Anhui provinces. Some took up temporary residence there to avail themselves of teachers, bookstores, and mutual stimulation from others also seeking to succeed as *chü-jen*. Nanking was attractive as the place to establish one's reputation. It was the site of the 1630 general meeting of the Fu she, a literary society which Chang P'u (1602–41) had started in 1628. After the provincial examination in the autumn of 1630, which he passed, Chang invited some of the other successful candidates to a small gathering on a boat on the Ch'in-huai River. Among the guests were Yang T'ing-shu (1595–1647), who had ranked first in the examination, Ch'en Tzu-lung, Wu Wei-yeh (1609–72), who went on to be the top-ranked candidate in the *chin-shih* examinations the following spring, and Wan Shou-ch'i (1603–52). Huang Tsung-hsi and Shen Shou-min (1607–75), who both had failed, were also there.[48] In subsequent years, Ch'en Chen-hui (1605–56), Hou Fang-yü (1618–55), and Mao Hsiang (1611–93), all sons of men who had achieved high rank, went to Nanking in part to become better known as poets and writers.[49] Fang I-chih met all of them, and became the friend of some.

Another reason for going to Nanking was the pleasure quarter around the Ch'in-huai River where it entered the city from the southeast, near the Old Compound (*Chiu yuan* 舊院), the center of prostitution.[50] Yü Huai (1616–96) evoked its exterior wonders.

47. Fang I-chih, "Hsi yü hsin pi," *Ch'i tai*, 1a. T'ao Yuan-ming, in "Kuei ch'ü lai tz'u 歸去來辭," *T'ao Yuan-ming chi*, 136, wrote: "I lean on the south window and let my pride expand, I consider how easy it is to be content with just enough for my knees." Emended from J. R. Hightower, trans., *The Poetry of T'ao Ch'ien*, 269.

48. Huang Hou-ping, "Huang Li-chou nien-p'u," 23a, in Huang Tsung-hsi, *Huang Li-chou i-chu hui-k'an*.

49. Wu Wei-yeh, "Mao Pi-chiang shou hsu," *Mei ts'un wen-chi*, quoted in Hsieh Kuo-chen, *Ming Ch'ing tang-she*, 178.

50. For an extensive discussion of the Ch'in-huai quarter, cf. Howard Levy, *A Feast of Mist and Flowers: The Gay Quarters of Nanking at the end of the Ming*, which translates Yü Huai 余懷, *Pan-ch'iao tsa chi* 板橋雜記. Also see Wang Shu-nu, *Chung-kuo ch'ang-chi shih*, 200–02, and the description of the brothels along the Ch'in-huai river in Chang Tai, *T'ao an meng i*, 46.

Nowhere else in the empire is there the profusion of lanterned boats of the Ch'in-huai river. Strung along both banks are ten miles of river mansions with richly carved and painted balustrades and beautifully worked silk window curtains. There, when guests protest they are drunk, their host says they cannot yet go home. Boatmen plying back and forth point out for their passengers, "The famous courtesan So-and-so lives here at such-and-such riverside mansion. Having the number one provincial graduate is what she considers worthy of her." For a moment, as night falls and all of the boats with their lanterns are gathered together, the shimmering mass of lights is like the wriggling of a disorderly dragon, so bright as to light the sky. The throb of the drums to set the rhythm for the oars pounds against one's heart. From Assembled Treasure Watergate to Universal Help Watergate, the din goes on till dawn.[51]

The names and talents of many of the celebrated women there have come down to us,[52] and a few of the women were immortalized in romantic literature, among them Li Hsiang-chün, who had a famous love affair with Hou Fang-yü,[53] and Tung Hsiao-wan, the prostitute who became devoted to Mao Hsiang.[54]

The camaraderie that was possible in Nanking was also one of its attractions. Hou Fang-yü confessed that "just as soon as I had grown up and was literate, I was seeking friends in Nanking." Hou's father told him to call on an old friend, Fang K'ung-chao, when he arrived in Nanking, and it was then that Hou also met Fang I-chih.[55] Fang I-chih's assessment of Hou was that he was finely talented and dashing, and that he could not bear to be alone.[56] Mao Hsiang enhanced his reputation as a poet by entertaining lavishly, and Fang was in frequent attendance.[57] Playing on the word *yeh* 冶, meaning to melt or fuse metal as well as to seduce, and also used to refer to Nanking, Fang wrote, "Nanking being a place where sexual passion (*yeh*) is indulged [or, where one goes and smelting (*yeh*) occurs], literati from all over often form inseparable associations [i.e., are bonded] with other literati there."[58]

Drinking and singing, painting and poetry—these were the main motifs as Fang expanded his circle of friends in Nanking. The emphasis was on social, group endeavors, although some adopted a perhaps feigned attitude of being

---

51. Yü Huai, *Pan-ch'iao tsa chi*, 4. Also translated in Levy, *A Feast of Mist and Flowers*, 39. The section of river described runs from the east side to the southernmost gate of the city; see the map in Chu Chi, *Chin-ling ku-chi t'u k'ao*, following page 192. Also see Chu Chi, *Chin-ling ku-chi ming-sheng ying-chi*, photographs 22, 30, 31, 39, 303, and 304.

52. Cf. Wang Shu-nu, *Chung-kuo ch'ang-chi shih*.

53. They were celebrated in K'ung Shang-jen's drama, *T'ao hua shan*. Cf. Hou Fang-yü, "Li I chuan 李姬傳," in *Chuang-hui t'ang chi*, 5.11b–12b.

54. Mao Hsiang wrote an account of his relation to Tung Hsiao-wan in his "Ying-mei an i yü 影梅菴憶語," which was translated by P'an Tze-yen as *Reminiscences of Tung Hsiao-wan*.

55. Hou Fang-yü, "Yü Juan Kuang-lu shu 與阮光祿書," *Chuang-hui t'ang chi*, 3.2b. The meeting probably occurred in 1636.

56. Fang I-chih, "Hsi yü hsin pi," 24a.

57. E.g., in 1636 at Mao Hsiang's riverside pavillion. Fang I-chih, "Hsi yü hsin pi," 21b.

58. Fang I-chih, "Chou Yuan-liang 'Yu sheng' hsu 周元亮友聲序," *Fu-shan wen-chi*, 5.12b.

aloof from the ordinary world and its conventions, an attitude Fang had cultivated to some extent in T'ung-ch'eng. He recalled how

> when I came to Nanking, by chance I was with Lai-shang 瀨上.[59] As we were speeding in our horse carriage through the marketplace, he looked at me and said, "In this quarter there is someone who is truly able in poetry and calligraphy. He is not involved in the affairs of the ordinary world. He does not strive to establish a name for himself. He does not like guests. Nevertheless, he likes me, and liking me, he ought to like you." Thereupon, we went into [this person's] house. We drank my wine and we sang nineteen of his poems. Yet why did he peevishly lift up [his wine cup] at a distance from us? I looked at Lai-shang and said, "I frequently am not involved with the ordinary world, yet I must like [i.e., at least be respectful to] a guest even from the ordinary world. This morning[60] going through the marketplace, was there something impermissible [which I did]? When I see Hsiao-shan's 小山 attitude of raising [his cup] at a distance from us like that, I wonder why, when he has sung songs with us and lives in the Ch'in-huai quarter." Hsiao-shan said, "Let us just drink the wine. Why worry about someone's being distant or near?"[61]

Eventually Fang was accepted as a friend by Hsiao-shan. More typical was an outing Fang went on in the early 1630s to Swallow Cliff (Yen-tzu chi 燕子磯) overlooking the Yangtze north of Nanking. From the river the cliff looked like a soaring swallow, and there was an impressive panoramic view of the river from the mountain. The custom was to go there on the thirteenth day of the fifth month, when the crowds of men and women traipsing over the mountain looked like so many ants, and the stench of the smoke and steam from cooking was disgusting. Except on this day, the local people almost never went there.[62] Fang went by boat to Swallow Cliff on the appointed day with two older friends who were adept at painting, Yang Wen-ts'ung (1597–1645) and Cheng Yuan-hsun (1604–45). There they met others, including Sun Lin, and a party was organized. As the drinking progressed, "forfeits" were paid by performances of singing and playing the flute. When the two friends who had arrived with Fang were allowed to redeem themselves in the drinking bout by painting, someone joked, "When they impeach some official for receiving a 'Swallow Cliff scroll' as a bribe, I shall have been the informer." They moved on to a temple, behind which was a cliff with scenery that looked as if it were from the hand of Kuo Hsi, the Sung landscape master. There Yang produced an impression of the pines, stones, and mists at Swallow Cliff. combining the styles of Ni Tsan and Huang Kung-wang, whereas Cheng created a scene from the famous Yellow Crane mountain (Huang ho shan) in Hupei. That evening, after the party had broken up and the boats were returning to Nanking along-

59. I have not determined who Lai-shang was.

60. Reading 日 as 旦.

61. Fang I-chih, "Hsiao-shan shih shih-chiu shou hsu 小山詩十九首序," *Fu-shan wen-chi,* 2.26a.

62. Wu Ying-chi, *Liu-tu wen chien lu* (1900 edition), A. 7b–8a.

side one another, Fang's thoughts went back to the mountain as it had turned dark and the wind was picking up, with the moon coming up at the cliff and its light flooding the river. It was this scene that he set down on a scroll to add to Yang's and Cheng's.[63]

Fang may have been name dropping when he recorded his association with Yang Wen-ts'ung, for Yang was one of the most well known painters of his time.[64] Yang, from Kweichow, was a *chü-jen* in 1618.[65] He lived in retirement near Nanking, outside the Tame Elephant Gate (Hsun hsiang men 馴象門), west of Rival the Rainbow Bridge (Sai hung ch'iao 賽虹橋), where he had a beautiful garden with splendid views of the encircling mountains.[66] Fang thought Yang had the characteristics of a man from Chin times (A.D. 265–420), that is, aloof and untrammeled, and described Yang's style of landscapes as "loose" (*sung* 鬆).[67] Most commentators discern Yuan models in Yang's paintings,[68] and a Ch'ing writer thought Fang's landscapes also were in the Yuan style,[69] but it is difficult to be sure because so few paintings from Fang's early years seem to be extant.[70]

It was Fang's talent for poetry more than for painting, however, that quickly gained him a reputation in Nanking. When more than a hundred guests assembled for the banquet given by Li Yuan-su, Marquis of Lin-huai, for his thirtieth birthday, there was a poetry competition after the musical entertainments, and Fang gained the seat of honor by being the first to complete his

---

63. Fang I-chih, "Hsi yü hsin pi," 5a–b. For photographs of Swallow Cliff, see Chu Chi, *Chin-ling ku-chi ming-sheng ying-chi*, 71–72.

64. Chou Liang-kung, *Tu hua lu*, 3.8a–9a. Chou included a comment by Fang I-chih praising Yang Wen-ts'ung. Also see James Cahill, ed., *The Restless Landscape*, 119. Wu Wei-yeh included Yang in his celebration of nine contemporary painters (see Hummel, *Eminent Chinese*, under Yang Wen-ts'ung), and Yang's name received further notoriety if not fame as the character who painted the fan to transform the blood stains into peach blossoms in act 23 of K'ung Shang-jen's *T'ao hua shan*.

65. On Yang's life, see Hummel, under Yang Wen-ts'ung, and Sirén, *Chinese Painting*, vol. 5, 53.

66. Fang I-chih, "Hsi yü hsin pi," 4b. Rival the Rainbow Bridge was outside the southwest corner of Nanking's walls.

67. Fang I-chih, "Hsi yü hsin pi," 4b. Cf. Sirén, *Chinese Painting*, vol. 5, 54.

68. Ch'eng Hsi, *Mu-fei ts'ang hua k'ao p'ing*, 21–22. Also see Cahill, ed., *The Restless Landscape*, 119–20.

69. Chiang Shao-shu 姜紹書, *Wu-sheng-shih shih* 無聲詩史, quoted in Ch'en T'ien, *Ming shih chi shih*, 17.3050. Ch'eng Hsi, *Mu-fei ts'ang hua k'ao p'ing*, 28, also saw Yuan influence in an album probably painted by Fang after 1650.

70. The most extensive discussion of Fang's views on painting, especially his own and after 1644, is in Jao Tsung-i, "Fang I-chih chih hua lun," *Hsiang-kan Chung-wen ta-hsueh Chung-kuo wen-hua yen-chiu so hsueh pao* 7 (1974), 113–31. Sirén briefly discussed Fang I-chih in *Chinese Painting*, vol. 5, 139, and lists a few pieces associated with his name. There is a consideration of a hanging scroll by Fang dated 1642 in Cahill, ed., *The Restless Landscape*, 120–22. The assertion there (120) that Fang ". . . shared . . . [a] quality that suggests a local Anhui style" seems to be founded on very limited evidence.

poem.[71] He came to be ranked with Ch'en Chen-hui, Hou Fang-yü, and Mao Hsiang as the "Four Sons of Eminent Men" (*ssu kung tzu* 四公子),[72] who distinguished themselves as young writers involved in the lively Nanking society. Of the young men whom Fang knew, he seemed most impressed with Ch'en Tzu-lung (1608–47). Fang felt that he had never found anyone's discussion of poetry compatible with his own views until he met Ch'en.[73] They first met in 1631,[74] and they were together in Hangchow the next year.[75] Fang found in Ch'en's poems a nobility of spirit, a concern for the troubled times, and a genuineness that was generally lacking in contemporary poetry.[76] What impressed Ch'en was the several hundred poems in all styles that Fang showed to him.[77] Ch'en Tzu-lung spoke to Fang in such praise of Li Wen, a fellow poet and friend of Ch'en, that Fang, even though he was tired of traveling and wanted to return home before the imminent winter weather set in, went out of his way to call on Li in Sung-chiang. He arrived late at night but received a warm, informal welcome, and he and Li quickly became engrossed in discussing Ch'ü Yuan's *Encountering Sorrow* (*Li sao*). As Fang asked rhetorically, "Considering the rarity of two people's hitting it off so well, was our instant compatibility simply like the cases in antiquity of 'becoming old friends at first sight'?"[78]

Ch'en Tzu-lung and Li Wen were among the prime movers in the Chi she 幾社, a society which was organized in Sung-chiang in 1629 for the sake of friendship, poetry, and mutual stimulation in preparing for the examinations, but which also served to promote the "ancient" style of writing of which they were partisans.[79] The Chi she for most purposes can be regarded as a local branch of the more encompassing society, the Fu she, which had its roots in the 1620s. The ostensible initial aim of the leaders of the Fu she was the revival (*fu* 復) of ancient learning and literary styles, at the expense of the current fashion in writing, symbolized by Ai Nan-ying (1583–1646).[80] Ai promoted T'ang and Sung writers as the *true* embodiment of the principles behind the prose of the classics as well as that of Confucius and Mencius, and dismissed the writing of Chin and Wei times (i.e., the third to sixth centuries) and its later imitations as a

71. Fang I-chih, "Hsi yü hsin pi," 3a.

72. The term *ssu kung tzu* first appears in Han T'an 韓菼 "Mao Ch'ien-hsiao mu-chih-ming 冒潜孝墓誌銘," in *Kuo-ch'ao ch'i-hsien lei-cheng ch'u pien*, 14191, written in about 1694. Cf. Chin T'ien-ko, *Wan-chih lieh-chuan kao*, 1.22b (70).

73. Fang I-chih, "Ch'en Wo-tzu shih hsu 陳臥子詩序," in "Chi-ku t'ang wen-chi," *Ch'i tai i shu*, 2.10a; also in *Fu-shan wen-chi*, 2.29a.

74. Ch'en Tzu-lung, preface to "Po-i chi" 博依集, 3a, in *T'ung-ch'eng Fang shih shih chi*, 22.

75. Fang I-chih, "Hsi yü hsin pi," 8b. Also, Fang I-chih, "Hsiung Po-kan Nan-jung chi 熊伯甘南榮集," *Fu-shan wen-chi*, 5.21a.

76. Fang I-chih, "Ch'en Wo-tzu shih hsu," 10a–11a.

77. Ch'en Tzu-lung, preface to "Po-i chi," 3a.

78. Fang I-chih, "Sung Li Shu-chang hsu 送李舒章序," in "Chi-ku t'ang wen-chi," *Ch'i tai i shu*, 2.17b. Also in *Fu-shan wen-chi*, 3.32a.

79. Hsieh Kuo-chen, 187; Ch'ien Chi-po, *Ming tai wen hsueh*, 69. Atwell, ch. 3.

80. Hsieh, 146, 157.

derogation from the ideal of being straightforward and substantial.[81] Modern writing, Ai contended, could rescue modern writers from the malpractices in which they indulged.[82] On the other hand, Chang P'u, the leader of the Fu she, sought to revive the displaced mid-sixteenth-century fashions.[83] Wang Shih-chen (1526–90) had advocated taking the poetry of the middle T'ang as models and the prose of Han and Wei (i.e., as late as the third century) as manifesting the true spirit of the Chou classics' style. Li P'an-lung (1515–70), usually ranked with Wang Shih-chen as an arbiter of mid-sixteenth-century literary tastes, had earlier agreed with Wang's dictum, "Prose must be like that of Western Han, poetry must be like that of T'ang; nothing after the Ta-li reign (766–79) is worth reading."[84]

Ch'en Tzu-lung as a young man had established himself as a leading proponent of antique styles by publicly standing up against Ai Nan-ying.[85] Fang I-chih, being friendly with Ch'en, associated with the Chi she, although it was primarily for men of Sung-chiang,[86] and he was a member of the Fu she, but he did not follow a hard line in the literary controversies. His friends were on both sides. "Wu Ying-chi admires Ch'en Lung-men [i.e., Ch'en Chi-t'ai [?] who was the close collaborator of Ai Nan-ying] and also likes Chang Tzu-lieh. Chang Tzu-lieh is disparaging of Ai Nan-ying. Ch'en Tzu-lung [who was a friend of Wu Ying-chi] thinks Ai Nan-ying is not worth considering. Each has his point."[87] Fang's suggestion that T'ang and Sung models are more appropriate[88] and his stress on straightforward prose would relate him more to Ai Nan-ying than to Ch'en Tzu-lung.[89] Fang's critical position was opposed to the whole spirit of revivals. "Looking back over the last few years, one notices that it is not the case that there have been no 'changes of tune' [in literary fashion]. . . . When a change occurs, it becomes a tendency. When it is a tendency, then within the world someone arises who wants to rescue [those who follow the

81. Hsieh, 158.

82. Ai Nan-ying, "Fang shu ts'e ting hsu 房書册定序," quoted in Hsieh, 158. "Modern writing" is my translation of Ai's term, *chin-jih chih wen* 今日之文.

83. Chang P'u compiled the *Han Wei Liu-ch'ao pai san chia chi* 漢魏六朝百三家集 to circulate the models the Fu she was promoting. Ch'ien Chi-po, *Ming tai wen hsueh*, 69, 71. Also Hsieh Kuo-chen, *Ming Ch'ing tang-she yun-tung k'ao*, 160–61, and Hummel, under Chang P'u.

84. Quoted in Ch'ien Chi-po, *Ming tai wen hsueh*, 33. There was a sloganizing element in declarations of "acceptable" prose and poetry models, and they should not be taken too literally.

85. Hsieh Kuo-chen, 160; Atwell, "Ch'en Tzu-lung," ch. 2, Ch'ien Chi-po, 69.

86. Hsieh, 190. Cf. Fang's poem on drinking and singing with, among others, Ch'en Tzu-lung, Hsia Yun-i, and Hsu Fu-yuan, who were all involved in the founding of the Chi she; *T'ung-ch'eng Fang shih shih chi*, 23.9a.

87. Fang I-chih, "Hsi yü hsin pi," 22a. Cf. *Fu-shan wen-chi*, 1.9b for doubts about prose models.

88. Fang I-chih, "Wen-chang hsin huo" 文章薪火.

89. Cf. Ch'ien Chi-po, *Ming tai wen hsueh*, 71.

new tendency or fashion, as Ai Nan-ying had thought to do]. When rescuing becomes too extreme, then there arises someone who will rescue the rescuers [i.e., Chang P'u]."[90] Fang agreed with a friend's criticism of Chung Hsing (1574–1624), whose stress, in his selections published as *T'ang shih kuei* 唐詩歸 and *Ku shih kuei* 古詩歸, was on "lean" poems with no superfluities, a view which had dominated an earlier generation's critical opinion.[91] Fang added that it is exactly the slight differences that reveal a poet's individual character and make his poems interesting.

> Knobby trees and rocks with spots like mynah bird eyes are defective, yet men are more fond of them [than they are of such trees or rocks without such "defects"]. To be defective is to be different; to be different is to be rare. How could the lightness of effect in Yuan Ch'en's poems, simplicity in Po Chü-i's, coldness in Meng Chiao's, leanness in Chia Tao's,[92] as well as ghostly effects in Li Ho's, not be the tendency toward which each was going, [given the particular "defects" of his character]? Thus, the men in antiquity each had his particular time, place, and direction, although not fully realizing that it was fittingly so. Each had his "defect." On the other hand, when men of today single-mindedly try to imitate this or that defect of the men of antiquity, they are merely being negligent in their studies and doing what seems convenient to them.[93]

Fang, perhaps, was diligent in his studies of earlier poems, as suggested by his impressing Ch'en Tzu-lung with the range of styles in which he wrote, but he seems never to have found a distinctive voice in poetry.

Two prefaces that were written in 1632 for a collection of Fang's poems, even if we discount the expected rhetoric of prefaces, are evidence of the reputation which was accruing to the young poet. Ch'en Tzu-lung praised the talents and potential of his new "sworn brother" and appreciated his turning back to "ancient" styles, although he compared Fang to the Sung poet Li Chih.[94] The author of the other preface, Wen Chen-meng (1574–1636), the number one *chin-shih* in 1622, was unstinted in his commendation of Fang: "His talent is ten times mine. If you look at his rather eclectic spirit and his honest brilliance, then his talent simply cannot be measured."[95]

Fang I-chih thus was earning a reputation by devoting much of his time and effort to cultural pursuits in Nanking. Years later his activities were catalogued: "He was skilled in lyric poetry, prose writing, lyric metrics, songs, music, calligraphy, painting, various kinds of stone engraving, dice playing, and other games, as well as in playing the flute and drums, in staging theatricals, and in telling stories. There was no art which he did not master. He led an exuberant

90. Fang I-chih, "Hsi yü hsin pi," 8b.
91. Fang I-chih, "Hsi yü hsin pi," 9a. Cf. Ch'ien Chi-po, *Ming tai wen hsueh*, 99, 101.
92. These were conventional assessments of T'ang poetic standards.
93. Fang I-chih, "Hsi yü hsin pi," 9a.
94. Ch'en Tzu-lung, preface in *T'ung-ch'eng Fang shih shih chi*, 22.3a.
95. Wen Chen-meng, preface to "Po-i chi," in *T'ung-ch'eng Fang shih shih chi*, 22.1b.

life before the age of thirty. . . ."[96] There is the impression here of a dilettante, of a frivolous young man dissipating his talents. But such activities also had a serious aspect, for they represented the pursuits of a "man of culture" (*wen jen* 文人).

Yoshikawa Kojirō has sought to give a limited interpretation to the term *wen jen* by applying it to a "new kind of man" which developed from the fourteenth century and of which the prime example is Yang Wei-chen (1296–1370). Characteristically, these "new men" felt no affinity for philosophy or government service, and by choice devoted their lives primarily to poetry and painting, with overtones of aestheticism, sentimentality, and even self-indulgence.[97] Yoshikawa acknowledged that the term *wen jen* and even men who fit his definition existed before Yuan, but he defended his claim for newness by arguing that the earlier men, as in Southern Sung, were not important, representative figures, and they were not venerated by their contemporaries as were the *wen jen* in Yuan and Ming. In the Sung dynasty, according to Yoshikawa, cultural, political and philosophical pursuits were all held to be aspects of one Way. There is no reason here to be as insistent as Yoshikawa was on the newness of the mode of *wen jen*. Ku Yen-wu, for instance, wrote that men who ". . . really knew nothing about classical studies and did not understand ancient and modern history but denominated themselves 'men of culture' " had been numerous since T'ang and Sung.[98] What seems unarguable is that the relative importance and incidence of *wen jen*, "men of culture," was on the rise.

In Yuan and Ming times, many of the painters as well as poets best known to their contemporaries and posterity fit this narrow interpretation of a "man of culture" who preferred to keep his distance from official service. "While Sung scholar-artists tended to be government officials, many of the best known scholar-painters of Yuan lived in retirement."[99] Such a trend may be expectable

96. Chou Liang-kung, *Tu hua lu*, 2.8a; modified from the translation in Siren, *A History of Later Chinese Painting*, 125–26.

97. Yoshikawa Kojirō, *Gen Min shi gaisetsu*, 103–4. I have chosen "man of culture" as a neutral translation of *wen jen*; "aesthete" seems too pejorative, "man of letters" seems too restrictive.

98. Ku Yen-wu, "Wen jen chih to 文人之多," *Jih chih lu*, 19. In *chüan* 19 Ku was passingly disparaging of a number of literary practices which he felt were all too characteristic.

99. Susan Bush, *Chinese Literati on Painting*, 119. Bush focuses on what Tung Ch'i-ch'ang called *wen jen chih hua* 文人之畫, which she translates as "literati painting" and which she says "has been taken as the Ming equivalent of Su Shih's 'scholars' painting,' " i.e., *shih jen chih hua* 士人之畫. (169) Bush marks a difference by choosing the terms "scholars" for *shih* and "literati" for *wen jen*, but treats them as one and the same, interchangeable from Sung to late Ming, at the expense of distinctions that are suggested in passages she cites. She appears indifferent to the implications of her statement that in a late Ming writer's classification of painters, "a scholar's education, not office, is now the main distinguishing feature." (156; also see 152) Moreover, not all of her Ming examples support her concluding comment that there was ". . . a particular type of artist who was statesman, writer, calligrapher, and painter, ideally all in one; and the most important literati artists embody this ideal." (185) Also see 178–79.

under the Mongol government, but it continued in Ming.[100] For such men, who were only minimally involved in government, or not at all, arts were more than a pastime or entertainment, although no one perhaps set out to be a "man of culture" in this sense. While some painters especially were able to flourish on "gifts" from admirers, the "man of culture" usually had independent means, supported by his family's or patron's money, or sometimes even his own, gained from land, prior government service, or even commercial endeavors.[101] Seen in the best light, such "men of culture" eschewed ambitions of wealth and standing as officials in order to devote themselves to literature and art. In the worst light, they were regarded as parasites who squandered wealth, dallied in their leisure with miscellaneous amusements, and did no good. Both of these extremes are overdrawn. Moreover, it is difficult in the particular case to determine if the man was positively devoted to cultivating his art or negatively withdrawing from the rigors of the examination system and the hazards of official life. Usually both entered into his motives. At the same time, most educated men sought to be known for their cultural accomplishments as a further enhancement to their reputation, and this gave a competitive edge to the drinking and the singing, to composing poetry and dashing off handsome painting and calligraphy. Thus the ideal of the aloof, serious "man of culture" was debased in practice, but it continued to have currency. Some men put their efforts and trust into literature and books, calligraphy and painting, collecting and appreciating, as other men might put theirs into moral philosophy or politics.[102]

100. The great eighteenth-century historian Chao I (1727–1814) commented on the number (he listed twenty-two names) of men in Ming who as either first degree holders only or commoners achieved fame among their contemporaries for their prose, poetry, calligraphy, or painting. Chao I, "Ming tai wen jen pu pi chieh Han-lin 明代文人不必皆翰林," *Nien-erh shih cha-chi*, 34. Chao I was using the term *wen jen* in a broad sense which is implied by the translation, "man of culture."

101. Cf. Ho Ping-ti, Ladder of Success, 154. Ho also observed, "A large number of those who were intellectually alert, either due [*sic*] to hard luck in the examinations or owing to their personal preference for an easy comfortable life, chose to become men of letters. . . . The men of letters, while not strictly members of the ruling class, nevertheless constituted a formidable social force." Ho Ping-ti, "Salt Merchants of Yang-chou," *Harvard Journal of Asiatic Studies* 17 (1954), 165–66.

102. Although not treating the ideal of "man of culture" directly, Nelson I. Wu, "Tung Ch'i-ch'ang (1555–1636): Apathy in Government and Fervor in Art," in A. F. Wright and D. C. Twitchett, eds., *Confucian Personalities*, 260–93, provides much material that supports the "man of culture" concept while also exemplifying the difficulty of rigidly applying it to particular cases. As Nelson Wu observed, ". . . it is intriguing that, as a high official, he [i.e., Tung Ch'i-ch'ang] should have been thinking about placing himself in history as an important figure in art." (264) Although I am not able to argue the point at length, I would suggest that K'ung Shang-jen's play, *The Peach Blossom Fan*, involving as it does the figures of a number of Fang I-chih's friends in Nanking, can be taken as an elaborate memorial to the passing of the *wen jen* ambiance that had peaked in Nanking in the last two decades of Ming. I refer the reader to Richard E. Strassberg, "The Peach Blossom Fan: Personal Cultivation in a Chinese Drama" (Ph.D. diss., Princeton University, May 1975), and to Chen Shih-hsiang and Harold Acton trans., K'ung Shang-jen, *The Peach Blossom Fan*.

The recognition Fang I-chih achieved for his numerous artistic talents and social graces did not satisfy him; perhaps it had come too early and comparatively easily. In a letter to a friend he recalled much later, at a time when he was inclined to deprecate many of his activities as a young man, that "when I was with you in Nanking, we did not have any profound discussions. I was given over only to poetry and wine."[103] In much the same vein he wrote, "When young I was fond of elegant writing. Noble spirited and reckless, I regularly criticized everything.[104] I had a reputation which in fact was baseless, and I was profligate."[105] While in retrospect Fang disparaged the nature of his activities when he had been in Nanking, even at the time he seems to have been critical of what he was doing. "We have all been living in Nanking. The whole of our time is for banqueting and enjoying ourselves with our friends. For the most part our scholarship really does not come up to what it should."[106] Having spent several years in Nanking and in traveling, he had been energetically involved in the social life among other young men gathered at those places where wealth and talent were in competitive abundance. He had established a reputation with his poetry, painting, and mastery of other polite arts, yet he had not found the role of "man of culture," in its narrow sense, fulfilling his ambitions. There was an undercurrent of doubt.

Toward the end of 1632[107] Fang returned home to T'ung-ch'eng. In a poem probably written shortly thereafter, he conveyed feelings of misgivings about the way he had been spending his time.

> I traveled in the winter cold, the solstice was approaching.
> The north wind blew both day and night. Why was the cold so piercing?
> A snow cloud blanketed the earth at Curled Mallow Village.
> Despair had cried out to the night. They'd had to chop their mulberries down.
> At the fifth watch the wind abated, the sky was not yet light.
> With a shushing sound in the air above the rain was turning snow.
> I caught the long road in a glance that lowered and leveled the hills.
> A cock gave its call outside the gate. There were no tracks from carts.
> When wrapped in furs I mounted the horse and set off through the snow,
> Both of my hands held the whip that felt as cold as iron.
> A son who was away from home had now grown tired and weary.
> Why did he choose to live abroad so as to become a valiant?

103. Fang I-chih, "Yu chi Erh-kung shu," in "Chi-ku t'ang wen-chi," *Ch'i tai i shu*, 2.30a; also in *Fu-shan wen-chi*, 8.12a.

104. An allusion to Hsu Shao 許邵, who made it a habit to devote the first day of each month to criticizing everything.

105. Fang I-chih, *Fu-shan wen-chi*, 8.18b.

106. Fang I-chih, "Hsi yü hsin pi," 10b. Fang went on to report a sample of the detailed philological problems they had discussed.

107. I am not certain that this date is accurate; Fang's poem which is quoted here may refer to his returning in the winter of 1633/34. Certainly he was in Nanking in 1633 and in T'ung-ch'eng in the spring of 1634. Probably the poem refers to the winter of 1632.

Deserted fields were left unplowed, the signs of life were few.
The streams in the wilds were covered with ice. The bridges were all down.
I galloped a hundred *li* to return home for the very first time.
I entered the gate in the dark of night. The lamps were yet to be snuffed.
In the wind and dust the journey's road had been arduous and long.
Melancholy when we met, unable to speak a word,
My family and the rest of the house then all laughed at me,
"Year after year, year after year, always apart from us."[108]

The poem suggests that Fang was not so sophisticated and self-confident as he was sometimes taken to be in Nanking.

Doubts

In spite of the hopes for a return to order that accompanied the inauguration of the Ch'ung-chen reign in 1628, the tempo of turbulence only quickened. The threat rising to the northeast of the Great Wall did not abate. In 1629 the peoples who later called themselves Manchus even sent a large raiding party which moved almost at will and temporarily besieged Peking.[109] In Shansi and Shensi bandit gangs had become "bandit" armies with leaders who were beginning to manifest political intentions. Fang I-chih remained informed of all of this. Not only was his father a bureau director in the Ministry of War from 1628 to 1631, but the problems in the North were reported in the so-called *Capital Gazette* (Ti-pao 邸報), which was circulated in provincial editions to which Fang had access. Being mainly in Nanking he must have heard all of the latest news as well as rumors. He makes reference to the contemporary disorders as a grave problem demanding attention.[110] But it was not easy to comprehend the gravity of the mounting crises. Not untypically, Wu Ying-chi later recalled, "I still remember a friend telling me, when the difficulties began in the eighth month of 1618 in Liao-tung, that the state would have several tens of years of warfare, and my thinking that his words were absurd because the state was quite intact."[111] Fang recounted what a friend had told him had transpired in 1629 in Peking when a Manchu raiding party appeared at the walls of the city. The knees of high officials shook with fright at the clamor of troops moving to the defense and at the uncertainty of the situation. Grown men wept with each other. But his young friend remained unruffled. "He chatted and joked. He

108. Fang I-chih, "Ts'ung Yeh-fu tao chung huan chia 從冶父道中還家," *T'ung-ch'eng Fang shih shih chi*, 23.2b–3a. Yeh-fu is in the northeast of Lu-chiang district, east of T'ung-ch'eng.

109. Hummel, *Eminent Chinese*, under Abahai.

110. Fang I-chih, "Ni shang ch'iu chih shu 擬上求治書," *Fu-shan wen-chi*, 1.2a–b (written in 1630?).

111. Wu Ying-chi, *Liu-tu wen chien lu*, A.12a.

recited rhyme-prose and poems." Fang expressed awe at his friend's coolness.[112] Fang wrote these words in 1633 in Nanking, when the lower Yangtze had not yet been touched by Manchu marauders or Chinese peasant bands or, for that matter, Ming troops on campaign.

If the turbulence of the early 1630s seemed remote to the young Fang I-chih, it was brought home to him in a double sense in 1634 when he was back in T'ung-ch'eng. His father was there, too, having just completed three years of scrupulously observing the rites of mourning after the death of his own father,[113] when there was a "popular uprising" in their district. According to one contemporary account, for some months dissident elements, led by an indentured servant named Chang Ju, had been gathering strength. A secret group was organized around T'ung-ch'eng with Wang Kuo-hua as the leader, and Huang Wen-ting became one of the key figures because of his intrepid character. Their intention was to ally with one or another of the bandit armies which operated to the west. When no bandit army came east as expected, another plan to have an uprising in the sixth month was aborted by heavy rains. A new date in the ninth month was set, but word of the conspiracy leaked out. When officials began to investigate, the organizers had placards calling for rebellion posted in front of the local yamen and circulated rumors that they had enlisted tens of thousands of trained men and had contracted alliances with forces outside of T'ung-ch'eng. The wealthy families were in a panic and fearful even of their household servants, but they could not agree on a common defense. Apparently fortuitously, a fire started to the east of the city wall in the middle of the night on the twenty-third of the eighth month and precipitated an outbreak of violence. Fires destroyed hundreds of homes, the city gates were opened, and within the city "the cauldron boiled."[114] As Fang I-chih described it, ". . . a mob of commoners cut access to T'ung-ch'eng, burned, and looted. They formed strongholds, carried flags, and set fires in the night. All of the prominent families fled. This was a disturbance such as T'ung-ch'eng had never before experienced. Although T'ung-ch'eng was in fact prospering, a mean-spirited, deeply resentful current had been changing things for a long while. But who would have thought that there would be this outbreak with armed men?"[115] Fang added that at the time there was no magistrate in the district and that many of the indentured servants (*nu-p'u* 奴僕) were rebellious, although he gave no reasons.

One of Fang's contemporaries, Tai Ming-shih (1653–1713), later wrote about the uprising and explained why it happened in his home town. He suggested that in the 1620s and 1630s ". . . the established families and powerful

112. Fang I-chih, "Su Wu-tzu Chi-hsi tsa yung hsu 蘇武子薊西雜咏序," *Fu-shan wen-chi*, 2.22a (written in 1633?).

113. Fang I-chih, *Fu-shan wen-chi*, 5.29a. Fang Ta-chen died in 1631.

114. Chiang Ch'en 蔣臣, *T'ung-ch'eng jih-lu* 桐城日錄, quoted in Fu I-ling, *Ming Ch'ing nung-ts'un she-hui ching-chi*, 98.

115. Fang I-chih, preface to "T'ung pien 桐變," *T'ung-ch'eng Fang shih shih chi*, 25.1a.

clans were much given over to licentious and extravagant behavior. Their sons, younger brothers, and young male servants had continually been plundering poor commoners and acting illegally. Thus it was that the number of treacherous commoners accumulated and the two men [i.e., Huang Wen-ting and Wang Kuo-hua] became leaders of the disorders."[116]

During the disorders the Fang household supposedly ". . . was not destroyed because of their generations of virtue,"[117] but most of the local wealthy families suffered widespread losses. Fang K'ung-chao's public stance toward the dissidents was for leniency, but he covertly assisted the local officials in marshalling troops and supplies. In less than a month some thirty ringleaders had been killed and sixty others captured. Because the uprising was easily suppressed, K'ung-chao urged that care be taken that the troops not kill any law-abiding person. After T'ung-ch'eng had been calmed, "bandit" armies were still attacking many places north of the River. K'ung-chao suspected that they would move south, through T'ung-ch'eng, and he was instrumental in raising funds and making preparations for the defense of the walled city.[118] Fang I-chih wrote of his father, "He personally was in the forefront, day and night mounting the walls, working hard that there would be no shirking."[119]

Because of the threat of continuing disorder in T'ung-ch'eng, Fang K'ung-chao sent his second sister, who had been as a mother to I-chih when his own mother died, to Nanking with her elderly mother and some of the household.[120] They were not alone. In the 1620s there was a change in the reasons why people moved to Nanking. Previously, men engaged in commerce or studies had taken up residence there, but seldom brought their families. As the troubles with the Manchus grew, northerners began to arrive in Nanking, and with the Miao uprisings, officials from Yunnan and Kweichow began to remain in the Nanking area rather than go home. In the 1630s, as popular uprisings occurred in various districts in the Nanking Metropolitan Area, officials began to move their families to the city, and after the violence in T'ung-ch'eng, "nine out of ten of the rich and powerful families north of the River [in modern

---

116. Tai Ming-shih, *Chieh i lu*, 2a–b (2489–90). Mi Chü Wiens, "Cotton Textile Production and Rural Social Transformation in Early Modern China," *Journal of the Institute of Chinese Studies of the Chinese University of Hong Kong* 7 (1974), 529, speaks of ". . . the intensification of tension between landlords and their laborers . . ." as leading to uprisings and revolts in an atmosphere of "mutual suspicion and antagonism." To the extent that this generalization is a function of the growth in cotton textile production in the Yangtze valley, it does not apparently apply to the T'ung-ch'eng uprising, although one could argue for a ripple effect that altered social relations in all districts that had commercial connections with the main textile centers.

117. "Fang K'ung-chao mu-chih-ming," 2a, in *Ch'i tai i shu*. Tai Ming-shih, *Chieh i lu*, 2b (2490), also mentioned that the Fang family was the only one not attacked.

118. Ibid., 2a, 5a.

119. Fang I-chih, "Ssu yuan hsin 思遠心," *Fang shih shih chi*, 24.16a.

120. Fang I-chih, "Hsi yü hsin pi," 4a.

Kiangsu and Anhui] came here." People from Shantung, Honan, and Hu-kuang also began to crowd into Nanking.[121] Fang I-chih, having accompanied the women to Nanking, "craned his neck looking to the west" toward T'ung-ch'eng, where his father was continuing to prepare the defenses against the "bandits." Fang expressed his confidence that nothing untoward would happen so long as his father was there.[122] Soon rebel bands did surround the city, but met staunch resistance. After suffering a do-or-die attack on their camp and the death of their chief by a poisoned arrow, they withdrew.[123]

Subsequently, bands passed through the district five times, but they supposedly did not even dare send spies into the walled city, which remained more than well prepared.[124] With a great deal of hyperbole, Fang I-chih later wrote:

> For a long time the bandits wanted to attack T'ung-ch'eng, but because defenses in the city were mounted with such constant vigilance, the bandits merely went back and forth below the walls, not daring to come close. Assisting in the defense on the one hand were the distinguished worthies and men with ranks of nobility, and on the other hand, men qualified as officials and those with examination degrees. Time and again they were able to inflict losses on the bandits. T'ung-ch'eng's not falling was not only due to good fortune.[125]

The reality behind these brave words was a siege laid down by the bandits. After the city had been surrounded for three months, Ho Ju-ch'ung (d. 1641), exerting his residual influence from having been a Grand Secretary from 1629 to 1631, persuaded some officers to lead their troops to relieve T'ung-ch'eng. He promised contributions for the officers' expenses and provisions for their men. Fang I-chih and Sun Lin crossed the Yangtze and met up with the vanguard of the relief force, which entered the city (to collect on Ho's promises?). When the bandits were defeated, innumerable heads were cut off. This was, Fang commented, the first major victory for government troops north of the River for several years.[126] But the costs of the "disturbances" were substantial. An untold number of Fang's friends and relatives in the district were killed by what he said was called the "horde of three hundred thousand."[127] On top of that, agriculture was in ruins because the bandits did not leave until spring had passed and

121. Wu Ying-chi, *Liu-tu wen chien lu,* B.10b.

122. Fang I-chih, preface to "Ssu yuan hsin," *Fang shih shih chi,* 24.16a.

123. Fang K'ung-chao's tomb inscription, 5b. This incident apparently refers to the attack on T'ung-ch'eng by part of the bandit leader Chang Ta-shou's 張大受 forces as they moved southeast from Shensi in the winter of 1634. See Li Wen-chih, *Wan Ming min-pien,* 58. On p. 207, Li recorded that T'ung-ch'eng was attacked in the first month of the eighth year of the Ch'ung-chen reign, i.e., 1635.

124. Fang K'ung-chao's tomb inscription, 5b.

125. Fang I-chih, preface to "Teng p'i shou 登陴守," *T'ung-ch'eng Fang shih shih chi,* 24.15b.

126. Fang I-chih, "Hsi yü hsin pi," 6a. On Ho Ju-ch'ung, cf. Ma Ch'i-ch'ang, *T'ung-ch'eng ch'i chiu chuan,* 4.27b ff.

127. Fang I-chih, "Jih ch'ung huan 日重瓛," *T'ung-ch'eng Fang shih shih chi,* 24.15a.

the farmers had fled or died. Fang even heard it said that on the roads for a hundred *li* around T'ung-ch'eng there was no sign of human life.[128] As a local leader, K'ung-chao stayed behind in T'ung-ch'eng to help settle the suspicions and jealousies which had arisen when the immediate crisis had passed as well as to look after the family's interests.[129] He received credit for having pacified his home district,[130] and was recommended by court officials for his experience in military affairs.[131]

Later Fang K'ung-chao went to Nanking for his mother's birthday. After Fang I-chih and his brother had entertained her with poems and songs, their grandmother told them about the comparatively minor difficulties and travail her father and husband had undergone when they were young, and then she drew a lesson for them. "Because of the turmoil from the bandits, we have now moved house to live primatively south of the River [i.e., in Nanking]. How would we not resume seeking to prepare for the times? Moreover, you ought to become accustomed to toil and hardship in many things. Industrious and frugal, do not be self-satisfied [about your knowledge] or think of yourself as great.[132] This cannot be forgotten for even a single day."[133]

In Nanking Fang I-chih still seemed inclined to pursue the activities that had occupied him in his period of "roaming about." He acknowledged that at the time he did not really understand what was happening, but his widowed aunt sought to guide him with her warnings, and her eldest sister sent a letter from Shantung to admonish him:

> Your father in the past earned a reputation while serving in the Bureau of Operations and just now he has pacified the disorders and expelled the bandits. He is not sorry that he had not been reappointed to office, but is rightly apprehensive about [ill-conceived] discussions of military matters. Our household is on the battlefield, yet my nephew reads books and seeks "solid learning" (*shih hsueh* 實學). Why does he futilely moan in an embittered way and drink to excess? Your Heaven granted abilities are without limit. You ought to devote your attention to the real world.[134]

In a sense, his aunts were exhorting him to "grow up," to face realities, but Fang I-chih had to find his own way.

A course that was open to him was emulation of his great-grandfather, Fang Hsueh-chien (1540–1616).[135] He had gained fame for his writings and

---

128. Fang I-chih, preface to "T'ien chia huang 田稼荒," ibid., 24.17b.

129. Fang I-chih, "Hsi yü hsin pi," 4a.

130. *Ming shih*, 260.6744, and *Fu-shan wen-chi*, 8.11b.

131. Fang K'ung-chao's tomb inscription (*Ch'i tai i shu*), 2a.

132. Grandmother was closely paraphrasing from the *Book of Documents*, "Ta Yü mo 大禹謨."

133. Fang I-chih, "Hsi yü hsin pi," 6b.

134. Fang I-chih, "Hsi yü hsin pi," 4a.

135. Fang Hsueh-chien's dates, and the following account of his life, are derived from Yeh Ts'an, "Fang Ming-shan hsing-chuang," 1a–4a, in *Ch'i tai i shu*.

lectures on morality, and he is a good later example of a man who devoted himself to moral improvement at the expense of holding office.

Fang Hsueh-chien had been an intelligent child with impressive literary capacities by the age of ten. His father, who never advanced beyond the first degree, died when Hsueh-chien was still in his teens. He conscientiously observed the rites of mourning, and gave his entire portion of the inheritance, which amounted to a hundred taels of silver, to his elder brother, who was making a bare living as a teacher. Hsueh-chien's abilities had previously attracted the notice of Chao Jui, an elderly retired official who was looking for a suitable man to marry his only child.[136] After completing the mourning period for his father, Hsueh-chien married Chao Jui's daughter. As a young man, he continued to demonstrate a generous spirit. He shared the property that formed part of his wife's dowry with his elder brother's family, and Hsueh-chien argued against the punishment of a young boy from the Chao clan who tried to abscond with valuables he had stolen from Hsueh-chien's house. He and his wife lived for several years in simplicity and seclusion as he devoted himself to studying. For all of these unselfish actions, Fang's name was beginning to cause a stir by the time he was in his early twenties, when he had another opportunity to manifest his steadfast commitment to what was right.

Chang Hsu, who held the post of Instructor (*chiao-yü*) in T'ung-ch'eng, was an adherent of Keng Ting-hsiang (1524–96) and the T'ai-chou school of Wang Yang-ming's followers.[137] Chang was so effective in encouraging others to be good men and implement moral precepts that Fang, declaring Chang to be his master, had the aim of becoming a sage, which was a goal Wang Yang-ming had taught was accessible to everyone. Subsequently Keng Ting-hsiang, while serving as the supervisor of instruction (*tu-hsueh* 督學) in Nanking, issued an order that outstanding commoners were to be recommended for consideration by the government, presumably for appointment to the Imperial Academy and possibly to official posts. Chang put in Fang's name with the local magistrate, whereupon Fang ran away and hid in the hills so that the magistrate could not find him. When the recommendation process was over, Fang reappeared and was reprimanded by Chang, but Fang contended that "attaining official rank is a matter of fate. To depend on someone else's influence is to succeed on false pretenses. I would not do that." Chang then abdicated his seat as Fang's superior to apologize for having been wrong. Later, proceeding by the "right" route, Fang passed the lowest level examination for the first time when he was twenty-seven. Four years later he became a stipendiary student, but he failed seven times in the provincial examination at Nanking. He was over fifty when in 1593 he went to Peking as a "tribute student" (*sui kung-sheng*). After the examination

136. Chao Jui has a biographical entry in Ma Ch'i-ch'ang, *T'ung-ch'eng ch'i chiu chuan*, 3.6b–7a.

137. On Keng Ting-hsiang, see Huang Tsung-hsi, *Ming ju hsueh an*, 35.

at the capital to verify his eligibility for appointment, he passed through the city in southern Chihli where his eldest son, who had become a *chin-shih* in 1589, was serving as a Prefectural Judge (*t'ui-kuan*). Hsueh-chien was pleased with the effectiveness his son showed in administering justice, but after discussing with the local prefect the merits of remaining hidden away or offering oneself for service, Fang Hsueh-chien apparently decided to decline the Ministry of Personnel's appointment to office.

Fang Hsueh-chien's decision might seem to be based on the realities of his advanced age, the expectation that he could achieve only low rank because he did not have even a *chü-jen* degree, and the satisfaction (and possibly embarrassment) of having a son well placed to advance to high office. Yet one suspects he would have declined office even earlier if the choice had presented itself. It seems that he had been preparing for a different career during the twenty years he was a *sheng-yuan* sitting for the examinations. In his twenties he had formed a literary society with a few friends in T'ung-ch'eng, and he had had a number of students and followers. It was almost as if, finally confronted with a choice, his decision not to serve set him free to do what was more important to him. Returning to T'ung-ch'eng, Fang Hsueh-chien built a hall with a shrine dedicated to Confucius. He opened it to others who were interested in discussing morality, and day after day they met to analyze the meaning and import of such crucial points in Wang Yang-ming's doctrine as the "goodness of human nature" (*hsing shan*) and "innate knowledge of good" (*liang chih*). Fang also organized similar groups in other communities, and traveled to them to give lectures on his views of moral teachings. In 1611 he lectured at the Tung-lin Academy,[138] perhaps the highest unofficial honor his contemporaries could grant. Wherever he went, he sought to convey his conviction of the moral and philosophical correctness of the School of Mind (*hsin hsueh*). As Huang Tsung-hsi commented, Fang Hsueh-chien "was grieved at seeing that the world in discussing 'mind' often venerated [Wang Chi's teachings on] the 'absence of good' and the 'absence of evil,'" so that he set out to show the true meaning of "mind" as revealed in the classics and in the writings of later Confucians.[139]

Fang Hsueh-chien was still alive during the first few years of Fang I-chih's life, and his teachings remained gospel in the family as I-chih and his younger sister were growing up.[140] Nevertheless, Fang I-chih did not follow in his great-grandfather's footsteps. That does not mean he was unaffected by Fang Hsueh-chien's precedent. Being his great-grandson, and being born into a rich, promi-

---

138. A report of his discussions with members of the Tung-lin Academy on the occasion of his appearance there in the ninth month of 1611 is in Fang Hsueh-chien, "Tung yu chi 東遊記" *chüan* 1, in *Ch'i tai i shu*. Also, cf. Heinrich Busch, "The Tung-lin shu-yüan and Its Political and Philosophical Significance," *Monumenta Serica* 14 (1949–55), 43.

139. Huang Tsung-hsi, *Ming ju hsueh an*, 35.365.

140. Fang Chung-lü, "Ku-mu Sun Kung-jen chuan 姑母孫恭人傳," "Han-ch'ing ko wen chi" 汗青閣文集, A.41b, in *Ch'i tai i shu*.

nent, successful family, provided Fang I-chih with advantages that gave him a distinct edge in the social competition of his times. It also meant that more was expected of him, by his family as well as by society in general, and also by himself. The prefaces written for him in these early years almost make more of his great-grandfather, of his grandfather, who had been successful in his official career in judicial and censorial posts, and of his father, who had already seen service as director of a bureau in Peking and who seemed sure of reaching higher levels, than of Fang I-chih himself. He received praise as a worthy heir of all of this, as a young man full of promise, but repeatedly the implication was that "we notice him now not so much for what he has accomplished, but because his family's achievements might be repeated by him."[141] It was in this vein that he came to be known as one of the "Four Sons of Eminent Men" (*ssu kung tzu*). He was, in short, expected to achieve renown and respect such as the three preceding generations of the Fang family had. This expectation, coupled with the troubled times, as was impressed upon him by his grandmother, gave Fang I-chih further impetus to do something outstanding.

When Fang had first moved to the little house he called "Room for My Knees" at Nanking, his maternal uncle, who was about his age, came to visit and wrote a paired inscription to hang on the wall: "Laughing with fellow literati from the entire empire. Accumulating knowledge by reading the books of antiquity."[142] The reference to nearly contradictory activities was a good forecast of Fang's years in Nanking. Through the 1630s he remained involved in camaraderie and literary endeavors, but he also continued reading widely and pursuing what his aunt called "solid learning." As a child, "when I had extra time from my memorizing and reading in school, I liked to inquire into the 'principles of things' (*wu li*)."[143] For reading, he had the advantage of his family's extensive collection of books. His grandfather had collected books of anecdotes in Peking, and they had all of the classics, the twenty-one histories, the *Comprehensive Mirror for Aid in Government* (*Tzu chih t'ung chien*) and its derivatives, the extant works of the Hundred Schools of thought of Chou times, as well as large encyclopedic compilations (*lei shu*), collected works, and various oddities. The family's holdings of Sung and Yuan commentaries on classics, stories, and gazetteers were incomplete, and they had no rare books. As Fang traveled on his own after he was twenty he called on book collectors. He made copies of the lists of their holdings and borrowed books from them when they allowed it. He was unable to fulfill his plan to go to Shao-hsing, Chekiang, to see the famous Four Sections (*ssu pu* 四部) library of the Ch'i family,[144] but in

---

141. Cf. especially the preface by Wen Chen-meng, *Fang shih shih chi*, 22.1a–b.

142. Fang I-chih, "Hsi yü hsin pi," 1a.

143. Fang I-chih, "I hsueh hsu," *Fu-shan wen-chi*, 3.41a.

144. Ch'i Ch'eng-yeh 祁承爍 and his son, Ch'i Piao-chia 彪佳 (1602–45), gathered one of the famous book collections at the end of Ming, which they described in a catalogue in 1625. Cf. Hummel, *Eminent Chinese*, under Ch'i Piao-chia.

Nanking he gathered some of the remnants of the Chiao and Ku families' collections which had been dispersed.[145] To make up for a deficiency in his own family's collection, he bought books of stories which were being printed in Soochow in large numbers.[146] Having access to all of these books, Fang had developed the habit of taking reading notes, and then notes on other occasions as well. "When Chou Ch'i and I lived at the 'Study Antiquity Hall' (Chi-ku t'ang 稽古堂),[147] whether I was at home or not, I would make a note of what I had come to know. Sometimes after a guest left I would make a note of what he had said."[148] He also kept notes of doubtful and difficult points he had encountered to await subsequent revision.[149] Whereas a few years earlier he had composed "hundreds of thousands of words" of poetry and rhyme-prose, he began to concentrate more on "ancient prose" (*ku wen*) style essays. He did not show these to others, nor did he discuss with others his findings on difficult points in the texts of classics and histories, ". . . for in a twilight period they despise another man's scholarship."[150] His friend Chou Ch'i described Fang's intentions: "He has wanted to exhort the empire [to rectify itself] by means of the Way of the ancients. If the empire were to try to read his writings and look at how he exhorts himself [to be righteous], then it could be so exhorted."[151] The implication here that contemporaries would not take morally and intellectually serious men seriously can be added to the other sources of Fang's doubts and uncertainties—his family's expectations, a world suffering disruptions of war, dissatisfaction with cultural self-indulgence.

These feelings provided the context for Fang I-chih's composition of the "Seven Solutions" in the mid-1630s. The dilemma that he assigned to the fictional protagonist was not unrelated to that he found in his own life—what was a talented, ambitious young man faced with a time of turmoil, to do with his life? It is part of the burden of such an advantaged young man that he is confronted with choice.

145. Fang presumably was alluding to the collection amassed by Chiao Hung 焦竑 (1541–1620). "A contemporary noted that Chiao Hung had a library which filled five rooms . . ." (Hummel, *Eminent Chinese*). I have not ascertained who the Ku family was; perhaps the reference is to Ku Ch'i-yuan 顧起元 (1565–1628).

146. Fang I-chih, "Shu T'ung ya chui chi hou 書通雅綴集後," in "Chi-ku t'ang wen-chi," *Ch'i tai i shu*, 2.21b–22a.

147. The "Study Antiquity Hall" was the name they gave to the place where they lived in Nanking, probably from 1635 to 1638 or so.

148. Fang I-chih, "Chi-ku t'ang tsa lu hsu," *Fu-shan wen-chi*, 2.35a.

149. Fang I-chih, "Hsi yü hsin pi," 11b.

150. Fang I-chih, "Yu chi Erh-kung shu," in "Chi-ku t'ang wen-chi," *Ch'i tai i shu*, 2.29b; also in *Fu-shan wen-chi*, 8.11b.

151. Chou Ch'i, preface, *Fu-shan wen-chi*, 2.1a–b, dated 1639.

3   Examination Man

Pao-shu Tzu Is Urged to Succeed

One day going through the marketplace,[1] he met Literatus Expectation[2]
and Clansman Grasper[3] on the street. He clasped their hands as they went
along together without speaking. In the distance they saw Sir Brazen[4]
driving toward them in a cloud of dust. Alighting from his carriage, he
bowed deeply. Elder Tough-Nut[5] was there in the marketplace, where he
had let down a screen [to tell fortunes].[6] There was someone named Old
Hollow-Deceit[7] who, living there temporarily, shared half a mat in the
market to sell drugs. His Worship Cunning-Courage[8] had come to consult
the fortune-teller. Seeing the other gentlemen standing in the sun, he
shouted for them to go inside and be seated. When they were settled, they

1. The interview with the would-be advisors takes place in an unspecified marketplace, but in light of its being within easy walking distance of a river where pleasure boats ply, as shall be seen in due course, the imagined site may well be one of the markets for gifts and luxury goods in the Ch'in-huai section of Nanking.

2. Feng-wu's name suggests "to meet" and "to welcome," to welcome or receive a guest, to act according to what is expected, to please, to meet the times, to be opportune, to seek success. His label is *shih* 士, a literatus, a man who has not yet achieved rank in the examinations but who is trying. Literatus Expectation.

3. Wo-ch'e's name connotes "to grasp" and "abrupt, hasty." He is called a *shih* 氏, which suggests he is a member of a clan, but has no further claim to social status. Clansman Grasper.

4. Heng-shih's name means "to be overbearing, unruly, to act outrageously," and "the ordinary world." He is a *chün* 君, a sir, implying he has hereditary rank. Sir Brazen.

5. Chen-li's name means "densely woven" and "nut-hard," something minute and fine, firm and durable. He is called *hsien-sheng* 先生, elder or teacher. Elder Tough-Nut.

6. On 垂簾, or 下簾, see *Han shu* 72.3056. A certain Yen Chün-p'ing 嚴君平, who performed divinations for others in the marketplace in Ch'eng-tu, Szechwan, when he had earned a hundred cash, enough to keep him in food, would close up shop, *lower a screen*, and teach the *Lao Tzu*. We should infer that Elder Tough-Nut, like Yen Chün-p'ing, was more than a teller of fortunes.

7. Wang-lang's name could mean "there is no, without," or "to befuddle, deceive," and "a hole," deceiving and vacuous. He is a *lao-jen* 老人, the old man. Old Hollow-Deceit.

8. Ch'eng-yung's name brings to mind "a small measure, degree" or "to measure," and "courage, bravery." In the "Ju hsing" section of the *Book of Rites* (*Li chi*), there is a passage, "When predatory birds and beasts attack and seize, they do not measure their courage (*ch'eng yung*)." His label is *kung* 公, suggesting nobility, probably official rank. His Worship Cunning-Courage.

all wanted a word with Pao-shu Tzu.[9] They had seen that Pao-shu Tzu
was in a black humor and that his mind was in a state of extreme disquiet.
Someone said, "How have your depressed and embittered feelings come
to such a state? All of us have advice for you. Are you willing to listen?"

Pao-shu Tzu said, "Well, yes and no.[10] In any case, I shall respectfully hear your commands."

Literatus Expectation said, "Is your state of mind not due to being
unsuccessful?

"Do not take umbrage at my chiding you. I see you as one who did not
work hard at the task of succeeding. [As one who could easily master rather
than be ruined by studying] the Han-tan walk, you could proceed apace
and reach the goal.[11] The sound of [Po Ya's celebrated zither called] the
Ringing Bell could be strummed again by you.[12] With your abilities, why
would this be difficult?

"Instead, you loftily devote yourself to classics and histories and to
carving and polishing lyric metrics and rhyme-prose. Your body debili-
tated[13] and your vital spirits enervated,[14] you might produce a lengthy
piece of work. Even if it were a thousand chapters reaching to the rafters,
you would not be recognized in the eyes of the men of this age. After three
years of fruitless literary exercises you would be as hungry as the dwarfs

32a

9. The name Pao-shu suggests "to hug in the arms," and, taking *shu* 蜀 to stand for *tu* 獨,
"alone, lonely," standing alone, on one's own. The phrase *pao shu* occurs in *Kuan Tzu*,
"Hsing shih 形勢," 1.5a: "With the ruler is inactive, the commoners are employed to their
own ends. He holds (*pao*) the ritual vessels (*shu*) and does not speak, but the ancestral hall is
thereby ordered." Instead of glossing *shu* as "ritual vessels," another tradition suggests *shu* be
taken as "one" (*yi* 一), which would have the ruler "embracing oneness." Both interpreta-
tions are relevant, but neither seems wholly adequate as an explanation of Pao-shu's name.
The name also resonates with Pao-p'u 抱朴, "Embracing the Simple," the sobriquet given to
Ko Hung (ca. 280–340) by his neighbors. (Cf. Ko Hung, *Pao-p'u Tzu*, 50.2b; J. R. Ware
translated the name Pao-p'u as *Simplex*.) The protagonist of the "Seven Solutions" is called a
tzu, 子 a title of respect which conveys the idea of a young master. Master Clinging-Alone
is a possible translation, but I have preferred to leave his name in transliteration.

10. On 唯唯否否, see "T'ai-shih-kung tzu hsu," *Shih chi*, 130.3299.

11. On 邯鄲之步, see "Ch'iu shui 秋水," *Chuang Tzu*, 136. (Cf. B. Watson, trans., *Complete
Works of Chuang Tzu*, 187.) A young man, according to Chuang Tzu, went to the city of
Han-tan to learn its residents' famous mode of strutting, but rather than mastering it he
forgot what he already knew—how to walk—and had to crawl home. The point that
Literatus Expectation is making, of course, is that Pao-shu Tzu is so clever that he could learn
something "unnatural," i.e., examination essay writing, without destroying his integrity in
the process.

12. On 號鍾, see *Ch'u Tz'u*, "Chiu t'an 九歎, Min ming 愍命." (Cf. David Hawkes, trans.,
Songs of the South, 164: "Now the Ringing Bell of Po Ya has been broken,/And they hold a
cheng and strike its jangling strings.") The point is that Pao-shu Tzu is so clever he could
"play" what is broken, i.e., the examinations.

13. The text in *Ch'i tai i shu* has 聲; I follow *Fu-shan wen-chi*, which has 身.

14. On 偏身 and 蔚氣, see "Shu chen hsun 俶眞訓," *Huai-nan Tzu*, 2.18a and 19b.

were full;[15] *grinding away at the five classics, you would not be as well off as tending pigs.*[16]

"*Men follow what is convenient in order to obtain the blue and purple [ribboned seals of high office].*[17] *The technique is exceedingly easy. What use is extensive knowledge and arduous preparation, or being harnessed to one's studies for months and years? Moreover, the men of this age on the whole regard what is convenient and at hand as the task to be pursued; anyone who is devoted to antiquity is looked upon by them as an enemy. If estimable sons and younger brothers who show the slightest inclination toward emulating the righteous*[18] *are scoldingly clamped into school by their strict fathers and clever elder brothers, then why do you choose to do it? Since those who speak of examination essays as the means to fame are numerous, what is the need for your interest in the classics and histories, in lyric metrics and rhyme-prose? I wish you would be critical of your way. What about closing yourself behind your gate and laboring over your studies [for the examinations]?*"[19]

Without self-satisfaction, Pao-shu Tzu said, "I quite agree with what you have said, but each individual by his nature has his own propensities and he absolutely cannot be compelled to go against them. If [we contrast] what men of the present day take as worthy tasks [with what is truly worthy], then 'drumming on the book box' is not 'becoming versed in the "Lesser Odes"';[20] *'memorizing and reading' is not [knowing] 'nine thousand*

15. On 餓於侏儒, see "Tung-fang Shuo chuan," *Han shu*, 65.2843. Tung-fang Shuo, miffed that his stipend at court was so small, jokingly complained to the emperor that he received the same allowance in grain and cash as the dwarfs, but since he was three times as large he was starving on what was surfeiting for them. (Cf. B. Watson, trans., *Courtier and Commoner in Ancient China*, 81.) Tung-fang Shuo had claimed to have spent three winters (years) in his studies. *Han shu*, 65.2841.

16. On 三冬, 篆刻, and 鑽厲, see Jen Fang 任昉, "Wei Fan Shang-shu . . . ti-i piao 爲范尚書 . . . 第一表," *pien* 348, *Wen hsuan*, 38.21b: "He really ground away at his studies, but without putting one classic at his command; he labored in crafting his art, but he had achieved nothing in three years."

17. On 青紫, see "Hsia-hou Sheng 夏侯勝 chuan," *Han shu*, 75.3159. Hsia-hou, one of the most eminent scholars of his time, would lecture his students, "A gentleman (*shih*) worries lest he does not understand clearly the texts of the classics. If one understands them clearly, he obtains the blue and purple like looking down and picking straw up off the ground." Literatus Expectation was overlooking the crucial preparatory step.

18. 翹風慕義, quoted from "Liu hou shih chia 留侯世家," *Shih chi*, 55.2040. (Cf. B. Watson, trans., *Records of the Grand Historian*, vol. 1, 140: The king of Han was advised that if he restored the descendants of the old aristocratic states, everyone would ". . . turn in longing toward your righteousness and beg to be your subjects.")

19. On 揣摩, see *Chan-kuo ts'e*, "Ch'in ts'e 秦策," 19. (Cf. J. Crump., trans., *Chan-Kuo Ts'e*, 57). Su Ch'in, after being rejected by the King of Ch'in, went home and pored over his books, even stabbing his thigh to keep himself awake at night, in order to prepare himself as the indispensable advisor. Literatus Expectation, like Su Ch'in, held that a period of "laboring over one's studies" could lead to "success" in gaining a place in government.

20. See *Li chi*, "Hsueh chi 學記." (Cf. S. Couvreur, trans., *Li Ki*, vol. 2, 32.) The students

characters';[21] *'enduring a long, soaking rain' is not 'making use of the* Han
History';[22] *'notching the candle' and 'striking the begging bowl' are not
'writing rhyme-prose and lyric poetry';*[23] *'mounting to a high place' is not
'being a high official.'*[24] *One may have mumbled only one chapter [of a*
classic] and memorized several thousand examination essays, but after a
year goes by these essays become unsuited [to the latest taste]. Then once
again one must collect and memorize the essays of those who have newly
achieved rank [by passing a provincial or capital examination]. I hold that
nothing compares to that as a source of suffering.

32b

 "He who is fond of antiquity plans in terms of a thousand years; he
who seeks success plans in terms of a single day. Of course that is impracti-
cable talk. One would not dare expect others to trust and follow it. Still, in
the present age those in the empire who have practiced [examination essays]
from childhood till they are distressed over them in their white-haired old
age[25] *and yet are unable to sell [their essays, and themselves, to the gov-*
ernment] are several hundred times more numerous than the literati who
are fond of antiquity. And why is it, then, that there are those who suddenly
attain high rank and enjoy fame without necessarily having spent a single
day 'laboring over their studies'? Why because of that, is my way wrong?
How can I avoid hostility and slander? Or could such talk be self-redeem-
ing?"[26]

---

were to become versed in the first three songs in the section of the *Songs* called the "Lesser
Odes" as the point of departure for becoming officials. They entered the school as the book
box was drummed and submissively went about their tasks.

 21. Ku Yen-wu asserted that in Han times if one could write more than nine thousand
characters at an examination one could become a historian/recorder. "Ching wen tzu t'i
經文字體," *Jih chih lu*, 16.

 22. See "Hsing Shao 邢邵 chuan," *Pei shih*, 43. At first Hsing Shao pursued a life of pleasure and did not take time out for serious endeavors, but once, during a long, soaking rain, he
read the *Han History* and by the fifth day was somewhat able to expound it.

 23. See "Wang Seng-ju 王僧孺 chuan," *Nan-shih*, 59. "Notching the candle" refers to the
practice of setting a time limit for the completion of the poems in a competition among an
evening's gathering of scholars. Someone complained that during the time it takes for one
inch of candle to burn, poems of four rhymes could be completed and that was not difficult
enough. The alternative was to strike a copper begging bowl, set the rhyme, and expect
everyone's poem to be completed before the sound died away.

 24. See "I wen chih 藝文志," *Han shu*, 30.1755, where a saying was quoted that one can be
a high official (*tai-fu* 大夫) if he is able to compose a poem when he has mounted to a high
place, such as a mountain top. The subsequent discussion adds that ability to quote from the
Songs also is the mark of a man worthy of office.

 25. On 童習白紛, see Yang Hsiung, *Fa yen* 法言, "Han Wei ts'ung-shu" (Pai pu ts'ung shu),
2.3a: "According to some, if one became accustomed to doing it in his youth, even in his
white-haired old age he will be disorderly."

 26. Pao-shu Tzu seems to mean either that his defense has redeemed his position or that
others in attacking him are trying to justify their own positions, or both.

"Success" (*feng shih* 逢時) in the context of the discussion in the "Seven Solutions" has a specific meaning: to pass the civil service examinations. Implied, of course, is the panoply of benefits attendant upon such success—recognized high status, legal privileges, informal influence, and enhanced opportunities for power and wealth, as well as the most important possibility of being appointed to office, which would bring more of the above and the chance to serve the wider community. In equating success with achieving degrees in the examinations, Literatus Expectation was not being unduly cynical, for ascending the scale in the examination hierarchy was *the* general contemporary index of success. Indeed, much of the modern literature on imperial China continues, tacitly or not, to share Literatus Expectation's assumption. Examination degrees, especially the *chin-shih* degree, tended and still tend to be taken as a more ready indicator of "success" than the height scaled in the bureaucratic hierarchy.[1]

From the middle of the fifteenth century the Ming government regularly recruited the overwhelming majority of its civil officials through the examination system.[2] Over a two-hundred-year period, normally every three years and sometimes more frequently, in prefectures and independent subprefectures all over China candidates sat for a written examination which, if they passed, earned them the title of *sheng-yuan* 生員 and the privilege of taking the qualifying examination (*k'o shih* 科試). Passing the qualifying examination enabled them to go to the provincial capital for the provincial examination (*hsiang shih* 鄉試), held in the autumn every three years. Although there was some shift in date, in general the candidates assembled at the examination compound on the ninth day of the eighth month, when their identity and eligibility were verified and they were each assigned to one of the hundreds of cubicles where they spent the night. The next day they wrote, and on the third day they handed in their papers and were allowed to leave the compound. The following day the pattern was repeated, and then a third time, so that the examination procedure took nine days to complete.[3] Failure in the provincial examination ordinarily meant one had to pass an "annual" examination (*sui shih* 歲試) to maintain his *sheng-yuan* status and his eligibility to take the next provincial qualifying examination. A relatively small but continually expanding group of *sheng-yuan* were awarded the title of "tribute student" (*kung-sheng*) or one of its variations, and thus were

1. Ho Ping-ti's *The Ladder of Success in Imperial China: Aspects of Social Mobility, 1368–1911* focuses primarily on examination degrees and secondarily on rank in the bureaucracy. Monetary success is treated to the extent it could be translated into examination and official rank. Other kinds of success, such as military or literary achievement, are almost completely neglected by Ho and most others writing on society in imperial China.

2. Ho Ping-ti, *Ladder of Success*, 14–15. The first Ming metropolitan and palace examinations in 1371 selected 119 *chin-shih*; the second, in 1385, selected 472. Cf. Ho, *Ladder*, 14–15, 186. Also see the lists of *chin-shih* in *Ming Ch'ing li-k'o chin-shih t'i-ming pei-lu*.

3. Shang Yen-liu, *Ch'ing tai k'o-chü k'ao-shih shu lu*, 60–63. A convenient summary of the examination hierarchy that prevailed in Ming and Ch'ing is in Wolfgang Franke, *The Reform and Abolition of the Traditional Chinese Examination System*, 8–11.

exempted from the "annual" examination. They were eligible to go to Nanking or Peking to study at the Imperial Academy (*Kuo-tzu chien*) and be appointed to minor posts.[4] Passing the provincial examination earned one the title of *chü-jen* and eligibility to be appointed to a minor office, commonly as an education supervisor or even as a district magistrate. More consequentially, *chü-jen* were eligible to go to Peking in the spring for the metropolitan examination (*hui shih* 會試).

At Peking the same nine-day cycle as at the provincial capitals was followed. The content of the metropolitan examination varied over the course of the dynasty, but the examination of 1645 can be taken to represent the system prevailing at the end of the Ming. At the first session, the candidates were assigned to write seven "essays on the meaning of the classics" (*ching i* 經義), three of the topics set by the examiners from the Four Books and four from the one of the Five Classics in which the candidate had chosen to specialize. For the second session, there was a "discussion" (*lun* 論) on a topic drawn, in 1645, from the *Book of Filial Submission* (*Hsiao ching* 孝經), although the source of the topic could be taken even from Sung Neo-Confucian writings; there also were five "judgements" (*p'an* 判) and the choice of a short "proclamation" (*chao* 詔), or an "announcement" (*kao* 誥), or a "memorial" (*piao* 表) to demonstrate command of bureaucratic forms. At the third session the candidate was asked to compose five "plans" (*ts'e* 策) on hypothetical current affairs topics.[5] The maximum number of characters for each type of essay was fixed, but the number varied over time. Lang Ying (1487–after 1566) gave them for the mid-sixteenth century, although he implied they were unchanging: "In the examinations of our dynasty, from the third year of the Hung-wu reign [1370] each 'essay on the meaning of the classic' in the first session has been limited to 500 characters and each essay on the Four Books has been limited to 300. In the second session, a 'discussion' of the Rites or Music has been limited to 300 characters. The 'plans' in the third session could be more than a thousand characters as the emphasis was on straightforward discussion rather than literary flourish."[6] Lang Ying also defined the criteria by which examiners judged each essay. "In terms of horse riding (*ch'i* 騎), they look at the vigor and facility [with which it was written]. In terms of archery (*she* 射), they look at how it hit the set number [of characters]. In terms of calligraphy (*shu* 書), they look at the strokes of the brush and at whether the standard style was followed. In terms of legal codes (*lü* 律), they look at whether the argument was expounded with detailed judiciousness."[7] Normally, the candidates who were deemed successful in the metropolitan examination were assembled for the palace examination

---

4. Cf. Ho Ping-ti, 27–29, on the five main types of *kung-sheng*.

5. Shang Yen-liu, 63.

6. Lang Ying, *Ch'i hsiu lei kao*, vol. 1, 202. In Ch'ing the allowed number of characters in the *ching i* essay continued to grow larger.

7. Lang Ying, 202. Cf. *Ming shih*, 70, 1694.

(*tien shih* 殿試), when the emperor set them a topic on which they wrote a "plan."[8] The final rank order of the candidates was then decided, in theory by the emperor himself, and the successful ones were formally confirmed as *chin-shih*.[9] The top several *chin-shih* were commonly appointed to the Han-lin Academy, where in effect they began training as administrative assistants to the emperor, and could have every expectation of rising to high level office in the capital. Other *chin-shih* were appointed to posts in the capital or provinces, especially as district magistrates, or were put on lists of "expectant" officials awaiting a suitable opening.

If passing the examination was a definition of success, the key to passing by the second half of the fifteenth century was facility in producing "essays on the meaning of the classic" which adhered to the rigorous form known as "explication of the meaning" (*chih-i* 制義) essays, or "current essays" (*shih-wen* 時文), or, most popularly, as "eight-legged essays" (*pa-ku wen* 八股文).[10] Mere competence was all that was required for the "discussions" and "plans"; the sheep were separated from the goats primarily on the basis of the "eight-legged essays." For the first century of Ming the essay on a topic from a classic had followed the style used in the Sung examinations.[11] According to Ku Yen-wu, "Through the T'ien-shun reign [1457–64], the 'essay on the meaning of the classic' (*ching-i*) did no more than explicate and interpret [the set passage]. Some parts were paired, some were loosely organized. At first there was no fixed form, and [the essay's] simple sentences and themes were few."[12] But "pairing" (*pi* 比) was a characteristic from the beginning of Ming.[13] The idea of "legs" derived from a complicated interplay of opposites in the composition of each essay—negatives with affirmatives, abstract statements with concrete ones, simplicities with profundities.[14] Rigid and rigorous, the form of the eight-legged essay never became fixed, as the rules of composition continued to evolve and the relative importance of the parts changed. "The first two, or sometimes

8. Lang Ying, 202.

9. A translation of a description of the ceremonies and customs attendant on the metropolitan and palace examinations of 1667 is in John Meskill, "A Conferral of the Degree of *Chin-shih*," *Monumenta Serica* 23 (1964 [1966]), 351–71. The description was written by Miao T'ung 繆肜 (1627–97), who was thirty-sixth in the metropolitan examination and first in the palace examination that year.

10. Other names for the same style essay include *chih-i* 制藝, *shih-i* 時藝, and *ssu-shu wen* 四書文. Cf. Shang Yen-liu, 227. Shang devoted a chapter to the origins, form, and development of the "eight-legged essays" and other examination forms. Fang I-chih often called the examination essays *t'ieh kua* 帖括, which was a term from the T'ang dynasty.

11. *Ming shih*, 70.1693.

12. Ku Yen-wu, "Shih wen ke shih 試文格式," *Jih chih lu*, 16.

13. Shang Yen-liu, 227, in contradiction to Ku Yen-wu, wrote that the "eight-legged" form was fixed at the beginning of Ming and became "fully developed" during the Ch'eng-hua reign (1466–87), which Ku contended was the reign during which the form was developed. Cf. Shang Yen-liu, 63.

14. Ku Yen-wu, "Shih wen ke shih."

three or four, sentences which assert the preamble are called 'breaching the topic' (*p'o t'i* 破題). The high incidence of paired sentences in general is a style inherited from Sung writers. (It stems from the rhyme-prose style of T'ang.) Next, the essay sets forth its idea in four or five sentences, called 'advancing the topic' (*ch'eng t'i* 承題). After that the essay cites why the Master (or Tseng Tzu, Tzu-ssu, Mencius or other similar [authors of the quotation set as the topic by the examiners]) spoke these words; this is called 'the origins of the topic' (*yuan t'i* 原題)."[15] And so on. "By the middle of the Wan-li reign [i.e., the end of the sixteenth century] the 'breaching' was only two sentences, the 'advancing' was only three sentences, and the 'origins' was not used. At the end of the essay the author explicates the words of the sages and as a last thing expresses his own ideas; this is called the 'grand conclusion' (*ta chieh* 大結)."[16] By the beginning of the seventeenth century the "grand conclusion" was only three or four sentences.[17] The bulk of the essay was contained in the four pairs of "legs," called "pairing which brings forth [the topic]" (*t'i pi* 提比), the "central pairing" (*chung pi* 中比), the "anterior pairing" (*hou pi* 後比), and the "pairing which binds together" (*shu pi* 束比) or "end pairing" (*mo pi* 末比), and in time even the "end pairing" legs atrophied.[18] The essay, then, emphasized the play of words and sentences against each other, with negation and counterbalancing of statements impeding the formulation of what we might consider an argument.

As the form of the essay became more rigid, another change was taking place which in part accounts for the emphasis placed on formal requirements. According to Ku Yen-wu, in the essays for the examinations at the beginning of Ming, one could make reference to contemporary affairs, but as the system developed only previous dynasties could be mentioned.[19] Some historians have seen in the prevailing standard for examination essays a manifestation of the tenor of the times—open and simple in the fifteenth century, peaking in quality in the first half of the sixteenth century, and becoming increasingly mechanical, so that mere cleverness came to be valued. By the seventeenth century disputatious, self-indulgent, undisciplined essays were being produced.[20] The implied conclusion of such arguments was that as the style of the essays became more

15. Ku Yen-wu, "Shih wen ke shih." Cf. Shang Yen-liu, 227. Shang, 229–30, gave quotations to show that the "pairing" (*pi*) approach was present in the examinations from T'ang and was well established in Sung. An even earlier source is the *p'ien-t'i* 駢體 style of the Six Dynasties.

16. Ku Yen-wu, "Shih wen ke shih." (Shang Yen-liu, 232, punctuates this passage with a comma after 畢.)

17. Ku Yen-wu, "Shih wen ke shih." The "grand conclusion" was abandoned in the K'ang-hsi reign. Shang Yen-liu, 234.

18. Shang Yen-liu, 233–34.

19. Ku Yen-wu, "Shih wen ke shih." However, as Ku Yen-wu also noted, at some examinations the topic set *alluded* to some contemporary event.

20. See Liu Lin-sheng, *Chung-kuo p'ien-wen shih*, 116. Shang Yen-liu, 238–39, discussed periodization in a similar fashion.

offensive, the practices of the literati (*shih*) became more decadent, which, of course, undermined the state and led to the fall of the dynasty. Ku Yen-wu concluded, "Thus, [by the middle of the Wan-li reign] affairs of state being muddled and officials in high position being fearful was foreshadowed in [the standard of] the examination essays."[21]

Effects of the Examination System

With the general perception that the eight-legged essay was the key to success and afforded opportunities more accessible to a broader spectrum of the population, the focus of education tended to be quite specific. From approximately the middle of the sixteenth century, books of model examination essays were published to meet a considerable demand.[22] In the late seventeenth century, bookstores supposedly paid as much as 4000 taels of silver to Lü Liu-liang (1629–83), who enjoyed great success as a compiler of "current style" essays.[23] As more men tried their minds at eight-legged essays, preparation for taking examinations came increasingly to be disparaged as a childish endeavor. Kuei Yu-kuang, with some hyperbole, described the situation in the mid-sixteenth century: "As a reserve for talent and a place where letters flourish, Wu [modern Kiangsu, around Soochow] is first in the empire. Its people are ashamed of any other occupation [than that of preparing for the examinations]. From the time they are young children, everybody is able to recite examination essays."[24] Preparation was not quite intellectually respectable, and men who thought themselves high-minded were loath to punish themselves, or even their sons, with eight-legged essays. The stultifying form of the eight legs itself has been credited with some of the blame for the decline in quality of literary output during Ming.[25] The emphasis on the examination was blamed for the decline in Confucian scholarship,[26] and for promoting the idea that studies should be

21. Ku Yen-wu, "Shih wen ke shih." An implicit reason for Ku Yen-wu's placing more emphasis than most later historians on the fifteenth-century origins of the eight-legged essay was to support his point that the essays were a derogation from the practice of the beginning of the dynasty and a contributory factor in the decline of the dynasty.

22. Ku Yen-wu, *Jih chih lu*, 16.9b–10b. Ku's remarks are referred to in Ho Ping-ti, *Ladder of Success*, 214, and in Tadao Sakai, "Confucianism and Popular Educational Works." 335. Cf. Wu, "Ming Printing and Printers," *Harvard Journal of Asiatic Studies* 7 (1942–43). Chapters 13 and 18 of the *Ju lin wai shih* contain sardonic descriptions of the compilation of these books of model essays.

23. Wang Ying-k'uei 王應奎, "Liu-nan hsu pi shuo" 柳南續筆說, quoted in Hsieh Kuo-chen, *Tang she yun-tung k'ao*, 146.

24. Kuei Yu-kuang, *Ch'üan chi*, 102.

25. Cf. *Chung-kuo wen-hsueh fa-ta shih*, 847.

26. Huang Tsung-hsi, quoted in Wilhelm, "On Ming Orthodoxy," *Monumenta Serica* 29 (1970–71), 5.

pursued solely for personal profit.[27] These later criticisms notwithstanding, the main goal of many men in the Ming dynasty was to pass the *chin-shih* examination.

Kuei Yu-kuang (1506–71) is an illustration of the hold the examination system could have on men's lives. As he observed, "From my youth I sat for the examinations, but continually blocked, I was unsuccessful (*pu yü* 不遇)."[28] In spite of learning how to write prose by the time he was eight, Kuei was not able to pass the provincial examination until 1540.[29] Over the next twenty-five years he failed in the metropolitan examination eight times. Meanwhile he was becoming one of the famous literary figures of the time, and was well known to later generations for the quality of his examination essays.[30] As he recognized, his reputation did not necessarily help him in the examinations. Kuei wrote of how in 1559, after he had failed for the seventh time at Peking, someone said to him that the Grand Secretaries in the Han-lin Academy, feeling sorry for him, wanted to intercede on his behalf but could not locate his papers. Someone else then told Kuei that although his reputation was such that everyone everywhere respected him, someone from his home town of K'un-shan had arranged that Kuei's examination papers be destroyed before the chief examiner and Grand Secretaries could review them. Kuei disagreed with those who expressed indignation at these reports. He contended that whichever side won out between those who wanted to pass him and those who wanted to block him was right, and the other wrong, because whether he passed or failed was due to Heaven, to fate. Kuei recalled that in two preceding examinations a Grand Secretary had sought to intercede on his behalf, but without avail; one need not assume that on those previous occasions there were those who wanted to block him. Kuei quoted Confucius's remark that "it is fate that the way forward is open; it is fate that the way forward is obstructed."[31] It was an illusion, according to Kuei, to believe that his failure on his seventh attempt should be attributed to those who would do him ill; they were as harmless as an imitation snake made of lacquer and horn. In spite of the ironic tone of Kuei's piece, "Allaying Suspicions,"[32] it is clear from his case that literary ability, reputation, perseverance, and connections in high places, even taken together, could not guarantee "success" in attaining the highest degree in the examinations. It was

27. Ku Yen-wu, *T'ing-lin shih wen chi*, 173.

28. Kuei Yu-kuang, *Ch'üan chi*, 72.

29. Kuei Yu-kuang's biography in *Ming shih*, 287, "Wen yuan lieh-chuan," quoted in *Kuei Yu-kuang ch'üan chi*.

30. Kuei Yu-kuang's biography in *Ming shih*. Also cf. Nivison, "Protest against Conventions," 348, and Shang Yen-liu, 239.

31. *Analects*, 14.38. Cf. Waley, trans., *Analects of Confucius*, 189–90: "If it is the will of Heaven that the Way shall prevail, then the Way will prevail. But if it is the will of Heaven that the Way should perish, then it must needs perish."

32. "Chieh huo 解惑," in *Kuei Yu-kuang ch'üan chi*, 52–53.

on his ninth attempt that "fate" was on Kuei Yu-kuang's side. He became a *chin-shih* in 1565 and died in office a few years later.[33]

Not everyone was able to adopt Kuei's detached, mocking view of failing. There were many who did not have anything approaching Kuei's lofty literary reputation, which suggested that he was an intelligent, talented man, whatever the outcome of the examination competition. There were also many for whom passing was the only conceivable means of bettering the livelihood of their family. For everyone it was *the* way to rise in social status. As the pool of literate men grew, a fierce competition developed, as there was only a slow increase in the quotas which had been imposed to keep the numbers who passed in the provincial and national examination at levels commensurate with the bureaucracy's staffing requirements. From the mid-fifteenth to the mid-seventeenth centuries, tens of thousands of candidates were qualified to sit for the triennial provincial examination, for which quotas for the entire empire allowed roughly 1000 to 1200 to become *chü-jen*. On the order of 300 *chü-jen* normally passed the triennial metropolitan examination to become *chin-shih*.[34] Many dropped out of the competition after successive failure at the provincial level. There were also old men who, not having Kuei Yu-kuang's "good fortune" at the age of sixty, were figures of sadness as well as fun as they continued year after frustrating year to labor over eight-legged essays in order to acquire the facility to pass, and regularly sat for the examinations in order to keep open the option that fate might smile on them, too. A high incidence of failure and frustration went along with the "ladder of success."

A tradition of protesting some of the ill effects of the examinations had grown with the system itself.[35] One form of criticism tended to come from men, who, believing themselves to be of uncommon intellectual cast, disparaged the distasteful pursuit of the examination degree to which lesser men devoted themselves for their own profit.[36] For example, Ch'en Ch'un in Southern Sung had practiced writing examination essays when he was young, but his master told him "that was not the concern of the sages and worthies," and instead taught

33. Kuei Yu-kuang's biography in *Ming shih*, 287.

34. Cf. Ho Ping-ti, *Ladder of Success*, 173–78, 183–90. C. O. Hucker, in "Governmental Organization of the Ming Dynasty," *Harvard Journal of Asiatic Studies* 21 (1958), 14, noted that an average of 276 men passed in each of the 90 *chin-shih* examinations during the course of the Ming dynasty. Quotas on lower levels were not effectively enforced, so there was a steady growth in the number holding some lower-degree status. Ku Yen-wu estimated the number of *sheng-yuan* at any one time to be 500,000 (out of a population between 100,000,000 and 150,000,000 in the seventeenth century). He arrived at his estimate, apparently, by supposing each district could be reckoned to have 300 *sheng-yuan* (and there were on the order of 2000 districts). Ku Yen-wu, "Sheng-yuan lun shang 生員論上," *Ku T'ing-lin wen-chi*, 1.22.

35. Cf. the excellent discussion in Nivison, "Protest against Conventions and Conventions of Protest," *Confucian Persuasion*; also Wolfgang Franke, *Reform and Abolition of the Examination System*, 16–27.

36. Cf. Nivison, "Protest against Conventions," 179.

him the Confucian anthology entitled *Reflections on Things at Hand* (*Chin ssu lu*).[37] But many critics, from Han Yü to Wang Yang-ming, argued that the superior man is able to preserve his integrity while preparing for competition in the examinations, and so long as he can do so there is no reason not to participate in the system. Thus Chu Hsi observed, "Even though he [a scholar of lofty vision and broad understanding] constantly works at preparing for the examinations, he is undisturbed. If Confucius were to come back to life now, he would not avoid the examinations; but surely they would not disturb him."[38] Chu Hsi even contended that there was nothing particularly laudable in choosing to avoid taking the examinations.[39] Wang Yang-ming was more sensitive than Chu Hsi to the detrimental effects the examination competition commonly had on one's attempts to remain unsullied by the selfish pursuit of gain and fame, but he also could recommend that ". . . if one can firmly fix his aim, in all his pursuits fully keep to the Tao, and not be influenced by desire of success or by fear of failure, then though he studies for the examinations this will be no real hindrance to his learning to become a virtuous man."[40] In both cases, the advice is that one can take the examinations and still preserve his moral and intellectual integrity, even though that is by no means an easy synthesis. On his low level, as when he suggested that Pao-shu Tzu would not be ruined by trying to learn the Han-tan walk, Literatus Expectation was continuing Chu Hsi's and Wang Yang-ming's claims. Pao-shu Tzu went further and denied that the two tasks were any longer compatible.

Fang and the Examinations

Fang I-chih in an essay entitled "On the Practices of the Literati" (*Shih hsi lun* 士習論) discussed more fully the social, rather than the personal, costs of what he saw as a misplaced emphasis on the examinations as the means of recruiting officials. Fang gave a neat definition of the literati: "As a group the literati (*shih*) lie between the various officials and the ordinary people."[41] Individual literati who were of no value were merely like the ordinary people, while those who had the skill demanded at the time could be presented at the court and become officials. Equally importantly, in Fang's view the greater part of the customs and values of the ordinary people came to them from the literati. No matter what

37. Huang Tsung-hsi, *Sung Yuan hsueh an*, 68.

38. Chu Hsi, *Chu Tzu ch'üan shu*, 65.26a; translated in Nivison, "Protest against Conventions," 190.

39. Chu Hsi, *Chu Tzu ch'üan shu*, 75.27b; translated in Nivison, 191–92.

40. Wang Yang-ming, *Wang Wen-ch'eng kung ch'üan shu*, 4.187. Also translated in Nivison, 180, as emended from Henke, *Philosophy of Wang Yang-ming*, 453; and in Julia Ching, trans., *The Philosophical Letters of Wang Yang-ming*, 46.

41. Fang I-chih, *Fu-shan wen-chi*, 3.8a; also in *Ch'i tai i shu*, 2.13a.

they do, the whole empire will follow them in doing it.[42] It is their two-fold influence, as potential officials and as the setters of community values, that make the "practices" of the literati crucial. Fang contended that these practices were in a state of deterioration. He saw that his contemporaries were ashamed to be called humble, loyal, generous, yielding, or straightforward, for such a man, in their minds, was of no use, was unemployable. On the contrary, they were greatly pleased to be thought aggressive and dissembling, ready to find fault with others.[43] Because those who were unsullied and respectful in their conduct were ridiculed, while those who were extravagant and intimidating were respected, the literati followed the latter mode. The poor ones lost any sense of shame and acted without any moral inhibitions. The sons of the rich were increasingly arrogant and profligate.[44] There were those who regarded the acquisition of literary skills merely as a means of "tricking the world and achieving success (*feng shih*)."[45] Broad learning (*po hsueh*), which the *Analects* says a gentleman has,[46] and being profoundly accomplished (*shen tsao* 深造) in the Way, which the *Mencius* says a gentleman is,[47] were neglected.[48] An accomplished literatus, in Fang's view, is able in such diverse endeavors as preparing a philosophically profound essay, discussing a wide range of topics, drafting state documents, assessing the laws and institutions of the dynasty, as well as planning and administering the policies of the government.[49] Why was all of this disregarded by the contemporary literati? Because they were concerned only with the "explication of a classic" (*chih–i*) essays for the examinations.[50] And why did the literati disregard important matters to concentrate on these essays? Because, Fang contended, the "explication" essay had become the fundamental part of the *chih-shih* examination, which was the only type of examination after the *ming-ching* 明經 and *hung-tz'u* 宏詞 examinations were not revived under the regulations from the Hung-wu reign (1368–98). Moreover, the *chin-shih* examination had come to overshadow the other two methods of recruiting officials, "recommendation" (*chien-chü* 薦舉) by high officials and the "annual

42. *Fu-shan wen-chi*, 3.8a; *Ch'i tai i shu*, 2.13a.

43. *Fu-shan wen-chi*, 3.10a; *Ch'i tai i shu*, 2.15a.

44. *Fu-shan wen-chi*, 3.9a; *Ch'i tai i shu*, 2.14a–b. Fang I-chih, it will be remembered, was one of the sons of the rich.

45. *Fu-shan wen-chi*, 3.8b; *Ch'i tai i shu*, 2.14a.

46. *Analects*, 6.25 (Cf. Waley, trans., *Analects of Confucius*, 121: "A gentleman who is widely versed in letters and at the same time knows how to submit his learning to the restraints of ritual is not likely, I think, to go far wrong.") Also see *Mencius*, 4B15. (Cf. D. C. Lau, trans., *Mencius*, 130: "Learn widely and go into what you have learned in detail so that in the end you can return to the essential.")

47. *Mencius*, 4B14. (Cf. D. C. Lau, trans., *Mencius*, 130: "A gentleman steeps himself in the Way because he wishes to find it in himself.")

48. Fang I-chih, *Fu-shan wen-chi*, 3.8b; *Ch'i tai i shu*, 2.13b.

49. *Fu-shan wen-chi*, 3.8a, 3.11a; *Ch'i tai i shu*, 2.13b, 2.16b.

50. *Fu-shan wen-chi*, 3.8b; *Ch'i tai i shu*, 2.13b.

tribute" (*sui-kung* 歲貢) of candidates sent from each district to the capital.[51] As Fang asked elsewhere, "How is one to be presented [to the court for appointment to office, as a *chin-shih* was,] only on the basis of fine writing? Nowadays everyone in the empire works only on examination essays. The plans and words of the earlier monarchs are not known in the slightest. But why blame it on the paucity of honest men with a sense of shame!"[52]

There were two, interconnected reasons why concentrating on the "explication" essays had such deleterious effects on the practices of the literati. The first was that they only memorized essays and no longer read books or sought to understand what was fundamental to government and morality.[53] The rationale behind the development of recruiting officials through competitive written examinations based in large part on the classics was that as a man became familiar with the classical texts, the ethical principles inherent in them would be increasingly internalized by him so that he would not just *know* virtue, but *act* with filial submission, brotherliness, loyalty, sincerity, propriety, righteousness, incorruptibility, and a sense of shame.[54] There were, of course, protests against this rationale. Wang An-shih in the eleventh century wrote: "The present method of selecting officials is as follows:—If a man has a colossal memory, can repeat extensive portions of the classics, and has some skill in composition, he is termed specially brilliant or worthy, and chosen for the highest grades of State ministers. . . . It should need no discussion to show that the knowledge and skill which these men display in no sense in itself fits them for such places of authority and distinction."[55] Wang denounced the contemporary practice of students' memorizing and writing essays to prepare for the examinations. "Not only does the present method of instruction fail to produce the type of men required, it actually spoils them so that they cannot become capable administrators. A man's capacity for government is best educed by specialization, and ruined by too great a variety of subjects to be studied. . . . The students of the present day ought to study methods of practical administration."[56] In spite of such protests, the prevailing assumption was that knowledge of the classics, as revealed by his performance in the written examinations, would be the tip of the iceberg of the man's character. Imbued with the ideas and precedents in the classics, he was a likely choice to be entrusted with the responsibilities of government office. But a man might short-circuit the process by becoming proficient

51. *Fu-shan wen-chi*, 3.8a; *Ch'i tai i shu*, 2.13b.
52. Fang I-chih, *Fu-shan wen-chi*, 1.1b.
53. *Fu-shan wen-chi*, 3.10a; *Ch'i tai i shu*, 2.15b.
54. See, for an example of this assumption, the summary of the 1436 order to the newly established education intendants in Tilemann Grimm, "Ming Educational Intendants," in C. O. Hucker, ed., *Chinese Government in Ming Times*, 135.
55. Wang An-shih, "Ten Thousand Word Memorial," translated in H. R. Williamson, *Wang An-shih*, vol. 1, 69.
56. Ibid., 61–62.

enough to pass the examinations without reading the classics and internalizing their values. An emperor in the mid-fifteenth century noted that it had been reported to him that students "were unwilling to devote earnest study to the Four Books and the Five Classics or to discuss the commentaries but only memorized old compositions, waiting for the next examination in anticipation of happy success."[57] The institutional response to the problem was to appoint, beginning in 1436, and continuously from 1462 after a temporary abeyance, education intendants (*t'i hsueh kuan* 提學官).[58] But the intendants were not able to supervise personally every candidate in their territory and so themselves tended to rely on written examinations.[59] Fang I-chih described the situation as he found it in his own time.

> I have observed that only with the impending arrival of the education intendant do the literati show an urgency in doing their lessons. Since the establishment of the office of education intendant, the system of local selection is nonoperational as responsibility has been delegated as a specialized duty by the prefects and district magistrates. The education intendant only arrives once every few years in any particular locality. Due to the complexity of the matter and the shortness of time, the visit is insufficient for providing any instruction, so he gives an examination. With wealth taking precedence over skill, recruiting literati with examinations is like winning at gambling![60]

The education intendants were thus unable, if indeed they felt any longer that it was their assignment, to do anything about the literati who did not read books but only memorized model essays in order to prepare for the examinations.[61] The indoctrinating function of studying the classics was thus minimized or even lost.

The second, related reason for the deteriorated state of the practices of the literati, according to Fang I-chih, was that the examinations did not in fact discover a man's virtue. Worse, they did not necessarily screen out the undesirables. Fang asks us to agree with the comment by Hsiang An-shih, a *chin-shih* in 1175: "Those who pass these examinations, even if they are malevolent or doltish, must be employed, whereas those who do not pass these examinations, even if they are as [worthy as Confucius's two disciples] Yen Hui and Min Sun or as [renowned for their humanity and righteousness as] Tseng Tzu and Recorder

57. Translated in Grimm, "Ming Educational Intendants," 134, from *Ming Ying-tsung shih lu* 明英宗實錄 (1962 reprint), 17.12b.

58. Grimm, 131–34. The full title of intendants was *t'i-tiao hsueh-hsiao kuan* 提調學校官, "officials in control of schools" (p. 131).

59. Grimm, ibid., provides an excellent discussion of the form, intent, and practice of the office of education intendant.

60. *Fu-shan wen-chi*, 3.10a; *Ch'i tai i shu*, 2.15b.

61. Ku Yen-wu held that the practice of memorizing model essays and only "likely" parts of the classics was the greatest defect of the examination system in his time. "Ni t'i," *Jih chih lu*, 16.

Ch'iu, must be dismissed [from consideration for employment]."[62] It was this circumstance, that doltish and malevolent men were able to aspire to pass the examinations and become officials, which led literati in general to be unconcerned with cultivating their virtue, or even to think that it was useless. Since it was only one's examination papers and not his conduct or character that were being judged, everyone's sights were lowered. "Worthy fathers and elder brothers, instructing their sons and younger brothers, say, 'Exert yourself in carrying out [your preparation for the examinations]. Soon you will be past the struggles, and then how can the ample wealth and high station that will be yours be calculated?'"[63] No mention was made of broad knowledge or of rectifying oneself.

Fang I-chih's recommendation for correcting the situation was a function of his perception of what was wrong. If one assumed that most literati wanted to become officials, and if it had been demonstrated that the current means of selecting officials did not encourage them either to acquire learning or develop virtue, then what was called for was a change to a process for selecting officials that would encourage them in the desired direction. Fang recalled that before the examinations' emphasis on empty literary skills had achieved its present hegemony, there had been a system under which local elders guaranteed the conduct of a literatus, and then local officials, after examining and schooling him, in their turn guaranteed his conduct when he was again to be examined for consideration for appointment.[64] The key to the system was that the conduct of a literatus was to be given great weight in the process of selection, and that his conduct would be vouched for by those who had a chance to know him. Fang cited the pragmatic criticism that Mao K'ai (1506–70), who became a *chin-shih* in 1535 and served as a censor, had directed at the recruitment system. "With recruitment of literati by recommendation, they are selected and only afterward are they employed in office; the rate of failure [to be worthy of reappointment] is one or two of ten. With recruitment by examination, they are employed in office and only afterward are they selected; the failure rate is eight or nine out of ten."[65] Censor Mao's proposal was that officials in each district and prefecture should, after due local inquiries and consultations, recommend a quota of tal-

---

62. *Fu-shan wen-chi*, 3.9b; *Ch'i tai i shu*, 2.15a. For Yen Hui, see *Analects*, 6.2 and also 11.6, where Yen Hui is named by Confucius as the one "who loved to learn;" see *Analects*, 6.7, where Min Sun declines improper appointment to office, and 11.4, where his filial piety is praised by Confucius. Tseng Ts'an 曾参 (i.e. Tseng Tzu) was one of Confucius's disciples; Recorder Ch'iu 史鰌 (or Yü 魚) was praised in *Analects*, 15.6, for being upright. (*Tseng Ts'an* is commonly read *Tseng Shen*, but see D. C. Lau's argument in *Asia Major* 16 [1971], 231.)

63. *Fu-shan wen-chi*, 3.8b; *Ch'i tai i shu*, 2.14a.

64. Fang I-chih, *Fu-shan wen-chi*, 3.10b; *Ch'i tai i shu*, 2.16a. Fang did not make clear when he thought this system had been in practice. He merely called it the "old system" (*chiu fa* 舊法). Such a system prevailed in Sung, but I believe Fang was referring to methods used in the early decades of Ming.

65. Quoted in Fang I-chih, *Fu-shan wen-chi*, 3.10b; *Ch'i tai i shu*, 2.16a.

ented, knowledgeable men whose conduct they guaranteed as faultless to a special examination for those who were "filial and scrupulous" (*hsiao lien* 孝廉). If these literati were to receive preference over those recruited through the regular examinations, students would venerate competence in the classics and emphasize righteous conduct, and men in general would pay more attention to self-regulation.[66] Fang acknowledged that his proposal, and others like it, if instituted would give rise to corrupt practices when lawless officials prone to do ill were in a position to make the recommendations, and so the system would be dependent on the integrity of the prefects and district magistrates.[67] Nevertheless, a method like this, where recommendations would be based on conduct, and mere proficiency in an examination essay would be discounted, was the means, according to Fang, both to have loyal, efficacious officials and to reform the practices of the literati.[68]

Fang I-chih's recommendation depends largely on the integrity of the local officials who would assess and recommend the literati, and how could he presume on their integrity when they had been recruited through the indiscriminatory examination process? This stumbling block of which comes first, virtuous literati to become officials or virtuous officials to recommend literati, was part of the justification for moving away from dependence on personal recommendations in favor of impersonal examination essays. The idea of recruiting officials by recommendation has been called ". . . basically a piece of Confucian feudal utopianism,"[69] and certainly there are enough examples where that description applies. Hu Chü-jen, for instance, in the fifteenth century, wrote, "If we are not able to implement the methods of 'promotion by the villages and selection by the lanes' of the early Chou dynasty, we should only recruit men by the method of recommendation; the examination system of the present day is absolutely without redeeming points."[70] Fang I-chih did not go so far, but rather was proposing a practicable system, in which personal recommendation would still be subject to verification by a special examination. He was not being a "feudal utopian" by suggesting that exclusive reliance on the eight-legged essay was not the best way to recruit administrators.[71] Fang's argument here was not with

66. *Fu-shan wen-chi*, 3.10b–11a; *Ch'i tai i shu*, 2.16a–b. "Filial and scrupulous" was a category under which men in Han times were recommended for office.

67. 3.11a; 2.16b.

68. 3.11a–b; 2.16b–17a.

69. Nivison, "Protest against Conventions," 346, n. 13.

70. Hu Chü-jen, *Chü yeh lu* 居業錄, 5.6; quoted in Jung Chao-tsu, *Ming tai ssu-hsiang shih*, 29. Cf. *Hou Han shu*, Chang-ti shu and An-ti chi, for the term *hsiang chü li hsüan* 鄉舉里選, which denotes the method of recruitment described in the *Chou li*, "Ti kuan ta ssu t'u" 地官大司徒.

71. Ku Yen-wu took a similar position. It might be noted that in the People's Republic of China there have been attempts to use local recommendations of persons of the right "character" in order to avoid the defects of competitive written examinations for gaining a place in an institution of higher education.

official service itself, which might be, at least implicitly, still taken as intrinsically worthwhile, but rather with the costs involved in making oneself eligible for appointment: prostitution of the intellect in gaining the necessary competence in examination essays, contamination of moral integrity in pursuing "success," risk of frustration through failing to pass. By concentrating on a specific end—passing the examinations and gaining a higher degree—the literati were acting as if any means were acceptable. Fang, then, was reacting against the easy acceptance of what constituted "success." To move up the examination hierarchy was a tangible, readily determinable manifestation of success and some, at least, were able to disregard the means by which that was achieved. For Fang, that was not a "success" which he would choose to seek.

Fang I-chih as a young boy had not been required by his family to devote great effort to memorizing examination essays,[72] but he acquired a facility in writing them, just as had almost all of his friends at Nanking. Some even published collections of their model eight-legged essays.[73] Fang and his family may have taken it for granted that he would duplicate his grandfather's and father's success in passing the *chin-shih* examination. There is a conspicuous lack of reference to the examinations in his writings from his years in Nanking, yet he later recalled that when he was twenty he had thought he would be dedicating his years from twenty-six to thirty-five to establishing his merit at court,[74] which suggests that he had expected to pass the metropolitan examination when he was in his mid-twenties.

Perhaps as early as 1630, but probably in 1633 and 1636, Fang sat for the provincial examination at Nanking. He certainly took the one in 1639 because that year he passed and thus became a *chü-jen*.[75] His success marks the end of a period in his life. He was never again to enjoy Nanking's pleasures in the way he had through the 1630s as a carefree young man. Fang left Nanking to go to Peking, along with the other newly passed *chü-jen* who planned to try the metropolitan examinations. Fang, though, had another reason for going to the capital. At the end of 1639 his father was impeached while serving as governor of Hu-kuang province and sent to prison in Peking. Fang went there to aid him, and it was said that because of the presence of various enemies of his father, Fang feigned that he would forgo the *chin-shih* examination in the spring of 1640, but then covertly entered the examination compound.[76] For whatever reasons, he

72. Fang I-chih, "Yu chi Erh-kung shu," in "Chi-ku t'ang wen-chi," *Ch'i tai i shu*, 2.29a; also in *Fu-shan wen-chi*, 8.11a.

73. Atwell, "Ch'en Tzu-lung," ch. 2.

74. Fang I-chih, "Yu chi Erh-kung shu," 2.29a.

75. Fang Chung-t'ung, in a note to "Shui-ching" 水晶 *t'iao* in *Wu li hsiao chih*, 7, said that in 1639 his father became a follower of Yü Yang 余颺, who was an examiner that year. Liao Ta-wen et al., *T'ung-ch'eng hsu-hsiu hsien-chih*, 14.3b (514), gives 1639 as the date that Fang became a *chü-jen*.

76. Wang Fu-chih, "Fang I-chih chuan," in *Ch'i tai i shu*, 1a. Cf. Wang Fu-chih, *Yung-li shih lu*, 5.2a–b (*Ch'uan-shan ch'üan chi*, 8955–56).

passed. He thus achieved the success that he had disparaged, but he had tried to remain unsullied by pursuing "more important" matters all the while he was preparing. He had taken the examinations without submitting to them. He had learned the "Han-tan walk," and his success only rendered his criticisms of the system less self-serving.

The most consequential effect of the examination system on Fang I-chih was not that he passed, but that even before passing he had joined with a critical opinion which had accumulated against them and their erosion of moral and intellectual values. By the 1630s, as some literati—and Fang I-chih must be counted among them—continued to disparage the empty memorizing, the shallow learning, and the moral corruption associated with the examinations, there was increasing impetus for the development of an alternative, more credible form of intellectual endeavor with other values and unrelated, at least directly, to personal aggrandizement.[77] In this context, difficult preparation and solid learning were potentially attractive, and there is repeated emphasis by a variety of writers on the difficult (*nan*) and the solid (*shih*). It was observed by Hsieh Chao-che (1567–1624) that "nowadays those who are called fond of learning are men who think gaining an examination degree is their most important duty. Not one in a hundred tries to leave a heritage of wise words for posterity. They do not give a thought to self-cultivation or their own conduct."[78] In reaction to this situation, during the seventeenth century there was an important minority of men who sought to distinguish themselves from what "everybody" did: devote himself to the eight-legged essay.

Ku Yen-wu as a young boy had not been set to laboring over examination essays by his grandfather,[79] and though he later acquired a competence in them, he never passed the provincial examination. He later wrote, "Rejected in the autumnal triennial examination of 1639, I retired and read books."[80] He never again sat for an examination. Neither did Huang Tsung-hsi study for the examinations when he was young.[81] He failed in 1630 when he first went in for a provincial examination. The next year, ostensibly in accord with his father's final behest of five years earlier, Huang began an intensive, two-year study of history and did not sit again for the examinations until 1636. Like Ku Yen-wu, Huang never succeeded in passing the *chü-jen* examinations, and when he was in the capital in 1642, he refused an attempt to recommend his name for a minor

---

77. Ch'ien Mu, *Chung-kuo chin san-pai nien hsueh-shu shih*, 141, also observed that interest in scholarship in early Ch'ing was partly in response to the examination system.

78. Hsieh Chao-che, *Wu tsa tsu*, 13.4b (1060).

79. Cf. W. Peterson, "The Life of Ku Yen-wu," *Harvard Journal of Asiatic Studies* 28 (1968), 125.

80. Ku Yen-wu, "T'ien-hsia chün-kuo li-ping shu hsu," *Ku T'ing-lin shih-wen chi*, 6.137. Cf. W. Peterson, 131.

81. Chiang Fan, *Kuo-ch'ao Han-hsueh shih-ch'eng chi*, 8.1a.

post.[82] Ku and Huang, like Fang, excoriated the deleterious effects of examination essays and the examination system as the primary means of recruiting officials. An alternative to seeking success in the examination halls was being sought, and Pao-shu Tzu gave voice to that desire.

82. Hsieh Kuo-chen, *Huang Li-chou hsueh-p'u,* 3–4; Huang Hou-ping, "Huang Li-chou nien-p'u," 23 a–b, 24b–26b, in Huang Tsung-hsi, *Li-chou i-chu hui-k'an.*

4 Rich Man

Pao-shu Tzu Is Urged to Make Money

Clansman Grasper said, "Literatus Expectation does not need to worry so much about you. For someone who surpasses others in perspicacity, a single day's work can be equivalent to an entire month [of lesser men's efforts]. What is the use of suffering [over your studies] morning and night? How do you know that you will not be finished with them in a morning and a night?"

Pao-shu Tzu answered, "I would suffer, morning and night, if I really could not suffer over them. How would you, sir, have me escape from my sufferings?"

Leaning forward with his hand on the table, Clansman Grasper said, "I understand why your anxiety waxes.[1] Your home district is devastated and your fields have gone to weeds. Your scrupulous family has been living away from home and is impoverished. For your part, you are fond of zealously helping others, and treat them with a quiet magnanimity. Easy going, you do not take care of your possessions, and the destitute in your village all make demands on your charitable benefactions. Your relatives and friends, seeing they do not have enough, look to you in their adversity. There is a steady stream of men who, offering their calling cards after hearing of your reputation, expect you to carouse with them. In so doing, you would certainly become like the man who made no sign when his robe was scorched [by lightning].[2]

"Why not become familiar with the techniques of Chi-jan?[3] Have a

33a

---

1. On 愈愈, see *Songs*, "Hsiao ya, Cheng yueh 正月." (Cf. Legge, trans., 2.4.8.2: "The sorrow of my heart becomes greater.")

2. On 衣焦不申, see *Shih shuo hsin yü*, "Ya liang," 6.89. Hsia-hou Hsuan 夏侯玄 was sitting under a cassia tree practicing his calligraphy during a thunder shower. Lightning split the tree and scorched his robes, but his appearance remained unchanged as he continued with his calligraphy, although his attendants were all bowled over. Also see "Hsia-hou Hsuan chuan," *San kuo chih*, Wei, 9.299. Implicated in a court intrigue at the age of forty-six, Hsia-hou Hsuan and his relatives were condemned. When he was being led to his execution, he was calm and his expression remained unchanged. Grasper's point seems to be that Pao-shu Tzu might become completely indifferent.

3. On the technique of Chi-jan 計然 (or Chi-yen 計研), see "Huo-chih 貨殖 chuan," *Shih*

prosperous life by making loans. Be involved in money-changing by doing the calculations. Everyone around you acts with duplicity and you will only be ruined [unless you heed my advice]. Pursue 10 percent profit. Be concerned with differences in price. Sell all of your books, zithers, swords, and curios. Become a broker in fish and salt and you will never lack a surplus. What is more, if you are able to eat at home and be frugal and if you break off with those with whom you have been associating, in a few years you could become rich."

With condescension in his voice, Pao-shu Tzu sighed, "Planning for management of his livelihood is a most important matter for a scholar (ju). But what if he is careless and improvident?[4]

"When you rise in the morning you ask how much is in your grain bins and how much cash has been dispersed. You do not shirk this bothersome task. You must have your servants make this accounting. Otherwise, they might cheat[5] *you out of 50 percent before you expose them and demand repayment. It is certainly difficult to find even a few men who are as scrupulous as Pao Shu [was in money matters].*[6] *Yet were my servant, when I was laughing and chatting*[7] *with my guests, to bring the records showing the accounts of dispersals and receipts and want me to audit and approve them down to the smallest detail,*[8] *could I be other than annoyed and wave him away?*[9] *Even when I sense his unchecked shrewdness, I still*

---

chi, 129.3256; also in *Han shu*, 91.3683. (Cf. B. Watson, trans., *Records of the Grand Historian*, vol. 2, 479–80.) Chi-jan advised the King of Yueh that if one understands how to wage war, he prepares, and if one understands timely use of resources, he understands the nature of goods to be traded. When these two points are understood, one perceives what need be known about trading the ten thousand commodities. "To invest in boats in times of drought and invest in carts in times of flood is the 'principle' of [trading] things." Yen Shih-ku was more explicit in the *Han shu*: "When drought reaches its extreme, then wet weather is coming; when flooding reaches its extreme, then dry weather is coming; therefore, in times of drought prepare [for what is coming] by accumulating boats, in times of flooding prepare by accumulating carts, so as to wait for when those items become expensive and you reap the profit." In other words, Chi-jan's "technique" is to buy cheap and sell dear. Cf. Rhea C. Blue, "The Argumentation of the Shih-huo chih chapters of the Han, Wei, and Sui Dynastic Histories," *Harvard Journal of Asiatic Studies* 11 (1948), 32.

4. On 儻葸不備, see "Shih Tan 史丹 chuan," *Han shu*, 82.3379: ". . . Although he had the appearance of being careless and improvident, his mind was meticulous."

5. On 乾沒, see Ku Yen-wu, *Jih chih lu*, 32. Ku reviewed the early occurrences of the term and concluded that it basically conveyed the idea of desiring, and taking, profits. However, it had come to connote illicit gain.

6. 廉如 (or 若) 鮑叔, quoted from "Tung-fang Shuo chuan," *Han shu*, 65.2841. Pao Shu became a byword for being generous because of his unstinted support of his friend Kuan Chung as the latter went through his formative troubles.

7. The *Ch'i tai i shu* text has *t'an* 談 for *t'an* 譚, as in the *Fu-shan wen-chi*.

8. On 米鹽靡密, see "Hsun-li 循吏 chuan," *Han shu*, 89.3629; literally, "to the fineness of grains of rice and salt."

9. Reading *hui* 撝 as *hui* 麾.

am indulgent.[10] *I might begin by being irritable and angry, but in a short*
while I may be doubtful and forgiving. Were I just to desire the clamor of 33b
Five Gates and only hear the sounds of piglets,[11] *who would tend to this*
for me?

"*With regard to the other part of your proposal, that I sell the various*
items I have in my collection, all my life I have not had many curios. I have
smiled at the men of this age who think having curios constitutes 'being
fond of antiquity.' Rather, I am stupid and simple; I live my life amidst
unrefined objects. Even if I were to sell everything,[12] *I would not obtain*
much silver. If I were to load thirty carts with my books[13] *but, in effect,*
have to give them away, why then load them? Of course, the bronze
ritual vessels and jade ornaments which I may have obtained for a few
taels of silver could be estimated to be worth several hundred taels were I
to say, 'These are objects from the Ch'in, Han and even Three [i.e., Hsia,
Shang-Yin, and Chou] dynasties.' As a result, do I not already have in my
collection what is ten or a hundred times more valuable than fish or salt?"

Pao-shu Tzu rose and, with a fan in front of his face [so that Grasper
might not hear], said with a sneer, "If that is the profit from trading in fish
and salt,[14] *it is not as much as what is to be had from seeking official salary*
and preferment. It is not as much as what is to be had from 'gifts' received
for managing someone else's affairs. It is not as much as what is to be had
in the middle of the night by a petty thief. It is not even as much as what is
to be had by a thug who robs by force in broad daylight!"

Clansman Grasper, overhearing these last remarks, said, "You are
unable to do any of the things you have just mentioned. For those, one ex-
hausts one's wits and capacities and only fears they will be inadequate [to
the task]. You are just singing about the true kings of earlier times.[15]

---

10. Reading *tiao* 雕 as *tiao* 刁.

11. In the town of Five Gates (Wu-men 五門) in Han times, a family of brothers raised pigs to sell as pork. The local people made up a ditty by playing on the name of their town and the fact that the imperial court was sometimes referred to as the Five Gates.

> Three Lords in the park,
> Two Chiefs in the hall.
> Five Gates' clamor?
> Pig sounds, that's all.

苑中三公, 舘下二卿, 五門嘩嘩, 唯聞豚聲. See Chao Ch'i, *San fu chüeh lu*, 26b.

12. See "Ch'ü li 曲禮," *Li chi*. (Cf. Couvreur, trans., *Li Ki*, vol. I, 77–78: "Un grand dignitaire, fût-il pauvre, ne vend pas les instruments qui lui servent pour les sacrifices!")

13. 藏書三十乘 Quoted from "Chang Hua 張華 chuan," *Chin shu*, 36.36a. Chang Hua rose from poverty to high office; when he was executed his family had no great wealth, just a mass of books. There were so many they filled thirty carts.

14. I follow the *Ch'i tai i shu* text, which has 魚鹽; *Fu-shan wen-chi* has 如鹽.

15. On 咏歌先王, see "Tung-fang Shuo chuan," *Han shu*, 65.2870. Tung-fang Shuo wrote, in the voice of a fictional character, "For this reason none of the gentlemen (*shih*) interested

Those who would not regard you as so much refuse are few indeed. I think you do not really have the guts [to do any of those things]."

The concern in this chapter is to show that Fang I-chih's attitudes toward the effects of commercial developments and government policies on the mores of his time shaped his intentions with regard to evolving a "new" orientation in intellectual endeavor. Rather than to attempt to set out a comprehensive account of the economic changes which occurred in the sixteenth and seventeenth centuries, it will be sufficient to indicate the character of late Ming perceptions of wealth. Fang I-chih, it will be seen, sought to reestablish the integrity of the literati by distinguishing their "proper," public values and motives from those that he saw as pervasive in the society at large.

Economic Change in Late Ming

In the last century of the Ming dynasty certain regions experienced a reinvigorated domestic trade that was reciprocally related to population growth and general economic expansion.[1] The increasing quantity and complexity of trade involved agricultural and handicraft products from villages, commodities such as metal, lumber, and valuables, and, significantly, items manufactured in workshops—lacquer ware, copper utensils, pottery, pewter. The scale of manufacture was sufficient for some of the trade names to become famous and some of the manufacturers rich enough occasionally to be treated on a nearly equal footing with officials.[2] Socially competitive with the "old" form of wealth derived primarily from landowning, this "new," commercial wealth centered especially in the Chiang-nan region.

Chiang-nan throughout the Ming dynasty was a most productive region agriculturally, a fact which was reflected in the large proportion of the empire's

---

in promoting their longevity are willing to enter [government service]. They dwell deep in the mountains, build their houses out of mud, make their doors from brambles, and sit there strumming their zithers while singing tunes celebrating the kings of earlier times. For their part, they can find happiness and forget about dying." (Cf. B. Watson, trans., *Courtier and Commoner*, 102–3.)

1. Cf. Fu I-ling, *Ming tai Chiang-nan shih-min ching-chi shih t'an*, 1–2. I leave aside the controversy over whether the last hundred years of Ming was a time of "sprouting capitalism." Explicitly rejecting the "sprouts of capitalism" theory, Huang Jen-yü (Ray Huang), "Ts'ung 'San-yen' k'an wan Ming shang-jen" ("Merchants of the Late Ming as Presented in the *San-yen* Stories"), *Journal of the Institute of Chinese Studies of the Chinese University of Hong Kong* 7.1 (1974), 133–54, draws together material from the collections of stories, published in the 1630s, in order to illustrate the social place and the operations of small-scale merchants.

2. Chang Tai, *T'ao an meng i*, 63. Cf. Fu I-ling, 48–49.

tax revenues for which it was responsible.[3] In late Ming, Fang I-chih's home district of T'ung-ch'eng exported large quantities of rice, which was shipped down the Ts'ung-yang River to the Yangtze to be distributed for sale.[4] Land in T'ung-ch'eng was thus a profitable and preferred form of investment,[5] and owners were drawn into the expanding trade in the Yangtze valley. By the time of Fang I-chih's birth, his family almost certainly was among those with extensive holdings. Although his great-grandfather had not inherited much property from his own father, he married the only child of an elderly retired official. With the property from his wife's dowry and trousseau he was able both to be more than generous to his poor elder brother and to lay the foundations for his own family's rise. Two of his three sons and two of his eight grandsons became *chin-shih* as the family consolidated and no doubt expanded its wealth by holding both office and land.[6]

A government post gave one access to more than the salary to be used in the purchase of land. Fang Ta-mei (*chin-shih* in 1586), who was some degree of cousin to Fang I-chih's grandfather,[7] explained to his sons how, as a scrupulous man, he had come to increase the family's wealth with the purchase of 350 *mou* of land plus having 1700 taels of silver held in reserve. "These are not things from my holding office but are from presents given by friends. Your departed mother worked long and hard for this result [i.e., the family's financial security], but she only worried that her sons might think that this property was obtained from holding office."[8] It was, of course, obtained from his having office, even if indirectly and not illegally, for the "presents" would not have been forthcoming on the same scale had Fang Ta-mei not been an official.

The large reserve of silver Fang Ta-mei accumulated reflects the unprecedented economic importance which was accorded to the metal from the six-

3. Cf. *Ming hui-yao*, 56 ("Shih-huo, erh, T'ien-fu"), and Hou Wai-lu, *T'ung shih*, vol. 4, 1107.

4. Fang Tu-han 方都韓, "Ts'ung-ch'uan ch'ü tao i 樅川榷稻議," in *Ku chin t'u-shu chi-ch'eng*, "Ts'ao mu tien 草木典" 28; quoted in Han Ta-ch'eng, "Ming tai shang-p'in ching-chi te fa-chan yü tzu-pen chu-i te meng-ya," in *Ming Ching she-hui ching-chi hsing-t'ai te yen-chiu*, 24.

5. Ho Ping-ti, *Ladder of Success*, 141 and 334, made this point, which he supported by referring to the whole of Ma Ch'i-ch'ang's *T'ung-ch'eng ch'i chiu chuan*, but the point seems to depend on inference rather than direct evidence. Chang Ying 張英 (1638–1708), a high official from T'ung-ch'eng in the K'ang-hsi reign, wrote a well-known set of instructions to his clan on managing property, the "Heng ch'an so-yen 恒產瑣言," in *Tu-su t'ang wen-chi* 篤素堂文集. For a translation of the "Heng ch'an so-yen," and on landowning in general in T'ung-ch'eng, see Hilary J. Beattie, "Land and Lineage in China: A Study of T'ung-ch'eng County, Anhwei, in the Ming and Ch'ing Dynasties" (Ph.D. diss., Cambridge University, 1973).

6. Yeh Ts'an, "Fang Ming-shan hsing-chuang," in *Ch'i tai i shu*, 1a–b, 2b, 4a.

7. The supposition of kinship is based on the occurrence of Ta 大 as the first character in his personal name and in the names of Fang I-chih's grandfather, Ta-chen, as well as Ta-chen's two younger brothers.

8. Ma Ch'i-ch'ang, *T'ung-ch'eng ch'i chiu chuan*, 4.14b.

teenth century as the volume of trade expanded. Silver became the primary medium for larger transactions and increasingly important as a tax medium,[9] changes which entailed adjustments that ran through the entire society. One of the most persistent questions was whether there was sufficient silver in the empire to meet the growing use to which it was put. About 1570 an official memorialized on the problem and incidentally gave testimony on the pervasive use of silver.

> We have observed that in the empire the commoners' anxiety that they might become impoverished is not due to any insufficiency of cloth or grain, but to an insufficiency of silver. Silver cannot be worn when one is cold, nor eaten when hungry; it must be exchanged for things of use as food and clothing.[10] Yet what alternative has there been but to employ silver and throw aside copper cash? As copper cash increasingly has been thrown aside, silver increasingly has dominated in circulation, and as it increasingly has dominated in use it has increasingly been removed to storehouses, and so silver has become increasingly expensive. But as goods have become increasingly cheap [relative to silver], the transaction of converting their produce into silver to pay taxes has become increasingly difficult [for the commoners]. Exploiters have taken advantage by buying cheaply [when the commoners all have to pay their taxes] and then selling when prices have become more expensive. The silver which has come to be hoarded by those exploiters continues to pile up, while what circulates in the empire diminishes. If this were to go on for a few decades more, we do not know where it will end.[11]

Although the protest was aimed primarily at the court's rapacious accumulation of silver at the expense even of the government treasury, the framework of the protest was concern over the adequacy of the money supply for the empire's needs. Through the Wan-li period (1573–1619), the amount of monetary silver in China continued to increase with the importation of significant quantities of silver from Peru and Mexico by way of the Philippines and from Japan.[12] However, demand grew even more rapidly. At the local yamen, small landowners only marginally involved in interregional trade were required to pay their taxes in silver. In the marketplace, the supply both of silver and copper cash did not maintain a balanced growth in pace with rising demand for money. Economic disruption accompanied economic growth.[13]

9. Cf. Liang Fang-chung, *The Single-Whip Method*. Also, Fu I-ling, *Chiang-nan shih-min*, 2.

10. Cf. A. Waley, *Po Chü-i*, 62, for a parallel sentiment expressed in the T'ang dynasty about copper cash.

11. "Chin Hsüeh-yen chuan 靳學顏傳," *Ming shih* 214.5669–70.

12. Millions of Spanish silver pesos were imported to Manila (and mostly traded to China) from the 1580s through the 1630s. See Ch'üan Han-sheng, "Ming Ch'ing chien Mei-chou pai-yin te shu-ju Chung-kuo" ("The Inflow of American Silver into China from the Late Ming to the Mid-Ch'ing Period"), *Journal of the Institute of Chinese Studies of the Chinese University of Hong Kong* 2.1 (1969), 59–79. Also see Liang Fang-chung, "Ming tai kuo-chi mao-i yü yin te shu-ch'u-ju," *Chung-kuo she-hui ching-chi shih chi-k'an* 6 (1939), 266–324.

13. Cf. Ch'üan Han-sheng, "Mei-chou pai-yin," 178–80.

The disruptions caused by the increase in trade, the use of silver, and the attendant commercializing of agriculture and the village economy were resented and denounced by men whose interests rested on landowning and office-holding. An example is the overdrawn summary of economic and social transformation that occurred over the sixteenth century which appeared in the gazetteer, probably completed in the early 1600s, of a prosperous district in southern Anhui.

> Our state's material prosperity and moral well-being reached their peak [here in She-hsien] in the Hung-chih reign [1488–1505]. In that time, households and individuals were amply provisioned. There were adequate houses for dwelling. There were sufficient fields for tilling. There were forested mountains for firewood. There were fertile gardens for planting. There was no vexatious pressing for taxes. No banditry arose. Marriages were carried out at the proper time. Villages were peaceful and secure. Spinning was done by the wives. Men concerned themselves with mulberry [wood for bows] and *p'eng* [bramble for arrows]. Indentured servants bore their burden. Neighbors were helpful. . . . Coming down to the end of the Cheng-te [1506–1521] and beginning of the Chia-ching [1522–1566] reigns, the situation was different. As merchants and traders became more numerous, farming was not emphasized. Property was exchanged. Prices fluctuated. Those who were able were successful. Those who were a bit slow were ruined. The family on the east might become rich while the family on the west was impoverished. As the equilibrium between those of higher and lower status was lost, everyone struggled over paltry sums. People were mutually exploitative; each sought to further himself. Thereupon, deceptive practices sprouted, contentions arose, recreations were off-color, extravagance was everywhere. . . . By the end of the Chia-ching [1522–1566] and the Lung-ch'ing [1567–1572] reigns, the situation differed even more. Instances of wealth from the superfluous [i.e., commerce] were numerous, and instances of wealth from the basic [i.e., agriculture] were few. The rich became richer and the poor got poorer. Those who had risen were overbearing. Those who had fallen were skittish. Property thus was oppressive, and possessions did not stay long with anyone. Trade was a tangle. Unchecked desires made people calculating. Powerful persons who did wrong created turmoil. Men without scruples preyed on others. . . . Today [i.e., about 1600], another thirty-some years after that, the differences are virtually incomparable [to the condition of society in 1500]. One out of a hundred is wealthy, but nine out of ten are impoverished. The impoverished are unable to oppose the wealthy, so that, contrary to what should be, the few control the many. Silver and copper cash seem to dominate even heaven and earth.[14]

Explicitly recalling the earlier era as a happy springtime, the account implicitly predicted a winter of discontent because of the expansion of commerce.

Against the background of these changes, it is possible to see a clash in which the "old" social forces sought to suppress men of the "new" wealth,

---

14. Ku Yen-wu, "She (-hsien) chih feng t'u lun 歙縣志風土論," *T'ien-hsia chün-kuo li-ping shu, ts'e* 9, 76a–b. Quoted in Hou Wai-lu, *Chung-kuo ssu-hsiang t'ung shih*, vol. 5, 3–4, whose textual variants and hiatuses I have followed.

especially that accumulated from trade in "manufactured" goods.[15] But such an easy dichotomy is blurred by the difficulty of sorting out the "new" men from the "old." Many landowning officials were willing to reap profits wherever they were to be found—in pawn shops, in dealing in salt and alcohol, in various kinds of stores.[16] Landowners in Chiang-nan derived income both from agriculture and trade, from "fields and gardens, and from the marketplace and shops."[17] When Fang I-chih's great-grandfather married the daughter of a retired official in the mid-sixteenth century, his wife brought as part of her trousseau (to be distinguished from the dowry) more than ten *mou* of fields and a shop in the marketplace.[18] Investments were made in overseas trade, mainly to southeast Asia and the Philippines, and in spinning and weaving cloth.[19] At the same time, those with commercially derived wealth used official status to protect and enlarge their holdings, not only by buying such titles as Student in the Imperial Academy (*chien-sheng*), but by "sheltering" their possessions under the names of men who had achieved rank in the examination or official hierarchies. A memorial in the Ch'ung-chen reign explained the symbiotic relationship.

> We have observed first degree holders, in such desperate straits that in the morning they do not give a thought for what will come of them in the evening, become inexhaustibly rich as soon as they receive the *chü-jen* degree. Such men, on passing the highest examination, live a life of luxury; they have several hundred thousand in silver if not several million. Consider how and why this is so. . . . They pay no tax on their person, no labor service on their property, no grain tribute on their fields, no commercial duties on their goods. Moreover, by sheltering dishonest men from *their* tax, labor service, grain tribute and commercial duties, their income is unending.[20]

This description is overdrawn, but it suggests the involvement of degree holders in local, private economic affairs.

One of the social effects of the increased commercialization under way in the sixteenth and seventeenth centuries was, supposedly, a whetted appetite for

---

15. Cf. Fu I-ling, *Chiang-nan shih-min*, 49–50. Such a clash, or contradiction, is asserted to represent the tension between old, feudal elements and "sprouting capitalism" with its developing bourgeoisie.

16. Huang Hsing-tseng, *Wu feng lu*, 5b. Also quoted in Fu I-ling, *Chiang-nan shih-min*, 40. Huang (1490–1540) wrote in the first half of the sixteenth century, when many of these developments were just getting under way. Ho Ping-ti, *Ladder of Success*, 81, and Albert Chan, "Peking at the Time of the Wan-li Emperor," 122, also referred to Huang's comments.

17. Kuei Yu-kuang, *Wen-chi*, quoted in Fu I-ling, 50.

18. Yeh Ts'an 葉燦, "Fang Ming-shan hsing-chuang 方明善行狀," in *Ch'i tai i shu*, 1b.

19. Fu I-ling, 50.

20. Ch'en Ch'i-hsin 陳啓新, quoted in Chi Liu-ch'i, *Ming chi pei lueh*, 12.2b–3a (480–81). Fictional, but vivid, examples of such practices are given in ch. 3 of *Ju lin wai shih*, by Wu Ching-tzu, and in ch. 1 of *Hsing-shih yin-yuan chuan* by P'u Sung-ling.

wealth. Ho Liang-chün (1506–73) argued on the basis of a few contrasting examples that prior to the latter part of the fifteenth century high officials did not accrue great wealth, but from the Cheng-te reign (i.e., the beginning of the sixteenth century) they owned businesses and took profits, so that some had fortunes of more than a hundred thousand taels in silver, enough, they thought, to last their descendants for hundreds of years.[21] The new developments furthered "the desire of the wealthy families of Chiang-nan in the pursuit of silver and the accumulation of copper cash."[22] Commercialization and silver together demolished any sharp distinction between landed interests and trade interests, which were even perceived to be allied as victims of supplemental taxes and extortions by eunuch agents of the Wan-li court.[23] The substantive impediments to the growth of the "new," commercially based wealth stemmed not so much from landowners *per se*, even large scale landowners, as from exactions imposed by all strata of government.[24]

There was no clear lineup of "new" commercial interests and "new" trends in thought against landed interests and "old" thought. If the latter is taken to stand for "Confucianism," Confucianism's bias against profit seeking did not render it inevitably hostile to trade, as the tradition made room for merchants in a harmonious social order.[25] There have been attempts to demonstrate a close relationship between involvement in commerce and the "progressive" thought represented by the Tung-lin movement.[26] (The claim has been made that the Tung-lin movement, although its call was for a rededication to traditional moral values, was in the vanguard of morality in the first quarter of the seventeenth century, and thus it was "progressive" to the extent that it was associated with emerging "bourgeois" values, if such indeed can be said to exist at this time.) Ku Hsien-ch'eng and Kao P'an-lung, the founders of the revived Tung-lin Academy, had family connections with trade. Ku's father had raised his family from extreme poverty by his efforts as a merchant, and one of Kao's ancestors had been a merchant out of necessity.[27] Although the Tung-lin movement was not a function of commercial interests, Tung-lin members supported

21. Ho Liang-chün, *Ssu-yu-chai ts'ung shuo che ch'ao* 四友齋叢說摘抄, 6.1a–b (353–54).

22. Fu I-ling, *Chiang-nan shih-min*, 49.

23. E.g., *Ming shih*, "Shih huo 5," 81.1972.

24. Hou Wai-lu discussed the rapacious character of tax collecting at the end of the sixteenth and beginning of the seventeenth century and observed it had blocked the development of capitalism. Cf. *Chung-kuo ssu-hsiang t'ung shih*, vol. 4, 1107–8. On the other hand, Ray Huang, "Fiscal Administration during the Ming Dynasty," in C. O. Hucker, ed., *Chinese Government in Ming Times*, 119–22, cast doubt on assertions that the land tax collections in late Ming are justifiably labeled as "exorbitant." There may in fact be little conflict between these two views; the one focuses on contemporary perceptions of the tax burden, the other on the revenue raising potential of the economy.

25. Cf. the discussion in Thomas A. Metzger, "The State and Commerce in Imperial China," *Asian and African Studies* 6 (1970), especially 25–38.

26. E.g., Hou Wai-lu, *Chung-kuo ssu-hsiang t'ung shih*, vol. 4, 1096–1120.

27. Hou Wai-lu, *Chung-kuo ssu-hsiang t'ung shih*, vol. 4, 1105.

and sympathized with traders and merchants, and vice versa. Tung-lin members urged reductions in the duties paid by merchants and better treatment for them, and called for government sympathy to be extended to the wealthy as well as the poor.[28] They tended to take the part of commercial interests against excessive exploitation and arbitrary exactions imposed by the court. Tung-lin members were prominently outspoken[29] against the rapacity of the Tax Commissioners (*shui shih* 稅使), posts created in 1579 in each province and filled by eunuchs,[30] and the Mining Inspectors (*k'uang chien* 礦監), mainly eunuchs sent out ostensibly to locate and develop new copper and silver mines to meet monetary needs but who instead used the mandate to collect forfeits from landowners who did not want to suffer "mine exploration" on their properties.[31] Similarly, Fang I-chih's grandfather, who was in accord with the Tung-lin criticisms of government practices and the need to reinvigorate morality, as a censor in Peking had memorialized in 1602 against the abuses by Tax Commissioners and Mining Inspectors,[32] and had urged reforms in the salt monopoly as well as in tax collection in Chiang-nan. Thus, "righteous" men could take the middle position of acknowledging the realities of the increase in commerce, in the use of silver, and in merchants' wealth, and could defend these changes without being actively involved in them.[33]

There is another dimension to the sympathy for merchants on the part of Tung-lin leaders. They were working with the heritage both of Wang Yang-ming's teachings that the street is full of sages[34] as well as the efforts, especially by those associated with the so-called T'ai-chou school, including Fang I-chih's great-grandfather, to make the teachings accessible to a wide audience. Merchants were no more excluded than were artisans and field laborers.[35] Through the sixteenth century there were recurrent attempts by a variety of thinkers to blur social distinctions in the effort to promote morality and social harmony.[36]

28. Hou Wai-lu, 1114–15.
29. Hou Wai-lu, 1109–12.
30. *Ming hui yao* 57, "Shang shui" 商稅.
31. *Ming shih chi shih pen mo*, 65, and *Ming shih*, "Shih-huo 5," K'eng yeh 坑冶, 81. 1972.
32. "Fang Ta-li chuan," in *Ch'i tai i shu*, 1a.
33. At least it has yet to be shown that they were actively and directly involved. Hou Wai-lu, *Chung-kuo ssu-hsiang t'ung shih*, vol. 4, 1116, wrote of the Tung-lin men as compromisers, as reformers of a class in the "middle," which still distinguishes them from the commercial stratum. Tso Yun-p'eng and Liu Ch'ung-jih, "Ming tai Tung-lin tang cheng te she-hui pei-ching chi ch'i yü shih-min yun-tung te kuan-hsi," *Hsin chien-she* 1957 (10), 33–38, also attempted to associate Tung-lin protests with new commercial interests against a rapacious "feudal" government. They proposed (p. 38) that the Tung-lin struggle was different from other factional conflicts in Chinese history because of the Tung-lin support for urban merchants, and vice versa.
34. Wang Yang-ming, *Wang Wen-ch'eng kung ch'üan shu*, 3.150. Cf. W. T. Chan, trans., *Instructions for Practical Living*, 239.
35. See Huang Tsung-hsi, *Ming ju hsueh an*, 32.319–20.
36. I have in mind such prominent figures as Wang Yang-ming, Ho Hsin-yin, and Lü K'un.

Fang's Attitudes Toward "New" Wealth

In contrast to the Tung-lin generation, Fang I-chih and his generation, perhaps by implication more than by intention, were reasserting the distance
between "true" literati, as an educated elite unsullied by motives of personal
profit, and the commoners (*min*), who were all too involved in commercial
endeavors. It was not so much that Fang and the others had a weaker consciousness of the problems of the marketplace.[37] Certainly Fang was cognizant of the
economic realities of his time, but his attitude was not one of defense of the
changes.

He wrote a short piece entitled "Proposals Concerning Monetary Policy"
(*Ch'ien ch'ao i* 錢鈔議) in the second half of 1643, when the financial condition
of the government was perilous and the emperor had ordered his Minister of
Revenue, Ni Yuan-lu (1594–1644), to proceed with a plan to issue quantities of
paper notes as money.[38] Fang doubted the efficacy of any attempt to issue notes
without establishing their credibility. The best government policy, he maintained, is in accord with the feelings of the people, and how, he asked, was
ordering them "to regard sheets of paper as valuable" in accord with their
feelings?[39] Merchants did not seem to warrant such consideration. Fang suggested that they could be ordered to transport grain to the border areas for use
by the military and they would receive as compensation certificates (*ch'ao* 鈔)
redeemable for salt in the centers of production around the Huai River in northern Kiangsu (4.26a). The implementation of Fang's suggestion would have meant
a revival of the policy, begun in the Hung-wu reign, of giving merchants salt
certificates for grain they delivered to designated granaries, instead of the then
current practice of making the delivery of silver to the frontier the cost of being
legally able to deal in salt.[40] With suitably stringent regulations against their
being forced on merchants or the merchants not receiving the full amount of
salt, the certificates, Fang contended, could also relieve some of the demand for

37. Cf. the assertion by Hou Wai-lu, vol. 4, 1146, that some of Fang I-chih's writings
manifest " . . . the weak civic consciousness of men of the Fu she."

38. Ray Huang, "Ni Yuan-lu: 'Realism' in a Neo-Confucian Scholar-Statesman," *Self
and Society*, 427. Fang I-chih noted (*Fu-shan wen-chi*, 4.26a) that his fellow townsman Chiang
Ch'en 蔣臣, who was serving as Ni Yuan-lu's "executive officer" at the Ministry (Ray Huang,
422), submitted the proposal on paper money on which the emperor ordered Ni to act. The
proposal, it may be added, was shortly abandoned. Cf. *Ming shih*, 81.1969.

39. Fang I-chih, "Ch'ien ch'ao i," *Fu-shan wen-chi*, 4.26a–b. Ni Yuan-lu also recognized
the importance of establishing confidence in the paper notes (Huang, 427).

40. *Hsu wen-hsien t'ung k'ao*, 20, "Cheng-chüeh, yen t'ieh" 征榷鹽鐵. In 1617 the salt
system had been revamped by, among other changes, allowing hereditary privileges for
certain merchants to ship salt, but the requirement that the merchants deliver silver to the
frontier was not abandoned until early Ch'ing. Cf. Thomas A. Metzger, "The Organizational Capabilities of the Ch'ing State in the Field of Commerce: The Liang-huai Salt
Monopoly, 1740–1840," in W. E. Willmott, ed., *Economic Organization in Chinese Society*,
21–24.

a convenient medium for long distance payments, which would then make it more possible to prohibit the free use of silver (4.25b–26a). He pointed out that in the Ch'in dynasty and under Han Wu-ti (140–87 B.C.) the circulation of silver had been prohibited, although gold was used as money, and in the first reigns of the Ming dynasty trade in gold and silver articles was banned (4.25b). (Fang did not need to add that the ban was in an attempt to support the circulation of paper notes, which the Ming government tried to revive but without achieving the effectiveness that had been attained in the first half of the Yuan dynasty.)[41] By banning the circulation of silver, the government could derive profits from the coins it issued, as well as from salt certificates which had established credibility (4.25b).

Silver, used by weight, was almost completely outside of government control. Copper coins, on the other hand, could legally only be minted by the government. Fang calculated that since the mints added zinc carbonate (*wo ch'ien* 倭鉛 or *lu-kan* 盧甘)[42] to constitute 40–60% of the melt with the copper in making good quality yellow coins that ring when dropped, more than 300 coins weighing one *ch'ien* 錢 each are made from 160 *ch'ien* of copper. Since officials sent to southern Kiangsi to buy copper on the market pay the equivalent of 0.133 taels of silver for 160 *ch'ien* of copper (and, I add, the exchange rate between silver and copper cash ideally ranged between 900 and 1200 coins for a tael of silver), and copper from Kwangtung and Japan was cheaper, there was a profit to be made by the government. Fang raised the possibility that the minting of coins be moved from Peking to the south, where the cost of rice and labor, as well as firewood and charcoal, was cheaper, with the implication that the profit margin could be raised. He acknowledged, however, that the officials of the Ministry of Works and Ministry of Revenue had a vested interest in continuing to operate their mints in the north. The trouble was that in order to derive a greater surplus in minting the coins, sometimes the amount of zinc carbonate was doubled, which produced darkish coins that shattered when dropped. Not only was it difficult to circulate these debased coins, but such practices had eroded confidence in copper cash so that people preferred to hold silver. Thus the coins minted by the government "are unable to compete with silver."[43] More than that, local officials have come to refuse to accept copper cash as payment of taxes because with silver they can add on supplementary amounts, such as the "meltage fee" (*huo-hao* 火耗). Just as paper money which is unac-

41. Cf. Gordon Tullock, "Paper Money—A Cycle in Cathay," *Economic History Review* 9 (1956–57), 393–407.

42. On these two terms for zinc carbonate, see Joseph Needham, *Science and Civilisation*, vol. 5, part 2, p. 199. Fang I-chih also referred to the terms in *Wu li hsiao chih*, 7; e.g., under "T'ung-k'uang 銅鑛."

43. Fang, "Ch'ien ch'ao i," 4.25a. For a brief review of minting policy proposals and changes during the Ch'ung-chen reign, see *Ming shih*, 81.1968–69. The perennial problem was that profit margins were not enough to ensure that sufficient cash of acceptable quality was minted.

ceptable for tax payments suffers in circulation, copper cash was not credited by the people (4.25b). "If credibility is not established," Fang asked, "how will there be any benefit [from issuing paper notes or copper cash] even if there are severe punishments and repeated imperial commands?" (4.26a) Fang urged that copper cash be used for tax payments (4.25b), and he cited precedents to show that there was no need for copper mines in Yunnan and Kweichow to be closed, as long as civil officials administered them and eunuchs were not sent to supervise them without good cause.[44] His main point was that there should be a shift away from reliance on silver, and its place should be retaken by a reliable copper cash in sufficient supply. "When the government mints a million strings [each "string" contained 1000 coins, in theory], then the economic life of the whole world has the use of another million strings, and how would this be a plan only for the merchants to derive more revenues!" (4.25a) Rather, Fang thought he had shown, it would be the government which would profit most. It is important to notice how "traditional" Fang's attitudes were: use of silver should be diminished or prohibited; merchants should be manipulated to perform burdensome tasks for the government in return for privileges to deal in salt; copper cash should be the medium in the marketplace and for tax payment. His attitudes are to be identified more with the "old" than with the "new" wealth.

Fang I-chih especially regretted that there were those who held that "in this age one cannot but try to increase his wealth,"[45] and to rebut this view he created the figure of Mr. Tranquility (Tan-po hsien-sheng 澹泊先生), who explained what was wrong with wanting to "increase wealth." He allowed that, as Tung Chung-shu had said, "It is clear that to be obviously seeking profit and always to fear impoverishment is the concern of commoners."[46] The trouble was, Mr. Tranquility argued, that "nowadays among princes, lords, and high officials on down to literati (*shih*) and commoners, rare is the man who does not have this view of being concerned to increase his wealth. They may each be different in social standing, but the reasons for their being fond of [wealth] are identical."[47] That is, they have all observed the merchants who, always selling their goods more expensively than they bought them, "expand their wealth several tens of times" to become richer than a noble family of a thousand chariots was in antiquity (3.4a). In consequence, money grubbers in the villages lend at compound interest and deal for unconscionable profits (3.4a). Others derive profit by settling disputes and disentangling problems which they have made it their concern to provoke or inflame (3.5a). Literati, ". . . once they earn a little something or perhaps collect a debt for someone and receive thanks [and

---

44. Fang, 4.26a. Ni Yuan-lu as Minister of Finance protested against opening new government mines (Huang, 426).
45. Fang I-chih, preface to "Huo-chih lun 貨殖論," *Fu-shan wen-chi*, 3.3a.
46. Fang I-chih, "Huo-chih lun," 3.4a, quoting from Tung Chung-shu.
47. "Huo-chih lun," 3.3b.

a portion of the proceeds],[48] take to sitting around in restaurants poring over contracts [in hopes of finding other 'business'].''[49] Then there are the literati who, particularly good at ingratiating themselves with officials by being flattering or amusing or of some petty service, enrich themselves by their known proximity to the powerful (3.5a–b). As soon as officials assume their posts, they start to accumulate riches, while government underlings twist the law to extract their own profits from the poor people (3.4a–b). Even princes and other nobility personally attend to money matters and are niggling over trifling amounts, "so how much more so, then, will be the tightfisted country fellow?" (3.4a) And of course, Mr. Tranquility added, the ordinary people want the luxuries and comforts they see the rich enjoying, with their extensive properties, lavish houses, elaborate meals, numerous women and servants, "with everything they like in profusion, with every whim satisfied" (3.4b). However, since in any struggle it is the side with the greater force that wins out, it is the powerful and influential who come to possess the greatest wealth and victimize the less well placed (3.6a–b). "Power," he observed, "is the basis of influence, and profits accrue to influence. In the present day, the uncorrupted and respectful are ridiculed by the rest of the world, while the powerful and influential are envied and increasingly prosper" (3.6b).

According to Mr. Tranquility, it was the example of merchants accruing fortunes that promoted avarice and contentiousness. For this same reason, Fang I-chih regretted that Ssu-ma Ch'ien in the *Records of the Grand Historian* had devoted a chapter to commoners who had vastly "increased their wealth" through trade, even those in such humble items as lard, soy sauce, cooked sheep's tripe, and horse medicine.[50] Fang quoted the judgment that "the eminence of some emperors, princes, generals, and ministers was not necessarily included in biographies by the Grand Historian [i.e., Ssu-ma Ch'ien], yet he included the 'increasers of wealth.' That everyone has heard of them is due to the Grand Historian's influence."[51] To counter the justification which the profit seekers found in the *Records of the Grand Historian*, it was suggested that the biographies of the men who had made fortunes should be taken in the same way one should take the story in the *Chuang Tzu* of Robber Chih's animalistic amorality in humiliating Confucius—that what was right was being indicated by speaking as if the opposite were correct.[52] This, of course, would be to turn on its head Ssu-ma Ch'ien's point in including the names of humble men who accumulated

48. Fang I-chih was taking the phrase 爲人起債, 分利受謝, from "Ku Yung 谷永 chuan," *Han shu*, 85.3460.

49. Fang I-chih, "Huo-chih lun," 3.4a.

50. Fang I-chih, "Huo-chih lun," 3.3a, 4a. Cf. "Huo-chih chuan," *Shih chi*, 129. *Also see* B. Watson, trans., *Records of the Grand Historian*, vol. 2, 499. (Watson, it may be noted, translated the title of the chapter as "The Money-makers.")

51. Fang I-chih, "Hsi yü hsin pi," 11a.

52. Fang I-chih, "Hsi yü hsin pi," 11b. Cf. *Chuang Tzu*, tsa-p'ien, "Tao Chih."

wealth. Ssu-ma Ch'ien took them to be men who in their own way benefited society while making a profit for themselves and their families, and by implication they were more than historically notable as a type; they were more laudable than the useless pedants who wrung their hands over Mencius's admonitions against "profit" but were unable to do anything themselves.

Fang I-chih, on the basis of the argument he assigned to Mr. Tranquility, might be taken to be firmly stuck in the narrow tradition of Confucian deprecation of all commercial endeavors as sullied with morally reprehensible profit-seeking. The confrontation Fang constructed between the old, aloof, moralistic, landowning Mr. Tranquility and a young, involved, straightforward merchant seems to symbolize the conflict between the "old" and "new" forms of wealth, although in Fang's presentation of the conflict there is no reference to the domination of the old over the new other than in terms of moral appeal, the patent superiority of Mr. Tranquility's ethic, once understood. But even the worthy Mr. Tranquility, who was described as living amidst the several hundred *mou* of land he owned, a rather substantial holding in agriculturally rich Chiang-nan, distinguished between the unproductive, avaricious profit-seeking of officials, middlemen, and the like, and the merchant's tasks of "grasping the calculating rods, reckoning 10 percent [profit margins on his sales], and increasing his stock of goods."[53] The fictional occasion for Mr. Tranquility's tirade against the avarice that results from a general attitude of wanting to increase one's wealth was an interview he had with a young man who had become a broker in order to liberate his family from the humiliation of having to eat bean soup (3.7a). This young man made several million in his travels across the empire by buying where goods were cheap and selling them where they were more dear. Nevertheless, he continued to remain satisfied with simple clothes, his humble village, and an unostentatious life, and he continued to be charitable, honest, righteous, and industrious (3.3a). In short, he was the hypothetical "good merchant." Mr. Tranquility even told him that "if everyone increased their wealth [as scrupulously] as you, then the empire would be well ordered" (3.6b). But when the young man, out of respect for Mr. Tranquility, offered to teach him the techniques of making money through trade, Mr. Tranquility, who was so aloof from the rest of the world that he was also called Mr. Indifferent (Tan-po hsien-sheng 淡泊先生) (3.3b), lamely protested that he was too old and did not have the strength to work so hard at "increasing wealth" in the way the young merchant had, just as he was not thick-skinned enough to "increase his wealth" in the unscrupulous ways most of the world did (3.6b). More than that, his argument that the desire to make money had led to all manner of contention and avarice persuaded the young merchant to abandon his trade and join old Mr. Tranquility in retirement (3.7a). The implication of Mr. Tranquility's view is that there would be a place in society for merchants

53. Fang I-chih, "Huo-chih lun," 3.4b.

if they would keep their place, and their values were not allowed to spread and corrupt everyone else, from prince to villager. It is avarice, ostensibly, not simply profit, which is to be condemned, but the ideal of "increasing one's wealth" had so established itself that Fang I-chih asked if one could stand against the fashion without drawing ridicule.[54]

Regardless of ridicule, some of Fang's contemporaries had a similar disdain for chasing profits, whether as an official, merchant, or whatever. There also is no doubt that Fang's attitude toward the sordid struggle to make money which he saw all around him was in part made possible by his family's being so well fixed. In spite of the disruptions in T'ung-ch'eng, during his years in Nanking he was able to maintain a reputation for generosity and was under no compulsion to be part of the large pool of men who had to be concerned with earning a living. One might suspect Fang of being merely hypocritical in denouncing the avarice of others. He might be charged with simply using his words to impede others from duplicating his own family's rise from the relative poverty of his great-grandfather's youth. He may have been speaking as a representative of an established family who owned land and who was primarily interested in resisting encroachments of its high place from newcomers, no matter how they derived their wealth. Whatever Fang's motives, he was part of a hardening of attitudes toward men of "new" wealth, especially that based on trade, that arose in the 1630s as the empire's turmoil rendered everyone more uncertain and more defensive than had been the case in the Tung-lin generation during the first quarter of the seventeenth century.[55] Yet it also must be noticed that Fang was criticizing not only merchants and *nouveaux*, but also established men who would uncritically, even insensitively, seek to increase their wealth. This parallels his criticism of those who, whether from old or new families, sought to rise in status by passing examinations without much concern for learning. In both cases, Fang was against self-seekers, men who would benefit themselves without regard for wider responsibilities. Money and degrees, Fang was saying, are not everything, although his prospects for having both were always very high.

Whatever lay at the back of Fang's mind, and however we assess his economic interests, we can still notice a negative correlation between "new" wealth derived from commerce and leading proponents of "new" learning.[56] Fang and Ku and Huang to some extent may have been on the side of merchants in criticizing previous occurrences of rapacious tax collecting and eunuch interference on the local level, but they were not advocates of the increasing monetization

54. Fang I-chih, "Huo-chih lun," preface, 3.3a.

55. In a cogent unpublished paper, William S. Atwell has argued that the economy in the late 1630s was suffering under a severe contraction in the amounts of silver imported annually from Manila and Japan. The effects of the contraction on attitudes toward silver, commerce, and merchants remain to be studied.

56. For an example of the opposite view of the correlation, see Shang Yüeh, *Chung-kuo tzu-pen chu-i kuan-hsi fa-sheng chi yen-pien te ch'u-pu yen-chiu*, 257 and 145–271 in general.

of the economy. They decried the increased reliance on silver as disruptive of social harmony. They wanted increased social and political emphasis on agricultural production without denying the necessity of commercial pursuits.[57] Thus, their writings were not contributing to the improvement of the position of the merchants in society. Secondly, they may have opposed the "old" learning propounded by too many of their contemporaries as remote from real world concerns and begun to formulate a "new," socially relevant learning founded in fact, and thus, it has been claimed, in some way congruent with tastes associated with new wealth. Nevertheless, their emphasis on command of the written tradition and the difficult, sometimes abstruse scholarship they developed hardly had an obvious appeal to a newly important urban culture that supposedly grew with the sprouts of capitalism. The contrast between the "ancient style" prose of the "Seven Solutions" and the nearly vernacular prose of contemporary short stories represents the distance between the scholars of the "new" learning and the readers of a more nearly popular genre.[58] Although Fang, Ku, and Huang were familiar with the "big city" because of their sojourns in Soochow and Nanking, their ideas did not have a particularly urban cast.

Regardless of what some writers have identified as "progressive" elements in seventeenth-century thought, a thread which runs through much of the criticisms and proposals made by Fang, Ku, and Huang is a need to revitalize the moral justification and social position of the literati as the only group properly standing between the imperial government and the commoners. In this sense, the "new" learning was in its origins in the 1630s allied to the "old" social order which was under stress from economic changes.

57. Cf. Huang Tsung-hsi, "Ming-i tai-fang lu," especially the three "Ts'ai chi 財計" essays, and Ku Yen-wu, "Ch'ien liang lun 錢糧論," in *Ku T'ing-lin shih-wen-chi*, 1.

58. Although the prose styles contrast, the moral values exhibited in the so-called vernacular stories of the seventeenth century were not always in contrast to the values of the "Seven Solutions." For example, Feng Meng-lung's story entitled "Two Magistrates Vie to Marry an Orphaned Girl" in *Hsing-shih heng-yen* compares old-style virtue with new-style wealth. The son of a millionaire, young Mr. P'an is beautiful, wears gorgeous clothes, devotes himself to drinking, whoring, and gambling, and never studies or works. Young Mr. Hsiao is the son of a poor but incorruptible official; he is ugly, indifferent to his clothes, and impoverished, but filial and studious. Mr. P'an vexes his father to death and ends up a starving pauper, while Mr. Hsiao passes the examinations and rises to be a government minister. And all of this happened, Feng told his readers, not too long ago in Chekiang. (See William Dolby, trans., *The Perfect Lady by Mistake*, 114–17.)

5 Another Man's Man

Pao-shu Tzu Is Urged to Find a Patron

Flushing with agitation, Sir Brazen stood up and, in an imposing, brag-gartly manner, said, "A real man, having been born in the world, is going to be of use in this world. Why be so constricted?[1] Can we not be impressed when observing the person who distributes a thousand in precious metal[2] in an instant and then who gains a thousand in precious metal in an instant? All of the impetuous, noble-spirited gentlemen (shih) who earned praise in the past were broad in their associations, and of those associations priority was always given to those involving men of high office. [Although so poor as to have] a mat as his door covering, [Ch'en P'ing] had carriage tracks left by numerous eminent callers.[3] Ning Ch'i, who was elevated by Duke Huan of Ch'i,[4] and Chia I, whose ability was made known by Lord Wu,[5] were both commoners and yet caused men with teams of the most majestic horses to come to them.[6] Feeding [Su Ch'in] meat from the best horses[7] and presenting [Po Kuei] moon beam [jade][8] were not considered extravagant.

1. On 拘拘, see "Ta Ts'ung shih 大宗師," *Chuang Tzu*, 54. (Watson, trans., *Complete Works of Chuang Tzu*, 84, gives "crookedy.") Pao-shu Tzu's malaise is mental, whereas in *Chuang Tzu* the term refers to a physical constricting.

2. An allusion to Fan Li 范蠡, who in the space of nineteen years three times made a fortune of a thousand in precious metal and twice gave his wealth away to his poor associates and relatives. "Huo chih chuan," *Shih chi*, 129.3257.

3. See "Ch'en Ch'eng-hsiang 陳丞相 shih chia," *Shih chi*, 56.2052. Ch'en P'ing 陳平 eventually was enfeoffed.

4. See "Tsou Yang 鄒陽 chuan," *Shih chi*, 83.2473. Ning Ch'i 甯戚 was feeding his ox among the carts and carriages at the city gate when he attracted the attention of Duke Huan of Ch'i 齊桓, who subsequently employed him as a minister. The incident is referred to in a number of places, including the "Li sao," *Ch'u tz'u*, 116, and *Huai-nan Tzu*, 12.8a–b.

5. 洛陽 was the home of Chia I and the name here refers to him. See "Chia I 賈誼 chuan," *Shih chi*, 84.2491. Lord Wu 吳公 was a governor who recommended Chia I to court.

6. 結駟連騎, quoted from "Chung-ni ti-tzu 仲尼弟子," *Shih chi*, 67.2208. When Tzu-kung 子貢 was a minister in Wei, he went with teams of the most majestic horses to call on another former disciple who was living in retirement. Cf. *Huai-nan Tzu*, 11.2a.

7. See "Tsou Yang chuan," *Shih chi*, 83.2472. The king was so angered when there were complaints about his minister, Su Ch'in, that he fed him with the rarest food to show his contempt for the criticisms.

8. Ibid., 2472. The Lord of Wei, in response to complaints about Po Kuei 白圭, presented him with a disc of moonbeam jade.

Plunking on a rush-bound sword handle[9] *and sweeping a high official's gateway*[10] *were not considered shameful.*

"A man who has integrity and is noble-spirited but who is unable to make himself known because of his poverty and low standing goes to make the acquaintance of a person of rank in order to achieve repute. Nowadays, if those who have a grasp of the common arts of medicine or fortune-telling or who rely on the petty skill of knowing simple number astrology[11] still are able to fetch fat sums by attracting the attention of men of high station, how much more [profit is there] for someone who is literate[12] and grasps the strengths and weaknesses of others.[13] Why not surrender a little of your haughty demeanor and be more pliant?[14] At best, you could then make your good name more widely known. At the very least, you would not lose out at making a living.[15] Those impoverished, bookish literati (shih) all around who are incapable of doing either good or ill for others can be avoided. You just want to crouch hugging your knees and moan and sing[16] while waiting for the time when there will be someone who understands you, someone who adapts his standards[17] and befriends you. In today's world, who makes it his business to understand others and esteem talent!" 34b

9. See "Meng-ch'ang Chün 孟嘗君 chuan," *Shih chi*, 75.2359. Feng Huan 馮驩 went to offer himself as a "guest," that is, a retainer, to Meng-ch'ang Chün. Extremely poor, with only one sword and a rush-covered hilt binding, Feng repeatedly plunked on his sword and lamented until Meng-ch'ang gave him what he wanted. (Also see J. I. Crump, Jr., trans., *Chan-Kuo Ts'e*, 189–90.)

10. See "Yeh-chien lei 謁見類," in Hu Wei-ts'ung, *Shu yen ku shih ta ch'üan*, 7.21b. Wei Po 魏勃 wanted to have an audience with Ts'ao Ts'an (sometimes read Shen) 曹參, Minister of Ch'i, but was too poor to make the requisite gift, so he swept the ground in front of the gate of one of Ts'ao's retainers, who wondered at it, and when Wei Po explained his motive, the retainer introduced him to Ts'ao.

11. 三五之賤伎, quoted from Chiang Yen 江淹, "I chien P'ing wang shang shu 詣建平王上書," *Wen hsuan*, 39.16a.

12. 能操觚, literally, "able to grasp the wooden tablets" on which one wrote.

13. On 持長短, see "K'u li 酷吏 chuan," *Shih chi*, 62.3135. Ning Ch'eng 寧成, who had dominated the government underlings in his command as well as the officials of superior status, after being punished retired to devote himself to making a fortune. Soon, "with possessions worth several thousand in precious metal, he acted as a righteous *hsia*; grasping the strengths and weaknesses of the local officials, he could go out accompanied by several tens of riders." (Cf. B. Watson, trans., *Records of the Grand Historian*, vol 2, 424.) In short, with his new wealth and old political acumen, Ning Ch'eng could do as he wished.

14. On 委蛇, see *Songs*, "Shao Nan 召南, Kao yang 羔羊." (Cf. Legge, trans., 28: "Easy are they, and self-possessed.")

15. The *Fu-shan wen-chi* text has 糊口; the *Ch'i tai i shu* has the more common 餬口.

16. An allusion to Pao-shu Tzu's behavior as he became depressed, and to Chu-ko Liang's before Liu Pei called on him. See "Chu-ko Liang chuan," *San kuo chih*, Shu, 35.911.

17. On 折節, see "Tuan Chiung 段熲 chuan," *Hou Han shu*, 65.2145. "When he was young Tuan Kung had practiced archery and horsemanship, looked up to *hsia*, and disparaged wealth. When he grew up he adapted his standards and was devoted to the learning of antiquity."

Pao-shu Tzu replied, "I understand that all too well.

"There are flippant, cunning men who dress in the finest, softest garments, wear ornate swords, and have carriages shined to a mirror finish. The young servant boys who attend them bellow [for others to yield the way] on the highways and squabble with official retinues. In the marketplaces everybody makes way for them and no one understands where they have come from. On the other hand, the truly worthy man, living in a low, cramped house,[18] having neither carriages nor horses at his gate, has his poor sandals, travel bag, and parasol [ready to go if called].[19] As he receives no welcome when he travels about, men in the market[20] begin by looking down on him and follow that by cursing him. His relatives, not taking him seriously, ridicule him. How sad! When things have come to such a pass, how can we expect a man not to seek influence and personal gain even if he does not want to? Thus, if one became familiar with appointment to office and discussed court affairs by being in touch with the Three Lords and Five Nobles,[21] going to attend them regardless of cold or heat, and drinking on intimate terms with them, after a while even officials[22] would be pleased to converse with one. More than that, he might always be insolent before other, more highly placed men. By depending on others to do things for me, and by using my connection to venge myself on my enemies, I could have wealthy men provide me with benefits; I could have villagers in awe of me; I could have inconstant literati, insincere in their commitments, as my adherents.[23] How grand! Nevertheless, I have frequently seen the retainers of men of high station haggling over a few coins[24] with the gatekeeper to send in a calling card. Once inside, they are not seated in the proper order and pace idly below the eaves. This is really a distressing situation in which to be placed. In their long robes they squirm around and press to interject what they have heard. They say, 'I have it from Mr. So-and-so' and 'Such-and-such happened at Mr. So-and-so's.'

35a

18. On 湫隘, see *Tso chuan*, Ch'ao 昭, 3rd year. (Cf. Legge, trans., *The Ch'un Ts'ew, with Tso Chuan*, 589: "Your house is near the market, low, small, noisy, and dusty. You should not live in it.")

19. Reading *ying* 贏 for *lei* 羸, as in the *Ch'i tai i shu* text, and for 贏, as in the *Fu-shan wen-chi*. 粗蹻贏蓋, quoted from "Fan-lun hsun 氾論訓," *Huai-nan Tzu*, 13.17a. Su Ch'in, who was to go on to dominate all the aristocrats, as a lowly commoner had started out with just his sandals, travel bag, and parasol.

20. Reading 厓 as *ch'an* 廛.

21. The term 三公 was used from Chou and Han times to designate a changing set of three high officials; 五侯 was used especially in Han to designate five important holders of fiefs. Here the two terms are rhetorical for "men of the highest standing," not necessarily with hereditary titles.

22. 縉紳, literally, "red sashes," those with official rank.

23. The shift in pronoun from "one" to "me" is in the text.

24. 肉好 is a term used in Han for round coins with a hole. As Fang I-chih explained in *T'ung ya* 27.2a, 肉 refers to the (metal) disc, and 好 refers to the hole.

"*As I do not have the face to do that, how would I be able to make clever talk like some sort of a reed in a wind instrument to compel the attention of highly placed men? I would rather live in a humble lane and find contentment in being 'useless' [compared to being 'used' in the way you propose].*"

Sir Brazen's recommendation that Pao-shu Tzu should associate with men of influence, that is, put himself in the entourage of someone powerful in order to be of "use" in the world, grows out of the tradition of the *hsia* 俠, a term commonly translated as "knight" or "adventurer," but which here might best be taken, however awkwardly, as a "man of action."[1] Two main aspects of the *hsia* can be distinguished.[2] First, there is the personal aspect of *acting*, usually with some force, as a matter of individual duty on behalf of others to effect justice. Secondly, there is the collective aspect of joining or *associating* with like-minded men, often as their "guest" (*k'o* 客), to have greater efficacy in realizing goals.

Acting on Behalf of Righteousness

The most conspicuous attention paid to *hsia* is the chapter in the *Records of the Grand Historian* devoted to them.[3] *Hsia*, according to the ideal at least, were proud, bold men, expert in the martial arts, rootless but firm in friendship, contemptuous of personal wealth, and self-sacrificing in their eagerness to avenge wrongs, especially on behalf of the helpless.[4] Ssu-ma Ch'ien set out the characteristics that he found praiseworthy about certain *hsia*: "Although their actions may deviate from perfect righteousness, they always keep their word.

1. Ch'ü T'ung-tsu, *Han Social Structure*, 186–87, suggested *hsia* might be rendered "redressor-of-wrongs," but that seems too laudatory to fit many contexts. Ch'ü preferred to leave the word untranslated, a practice with which I agree. The term *yu hsia* can mean either *hsia* who wander (*yu* 遊) or *hsia* who associate with others (*chiao yu* 交遊). As Ch'ü pointed out, the "associating" aspect is stronger in most contexts, so that "wandering knights" or "knights errant" are less appropriate as translations. Ch'ü's discussion (pp. 185–95, 245–47) of *hsia* as a social group in Han times draws together much of the relevant material. T'ao Hsi-sheng 陶希聖, *Pien-shih yü yu-hsia*, also included much interesting material; his concern was mainly with the social origins of "free floaters" in the Warring States period.

2. T'ao Hsi-sheng, 75, made much the same distinction, though in a different context.

3. *Shih chi*, 124. Translated in B. Watson, *Records of the Grand Historian*, vol. 2, 452–61. The *Chan kuo ts'e* also includes accounts of the exploits of *hsia*. Numerous examples, of course, are cited in James J. Y. Liu, *The Chinese Knight-Errant*.

4. Cf. James J. Y. Liu, *The Chinese Knight-Errant*, 4–7, for a list of ideals associated with *hsia*.

They fulfill their tasks and carry out what they promise. Without caring about their own lives, they go to other gentlemen (*shih*) in distress. When they have preserved the life of another who might have perished they do not brag of their capabilities, and feel ashamed to boast of their kindness to others."[5] But Ssu-ma Ch'ien, as Fang I-chih pointed out, later was often criticized for dignifying the *hsia* with his attention.[6] In times of order they were commonly regarded by the authorities as lawless troublemakers, and it was on these grounds that there were attempts to suppress them early in the Han and later.[7] Pan Ku asserted in the *Han History* that in the Warring States period, as *hsia* came to be patronized by men of noble rank, the spirit of attending to one's governmental responsibilities and serving one's superior declined and increasingly there was talk of turning one's back on the public good and dying for one's friends, so that even when order was reestablished under the Han dynasty they still offended the law with their pursuit of private justice, and they still were assembled in the retinues of nobles.[8] In spite of reprovals by Pan Ku and subsequent historians' general neglect of *hsia* as a praiseworthy type, the romantic ideal of the *hsia* was continued in the plays and novelistic narratives which celebrated the swashbuckling, avenging "knight errant" as a hero standing against convention and for the reparation of wrongs.[9] The qualities of the "guest" Feng Ming-ch'i in the *Scholars* (*Ju-lin wai shih*) stand in strong contrast with the effete, grasping scholars (*ju*) around him. He is not only iron-strong, he gratuitously helps those in trouble when their friends avoid them, he thinks for his social superiors, he is considerate toward his inferiors, he is unselfish with money, and he accepts no thanks. Feng Ming-ch'i, portrayed as a renowned champion of the wronged who has everyone in awe of him, and who fears no one, is a good example of the fictional type.[10] To act as a *hsia* in the real world, however, was more difficult.

Confucius defined lack of courage (*yung* 勇) as "to see what is right and not do it,"[11] which Fang I-chih took to mean that Confucius was ashamed when

5. *Shih chi*, 124.3181. I have followed, with some modification, the translation in Ch'ü T'ung-tsu, *Han Social Structure*, 186. The passage is also translated in Liu, *Knight-Errant*, 16, and in B. Watson. vol. 2, 453.

6. Fang I-chih, "Jen lun 任論," *Fu-shan wen-chi*, 5.39a.

7. Ch'ü T'ung-tsu, *Han Social Structure*, 135, 196. Cf. Lao Kan 勞幹, "Lun Han tai te yu-hsia," *Wen shih che hsueh-pao* 1 (1950), 247–48.

8. *Han shu*, 92.3697–99. Cf. B. Watson, trans., *Courtier and Commoner*, 222–25.

9. Cf. Robert Ruhlmann, "Traditional Heroes in Chinese Popular Fiction," in A. F. Wright, ed., *Confucian Persuasion*, 141–76, and Liu, *The Chinese Knight-Errant*. Both are primarily interested in *hsia* as they appear as literary, rather than historical, figures.

10. Wu Ching-tzu, *The Scholars*, 543–66, 569–71. Other fictional examples, some of them ambiguously representative of *hsia*, are considered in Y. W. Ma, "The Knight-Errant in Hua-pen Stories," *T'oung Pao* 61 (1975), 266–300.

11. *Analects*, 2.24. (Cf. Waley, trans., *Analects of Confucius*, 93: "Just as to sacrifice to ancestors other than one's own is presumption, so to see what is right and not to do it is cowardice.")

someone did not do what he knew to be right.[12] The persistent problem of how to *act* on behalf of righteousness was difficult enough if one had executive powers in government. The problem was compounded for men not in government, for they, too, could feel a sense of duty (*jen* 任), a need to be of use (*yu yung* 有用). In Fang's view, Ssu-ma Ch'ien had been correct to honor the *hsia*, for their origins lay in men with a strong sense of duty (*jen*). Because those in government were proving incapable of acting according to what was right (*cheng*) and righteous (*i*), they had taken it upon themselves to act.[13] Duty, Fang reminded his readers, was prescribed in the *Rituals of Chou* (the "Ti kuan ssu t'u" section) as one of the six aspects of good conduct to be followed by the people in the villages, along with filial, friendly, harmonious, proper marital, and sympathetic behavior. In this ancient context, "duty" meant putting forth effort and shouldering responsibilities when the entire community was confronted with difficulties. The *hsia* represented an outgrowth of "duty" in this sense.[14] They came from the villages and narrow lanes and served the needs of the little man who, wronged by those more powerful than he, received no justice from a neglectful government.[15] What went wrong, according to Fang I-chih, was that *hsia*, instead of always acting out of duty and on behalf of righteousness, began to use their own physical prowess, the collective force of their friends and "guests," and the influence they could exert through their noble patrons' power to derive personal benefit.[16] The ideal of the dutiful *hsia* (*jen hsia* 任俠) declined, to be replaced by the "associating," or roaming, *hsia* (*yu hsia*) who opposed the laws and did evil for his own gain.[17] The activities of such *hsia* thus came to be feared as a source of disorder.[18] Nevertheless, what Fang found praiseworthy was the willingness of the original *hsia* to act without regard for their personal interests, even their own safety, and without compromising their virtue (5.39a). In contrast, Fang saw that among his contemporaries

> the literati (*shih*) and gentlemen (*chün-tzu*) place highest value on discussing morality, and establishing a reputation comes second. But as soon as there is a disturbance they worry about the consequences and the legal prohibitions, and then they only fear that its ramifications will extend to them. Their legs quaking when they hear a sound, prostrating themselves when they see a shadow, they regard [the high esteem for

12. Fang I-chih, "Jen lun," *Fu-shan wen-chi*, 5.39b.

13. Fang I-chih, "Jen lun." *Fu-shan wen-chi*, 5.39a. As J. Liu, *The Chinese Knight-Errant*, 7, pointed out, the *hsia* "went beyond the call of duty" from a certain point of view.

14. Fang I-chih, "Jen lun," 5.39a. Fang was oversimplifying, needless to say. For a summary of the modern debate on the social origins of the *hsia*, see Liu, *The Chinese Knight-Errant*, 2–4, 10–12.

15. Fang I-chih, "Jen lun," 5.39b. Cf. Ch'ü T'ung-tsu, *Han Social Structure*, 189–90.

16. 5.39a.

17. Ibid.

18. Fang I-chih, "Fang luan 防亂," *Fu-shan wen-chi*, 5.56a.

friendship exhibited by] Ch'en Ch'ung, Lei I, Lien Fan, and Ch'ing Hung as common. When the adverse or unexpected occurs, they close their gates and flap their hands, but they do not put their heads outside. Such is their "virtue." . . . They boast and brag about morality, reputation, and their own sense of duty, yet in the train of such talk, they do not take involvement in any affair as their responsibility.[19]

In the sixteenth century there had been men who tried to live the *hsia* ideal. Yen Chün (died about 1550) attracted contemporary notice for performing acts of outstanding loyalty by accompanying a friend who had been banished, and by recovering and burying the remains of his teacher who died in a battle in Yunnan. After his own death, Yen was praised as "a Confucian in his learning, a *hsia* in his conduct."[20] With less praise, it was later observed that Yen Chün "as a *hsia* liked to go to the aid of others in distress."[21] One of his followers, Ho Hsin-yin (1517–79), had become a *chü-jen* at thirty but then gave up the intention of becoming an official. An ardent supporter of Yen's spirit of acting on behalf of friendship, Ho has been described as a *hsia* for his emphasis on the need for concrete action (*shih hsing* 實行).[22] Ho wrote that just as an artisan, farmer, or merchant, if he is to rise in station, must perform in an outstanding way, so, too, if a literatus is to become a sage, he must act.[23] That Ho incurred the disfavor of most powerful men, that he was jailed for trying to defend his clan's newly organized community interests against pressures from the local government, that he lived a rootless, almost fugitive life, that he placed great stress on the virtue of friendship, that he died in jail—in all of these things Ho had the air of a latter-day *hsia*, although he was also distinguished for his intellectual contributions as a writer and teacher.[24] It was his expression of concern for the common good, against a contemporary fashion of emphasizing self-cultivation, that makes Ho close to being an example of Fang I-chih's ideal of a "dutiful *hsia*."

The desire to act continued to seek an outlet, although often enough the actions were but a pale reflection of the exploits of the original *hsia*. It tended to be that simply martial prowess rather than heroic action was taken to indicate

19. Fang I-chih, "Jen lun," *Fu-shan wen-chi*, 5.39b–40a. The names of Ch'en Ch'ung 陳重 and Lei I 雷義 of Later Han became a byword for inseparable friends. (See "Lei I chuan," *Hou Han shu*, 71.2688.) The names of Lien Fan 廉范 and Ch'ing Hung 慶鴻, also of Later Han, suggested devoted friendship, for they were compared by their contemporaries to the loyal friendship of Pao Shu for Kuan Chung. (See "Lien Fan chuan," *Hou Han shu*, 31.1104.)

20. The praise was from Keng Ting-hsiang, quoted in Jung Chao-tsu, *Ming tai ssu-hsiang shih*, 226; also in deBary, "Individualism," *Self and Society*, 179.

21. Huang Tsung-hsi, *Ming ju hsueh an*, 32, prefatory remarks. Cf. deBary, 179, and Chi Wen-fu, *Wan Ming ssu-hsiang shih lun*, 34.

22. Jung Chao-tsu, *Ming tai ssu-hsiang shih*, 226–27. On Ho's life, cf. deBary, 178–88; Ronald Dimberg, *The Sage and Society: The Life and Thought of Ho Hsin-yin*, 38–56; and Goodrich and Fang, *Dictionary of Ming Biography*, under Ho Hsin-yin.

23. Jung Chao-tsu, 227.

24. This point was made in Jung, 226, and in deBary, "Individualism," 186.

a man's *hsia*-like character. Fang I-chih's younger brother, Ch'i-i (1619–49),[25] was awarded student status at the age of fourteen,[26] and became a noteworthy calligrapher[27] as well as a competent poet.[28] But for all of his refinement, he also liked to act the part of a *hsia*.[29] He was an expert horseman, and so strong he could draw a 500 *chin* bow and so skillful he could hit the target repeatedly.[30] In putting his talents to use, Ch'i-i distinguished himself for his bravery during operations against bandit armies when his father was governor in Hu-kuang in the late 1630s.[31] A friend wrote that he brought to mind the spirit of the men in antiquity who on horseback killed bandits and off their horse drafted the reports of victory.[32] In a poem celebrating the literatus who acted like a *hsia*, Ch'i-i wrote, "The *hsia-shih* 俠士, emphasizing righteousness, is indifferent to vast wealth; not concerned with the superficial, he seeks to touch other men's souls. A hundred times he gives away all he has, without a trace of regret; entering fire he is not burned, in the water he does not drown."[33] His literary skills were hardly outstanding, but Fang Ch'i-i established a reputation as a "dutiful *hsia* who was a poet" (*sao jen jen hsia* 騷人任俠).[34] Fang I-chih's brother-in-law, Sun Lin, also had some attributes of a *hsia*, in that he, too, was practiced in the martial arts of archery and riding, and he manifested his bravery in the battles against bandits when his father-in-law was governor in Hu-kuang. Sun was so troubled by the times that he changed his name to Wu-kung 武公, the Martial One. He wore a short robe instead of a long scholar's gown and carried a cross-bow, so that no one took him for a Confucian (*ju*).[35] Their contemporaries could still find it remarkable for young men of Fang Ch'i-i's or Sun Lin's social and educational standing to be so involved in the martial arts, but the two were hardly unique. In the late 1620s Fang I-chih and his friend Chou Ch'i, in spite of their cultural refinement and their aim to be Confucians (*ju*), also learned to wear armor, ride at a charging gallop, and shoot arrows and stones. "How were these not, given the state of the empire, activities one had to do?" Fang asked.[36] In the last two decades of Ming, increasing turmoil led many to conclude that martial training was not extraneous, and often enough there was opportunity to put training into practice.

25. For Fang Ch'i-i's dates, see the tomb inscription by Ch'ien Ch'eng-chih, in *T'ung-ch'eng Fang shih shih chi*, 5.22a–26b; also in Ch'ien Ch'eng-chih, *T'ien-chien chi*.

26. Ibid., 22b.

27. Ibid., 24a.

28. Preface by Ch'en Cho 陳焯, in *T'ung-ch'eng Fang shih shih chi*, 4.3a.

29. Ma Ch'i-ch'ang, *T'ung-ch'eng ch'i chiu chuan*, 6.17a.

30. Preface by Ch'en Cho, 3a. Also see *T'ung-ch'eng ch'i chiu chuan*, 6.17-b, and Ch'ien Ch'eng-chih, 5.22b, 24b.

31. Preface by Ch'en Cho, 3b.

32. Ch'ien Ch'eng-chih, 5.24a.

33. Fang Ch'i-i, "Hsia-shih hsing 俠士行," *T'ung-ch'eng Fang shih shih chi*, 5.2b.

34. Preface by Ch'en Cho, 4.2b.

35. Ma Ch'i-ch'ang, *T'ung-ch'eng ch'i chiu chuan*, 6.5b.

36. Fang I-chih, "Sung Chou Nung-fu huan ku-hsiang hsu," *Fu-shan wen-chi*, 5.23a–b.

Even in less turbulent times *hsia*-like activities had attracted the attention of educated young men. A noteworthy instance is Wang Yang-ming, who in his youth had trained in military skills and associated with other "dauntless" young men, an experience which has been seen as contributory to the development of his emphasis on moral action.[37] Disparaging those who did not *do* what was morally right, the mature Wang Yang-ming explained that the criticism to which he was being subjected stemmed from men who did not understand that he was free-reined (*k'uang* 狂) because he could act directly and simply on the basis of his innate knowledge (*liang chih*) of what was truly good and bad.[38] Wang acknowledged that previously he had something of the "sincerity of the honest country fellow" (*hsiang yuan* 鄉愿),[39] which Confucius had identified as an enemy of true virtue,[40] in the sense that such sincerity is taken by unreflective minds to be virtue and so they are never led to the self-examination that will enable them to be genuinely virtuous. Rather than be trapped in such self-satisfaction, Mencius contended, it is better to begin either by being free-reined (*k'uang*) or cautious (*chüan* 狷). Neither was as good as following the middle way, but both were means to bring oneself to it. The term "free-reined" was glossed as rushing forward for something (*chin ch'ü* 進取), which was taken to imply that there also are some things for which the free-reined man will not rush forward; "cautious" meant there are some things which one will not do, which in turn implies there are things the cautious man will do.[41] The result in

37. See Wang's "nien-p'u" in *Wang Wen-ch'eng kung ch'üan shu*, 32.904. Wang alluded to this type of activism at the conclusion of his famous essay on "Pulling up the Root and Stopping up the Source" when he pleaded for "heroic literati" (*hao-chieh chih shih* 豪傑之士) to "rise up without delay." *Wang Wen-ch'eng kung ch'üan shu*, 2.102. (Cf. W. T. Chan, trans., *Instructions for Practical Living*, 124.) Wang Yang-ming's interest in *hsia*-like activities was referred to by his contemporaries, e.g., by Chan Jo-shui, in Wang's "mu-chih-ming," ibid., 37.1052. Cf. Julia Ching, "Wang Yang-ming: A Study in 'Mad Ardour,'" *Papers on Far Eastern History* 3 (1971), 99–100, and Tadao Sakai, "Popular Education Works," in *Self and Society*, 340.

38. Wang Yang-ming, *Ch'uan hsi lu*, in *Wang Wen-ch'eng kung ch'üan shu*, 3.150. Cf. W. T. Chan, trans., *Instructions for Practical Living*, 239. Wang Yang-ming's comment was made in 1523; cf. "nien-p'u," 34.958.

39. Ibid., 3.150.

40. *Lun yü*, 17.13. (Cf. Waley, trans., *Analects of Confucius*, 213: "The 'honest villager' spoils true virtue." D. C. Lau, trans., *Mencius*, 203: "The village honest man is the enemy of virtue.")

41. *Mencius*, 7B37. D. C. Lau, trans., *Mencius*, 202, renders *k'uang* as "wild" and *chüan* as "squeamish." There are numerous other possibilities for rendering this difficult pair of words. As an example of the application of the two terms, see Huang Tsung-hsi, *Ming ju hsueh an* 2.8, where Hu Chü-jen was assessed as close to being too cautious, or tight-reined, in contrast to Ch'en Hsien-chang's being almost too free-reined. Also see introductory comment, "Tu hsing 獨行 chuan," *Hou Han shu*, 81.2665, which expands on the gloss of *k'uang* and *chüan* in *Analects*, 13.21 and in *Mencius*, 7B37. It should be noted that Confucius (17.8) used the word *k'uang* to describe the shortcomings of the person who loves being courageous without loving learning.

either case is that one is *acting* on the basis of an evaluation, and thus beginning to move toward the way of morality. Wang Chi (1498–1583), who acted like a "dutiful *hsia*" (*jen hsia*) as a young man,[42] described the "sincerity of the honest country fellow" as earning the approbation of others to the extent that they regard you as flawless as a sage, but because you do not disassociate yourself from what is dirty and vile you are no more a sage than purple is vermilion, or than lewd music is elegant,[43] though uncritical people may be confused by the superficial similarities. To really begin to act like a sage, Wang argued, there can be no trace of covering up in your conduct, even when you are at fault. You must be free-reined, even at the expense of some of the petty social niceties.[44] The "sincerity of the honest country fellow" is entirely derived from outside of himself and merely aims at being pleasing to the rest of the world. He thinks he is right, and therefore cannot embark on the path of becoming a sage.[45] Or, as Mencius explained, "If you want to censure him, you cannot find anything; if you want to find fault with him, you cannot find anything either. He shares with others the practices of the day and is in harmony with the sordid world. He pursues such a policy and appears to be conscientious and faithful, and to show integrity in his conduct. He is liked by the multitude and is self-righteous. It is impossible to embark on the way of Yao and Shun with such a man. Hence the name 'enemy of virtue.' "[46] The emphasis in the sixteenth century, drawing its justification from Wang Yang-ming's doctrine of innate knowledge of good, was on *acting*, on *doing* what you know in your heart to be right rather than unthinkingly following what mere social convention dictated. Being "free-reined" in this light was a term of praise, and overlapped with being a *hsia* in the sense that Fang I-chih found praiseworthy.[47]

Some critics, however, saw being free-reined on the basis of one's innate knowledge of good as destructive of the moral teachings that were fundamental to social order. If everyone could make his own determination of right, and if, contrary to Wang Yang-ming's expectations, they could arrive at different conclusions, then there would arise a situation quite analogous to *hsia* pursuing their own vision of justice at the expense of the laws established by the imperial government. A free-reined individual's ideas could even be perceived as more disruptive than the weapon of a proud, bold man. The extreme of this possibility was

42. Chi Wen-fu, *Wan Ming*, 46.

43. Alluding to *Lun yü*, 17.18. (Cf. D. C. Lau, trans., *Mencius*, 203: "I dislike the music of Cheng for fear that it might be confused with proper music; I dislike purple for fear it might be confused with vermillion." A. Waley, trans., *Analects of Confucius*, 214: "I hate to see roan killing red, I hate to see the tunes of Cheng corrupting court music.")

44. Wang Chi, quoted in Chi Wen-fu, 33–34.

45. Wang Chi, quoted in Huang Tsung-hsi, *Ming ju hsueh an*, 12.102.

46. *Mencius*, 7B37, as translated in D. C. Lau, trans., *Mencius*, 203.

47. Cf. the discussion on Wang Ken and the "new heroism" in deBary, "Individualism and Humanitarianism," *Self and Society*, 169–71.

Li Chih (1527–1602), who late in life set out to challenge others with his ideas and ended up committing suicide in jail.[48] Shortly after Li's death a memorial to the emperor asked for imperial condemnation of all his writings and charged him with being *k'uang*, not in a laudatory sense but in the sense of wild and dissipated, even mad.[49] Li Chih had renounced his standing as a literatus and an official by adopting the garb of a Ch'an Buddhist monk, which made it easy for critics to attack his ideas, along with those of the men who were perceived as his predecessors, men such as Yen Chün, Ho Hsin-yin, and Teng Huo-ch'ü, who also became a monk; they were accused of mixing Ch'an (Zen) into Confucianism.[50] At issue was more than a matter of doctrinal purity. Li Chih represented the dangers of placing inordinate emphasis on making up one's own mind about values, just as the *hsia* disrupted established society by acting on his own standard of justice. In Ku Yen-wu's estimation, no one in all of history had been worse than Li Chih in fearlessly, recklessly daring to oppose the teachings of the sages.[51]

In other contexts, being fearless or reckless (*wu chi-tan* 無忌憚) might be taken as attributes of being "free-reined" (*k'uang*),[52] and in Li Chih's own time thoughtful men were not prepared to give up the interpretation that being free-reined was part of being a sage. Leaders of the Tung-lin Academy continued to recognize the need to avoid the pitfall of merely acting with the "sincerity of an honest country fellow" (*hsiang-yuan*) and still stressed risking being too free-reined or too cautious as a means to achieving the correct path of the sages.[53] But they placed perhaps more emphasis on being careful (*hsiao hsin* 小心), which is an opposite of being free-reined.[54] Because of examples like Li Chih, the ideal of being free-reined was tarnished. In the course of the seventeenth century the term *k'uang* was often used to condemn rather than praise a man who took a stand against traditional values, and the justification for acting independently out of a sense of moral duty was undermined.

48. A summary of Li Chih's career is in deBary, "Individualism," 188–213. Also see Jung Chao-tsu, *Li Chih nien-p'u*.

49. The memorial is quoted in Ku Yen-wu, "Li Chih," *Jih chih lu*, 18.

50. Huang Tsung-hsi's prefatory remarks, *Ming ju hsueh an*, 32. Essentially following Huang Tsung-hsi, Chi Wen-fu in *Wan Ming ssu-hsiang shih lun*, chapter 3, discussed the men who have been labeled the "wild Ch'an" (*k'uang Ch'an*). I have not determined when the two words were first combined as a term of opprobrium.

51. Ku Yen-wu, "Li Chih," *Jih chih lu*, 18.

52. Cf. Chi Wen-fu, *Wan Ming ssu-hsiang shih lun*, 65.

53. A selection of quotations which support this point is assembled in Ch'ien Mu, *Chin san-pai nien hsueh-shu shih*, 15–16, and the matter is referred to repeatedly in the chapters on Tung-lin members in Huang Tsung-hsi, *Ming ju hsueh an*, 58–61. Cf. the example of Ku Yun-ch'eng's views translated in Ian McMorran, "Wang Fu-chih and Neo-Confucian Tradition," *Unfolding*, 426.

54. Chi Wen-fu, *Wan Ming ssu-hsiang shih lun*, 65.

Associating as a "Guest"

The original *hsia* in the Warring States period may have begun as independent
men who used their abilities on behalf of the helpless, but as their fame spread
others came to associate with them as friends and fellow *hsia*, some becoming
"guests" (*k'o* 客).[55] The guests often were expected to perform various services
on behalf of their "host," and some of the hosts became even more renowned
than their guests.[56] In the Warring States period the Four Lords (*ssu chün* 四君)
were famous as the patrons of numerous (the usual number was 3000) guests,
ranging from noble-minded *hsia* to useful criminals.[57] Under the Han dynasty
there continued to be patrons who assembled crowds of guests, such as the
Prince of Huai-nan and the Prince P'i of Wu, who were criticized in the *Han
History* for doing so,[58] and the practice underwent a revival toward the end of
Han.[59] Liu Pei as a young man had liked to associate with "heroes" and *hsia*,[60]
and with crucial help from his guests he went on to be emperor of the state of
Shu Han. The guest relation had developed as a peer association, but as a host
was able to shelter his guests from the state's demands for taxes, labor and military service, and criminal prosecution, he was also able to have them function as
his retainers, with various gradations among the men assembled,[61] some performing military functions, some acting even as his servants and tenants.[62] In
later times, then, guests often were less like *hsia* than they were hangers-on, if
not outright dependents. To join the entourage of the powerful remained attractive, but it was regarded as debasing by the independent minded. Late in his
life Ku Yen-wu tried to dissuade a young man from going to the household of
Ku's nephew, a powerful official in Peking.

> Currently you are poor and hard-pressed and have the chance to go to a household
> of importance. This is something that all ordinary persons would desire. But moral
> standards decline day by day, and people's character daily becomes more obsequious.

55. Fang I-chih, "Jen lun," *Fu-shan wen-chi*, 5.39a.
56. Ssu-ma Ch'ien made this point in "Yu hsia chuan," *Shih chi*, 124.3183.
57. The Four Lords (*ssu chün*, or *ssu hao* 四豪) were Lord Meng-ch'ang 孟嘗, Lord P'ing-
yuan 平原, Lord Hsin-ling 信陵, and Lord Ch'un-shen 春申; all have biographies in *Shih chi*,
75–78. The latter two lords are mentioned in Wu Ching-tzu, *Ju lin wai shih*, chapter 10, as
examples of munificent hosts.
58. *Han shu*, 92.3698. Cf. Watson, trans., *Courtier and Commoner in Ancient China*, 224.
"Guests" as a special group in Han times are considered in Ch'ü T'ung-tsu, *Han Social
Structure*, 127–35.
59. Ch'ü T'ung-tsu, 130, 132.
60. "Hsien chu 先主 chuan," *San kuo chih*, Shu, 32.872.
61. Ch'ü T'ung-tsu, *Han Social Structure*, 129, 131.
62. See Chü Ch'ing-yuan, "San kuo shih-tai te k'o," *Shih huo* 3 (1936), 161–65, for a
survey of the range of terms for types of "guests" and their relations to their "hosts." Chü
claims that by the Three Kingdoms periob, large numbers of guests were practically owned
by their host/master, although they were free to leave, which slaves were not. Also see
Ch'ü T'ung-tsu, 134.

The more lofty his [Ku's nephew's] position becomes, the more numerous are his guests. The sycophants remain and the unbending leave. Now he intends to invite one or two scholarly gentlemen so as to cover up the hordes, but he does not understand that fragrant and fulsome cannot be stored in the same pot. As his sixty-four-year-old maternal uncle, I lodged in his household. Seeing the activities of those who hasten to him like flies and ants frightened me. . . . If you go, you will associate day and night with bullies and slaves. More than being unable to read or study, you will certainly suffer by associating with those villains.[63]

Fang I-chih was pessimistic about the contemporary possibilities of being a guest while maintaining the integrity of the original *hsia*. In antiquity, *hsia* associated as guests out of a desire to do what was right and what might otherwise be left undone, but Fang wrote that in his time men were merely posing as *hsia*.[64] Once guests had begun to pursue their own, their host's, or their friends' and fellow guests' personal interests, the ideal of such associations began to be perverted. The derogation continued until society could only be suspicious of the motives of those who assembled guests as well as the motives of the guests themselves. Fang observed that without money one could not attract an entourage, and too often the guests departed as soon as the money was gone.[65] To show that even with the best of motives one could not reactivate the ideal in the present day, Fang invented the figure of Master *Hsia* (Yu hsia kung-tzu 游俠公子) in a piece of rhyme-prose entitled "Associating with Guests" (Chieh k'o fu 結客賦). Master *Hsia* sought to emulate the Four Lords of the Warring States period by maintaining 3000 "guests" and roaming the empire to be brave and noble on behalf of others.[66] His intention was to induce righteousness and be magnanimous, to use his associations with his guests to repay enemies, and thus to earn undying fame (1.12a). In his wandering he heard of a worthy who lived in seclusion near the eastern outer wall and thus was known as Mr. Eastern Wall (Tung-kuo hsien-sheng 東郭先生). Mr. Eastern Wall tens of years earlier had acted as a *hsia* but now avoided contact with the rich and powerful. When Master *Hsia* arrived to humbly call on him and recruit him as another of his already numerous "guests" who would benefit him, Eastern Wall scoffed at the idea of trying to be heroic in the present age like the Four Lords in antiquity (1.11b–12b). "Alas for the decadent state of the world. Why is it that no bounds are observed, no virtue is practiced? It grieves the heart. Doing what they feel, people end up free-reined [or, more disparagingly here, unrestrained and wild]. Do you still not have your eyes wide open to see the state of the empire? The

63. Ku Yen-wu, *Ku T'ing-lin shih-wen-chi*, 174. Also translated in Hellmut Wilhelm, "The Po-hsüeh Hung-ju Examination of 1679," *Journal of the American Oriental Society* 71 (1951), 64.

64. Fang I-chih, preface to "Chieh k'o fu 結客賦," *Fu-shan wen-chi*, 1.11a.

65. Fang I-chih, "Sung Li Shu-chang hsu," *Fu-shan wen-chi*, 3.32b; also in *Ch'i tai i shu*, 2.18a. Cf. "Chieh k'o fu," 1.17a.

66. Fang I-chih, "Chieh k'o fu," 1.11a–b.

empire only chases after influence. The empire only crowds after profit!"[67]
The present day extravagant hosts and grasping guests who exploit others could
not be spoken of in the same breath as the stalwarts of the past, who were willing
to incur punishments in going to the aid of men in distress (1.15a). Eastern Wall
contended that the man of talent and high aims who wants an untroubled mind
and does not want to be drawn into doing what he knows he should not, would
do better to hide himself away, cutting off all links and not associating with
others (1.15b–16a). Master *Hsia* was humbled by Eastern Wall's words.

> Silently he struck the table, and then he said, "I have been so blind. I only thought
> that by scattering money and associating with many guests I, too, could become
> known by the empire. How could I realize that the clever superficiality of customs
> and the venom of human feelings had now come to this? I would like to cut myself
> off from all my guests and only follow your lead. For the rest of my life I shall seek
> to do nothing other than examine the changes that have occurred in the empire,
> submit to self-cultivation as practiced by men in antiquity, and stress what com-
> moners take as kindly. I shall be selective in my associations. I shall not do what would
> bring embarrassment to the truly wise. I shall only be ashamed of those wealthy
> families day and night manipulating their counting sticks [as they calculate their
> profits]. I shall not associate with other than men of my village. My name shall not
> be heard by the nobility. If I had continued only desiring rich emoluments, stealing
> high position, taking delight in owning fields and houses, lavishing money on teams
> of horses, drinking and eating fine food, dressing in pearls and feathers, then when
> I was old and at the point of death, I would have looked askance at my wife and
> children and wept, for although there might have been a mass of inscriptions of
> condolence on my coffin, there would be nothing of benefit [to others] recorded in
> my obituary and I would sincerely have been ashamed about what I had done in my
> life." (1.16b–17a).

Thus Master *Hsia* realized that associating with *hsia* as one's guests was imprac-
ticable in the present age. By implication, the same was true of being a guest.
Because of the times, the idea had become irrecoverably corrupted. With would-
be *hsia* and patrons of *hsia* coming together to pursue their own ends by taking
advantage of others, ". . . one should break off from associating [on such
terms], although doing so is difficult."[68]

Nevertheless, Fang I-chih was involved in attempts to invest contemporary
associations with the ideals of activism and righteousness. In the early 1630s he
and his brother-in-law Sun Lin had begun to participate in the Chi she, established in Sung-chiang by six young men, including Hsia Yun-i, Ch'en Tzu-
lung, Hsu Fu-yuan, and Li Wen.[69] The hundred members of the Chi she were,
of course, involved in the usual poetry and drinking as well as in collective prep-

---

67. 1.12b. Eastern Wall said that he, too, was "free-reined and contrary." (1.12a)

68. Fang I-chih, preface to "Chieh k'o fu," *Fu-shan wen-chi*, 1.11a.

69. Hsieh Kuo-chen, *Tang-she yun-tung k'ao*, 187. On Sun Lin's participation in the Chi
she, see *T'ung-ch'eng ch'i chiu chuan*, 6.5a–b.

aration for the examinations; the Chi she has been contrasted as more "inner directed" (*tui nei* 對內) than the "outer directed" (*tui wai* 對外) Fu she, for the latter was involved in organizing on a broad scale and having its collective weight felt in the government, while the Chi she members were more inclined to "reading behind closed doors."[70] But there was an element which distinguished the Chi she from being merely a literary society. It was their discussions of how to restore order and avenge the insults the dynasty had suffered that had inspired Sun Lin to slough off his youthful indifference and eagerly discuss military matters and practice the martial arts.[71] Other members of the Chi she, notably Ch'en Tzu-lung, also acquired military skills.[72] Among their contemporaries, "scratching in the ashes" and "heaping rice" to make model mountains for mapping military strategy were clichés for manifesting concern to do something about the disordered times. Ch'en Tzu-lung put great stress on acting for the community good, finding his justification in Mencius's assertion that "noble spirited men (*shih*) make the effort even without a King Wen [on the throne]."[73] Although much of the Chi she members' commitment to "action" might be dismissed as rhetoric or posturing, the conduct of many of them after 1644 attests their courage and perhaps their earlier resolve as well.[74] In this regard, the Chi she was echoing the associations of *hsia* in earlier times which were based on friendship and dedicated to serving justice in a corrupt world.[75]

Fang I-chih also was involved, along with all of the prominent Chi she members, in the larger, more encompassing Fu she, in which ". . . the spirit of 'being of use' (*yu yung* 有用) was regarded as important."[76] Fang referred only passingly to the Fu she,[77] and the arguments he assigned to Mr. Eastern Wall suggest he had reservations about members of the Fu she using their joint influence for personal gain. It has been observed, for instance, that one reason for the Fu she's rapid growth in membership was the apparent ability to influence the outcome of examinations in the 1630s.[78] Although they drew upon the reputation for self-sacrifice that had been gained by the Tung-lin martyrs in the mid-1620s, the motives of the Fu she were still suspect. The Ch'ung-chen emperor worried that they constituted a clique (*tang* 黨), and thereby continued the fac-

---

70. Hsieh Kuo-chen, 190.

71. Ma Ch'i-ch'ang, *T'ung-ch'eng ch'i chiu chuan*, 6.5b.

72. Atwell, "Ch'en Tzu-lung."

73. See Atwell, "Ch'en Tzu-lung." *Mencius*, 7A10. (Cf. D. C. Lau, trans., "Outstanding men make the effort even without a King Wen.")

74. Cf. Hsieh Kuo-chen's comment, 193.

75. Although friendship was emphasized, the Tung-lin and Fu she gained part of their widespread influence by developing a hierarchy of master-student relationships.

76. Jung Chao-tsu, "Fang I-chih ho t'a te ssu-hsiang," *Ling-nan hsueh-pao* 9 (1948), 100.

77. E.g., Fang I-chih, "Hsi yü hsin pi," 22a; *Fu-shan wen-chi*, 2.34a, on the occasion of Wei Hsueh-lien's copying out the *Hsiao ching* in his blood; cf. Hsieh Kuo-chen, *Tang-she yun-tung k'ao*, 175.

78. Hsieh Kuo-chen, 250; Atwell, "Ch'en Tzu-lung."

tional disputes which had torn the bureaucracy in the preceding reigns.[79] According to Fang, cliques were organized by men whose power and wealth inevitably attract adherents, even sycophants. "They slander what is right and praise what is wrong. If someone happens to be rapidly promoted, they maintain that 'it was I who was able to recommend him.' If someone happens to be guilty of a crime and severely punished, they maintain that 'it was I who really struck him down.' By making others afraid of them, they further their influence."[80] To be a clique in this sense, the Fu she would have to be seen as mixing up right and wrong and being the tool of the powerful. Obviously enough, Fang I-chih and his friends in the Fu she were not inclined to assess their political struggles, even their successes, as other than devotion to the cause of righteousness.

An incident which occurred late in 1632 reveals Fang's involvement in the maneuvers of the Fu she in connection with the examinations and politics. On his return to T'ung-ch'eng from a trip in the Soochow area, the center of Fu she activities, Fang met with a fellow townsman, Ch'ien Ping-cheng (1612–93).[81] Ch'ien and three of his older brothers, it seems, had become involved in a society organized in An-ch'ing, the prefectural city just to the south of T'ung-ch'eng. The society was covertly headed by Juan Ta-ch'eng (ca. 1587-1646),[82] who was attracting adherents with promises of recommendations and fame. The Ch'ien brothers, related by marriage to Juan's family, were unfamiliar with court politics and not aware of the unsavory reputation Juan had garnered for his involvement with the eunuch Wei Chung-hsien in the 1620s. Fang told Ch'ien, "What happens here in Wu is the 'outside' to the 'inside' of court doings. Previously, when like-minded men were distinguished [from the other, 'bad' set of like-minded men], the eunuch's clique [i.e., those allied with Wei Chung-hsien, including Juan Ta-ch'eng] were all expelled. How could we offer allegiance to one of them? How soon can you disassociate yourself from him?" Thereafter Ch'ien prepared for the examinations on his own and declined to go to the next meeting of the society Juan had organized so that everyone might know he was of a different mind than Juan. That winter Ch'ien was ranked first in the "annual" examination to reconfirm the status of the local *sheng-yuan.* Juan Ta-ch'eng tried to claim the credit for Ch'ien's ranking, but Ch'ien was told that, unbeknownst to him, he had been recommended to the examiner by Fang

79. Hsieh Kuo-chen, 74.

80. Fang I-chih, "Huo chih lun," *Fu-shan wen-chi,* 3.6b.

81. Ch'ien Hui-lu 錢撝祿, "T'ien-chien nien-p'u," in Ch'ien Ch'eng-chih, *T'ien-chien chi.* Ch'ien Ping-cheng later changed his name to Ch'eng-chih, by which he is usually known.

82. Chu Yen, "Ming chi T'ung-ch'eng Chung-chiang she k'ao," *Kuo-li chung-yang yen-chiu yuan li-shih yü-yen so chi-k'an* 1 (1930), 251–65. Cf. Robert B. Crawford, "The Biography of Juan Ta-ch'eng," *Chinese Culture* 6:2 (1965), 28-105, especially 57; and Hummel, *Eminent Chinese,* under Juan Ta-ch'eng.

I-chih's father.[83] Juan was trying to form a clique around him by peddling influence, but what of those who opposed him?

This incident was paralleled on a larger, public scale in the preparation and promulgation of the Manifesto of Nanking. A core of Fang's friends and acquaintances in the Fu she were annoyed at the presence of Juan Ta-ch'eng in Nanking after 1634, where he was receiving many callers, discussing military affairs, attracting a coterie of *hsia*-like men, and acting as if he hoped to reinstate himself as an official.[84] In 1636 Juan was thought to be threatening Wei Hsueh-lien with physical harm because Wei, who was in Nanking for the provincial examinations, continued openly to blame Juan for the death of Wei's father and elder brother in 1625. Wei had attracted even more sympathy than the sons of other men who had died for opposing Wei Chung-hsien by using his own blood to write a memorial to the emperor about the injustice inflicted on his family. As part of his protest, Wei declined to wear fancy clothes, eat more than a few dishes at a meal, or frequent prostitutes.[85] Wei's friends in the Fu she ostentatiously protected him from Juan, and after the examinations were over Wei provided a banquet in thanks. At the banquet were the sons of more than half a dozen men who had died for opposing the eunuch faction. Huang Tsung-hsi was among them, and Fang I-chih was also a guest. All of this served to intensify Juan's hatred for the lot of them.[86] When Juan tried to establish a rival society in Nanking as well as to ingratiate himself with Fu she members there, they felt further affronted.[87] Juan elaborately entertained three of Fang's friends, who were known for being fond of poetry, with the intention of so pleasing them with his new poems and beguiling them with wine that they would begin to like him. But, being members of the Fu she, they could not forgive him his past association with Wei Chung-hsien, and when the feasting was well advanced and Juan thought his plan was working, they suddenly reviled him: "You eunuch-like old woman! How could you hope to redeem yourself by being a poet?", and drawing a full forfeit of wine, they laughed at him uproariously.[88] Finally, in order to put an end to the irritation, and the potential danger, that Juan's attempts to regain respectability and influence in Nanking represented, in 1638 Wu Ying-chi drafted an astringent denunciation of Juan and circulated it

83. Ch'ien Hui-lu, "T'ien-chien nien-p'u," 3a. Also quoted in Hsieh Kuo-chen, 173, and in Chu Yen, 257–58.

84. Ch'ien Ch'eng-chih, quoted in Hsieh Kuo-chen, *Tang-she yun-tung k'ao*, 173–74.

85. Fang I-chih, "Hsi yü hsin pi," 21b.

86. Mao Hsiang, *T'ung jen chi*, quoted in Hsieh, *Tang-she yun-tung k'ao*, 174–75. Cf. Fang I-chih, "Hsi yü hsin pi," 21b.

87. Hsieh Kuo-chen, 176–77.

88. Wu Wei-yeh, "Mao Pi-chiang shou hsu," *Mei-ts'un wen chi*, quoted in Hsieh, 179. The story perhaps should not be taken too literally, but it is indicative of the vindictive feelings toward Juan. Also see the fourth act of K'ung Shang-jen's *T'ao hua shan*.

among his friends in the Fu she for their backing.[89] Just at this time Fang I-chih returned to Nanking from Hu-kuang, where his father was serving as governor. He went back to Hu-kuang the next year, but when the Manifesto became public in 1639 Juan supposedly thought Fang was one of the chief instigators.[90] Fang also later recalled that Juan had thought the Manifesto had emanated from him, although Fang assigned the credit to Wu Ying-chi and Ku Kao.[91] Most accounts agree that Fang's friends Ch'en Chen-hui and Ku Kao were the chief sponsors,[92] and Fang I-chih has only been described as a co-conspirator.[93] The publication of the Manifesto was not an action taken by the Fu she as a whole, or even by its leadership, which was involved with intragovernmental struggles in Peking. The Manifesto was the result of the efforts of a few hotheaded friends in Nanking who felt they were helping each other against a common enemy. We can glimpse this spirit in a small incident which also occurred in the autumn of 1639, when Wu Tao-ning, who was Fang I-chih's uncle and friend of Fang's own age, went to some lengths to seek out a Taoist priest in order to procure a pill that cured Huang Tsung-hsi of a fever. Huang appreciated that Wu acted out of pure friendship,[94] and the authors of the Manifesto, along with the 140 or so men who lent their names as signatories, also acted out of a sense of friendship. The difference, of course, is that the Manifesto was perceived as the concerted action of men who had a formal relationship with each other—membership in the Fu she—which went beyond friendship in its implications. The attack on Juan was admired as the courage of benevolent men, unselfish and public-spirited,[95] and it was so vitriolic that he felt compelled to leave Nanking.[96] The victory was celebrated with much wine and laughter,[97] for here was an efficacious action on behalf of righteousness and justice. Juan Ta-ch'eng's time for retribution came later, in 1645, when he availed himself of his friend Ma Shih-ying's control of Nanking to punish the young men who had attacked him in 1639.[98]

89. Ch'en Chen-hui, "Fang luan kung-chieh pen-mo," *Shu shih ch'i tse*, 7a–b. Also excerpted in Hsieh, 179–80. Cf. Crawford, "Juan Ta-ch'eng," *Chinese Culture* 6:2 (1965), 59.

90. Ch'ien Hui-lu, "T'ien-chien nien-p'u," quoted in Chu Yen, "Ming chi T'ung-ch'eng Chung-chiang she k'ao," 258.

91. Fang I-chih, "Chi Chang Erh-kung shu," *Fu-shan wen-chi*, 8.9a; also in "Chi-ku t'ang wen-chi," *Ch'i tai i shu*, 2.27a.

92. Ch'en Chen-hui, 7a–8a. Hsieh Kuo-chen, 179–80. Hummel, *Eminent Chinese*, under Ch'en Chen-hui.

93. Ch'en Chen-hui, 8a. Fang I-chih's name is not listed among those who signed; cf. Hsieh Kuo-chen, *Huang Li-chou hsueh-p'u*, 103–4.

94. Huang Hou-ping, "Huang Li-chou nien-p'u," 25b, in Huang Tsung-hsi, *Li-chou i-chu hui-k'an*. At this time, Huang Tsung-hsi, Fang I-chih, Ku Kao, Ch'en Chen-hui, Mao Hsiang, Hou Fang-yü and a few others supposedly were in daily contact with each other in Nanking.

95. Ch'en Chen-hui, 8a.

96. Ch'en Chen-hui, 8b–9a. Hsieh Kuo-chen, *Tang-she yun-tung k'ao*, 184. Hummel, under Ch'en Chen-hui and Juan Ta-ch'eng.

97. Hsieh Kuo-chen, 185.

98. Hsieh Kuo-chen, 185–86; Chu Yen, 260–64; Hummel, *Eminent Chinese*, under Juan

The great victory over Juan seems hollow, for he was hardly Wei Chung-hsien, the powerful enemy the fathers of some of the leading young men of the Fu she in Nanking had faced in their pursuit of the righteous course in the preceding reign.[99] As Fang I-chih asked rhetorically in his preface to "Associating with Guests," "Is forming a clique with those who are like you and opposing those who are different from you really what is called 'inducing righteousness by being true to your word'?"[100] The problem of acting on behalf of righteousness had not been resolved by the evolution of politically involved associations such as the Tung-lin and Fu she.

There is a basic contrast between the Tung-lin and the Fu she. Leaders of the Tung-lin were strongly motivated by moral considerations. Their willingness to risk failure as a means of proving their cultivated devotion to moral right seems inversely related to political sense.[101] The Fu she, on the other hand, once its aspect of being a literary society, or even an amalgamation of coteries,[102] is stripped away, has more of the characteristics of a formal political organization, "probably the largest and most sophisticated political organization"[103] of the elite in China before the twentieth century. Its political influence was quickly dissipated, and its failure to strike roots must have other dimensions of explanation than simply the Manchu conquest, as has been suggested by some.[104] In terms of their social status, it was in the interests of the literati " . . . to avoid creating institutions which might have brought society and polity together";[105] to do so would have compromised their crucial role as middlemen between the imperial government and the commoners. But the Fu she *was* organized. In terms of motivating ideas, part of the impetus was a desire to emulate the *hsia* ideal, in which acting in concert was a suitable means to carry out noble aims

---

Ta-ch'eng.

99. Cf. Atwell, "The Fu She," *Unfolding*, 354.

100. Fang I-chih, preface to "Chieh k'o fu," *Fu-shan wen-chi*, 1.11a. The allusion is to "Kuan Fu chuan," *Shih chi*, 107.2847: "He had no taste for literature but loved the feats of dutiful *hsia* and was absolutely true to his word. All his associates were rich or influential citizens, local bosses or gangster leaders." Emended from B. Watson, trans., *Records of the Grand Historian*, vol. 2, 118.

101. Cf. C. O. Hucker, "The Tung-lin Movement," in J. K. Fairbank, ed., *Chinese Thought and Institutions*, 161–62: "The Tung-lin men . . . seemed to feel that failure in the partisan struggle, or death, or even destruction of the state, would be preferable to the compromise of personal ethics. . . . Their political movement was in fact a glorious failure." Also cf. F. Wakeman, "The Price of Autonomy," *Daedalus* (Spring 1972), 47: ". . . Late Ming intellectuals *needed* to fail politically. . . ." Wakeman over-generalized the suicidal tendency of Tung-lin adherents; it is discernible in Yang Lien, but seems less perceptible in the founding generation.

102. Wakeman, "The Price of Autonomy," 54.

103. Atwell, "The Fu She," *Unfolding*, 358.

104. Factions continued to be an element in the early Ch'ing political scene, although large-scale organizations for even literary and philosophical purposes were forbidden from the first years of the dynasty.

105. F. Wakeman, "The Price of Autonomy," 55.

when government was deficient. As the Fu she grew in adherents and the scale of relationships changed, however, the *hsia* ideal was diluted. Even in the disorder of the 1630s, claims of being free-reined (*k'uang*) and associating (*chiao*) with like-minded men were suspect as cloaks for the activities of immoral men and opportunists. The names of Ku Yen-wu, Huang Tsung-hsi, and Fang I-chih were listed as members of the Fu she, but they were already developing interests that led them in other directions, away from organizations.

Fang I-chih, disgusted by self-seekers who attached themselves to men of influence, may have doubted the possibility of being of "use" outside of government as a modern day *hsia*, or "guest," but he also recognized the times demanded action. His problem was to discover an alternative in which one could exercise his sense of duty to a wider social good.

6 Emperor's Man

Pao-shu Tzu Is Urged
to Advise the Emperor

Flinging his arms out to the sides,[1] *His Worship Cunning-Courage said vigorously, yet with a soured tone, "How loathsome! How do you bring yourself to utter those vacuous vulgarities? Right now our sage, perspicacious ruler is too busy to eat at the proper time. He seeks men who are worthy and virtuous, foursquare and rectified,*[2] *to assist him in the administration of government. He will shatter convention and revive the glory of antiquity.*

"From the humble status of ordinary commoner one can proffer words [of advice or petition the emperor]. Folk songs which emanate from the remote countryside penetrate directly to the inner court.[3]

"With your sharp insight into ancient and modern times, you have judged what are ruinous and effective [policies]. You have a comprehensive knowledge of the state of our dynasty.[4] *You see before you the extent of the*

1. On 橫肱, see "Ch'ü li," *Li chi*, "When seated with others, one does not extend his arms." (Cf. Couvreur, trans., *Li Ki*, vol. 1, 21: "Assis à côté d'un égal, ne croisez pas votre coude sur le sien [ce serait le gêner]." Thus Cunning-Courage was offending etiquette.

2. On 賢良方正, see "Wen-ti chi 文帝紀," *Han shu* 4.116, where the emperor, because of a solar eclipse, said he wanted to bring into the government worthy and virtuous, foursquare and rectified men who would be able to remonstrate with him about his shortcomings. Also see "P'ing-chun shu 平準書," *Shih chi* 30.1424, where it is mentioned that gentlemen (*shih*) who had those characteristics, as well as learning, had been summoned to the capital and some had reached high office. (Cf. Watson, trans., *Records of the Grand Historian*, vol. 2, 85.)

3. This idea had wide currency. In T'ang times, it was generally believed that " . . .in old days there had been officials who went around collecting folk-songs which they then showed to the Emperor in order that he might know what was going on in people's minds." Arthur Waley, *Po Chü-i*, 48.

4. 通達國體, quoted from "Ch'eng-ti chi 成帝紀," *Han shu*, 10.313: "One who is knowledgeable about ancient and modern times and is penetratingly familiar with the state of our dynasty is called a 'po-shih' 博士. If he is not, then his studies should not be transmitted." I have rendered the term *kuo-t'i* with the ambiguous phrase, "the state of our dynasty," to refer to the condition but also to the institutions of the dynasty. L. S. Yang (in J. K. Fairbank, ed., *The Chinese World Order*, 293) pointed out that strictly speaking *kuo-t'i* "merely refers to the dignity . . . of the state," that is, to the *t'i-t'ung* 體統 or *t'i-mien* 體面 of the *kuo-ch'ao* 國朝, although that dignity is partly based on institutions (*t'i-chih* 體制). In the present context, however, the word "dignity" does not seem sufficiently inclusive.

turmoil inside and outside the empire.[5] *Why not offer your loyal services to our ruling house by preparing a petition trenchantly setting out the advantages and weaknesses of present conditions, instead of cherishing moral correctness and maintaining a stolid, wooden manner? You are content with mourning the times while grasping your wrist.*[6] *This cannot be called heroic."*

Pao-shu Tzu, groping for candid words to contradict him, said most sincerely, "In the present age, one may want to 'shatter convention,' but nothing would change as those below ostensibly carried out the new ways. In the present age, one may want to 'revive the glory of antiquity,' but it would merely create opportunity for corruption as those below adaptively followed along.

"In seeking to proffer words [of advice to the emperor] from the perimeter, the words themselves might be sent up and proffered, but in the end the feelings of those below would not succeed in penetrating to those on high.

"If one were to risk his life by rushing impetuously beyond his station in order to send up [advice], he certainly would be showing great concern for the contemporary situation. In straightforward, highly remonstrative terms, he might say what other men dare not say about the reasons behind what is erroneous or correct, right or wrong, nominal or real, rewardable or punishable. But as soon as the criticism is directed at the person of the ruler, there is peril to the speaker. As soon as the finger is pointed at those in close proximity to the ruler, there is even more peril. If, on the other hand, his words did not go beyond [proposals] that would bear on advantages or weaknesses for the whole empire and would not cut too deeply when implemented, and if his words were extracted from the works of others and discussed affairs[7] *as though they were from someone loyal and upright, they might then penetrate to the emperor and those who grasp the handles of power might accede to them.*

"Nevertheless, from the time it was permissible to send up petitions by prostrating oneself at the palace gate,[8] *there have been petitioners every-*

35b

---

5. In the *Ch'i tai i shu*, the text reads 天下內外撰撰如此; the *Fu-shan wen-chi* text has 天下外內冠撰撰如此. The hiatus indicates a reference to "barbarians" which was effaced to avoid offense to the Manchus.

6. Reading 掔 as 捥 or 腕. 搤腕 was a standard gesture for manifesting one's roused emotions. General Fan did it before donating his head to Ching K'o's plot to assassinate the King of Ch'in. Also see "Wei ts'e 魏策," *Chan kuo ts'e*, 214: "For this reason, the roving *shih* of the empire are all day and night grasping their wrists, glaring in anger, and gnashing their teeth. . . . " (Cf. J. Crump, trans., *Chan-Kuo Ts'e*, 402).

7. On 論列, see "Ssu-ma Ch'ien chuan," *Han shu* 62.2728. In his famous letter to Jen An, Ssu-ma Ch'ien asked how he would dare "discuss pros and cons" at court. (Cf. Watson, *Ssu-ma Ch'ien*, 60.)

8. Following the *Fu-shan wen-chi* text, which has 闕, rather than 闋, as in the *Ch'i tai i shu*. 伏闕上書 appears as a term in Sung.

where. There are unreliable men from the marketplaces and villages who have never recited the Songs *or the* Documents *but who know the minutiae expected of others.*[9] *[On the occasion of a government call for advice,] they might happen on to a dull idea*[10] *and sighing repeatedly they respond point by point. They then run to our 'Ch'ang-an' [i.e., Peking] to send up their petition. Old clerks, having become familiar with government regulations, send up their petitions. Soured old scholars, to be rid of what besets them and without any other means to requite themselves, send up their petitions. Supervisory clerks and connivers send up petitions, too, when they want to create confusion and mislead their superiors in order to involve others in litigation for personal motives, or when they are losing in a struggle with a great family with whom they are angered. In our day, the sending up of petitions has come to be so much in this vein that a gentleman feels ashamed to do it.*

"Moreover, someone's memorializing in the morning and being summoned to court that evening does not happen now in the manner implied by the old saying, 'How terrible that we have met so late.'[11] *Actually, he would have his contact who had accumulated favor [at court], who kept him fully informed, and who completely sheltered him.*[12] *Only then would he prostrate himself outside the court gate and hope for the 'unexpected' good fortune [of attending on the emperor]. Yet even such a man will not always escape if one morning there is an obstruction hanging [in the well and the jug] breaks against the tiles of the well wall.*[13] *Consider merely the* 　　36a
scholar who has not realized his ambitions; outside [the government] he

9. 咫尺之義, quoted from "Yu-hsia 游俠 chuan," *Shih chi*, 124.3182. (Cf. B. Watson, trans., *Records of the Grand Historian*, vol.2, 454: "Men who stick fast to their doctrines and observe every minute principle of duty, though it means spending all their lives alone in the world, can hardly be discussed in the same breath with those who lower the tone of their discourse to suit the vulgar, bob along with the current of the times, and thereby acquire a glorious name.")

10. The *Fu-shan wen-chi* text has *ch'ih* 持; the *Ch'i tai i shu* text has *te* 得. *Ning* 濘 is to be read as 懦, or *nuo* 懦. On 懦愚, see "Ch'i ts'e," *Chan kuo ts'e*, 97. By way of apology, Lord Meng-ch'ang said that he was so wearied by his court affairs and troubled by all the anxieties that his being had become dulled. (Cf. J. Crump, trans., *Chan-Kuo Ts'e*, 190).

11. 恨相見晚, close to 恨相知晚 in "Kuan Fu 灌夫 chuan," *Shih chi*, 107.2847, and in *Han shu*, 52.2384. The point of the saying is that a bond of trust was immediately established between the two men who had just met.

12. The rendering of this sentence is speculative.

13. 一旦重礙, 爲甕所轠, quoted from Yang Hsiung's "Rebuke about Wine," in "Ch'en Tsun 陳遵 chuan," *Han shu*, 92.3713. The piece contrasted an overly rigid gentleman (*shih*), who was like an earthenware water jug, with the easygoing, flexible gentleman (*shih*), who was like a leather wine pouch. "You are like a jug. Look at where the jug rests: on the rim of the well. Being high above but next to the depths of the well, it is always close to danger whenever it is being moved. Neither wine nor sediment enters its mouth; it gets its full from water. Not able to move either left or right, the jug is pulled by a rope. If one morning there is an obstruction hanging in the well, the jug will strike and be broken on the tiles [on the

has no one to draw on for prestige, and inside [the government] he has no one to aid or assist him. If he is not believed when he cries out a protest, then it is fetters and chains for him; his foot will trip in a hole.[14] *Then what is better than being in a carefree state*[15] *with husks for food and coarse hemp for clothes!"*

Under Ming law anyone, commoner or official, could hand in a petition for transmission to the emperor. As part of his legacy of instructions to his descendants, the Hung-wu emperor urged on them the necessity of allowing anyone who had something that should be said to the emperor to memorialize without being blocked by any government office. His intention was that in this way corrupt practices would be exposed and the sentiments of the governed would be known to the emperor. Those complaints or proposals that were justified were to be handed over to the relevant office for action.[1] This principle was thus established as a fundamental part of the Ming system.[2] But Cunning-Courage was appealing to a greater tradition than simply the possibility in Ming of a man of low standing being able to present a communication to the emperor. What he had in mind was that by proffering such telling advice the petitioner would attract the emperor's notice and thereby be catapulted to the top. Summoned to the emperor's presence, the newly arrived advisor would be so persuasive that he would be entrusted with the handles of power and thus could effect good works for the society at large without having had to spend a lifetime inching up to a position of administrative responsibility.

The Warring States period supplies many examples of such men, and the name of Su Ch'in must be among the most prominent. Without presuming to

---

walls of the well]. Its body will be cast into the Yellow Spring, its 'flesh and blood' will become clay, [from which it was made]. Being used in this way is not as good as being a leather wine pouch. The leather pouch is round and flexible, with a belly like a huge pot. For the whole day while it is filled with wine others repeatedly 'borrow' some. It constantly is a 'tool' of the state, assigned to a carriage [accompanying the emperor to supply him]. It goes in and out of the two palaces; it is involved in affairs in the houses of the lords. Because of this we might ask, how is wine [rather than the character of the jug, and the man], the transgressor?" (Cf. B. Watson, trans., *Courtier and Commoner in Ancient China*, 238–39, and the translation in David R. Knechtges, "Wit, Humor, and Satire in Early Chinese Literature," *Monumenta Serica* 29 (1970–71), 93.)

14. Reading 趾, as in the *Fu-shan wen-chi* text. 足蹟趾硌 is quoted from "Yuan tao 原道," *Huai-nan Tzu*, 1.25b. Speaking of the ordinary man's limits of perception and understanding when he is wrapped up in other things, the *Huai-nan Tzu* contended that "he is not aware of his foot tripping in a hole (or the Pit at Ch'u?) or of his head bumping a tree (or the Grove?)."

15. On 消搖, compare 逍遙遊, "Free and Easy Wandering," the title of the first chapter of the *Chuang Tzu*.

1. Chu Kuo-chen, *Huang Ming ta hsun chi*, 1.6a.

2. Hung-wu's admonition is quoted in the *Ta Ming hui tien*, 80.1a. (p. 1259)

enter the controversy over whether he was a historical person,[3] we may still recognize the continuing appeal of the story of his humble origins, his labors to prepare himself for the task of counseling a king, his winning the confidence of the king of Chao, and his efforts to save the rest of China from the encroachments of the state of Ch'in.[4] Su Ch'in represents a whole group of what have been called "persuaders,"[5] typically men who sought to purvey their military and political sagacity to a ruler in return for a share of wealth and power. Attempts to argue rulers into following a moral path, such as Mencius repeatedly sought to do, represent a ramification of this tradition by which men even " 'from the meanest alleys of poverty' could hope to rise rapidly if they were skillful enough and if they could gain the ear of someone in power—and this last consideration was crucial."[6] As the imperial system developed and access to the emperor's person was more limited, the possibility remained of catching his eye if not his ear by sending in a written statement.[7] Thus Han Yü (768–824), as yet unsuccessful in the T'ang examinations, thought to analyze contemporary problems and, by presenting his recommendations to the emperor, be appointed to a suitably high office.[8] The most famous example, however, in later imperial times is Wang An-shih (1021–86). After receiving his *chin-shih* degree in 1042, he served in local government positions, refused opportunities to be considered for appointment to the capital, and cultivated his reputation.[9] In 1058 he submitted a memorial on the contemporary state of the government, a document which came to be known as his "Ten Thousand Word Memorial" (*Wan yen shu* 萬言書). Its concluding sentences asserted his unselfish reasons for speaking out.

> These matters I regard as of the first importance to your own enlightenment. If I were to hold my tongue on such things, and just present for your consideration one or two matters of trifling importance, asking you to estimate their relative benefit or injury, it would merely muddle your mind and be of no practical help to the government of the country. To act in that way would be foreign to my ideas of loyalty, so I trust your Majesty will give my proposals careful attention, adopting such as you may think beneficial and appropriate. That I am convinced will make for the increased well-being of your people.[10]

3. Cf. J. I. Crump, Jr., *Intrigues: Studies of the Chan-kuo Ts'e*, 29–30, and H. Maspero, "Le Roman de Sou Ts'in," *Etudes Asiatiques* 2 (1925), 127–41.

4. J. I. Crump, *Intrigues: Studies*, 31–35, and Crump, trans., *Chan-Kuo Ts'e*, 55–58.

5. The term is advanced in Crump, *Intrigues: Studies*, 4. Also see T'ao Hsi-sheng, *Pien-shih yü yu-hsia.*

6. Crump, *Intrigues: Studies*, 4.

7. Cf. Ch'ü T'ung-tsu, *Han Social Structure*, 102: "Scholars could present memorials directly to the emperor to recommend themselves. It was said that about one thousand scholars attempted to show off their talents by this means in Emperor Wu's time."

8. Nivison, "Protest against Conventions," *Confucian Persuasion*, 185.

9. H. R. Williamson, *Wang An-shih, A Chinese Statesman and Educationalist of the Sung Dynasty*, vol. 1, 14–47, and James T. C. Liu, *Reform in Sung China: Wang An-shih and His New Policies*, 2–3.

10. Wang An-shih, as translated in Williamson, vol. 1, 84.

Although there was more than a ten-year lapse, including the accession of two new emperors and a hiatus of three years while Wang mourned his mother's death, between the memorial and his being given important responsibilities for the conduct of the government in 1069, the two events remained linked; the long memorial was the basis for Wang's political rise. The possibility which Cunning-Courage recommended to Pao-shu Tzu continued to exist, even if it was seldom realized. If one had sufficiently penetrating comprehension of the troubles which beset the state and made his proposals known to an emperor concerned with good government, as Cunning-Courage suggested, one then would have the opportunity to serve the society as an effective official.

By indicating the current realities behind Cunning-Courage's proposal, Pao-shu Tzu shows that it is not a suitable course for him. His first two points, that sending up petitions had degenerated because of the abuse of the privilege and that loyal, frank advice would now at best be met with indifference and at worst with punishment, were elaborated by Fang I-chih in a draft for a memorial which almost certainly was never sent. According to Fang, in his time petition writers did not speak forthrightly about what was wrong at court or exhort the emperor to labor for a more effective government, but instead wrote mainly to request appointment to high office or other favors.[11] Using words close to those he later put in the mouth of Pao-shu Tzu, Fang wrote, "Evil, scheming men from deep in the countryside and without any resources of their own, and frustrated, soured old scholars who find fault with others all send up petitions and disturb the afternoon sessions of the court."[12] Fang was referring to the submission of petitions by individuals seeking to instigate a legal proceeding for reasons of personal revenge or to benefit in some other way. The practice was of long-standing, for as early as 1429 it was called to the emperor's attention that " . . . the people of Szechwan were exceedingly fond of litigations and often on the slightest pretext submitted sealed memorials to the throne."[13] Although the Hung-wu emperor's admonition to his descendants had not considered the possibility, in later reigns it was found necessary to punish petitioners who used the opportunity to memorialize the emperor in the hopes of avenging a personal animosity.[14] Worse than the abuses themselves, had the submission of self-interested petitions, Fang asked, caused the emperors to view all of the literati and officials as unworthy of his attention?[15] Without answering his question, Fang contended that the emperor's inattention to petitions of substance, particularly frank remonstrations, coupled with his inaccessibility to

---

11. Fang I-chih, "Ni shang ch'iu tu-shu chien-jen su 擬上求讀書見人疏," *Fu-shan wen-chi*, 2.1a; also in *Ch'i tai i shu*, 2.1a. Fang, of course, denied that his writing advice was at all cast in that same mold.

12. Ibid., 2.3b.

13. Hucker, *Censorial System*, 99.

14. *Ta Ming hui tien*, 80.1a. (p. 1259)

15. Fang I-chih, *Fu-shan wen-chi*, 2.3b; *Ch'i tai i shu*, 2.3b.

personal interviews with officials, was a fundamental shortcoming in the government.[16]

There was good reason for Fang I-chih as well as Pao-shu Tzu to doubt that a well-intentioned petition containing frank advice would be heard. The Wan-li (r. 1573–1619), T'ai-ch'ang (r. 1620), and T'ien-ch'i (r. 1621–27) emperors had, from the 1580s, been conspicuous in their inattention to the affairs of government. The Wan-li emperor went for some thirty years with only rare appearances before his officials and conducted such business as he did principally through eunuch intermediaries.[17] The ill-fated T'ai-ch'ang emperor's attention was mainly devoted to being established and to dying, as he reigned less than two months. The T'ien-ch'i emperor was famous for his preoccupation with carpentry while the eunuch Wei Chung-hsien gathered the reins of power for himself and crushed those who thought to oppose him.[18] Aside from these three emperors, who in any case might be regarded as aberrations in the imperial system, there was a long-term trend, noticed by a wide variety of observers, for the position of the emperor to become increasingly elevated, remote, and inaccessible. Fang I-chih pointed out that Han Wu-ti (r. 140–87 B.C.) daily met with the assembled host of officials and that some memorable discussions took place,[19] and that under T'ang T'ai-tsung (r. 627–49) officials above the fifth rank were frequently invited in for an interview. Even the Hung-wu and Yung-lo emperors at the beginning of Ming, Fang observed, from time to time discussed affairs of state with all of the officials.[20] In spite of these precedents, the practice of the emperor's surrounding himself with his officials so that there was constant and full communication between them had not been maintained, and this, argued Fang, was a fundamental impediment to good government.[21] If the emperor encourages frank speech and stays informed by interviewing his officials, " . . . 'the affairs of the palace and the government office will be as one.' Concealment will not arise and plots by evil men will not be undertaken."[22] What Fang had in mind was the need to avoid a repetition of the T'ien-ch'i experience, when the bureaucracy was rendered almost powerless by Wei Chung-hsien's shutting them off from the legitimate source of authority for his own ends. Even though the Ch'ung-chen emperor involved himself in the ad-

16. These two contentions are the theme of his draft memorial, "Ni shang ch'iu tu-shu chien-jen su."

17. Meng Sen, *Ming tai shih*, 268.

18. Meng Sen, 304, 319. Hummel, *Eminent Chinese*, under Wei Chung-hsien.

19. Fang did not mention two sets of discussions in the presence of Han emperors which were the basis of books: the *Discourses on Salt and Iron* under Chao-ti (r. 86–74 B.C.), and the *Discussions at White Tiger Palace* under Chang-ti (r. 76–88).

20. Fang I-chih, "Ni shang ch'iu tu-shu chien-jen su," *Fu-shan wen-chi*, 2.3a; *Ch'i tai i shu*, 2.3a.

21. Ibid., 2.1b.

22. Ibid., 2.1b. The sentence "The affairs of the palace and the government office will be as one" is almost an exact quotation from the *San kuo chih*, Shu, 5.919.

ministration of the government, he remained wary of "frank advice," in part out of concern that it was continuing to serve factional interests. Thus Fang I-chih could conclude, "If our emperor wants his to be compared to Yao and Shun's government, then I propose that he begin by heeding the straight speech of his officials. His officials then will dare to speak of matters concerning handling troops and managing finances in order to prepare [alternative policies] for his selection."[23] There was no point, then, in sending up a petition containing excellent advice if it would not be heeded. Fang I-chih expressed his regret that a friend who had been in Peking in 1629 when a Manchu raiding party attacked the city had cast his cogent insights into contemporary problems in the form of a poem rather than as a petition for the emperor because he knew a petition would only be disregarded by the high officials.[24]

Dangers of Serving

Pao-shu Tzu's third point in rejection of Cunning-Courage's suggestion refers to the physical dangers involved in serving the Ming government. Although in the Sung dynasty officials were not subject to corporal punishment, it was not unprecedented, but it became a well-established practice, even a characteristic, of Ming government.[25] At the beginning of his reign the Hung-wu emperor had expressed his accord with the argument by Liu Chi (1311–75) that high officials should not be humiliated; if guilty of a serious infraction, they should be allowed to commit suicide rather than be executed. When the Minister of Works was sentenced in 1373 to a beating, the emperor intervened by saying an official of such high standing ought not be humiliated for a petty reason, but be permitted to forfeit his salary as amends.[26] The precedent thus set was overturned in Hung-wu's reign when a marquis (*hou*) and his son were whipped to death in 1380 and a Minister of Works beaten to death the following year. It became a common practice to administer beatings in court to add humiliation to the punishment of officials.[27] As late as 1425 a low-ranking official was

23. *Fu-shan wen-chi*, 2.4a; *Ch'i tai i shu*, 2.4a.

24. Fang I-chih, "Su Wu-tzu 'Chi hsi tsa yung' hsu 蘇武子薊西雜咏序," *Fu-shan wen-chi*, 2.22a. Although Fang may have been correct that good advice was not heeded, that does not mean no one tried. Censors submitted counseling memorials, for example, at a high rate during the T'ien-ch'i reign. (Cf. Hucker, *Censorial System*, 175.)

25. Cf. Hsu Daulin, "Ming T'ai-tsu yü Chung-kuo chuan-chih cheng-ch'üan" ("The First Ming Emperor and Chinese Despotism"), *Tsing Hua Journal of Chinese Studies* 8 (1970), 358.

26. "Hsing fa chih" 3, *Ming shih* 95.2329. Meng Sen, *Ming tai shih*, 81. In 1375 a beating was administered in court to an official. Cf. Hsu Daulin, "Ming T'ai-tsu," 358.

27. *Ming shih*, 95.2329; cf. 132.3860. Meng Sen, *Ming tai shih*, 81. Meng Sen added that for a righteous man to be beaten in court came to be regarded as bringing glory and respect to the victim. (p. 82) Cf. Hsu Daulin, "Ming T'ai-tsu," 358–59.

beaten and jailed for criticizing the emperor's personal conduct,[28] but from the Hsuan-te reign (1426–35) on, even though officials occasionally were humiliated by being forced to wear the cangue, the administration of beatings in court was regarded as a thing of the past.[29] The respite, however, was temporary, for the practice was revived by 1479. In 1519, 146 men were beaten, 11 of whom died, for their involvement in recommendations against the emperor's continuing to stay in the South. Five years later a similar scale of punishment, 134 men beaten and 16 dead, was imposed on officials for their objections to the emperor's plans to grant imperial honors to his mother and father after he had inherited the throne from his cousin. Through the Chia-ching reign (1522–66) the regulations were applied with such severity that even the highest officials did not escape being humiliated by a beating. During the middle forty years of the sixteenth century the number of court officials beaten and killed supposedly was several times the number of preceding reigns. The practice continued often enough under Chang Chü-cheng's (1525–82) domination of the young Wan-li emperor, but beatings were not administered after the Wan-li emperor withdrew into his inner precincts and cut himself off from his officials. Whether beatings were administered in any particular reign, or even how many, did not matter so much as the precedents that had been instituted during the course of the Ming dynasty. The official who spoke out to advise his emperor knew he risked incurring physical punishment as the reward for his effort.

The humiliation and injury of beatings in court were not the only means Hung-wu established at the beginning of the dynasty for the punishment of officials. He had more than a dozen minor officials put to death for drafting congratulatory memorials containing phrases which had near homophonic parallels that the emperor found insulting.[30] Hung-wu also demonstrated that officials could be killed for no further offense than provoking the emperor with their proposals. In 1377 Yeh Po-chü died in prison, where he had been consigned after sending up a three-pronged, "ten thousand word" memorial in which he had argued by a host of historical precedents that enfeoffing imperial relatives in the future might create a situation in which "the tail was too big for the dog." Hung-wu was particularly infuriated at the implied criticism of his own sons and threatened to kill Yeh with his own hands.[31] Li Shih-lu was put to death in front of the throne, where he had placed his court tablet in protest of the Hung-

28. Hucker, *Censorial System*, 113–15. *Ming shih*, 163.4422. Ku Chieh-kang, "A Study of Literary Persecution during the Ming," *Harvard Journal of Asiatic Studies* 3 (1938), 270–71.

29. *Ming shih*, 95.2329–2330. Cf. Hucker, *Censorial System*, 265. The points that follow in this paragraph are drawn from the account in *Ming shih*, 95.2330, on the history of beatings in court.

30. Examples are listed in Ku Chieh-kang, "A Study of Literary Persecution during the Ming," 260–63. Also see Hsu Daulin, "Ming T'ai-tsu," 357.

31. *Ming shih*, 139.3995; 3990–95 includes a condensed version of the offensive memorial. Meng Sen, *Ming tai shih*, 77–78. Ku Chieh-kang, 269–70.

wu emperor's unwillingness to heed repeated advice to circumscribe imperial patronage of Buddhism and Buddhists.[32] In both instances, the would-be advice-givers were "right" in the view of historians because in the one case the Prince of Yen's independent military command became the base for seizing the throne in 1402, and in the other case Buddhism's influence at court was greatly reduced even during the Hung-wu reign.[33] It was not the case that the Hung-wu emperor would not listen to advice. On the contrary, he often discussed matters with his officials and could be persuaded by them,[34] and he established the practice of permitting anyone to memorialize directly to the throne. Although Hung-wu recognized his need to have views occasionally contrary to his own, there was an unfortunately ill-defined line that a provocative official could cross, intentionally or not. The case of Wang P'u (*chin-shih* in 1385) is instructive of the limits of the emperor's willingness to tolerate contradictions, an official's pride, and the inevitable victor in a direct clash.

> Wang P'u's character was to be irritatingly blunt. He frequently argued with the [Hung-wu] emperor and was never willing to concede. One day when their wrangling had been especially vigorous, the emperor lost his temper and ordered his execution. On the way to the marketplace [where executions were carried out], an order came recalling [Wang P'u and the execution party]. The emperor asked, "Have you changed?" Wang P'u replied, "The emperor, not considering me unworthy, raised me to the office of censor. Why does he now seek to humiliate me in this way? If I was without fault, why was I ordered executed? If I was guilty, why should I live? Today I had wanted to go to a speedy death." The emperor became furious and urged them to proceed with the punishment. As they passed the historians' office, Wang shouted, "Let Secretary Liu San-wu record that on this date the emperor killed the guiltless censor, Wang P'u." He was executed.[35]

By such examples Ming officials were taught that to affront the emperor was to risk death.

Hung-wu went further than executing officials for acts over which they had personal responsibility. He rained down terror. The bureaucracy was decimated by the thousands of executions ordered after the emperor suspected Kuo Huan (d. 1385) and others of accepting bribes in the Ministry of Personnel, and when officials of the Ministry of Revenue in 1382 were suspected of colluding with provincial and local officials in fiscal affairs.[36] Some thirty thousand men were sentenced to be executed in the early 1390s ostensibly as a result of the emperor's receiving belated testimony that they had been implicated in ram-

32. *Ming shih*, 139.3988–89. Meng Sen, *Ming tai shih*, 78.

33. Comment in *Ming shih*, 139.3996. Cf. Meng Sen, *Ming tai shih*, 78.

34. Cf. examples in Meng Sen, *Ming tai shih*, 76–77. Fang I-chih, too, contrasted Hung-wu's meeting with his officials with the comparative isolation of the emperor in the later reigns. "Ni shang ch'iu tu-shu chien-jen su," *Fu-shan wen-chi*, 2.3a; also in *Ch'i tai i shu*, 2.3a.

35. *Ming shih*, 139.3999–4000. Meng Sen, *Ming tai shih*, 78.

36. *Ming shih*, 94.2318–19.

ifications of the rebellious plotting for which the powerful prime minister Hu
Wei-yung had been executed in 1380. A further fifteen thousand were ordered
executed following the denunciation in 1393 of general Lan Yü and other
enfeoffed servants of the throne for treasonous plots.[37] The Hung-wu emperor's
motives for the executions were complicated, with rapacity, megalomania,
paranoia, and "reasons of state" inextricably mixed; he may have been seeking
to create a new climate of opinion in the ranks of the officials, in which they
were to be wholly subservient to the throne. Whatever his intentions, one
effect was clear. The independence of the officials was being severely tested. In
the memorial that led to his death in 1377, Yeh Po-chü had already protested
the demoralizing effects of indiscriminate use of punishments. "In former
times, literati (*shih*) regarded promotion in office as an honor and dismissal as
a humiliation. Today, literati regard living in anonymity as a blessing and being
disqualified from service as their good fortune. They regard being sentenced to
military settlements or labor service as an unavoidable punishment and receiving a beating as a commonplace humiliation."[38] Yeh pointed out that in
recent years not a few officials had been executed, but rather than leading to
the absence of offenses, the executions had blurred the distinction between good
and bad so that less worthy officials did not seek to better themselves and the
ones who wanted to do good had become lax.[39] Because of the beatings and executions, many men of repute declined repeated summons to come to court
and serve in Hung-wu's government.[40] Terror executions demonstrated that
it was not necessary to make a false step while serving. Merely to be in the
government when someone else did could result in the loss of one's life.

Officials were treated more to their liking during the Chien-wen reign
(1399–1402),[41] but when the Prince of Yen in 1402 succeeded in taking the
throne from his nephew, terror executions were reapplied. Before he captured

37. *Ming shih*, 132.3866; 308.7908; Meng Sen, *Ming tai shih*, 70–75; Hsu Daulin, "Ming
T'ai-tsu," 358. One should suppose that the numbers given for those executed represent
orders of magnitude rather than accounting figures.

38. *Ming shih*, 139.3991. This segment of Yeh's memorial is also translated in R. B.
Crawford et al., "Fang Hsiao-ju in the Light of Early Ming Society," *Monumenta Serica* 15
(1956), 321–22.

39. *Ming shih*, 139.3992.

40. Ku Chieh-kang oversimplified the reasons for imposing punishments when he wrote
that the Hung-wu emperor " . . . occasionally ordered executions of scholars through
misunderstanding literary passages. Consequently, although he sought out and summoned
the virtuous by oft-repeated proclamation, there were very many scholars in retirement who
did not respond. . . . In a large majority of cases their reason was that the meshes of the net
of the law were too fine: one error on things under taboo, and it was difficult to escape destruction." Ku Chieh-kang, "Literary Persecution during the Ming," 256–57. It would be
mistaken to infer that all responsibility for the profligate application of the death penalty
should lie with the Hung-wu emperor. Officials, including some who themselves were later
to suffer execution, often instigated proposals that certain persons or actions deserved death.

41. Meng Sen, *Ming tai shih*, 85.

Nanking and the Chien-wen emperor's most respected minister, Fang Hsiao-
ju (1357–1402), the victorious Yung-lo emperor had been advised that even
though Fang would not submit, to kill him would alienate much of official
opinion. Nevertheless, when brought before the throne, Fang's defiant refusal
to recognize him as the rightful emperor and willingness to die so infuriated
Yung-lo that he ordered not only Fang's execution, but also that of all members
of his family and clan, in-laws, friends, and students, which amounted to more
than 800 persons. Still others, more distantly related to Fang, were banished to
the frontier.[42] Dozens more capital and provincial officials were killed, some
with the most cruel tortures, and hundreds from their families and clans were
executed or banished for refusing to acknowledge the legitimacy of the new
emperor. Still others killed themselves to manifest their loyalty to the deposed
emperor and protest the usurpation.[43]

A casualty of the usurpation was Fang Fa (d. 1403), an ancestor of Fang
I-chih. Fang Fa was serving as a judge (*tuan-shih*) attached to the Regional Military Commission (*tu-ssu*) in Szechwan when he refused to sign his name to a
congratulatory memorial to the newly enthroned Yung-lo emperor. One
reason for his resistance was that Fang Hsiao-ju had been the chief examiner
when he passed the *chü-jen* examination in 1399. Rather than be summoned to
Nanking and punished, Fang Fa took his family on a boat going down the
Yangtze and when it reached the border of his home prefecture, he drowned
himself in the river.[44] In his final poem, he held that his official rank was not too
lowly for him to commit suicide for his ruling house's troubles, that is, out of
loyalty to the Chien-wen emperor.[45] There were many who, not going so far
as Fang Fa, nevertheless privately held that to serve the Yung-lo emperor was
to be disloyal to the Ming dynasty. More than that, the Yung-lo emperor taught
the empire that merely to be associated with a man who insistently stood on
Confucian principles could cost one's life.

The Hung-wu and Yung-lo emperors' barbarity was not duplicated by
their descendants, but official service had been rendered less attractive by their
precedents for the man who felt he had to maintain his integrity at all costs. It
had become clear what that might be. There were, no doubt, many men who
were intimidated and held their peace. There also was a steady stream of men
who courted the risks of serving, and even of affronting, the emperor, in order
to exercise their sense of duty for the good of the state. Particularly when they

---

42. *Ming shih*, 141.4017–19. Meng Sen, *Ming tai shih*, 101–2. Crawford et al., "Fang
Hsiao-ju," *Monumenta Serica* 15 (1956), 303–27. Some of those involved committed suicide
to escape a terrible death.

43. Ku Ying-t'ai, *Ming shih chi shih pen mo*, 18 (Jen-wu hsün-nan 壬午殉難), gives more
than sixty cases of terror applied at the time of the Yung-lo emperor's succession.

44. *T'ung-ch'eng Fang shih shih chi*, 1.1a. Cf. the mention of Fang Fa's suicide in *Ming shih*,
141.4021.

45. Ibid., 1.1b.

suffered the consequences, they gained the praise of their contemporaries as well as of historians. In perhaps the most tranquil of times for officials in Ming, when the Hsuan-te emperor (r. 1426–35) persisted in treating infractions by officials with what some considered excessive leniency,[46] the risk was still present. Ch'en Tso, an investigating censor, submitted a memorial suggesting the emperor not neglect the lessons in the *Ta-hsueh yen i* 大學衍義, the collection of classical quotations and historical precedents compiled by Chen Te-hsiu in Sung to give concrete illustration to the precepts of the *Great Learning*. The emperor, angered at the implication that he was not sufficiently familiar with the *Great Learning*, a text which had come to be regarded almost as the ethical testament of the dynasty, imprisoned Ch'en Tso and members of his family. His father died in jail and Ch'en was not released until after the accession of a new emperor in 1435.[47] In a less than tranquil reign, Yang Tsui (d. 1540), chief minister of the Court of the Imperial Stud (*T'ai p'u ch'ing*), was beaten to death for remonstrating against the emperor's ingesting pills and drugs in a search for longevity at the expense of attention to government affairs.[48] Through the 1540s and 1550s the remonstration was repeated and the protesting officials were beaten and imprisoned in their turn. The most famous remonstrator in this succession was Hai Jui (1514–87), who had purchased a coffin and given his final instructions to his family before sending up a memorial in 1566 criticizing the emperor's indulgence in Taoist practices and consequent neglect of government affairs. The memorial and Hai's willingness to die gave the emperor pause, but later Hai Jui's arrest was ordered.[49] In spite of unenlightened emperors and repeated, disastrous losses of life, every reign in Ming had officials who conscientiously sought to follow the Way and serve the ruler, and in general the *esprit* (*ch'i-chieh* 氣節) of officials in Ming was much higher than in Ch'ing.[50]

Fang and the Recent Record

There was ample justification, then, from events in the history of the Ming dynasty for Pao-shu Tzu's third point, that even if one were accorded high office the risks were such that living in humble obscurity might be preferable.

46. Cf. Hucker, *Censorial System*, 126–28; 260–61; and passim. One wonders if Hsuan-te did not go to extremes of leniency and benevolence (or at least is portrayed by historians as doing so) to contrast his reign with that of his grandfather, the Yung-lo emperor.
47. Meng Sen, *Ming tai shih*, 131. Hucker, *Censorial System*, 133. *Ming shih*, 162.4401–02.
48. *Ming shih*, 209.5516.
49. *Ming shih*, 226.5930–31; Meng Sen, *Ming tai shih*, 249–51. Ku Chieh-kang, "Literary Persecution during the Ming," 272–73. Hai Jui was released from jail after the accession of a new emperor within the year.
50. Meng Sen, *Ming tai shih*, 78, 82. For a listing of outstanding remonstrations during Ming, see Yü Teng, "Ming tai chien-ch'a chih-tu kai-shu," *Chin-ling hsueh-pao* 6 (1936), 213–29.

Recent events in the T'ien-ch'i reign (1621–27) underlined that blood shed by officials was by no means a matter of the distant past. The practice of administering beatings at court was revived. An investigating censor was beaten in court when the newly enthroned emperor was offended by his demand for the punishment of the eunuch who had administered the "red pills" which were blamed for the T'ai-ch'ang emperor's death.[51] In 1624 two men died as a result of court beatings, and after the censorate had ineffectually protested, Yeh Hsiang-kao (1559–1627), the dominant Grand Secretary of the time, reportedly said, "For several dozen years this has not been done. Now under our administration it has occurred three times in a ten-day period. It absolutely must not be done again." As if to imply that the protest was effective, the *Ming History* added the comment that "Wei Chung-hsien thereupon abolished beatings at court. But those whom he wanted killed were sent to the prison of the imperial bodyguard."[52] They died in prison for being outspokenly critical of Wei Chung-hsien's influence over the emperor and thus the government. The memorial which precipitated Wei's retribution was Yang Lien's (1572–1625) denunciation of the eunuch's "24 crimes" to the emperor in 1624. Yang explicitly staked his head that he could loyally provoke the young emperor into saving the dynasty by withdrawing the powers Wei Chung-hsien had accrued: "If all this [which I have proposed, including the removal of Wei] is done and still Heaven's blessings do not return and men's hearts are not pleased. . . then I request that you behead me as an offering to Chung-hsien."[53] The emperor at best vacillated and Wei Chung-hsien, after an initial fright, kept his place. Yang Lien and Tso Kuang-tou (1575–1625), who had helped draft the memorial, became two of the "six martyrs" who died under torture in prison in 1625. More than a dozen other officials killed themselves or were killed under pressure of Wei Chung-hsien's efforts to suppress criticism of his role in the government.[54] Many were forced out of office and others felt compelled to resign. Among them was Fang I-chih's grandfather, Fang Ta-chen (1558–1631), serving as Vice Minister of the Grand Court of Revision (*Ta-li ssu shao-ch'ing*) at the peak of his career. Refusing an appointment as Chief Minister of the Court of Imperial Entertainments (*Kuang-lu ssu ch'ing*) at Nanking, he went

51. Hucker, *Censorial System*, 272.

52. *Ming shih* (Hsing fa chih), 95.2330. The *Ming shih* oversimplified the course of events. On at least one occasion after Yeh resigned as Grand Secretary, an official associated with him was beaten in court. (Hucker, *Censorial System*, 273) The *Ming shih* also did not mention Wang Wen-yen (Hucker, 194) among the three that stimulated Yeh's protest.

53. Translated in Hucker, *Censorial System*, 204. Hucker summarized and translated segments of Yang Lien's memorial, and provided an account of the main events in the attempts to dislodge Wei and the retribution suffered by the critics. Also see Hummel, *Eminent Chinese*, under Wei Chung-hsien, Yang Lien, et al. Meng Sen, *Ming tai shih*, 324–31.

54. Sixteen names are listed in Wu Ying-chi, *Ch'i-Chen liang ch'ao po fu lu*, 7.1a–b, as "loyal officials who were killed in Hsi-tsung's court."

into retirement in 1625.[55] Fang I-chih's father, just promoted from bureau director in the Ministry of War to Defense Intendant (*ping-pei*) in Kiangsi, was dismissed from office for opposing those allied to Wei Chung-hsien.[56] After the death of the T'ien-ch'i emperor in 1627, the derivative character of Wei Chung-hsien's power was demonstrated by the Ch'ung-chen emperor's carefully recovering control of the imperial apparatus and within three months forcing Wei's suicide.[57]

The accession of the Ch'ung-chen emperor and the demise of Wei Chung-hsien were welcomed as an end to the deadly strife at court, and many officials, including Fang K'ung-chao, who had felt compelled to retire in the preceding reign returned to Peking to accept appointments in 1628. The struggle within the bureaucracy was renewed, however, as political and even blood revenge was sought against officials who had allied themselves with Wei, and punishments continued to be liberally applied. The post of Minister of Justice has been cited as an example of the rapid turnover and unpleasant fates of officials through the Ch'ung-chen reign. In the course of seventeen years there were seventeen appointments to the post. The first minister was sentenced to death for his association with the eunuch faction, two were banished, two more were removed from the rolls of men eligible for appointment, one was reduced in rank after his trial, two died in prison, and one died in office. One minister was imprisoned, then reappointed and shifted to another ministry. Of the less unhappy cases, one retired before he had served a year, two were shifted to another ministry before they had taken up their Justice appointment, and one left office and refused a later reappointment. The last Minister of Justice of the Ch'ung-chen reign surrendered when the rebels captured Peking in 1644.[58] The risk of physical punishment and death remained. At any time, "the jug could strike against the tiles."

A most pertinent example occurred after Fang I-chih had written the "Seven Solutions." In the sixth month of 1638 his father, K'ung-chao, was appointed in Peking as an assistant censor-in-chief (*ch'ien tu yü-shih*) and governor (*hsun-fu*) of Hu-kuang province (modern Hunan and Hupei).[59] On his first day in office he inspected the ranks of his troops to manifest his concern for his military responsibilities, and he went on to achieve eight victories in eight battles with various rebel bands.[60] But in 1639 his troops were involved along

55. "Fang Ta-li chuan," 1a–b, in *Ch'i tai i shu.*

56. *Ch'ung-chen ch'ang pien*, 2.1b. *Ming shih*, 260.6744. Hsu Tzu, 610.

57. Hummel, under Wei Chung-hsien. Meng Sen, *Ming tai shih*, 338.

58. Meng Sen, *Ming tai shih*, 348–49, drawn from the *Ming shih*. Also see James B. Parsons, "The Ming Dynasty Bureaucracy: Aspects of Background Forces," in C. O. Hucker, *Chinese Government in Ming Times*, 177–81, for a summary discussion of the average rates of turnover of officials in Ming.

59. *Ming shih*, 260.6744. *P'ing k'ou chih*, 3.6b. T'an Ch'ien, *Kuo chueh*, 5813.

60. *Ming shih*, 260.6744. Also "Fang Chen-shu mu-chih-ming," in *Ch'i tai i shu.*

with those under two generals in a defeat inflicted by a rebel leader whose "surrender" had been accepted the previous year against Fang K'ung-chao's advice.[61] At least in part because he had voiced opposition to the strategy which led to defeat, Fang was impeached, dismissed from his post of governor, and sent under arrest to Peking,[62] where he was held in the West Prison.[63] While visiting his father in prison, Fang I-chih had more firsthand experience of the physical dangers of government service. He met three officials there who were waiting to be beaten. He warned them that if they took python gall as a sedative, as they intended, it might leave them impotent. He suggested an alternative prescription for rendering themselves insensitive to the pain that was to be inflicted on them.[64] Because of his father's troubles, Fang found that he had to send up a petition, not to offer advice, but to make a personally motivated plea. In the memorial, which he submitted in the third month of 1640, he summarized the events leading up to the military defeat to show that K'ung-chao was being unduly singled out for blame and he also reminded the emperor of the Fang family's generations of loyal service to the dynasty. But his main purpose in the memorial was to plead to be allowed to replace his father for any punishment for which he was judged liable.[65] K'ung-chao was sentenced to be executed, but due to Fang I-chih's display of filial devotion and K'ung-chao's record as an official, the punishment was reduced to banishment to Shao-hsing.[66] The story was told to Fang I-chih years later that one day the emperor in an informal setting had sighed and said, "Seeking a loyal official, one must go to the house of a filial son." The officials near him respectfully asked what he meant. That morning one of the young officials in court named Ch'en had performed all of his duties impeccably even though his father was in prison and about to be sentenced because of a recent error while governor of Honan. If the son is so unfilial, the emperor wondered, is he able to be loyal? The officials pointed out to the emperor that the conduct and costume of Ch'en in performing his court duties were minutely prescribed in the regulations. Realizing they did not understand his point, the emperor said that in such circumstances the official ought to resign, or at least manifest that he had some feelings. "At this time," the emperor continued, "there is a new *chin-shih*, Fang I-chih. His father, K'ung-chao, had been governor of Hu-kuang, and like that Ch'en's father, was guilty and imprisoned. I have heard that I-chih has a petition written in blood, and that each day he is outside the gate of the court to await the passing of all the officials. Prostrating himself and crying out, he seeks to have it made known that

61. *Ming shih*, 260.6744–45. Li Wen-chih, *Wan Ming min pien*, 79.
62. *Ming shih*, 260.6745. *P'ing k'ou chih*, 3.10a. Meng Sen, *Ming tai shih*, 360. According to T'an Ch'ien, *Kuo chueh*, 5853, the arrest occurred in the first month of 1640.
63. Fang I-chih, *Fu-shan wen-chi*, 8.12b.
64. Fang I-chih, *Wu li hsiao chih*, 5.20a.
65. Fang I-chih, *Fu-shan wen-chi*, 4.8a–b.
66. *Ming shih*, 260.6745. T'an Ch'ien, 5897.

he would die in place of his father. This, gentlemen, is a son." The emperor then sighed again and repeated, "Seeking a loyal official, one must go to the house of a filial son."[67] Whatever opportunity the incident gave Fang to show his filial devotion, it must have confirmed for him the perils of serving in government.

For all the risks, the political climate of the 1630s did not cause all talented, serious young men to turn away from government, but it did create the circumstances in which certain men appeared to find socially relevant scholarship an alternative to the frustration and hazards of holding office. Fang I-chih's friend Ch'en Tzu-lung, after some hesitation, went at the insistence of his ill stepmother to Peking for the 1637 metropolitan examination. He was successful and accepted an appointment as a prefectural judge, but before he had reached his assignment he had to retire to mourn her death. While in mourning he edited a compilation of writings on political and social questions, and, without our imputing a causal relationship, by 1639 he was declaring his intention to remain in retirement and not return to office. However, he was urged to serve, and his eighty-year-old grandmother not only denied he could use her age as an excuse, but also stressed his need to repay the family's obligation to the dynasty. Ch'en went to Peking in the spring of 1640 and, when his last minute request to be excused was denied, he took up another official appointment.[68] Ch'en Tzu-lung's conduct may be compared with Huang Tsung-hsi's, whose father died in prison in 1626 for his involvement in the Tung-lin attempt to unseat Wei Chung-hsien.[69] Huang Tsung-hsi's mother was adamant that as the eldest son he revenge her husband's death. She pasted eight words, "Have you forgotten the eunuch killed your father?" on the walls, and the boy would sob on his pillow at night.[70] By the time Huang reached the capital after the accession of the new emperor late in 1627, Wei Chung-hsien had committed suicide, but Huang was not satisfied with the posthumous rehabilitation of his father and a title granted him as the heir. He stabbed two men whom he held personally responsible for his father's death when they were on trial for, in effect, collaborating with Wei Chung-hsien, and supplied testimony that contributed to their both being sentenced to execution.[71] He cut off the hair of another former official to offer in a commemoration ceremony for his father and the other men who died in 1625–26.[72] Such bold revenge earned him the admiration of

67. Li Yao, biography of Fang I-chih, in *Ch'i tai i shu*, 3a–b. The probability that this story is apocryphal is rather high.

68. W. Atwell, "Ch'en Tzu-lung," 74, 78, 99–101.

69. Hsieh Kuo-chen, *Huang Li-chou hsueh-p'u*, 1–2. Also Hummel, *Eminent Chinese*, under Huang Tsung-hsi.

70. Hsieh Kuo-chen, *Huang Li-chou hsueh-p'u*, 2; Huang Hou-ping, "Huang Li-chou nien-p'u," 21b, in Huang Tsung-hsi, *Li-chou i-chu hui-k'an*.

71. Hsieh Kuo-chen, 2; also Chiang Fan, *Kuo-ch'ao Han-hsueh shih-ch'eng chi*, 8.1a, and "Huang Li-chou nien-p'u," 22a.

72. Hsieh Kuo-chen, 3; Chiang Fan, 8.1b; "Nien-p'u," 22a.

many, supposedly even the emperor,[73] but Huang did not pursue a political career. The injustice to his father being atoned, Huang left the capital. By 1631 he was home and devoting himself to historical studies, ostensibly in fulfillment of his father's wishes.[74] We cannot assume to understand Huang's motivations, but a connection between his father's political death and his own retirement to historical scholarship seems more than plausible.

Fang I-chih's family had not suffered punishment at court until his father's brush with a sentence of execution in 1640. Before that Fang may have expressed some ambivalence about serving, but it seems that he and others assumed all along that he would follow in his father's path as an official. When Fang was in Peking to help his father, and to offer his own life in lieu of his father's, he did not participate in the rounds of eating, drinking, and entertainment that were as available to him in the capital as they had been in Nanking. As he recalled, "When I was attending my father in the West Prison, I did not go to banquets, but hid myself in my lodgings and read books."[75] The inference can be drawn that immersion in books helped Fang cope with the tense situation. But more than that, and again without claiming we have fathomed Fang's motivations either, we can discern a connection between the political hazards and a developing devotion to scholarship. In the years 1640–43, while he was in Peking to aid his father and then to await appointment after he had surreptitiously passed the *chin-shih* examination in the spring of 1640, Fang began to assemble his notes and thoughts and prepare sections of the manuscripts of what eventually became his two best-known books, the *Comprehensive Refinement* and the *Notes on Principles of Things*.[76] Against a background of long-term trends and contemporary lessons in the frustrations and dangers of holding office, leading figures in the development of the new intellectual orientation had begun to direct their efforts away from government service before the Manchus occupied Peking in 1644.

Let me bring the discussion full circle. When the aim of aiding the emperor with good advice was perceived to be frustrated by blockage of the channels of communication and by the hazards of service in the bureaucracy, an alternative means for realizing that aim was possible. One could write a book to attract the attention of a ruler, present or future. Fang I-chih recognized this possibility. In the first few years of the Ch'ung-chen reign he had written that an effective emperor had to have contact not only with his officials but also with books. By reading widely, the emperor could penetrate what Fang regarded as obfuscations of the proper models for imperial conduct and government policy. He disparaged talk of Yao and Shun and the Three Dynasties of high antiquity and

73. Hsieh Kuo-chen, 3; Chiang Fan, 8.1b; "Nien-p'u," 22b.

74. Hsieh Kuo-chen, 3, quoted from Huang's tomb inscription.

75. Fang I-chih, "Shu T'ung ya chui-chi hou," *Ch'i tai i shu*, 2.22a. The West Prison (Hsi ts'ao 西曹) was the jail of the Ministry of Justice.

76. Fang I-chih, "Ch'ü Chi-ku-t'ang ke chung tsa lu ho pien chih yueh T'ung ya," *T'ung-ch'eng Fang shih shih chi*, 26.8b.

recommended instead study of the more accessible realities of T'ang and Sung. The emperor who would read books for guidance, Fang argued, should turn to historical overviews such as Ssu-ma Kuang's *Comprehensive Mirror for Aid in Government* and its abridgement, *Essentials of the Comprehensive Mirror*, compiled by Chu Hsi. For precedents from his own dynasty, the emperor should read not only the Hung-wu emperor's admonitions to his descendants, but also the *Supplement to the Elaborations of the Meaning of the Great Learning* (*Ta hsueh yen i pu*) by Ch'iu Chün (1418–95).[77] The books cited by Fang are noteworthy for being essentially historical in their approach to problems of governing the empire. In this mode of "advising the emperor," Fang and his contemporaries could find justification for producing their own contributions to clarifying the Way for the general good.

77. Fang I-chih, "Ni shang ch'iu tu-shu chien-jen su," *Fu-shan wen-chi*, 2.2a–3b; *Ch'i tai i shu*, 2.2a–3b.

7   Useless Men

Pao-shu Tzu Is Urged to Escape

. . . into Mountain Seclusion

With a respectful attitude while dividing the milfoils,[1] *Elder Tough-Nut pronounced with composure, "In antiquity when a worthy who had entered the service of his monarch did not find conditions adequate to realize his ambitions, he withdrew but had the means to look after his own affairs. You are ambitious and aloof, yet you have come aimlessely to this place [i.e., Nanking]. You are not acting as a literatus of noble character would.*

"I have heard you have a mountain tucked away between Mt. Ch'ien and Mt. Huo [both in Anhui, west of T'ung-ch'eng]. The perilous paths which connect it to the outside traverse deep, deserted valleys, inaccessible ravines and rope bridges.[2] *It is what is called 'a place which one man can defend against ten thousand.' The blocked passes in each direction are themselves sufficient to withstand the incursions of bandits. On this mountain there are several tens of li of fertile land. With plantings of mulberry and hemp [for clothing] and domesticated dogs and pigs [for meat], it would be like the terrain around a town, yet just by netting wild animals and gathering wild vegetables one could satisfy his needs. It is a Lung-chung ("In the Midst of Plenty"),*[3] *a place where one can 'sleep high,'*[4] *[away from the turmoil of the times]. Since you are not in accord with the times and the times do not make use of you, do you still want to attract attention to yourself, like a tree on the mountain or an oil flame?*[5] *Why not*

---

1. Reading as 蚼蚼. On 揲策, see "Kuei ts'e 龜策 chuan," *Shih chi*, 128.3224: "He divides the milfoils and determines the numbers."

2. The *Ch'i tai i shu* has 懸度 (read as 渡); the *Fu-shan wen-chi* has 縣度.

3. 隆中, in Hupei west of Hsiang-yang 襄陽, is where Chu-ko Liang lived as a farmer until he was made the chief aide of Liu Pei 劉備. See note in "Chu-ko Liang 諸葛亮 chuan," *San kuo chih*, Shu, 35.911.

4. On 高臥, see "Hsieh An 謝安 chuan," *Chin shu*, 79.7a. Hsieh An, who finally accepted an appointment after repeated refusals, was jokingly accused of having "slept high" in the mountains. The implication was that Hsieh was aloof from the ordinary world.

5. On 山木 and 膏火, see "Jen-chien shih 人間世," *Chuang Tzu*, 4.38: "The tree on the mountain induces its own destruction, the oil flame fries in its own fat." The point in the *Chuang Tzu* is that a man's talent or wealth is the cause of his destruction: to be "useless"

*go with all haste to escape from the world, enter your mountain, and live
in retirement? Be the cicada in sloughing off this dirty world; be the peasant[6] who without ambitions gathers nuts to eat and bark to wear. Though
it would be all right [to retire until you eventually] assess the times as
suitable and then go into [government service], instead you are a near nothing[7] here in the marketplace. Do you just want to sit back watching the
tumult here in Chiang-nan?*

"Let me make a prognostication for you."

Pao-shu Tzu said with a deep sigh, "Our times are difficult. Going
into [government service] now is not like [the service] of men in antiquity.
By the same token, living in retirement now cannot compare to [the retire-
ment] of men in antiquity. When one understand seminal forces, he should
be decisive. Do you think I am blind?[8] It is just that I am but a man of the
ordinary world. Sickly as well as refined and physically weak, I am not
able to work a plow.[9] The marriage arrangements for my sons and
daughters are not completed, and they are still dependent on me. I cannot
evade [my responsibilities] for them.

"Moreover, were I to enter the mountains without comrades and live
alone in a hut where I could see no neighbor's smoke, would native troublemakers not be suspicious of me even though I were wearing coarsely woven
cloth and eating wild plants? If you retort, 'Use kindness and munificence
to win them with virtue,' then my response would be that I certainly
could, but only by sharing each meal with them. Though they might be
filled up, I would be left destitute. Or if you retort, 'Use your prestige to
subdue them,' then my response would be that I certainly would have to
assemble many warriors and stout fellows to live with me. Were I to do this,
then to take a stroll one day I would have the expenses of moving an army.
Moreover, men in the mountains tend to be wide-eyed and startle-eared,
and there are officers and laws that incriminate them. How can one, on his
own authority,[10] kill others by using his own army? If he were to do that,
he might then have the passes blocked in all four directions, but he would*

36b

---

is the way to survive. (Cf. B. Watson, trans., *Complete Works of Chuang Tzu*, 66–67.)

6. Reading 萌 as 氓.

7. Taking *hsi* 邀 as *su* 邀, and reading *p'u-su* 樸邀 as 樸樕, which is glossed as 小木 and as
心木, from *Songs*, "Chao nan 召南, Yeh yu ssu chün 野有死麕." *P'u-su* has the extended meanings of "small abilities" 小材 and "humble circumstances" 鄙陋. In the original context,
Legge (1.2.12.2) decided it meant "scrubby oaks."

8. On 瞑瞑, see "Lan ming hsun 覽冥訓," *Huai-nan Tzu*, 6.11a: "Acting as a horse, acting
as a cow, his gait is stumbling, his vision is limited." Cf. n. 21 below.

9. On 躬耕 (or 畊), see "Chu-ko Liang chuan," *San kuo chih*, Shu, 35.911 and 920. Chu-ko
Liang, who was a tall man, plowed to support himself after his father died, and also to preserve his life during the chaotic times.

10. On 擅殺, or 專殺, see *Mencius*, 6B7. (Cf. D. C. Lau, trans., *Mencius*, 177: " . . . a feudal
lord should not exercise sole authority in the execution of a Counsellor.")

no more be able to hold [that place] than a great highway. Bandits already are nested in such places. I have heard it said, 'Live in town in times of lesser turmoil. Live in the hills in times of greater turmoil.' But what ought we to do when the empire is in between turmoil and no turmoil? [If one merely wants] heedlessly to preserve his life,[11] there must be a way to do this. Even with his great intelligence, Chu-ko Liang[12] could not live at Lang-ye [his native place in Shantung], but had to live abroad. After living everywhere, he found at Lung-chung in Nan-yang for the first time a place to hug his knees.[13] My intelligence does not attain to that of Chu-ko Liang, and I still do not know where to 'hug my knees.' I look in all four directions; in the general distress, there is nowhere to hasten.[14] You, sir, may have your milfoils and tortoise shells, but how are you able to make a decision for the here and now?"

. . . into Esoteric Practices

Old Hollow-Deceit, haughtily drawing attention to himself, said, "As someone who is truly good at calculating worldly affairs, are you also able to understand what is outside of this common world? Here in my pot is a drug. It can relieve your oppression[15] and bring a new dawning. Would you like to take some?"

Pao-shu Tzu said, "Even were I ill, I would not like to take any drug. Because the drugs of the men of the world all produce [rather than cure] illness, taking them is not as good as self-healing without drugs. Do I now see that you are one of those who drink the pure water of the dew? You must have secret formulas.[16] May I hear of them?"

11. 苟全性命 is quoted from Chu-ko Liang's "Ch'ien ch'u shih piao 前出師表," *San kuo chih,* Shu, 5.920: "Beginning as a commoner, I plowed at Nan-yang; I heedlessly preserved my life in a time of turmoil and did not seek to make my understanding known to the lords."

12. 武侯 refers to Chu-ko Liang, who was enfeoffed as Lord of Wu-hsiang 武鄉侯.

13. See "Chu-ko Liang chuan," *San kuo chih,* Shu, 35.911–12. After being compelled to leave his home in Lang-ye 瑯琊 (or 琅邪) after his father died, Chu-ko Liang lived as a farmer at Lung-chung, near Nan-yang 南陽 in southern Honan. Halfway up the mountain there was a "Hugging the Knees Stone" 抱膝石, traditionally where Chu-ko Liang hugged his knees and moaned. He also belittled one of his friends for feeling he had an obligation to return to his native place.

14. Quoted from *Songs,* "Hsiao ya, Chieh nan shan." (Cf. Legge, trans., 2.4.7.7: "I look to the four quarters [of the kingdom]; Distress is everywhere, there is nowhere I can drive to.")

15. On 苑結, see *Songs,* "Hsiao ya, Tu jen shih 都人士." (Cf. Legge, trans., 2.8.1.3: "And my heart grieves with indissoluble sorrow.")

16. On 上池之水 and 禁方, see "Pien-ch'üeh 扁鵲 chuan," *Shih chi,* 105.2785. Ch'in Yüeh-jen 秦越人, who was popularly known to his contemporaries as Pien-ch'üeh, embarked on a medical career after receiving "secret formulas," along with a drug which, when taken with

Old Hollow-Deceit replied, "Each man, in wanting to know,[17] of himself does violence to his way. [Once one can make distinctions as fine as] the space in a seam made with a needle and silk thread or the crack around a wedged piece of wood,[18] he will make his plans without actually going beyond his own body. When, penetrating deeper and deeper, he catches [the secret], he can act in accord with his physical desires. Could the Gateway of the Mysterious Female[19] be airy talk without a womb-principle?[20] Were you and I, stumbling along,[21] to sit [in meditation], in less than ten days we could have a clear view of the Yellow Hall and the Purple Palace.[22] The song of the wood gatherer in the open countryside, heard at the time of King Hsuan of Chou,[23] speaks exactly of this: 'swathe your head with the golden head wrapping, enter the heavenly gate, exhale the superior semen, and inhale the mysterious spring.'[24] After this, were beauties the likes of Yang-wen and Nan-wei[25] ranked before you by the hundred and you mounted them one after another, there would be no harm to yourself. That would be most agreeable. And by this means your eyes would be brighter and your hair darker, you would be resistant to disease and lengthen your life; of the drugs known to men, none then is better than this one. It all can follow on what is in my pot. Accept some."

37b

---

the "pure water of the dew" (i.e., water which has not been in contact with the element earth), would give one enhanced mental powers.

17. On 倜倜, see "Shu chen hsun 俶真訓," *Huai-nan Tzu*, 2.14a. With the coming of civilization and values, ". . . knowledge then arose; seeking to be enlightened, wanting to know, everyone parted with his childlike, ignorant heart. . . . "

18. 箴縷綫縗之間, 篸揆呪讕之郤. Quoted from "Yao lueh hsun 要略訓," *Huai-nan Tzu*, 21.4a. The phrases are descriptive of the concerns of the thirteenth chapter of the *Huai-nan Tzu*; by understanding how to make such distinctions, one is best able to discern and accord with change.

19. 玄牝之門. See *Lao Tzu: Tao te ching*, 6. (Cf. D. C. Lau, trans., *Lao tzu*, 62: "The gateway of the mysterious female;" and W. T. Chan, trans., *The Way of Lao Tzu*, 110: "The gate of the subtle and profound female.")

20. Taking *li* 裏, "within," as alluding both to *li* 理, "principle," and *pao-t'ai* 胞胎, "womb."

21. On 躓躓, see "Lan-ming hsun," *Huai-nan Tzu*, 6.11a: "Acting as a horse, acting as a cow, his gait is stumbling, his vision is limited." Cf. n. 8 above.

22. That is, two of the points within the body on which to focus in meditation; the Yellow Hall is usually taken to be above or below the navel, and the Purple Palace is at the top of the head or in the chest.

23. King Hsuan of Chou reigned 827–782 B.C.

24. These renderings are tentative; all of these phrases apparently have to do with esoteric meditation or (and?) sexual practices.

25. On 陽文, see "Hsiu wu hsun 脩務訓," *Huai-nan Tzu*, 19.7b: "Hsi-shih 西施 and Yang-wen were both one of those women whose very being can be pleasing, who with handsome face, bright teeth, and a beautifully boned, delicate figure, has no need for oils and powders, scents and polishes." (Cf. Evan Morgan, trans., *Tao, the Great Luminant*, 228.) On 南威, see "Wei ts'e," *Chan kuo ts'e*, 207: Nan-wei caused Duke Wen of Ch'in to forget about court affairs for three days, such was her allure.

Pao-shu Tzu: "*For a long time I have known that in the world there was this extraordinary art. Nevertheless, at home I have a wife who is prone to jealousy. How could I have compliant, voluptuous, long-robed[26] beauties on either hand? Every day my wife would grab my chin whiskers and display her anger in my house. Moreover, I do not have enough time to lay plans for gaining my breakfast and supper. How much less would I be able to imitate Tung-fang Shuo's repeated use of the gifts bestowed on him by the emperor to obtain new young wives in Ch'ang-an?*"[27]

Old Hollow-Deceit: "*Wang Chi sought fame from his single sack of clothes.[28] Ch'ih-i accumulated a thousand in gold.[29] Thus, why should one be in financial straits? Even in antiquity there was this means of obtaining [precious metals]. In less time than it takes the shadow cast by a sun dial to move, stone could be made into pure silver, coppers could be made into pure gold.[30] People suffer from being poor. For this reason, your wife and children share in the feeling that they have nothing to stir their enthusiasm and they dislike you for it. I am sure the looks on the faces of members of your family who might direct abuse at you would change if gold were plentiful, much of it were exchanged for ornaments of pearl and jade, beautifully worked cloth, amber and other gems, and the splendor laid out before them. Does a man of character not find it difficult to be estranged from his children?*"

38a

Pao-shu Tzu: "*One has to be an immortal before he can practice the ancient art of creating yellow gold and white silver. Men of this age are fond of these [precious metals] and therefore seek to acquire the art but never can. Immortals do not necessarily like these [precious metals] and therefore they could do it but never do.[31] Consequently, if someone [and I am looking*

26. The phrase 初初挑挑 is quoted from Ssu-ma Hsiang-ju 司馬相如, "Tzu hsu fu 子虛賦," *Wen hsuan*, 7.29b. (Cf. B. Watson, trans., *Chinese Rhyme-Prose*, 34.)

27. Man-ch'ien 曼倩 was Tung-fang Shuo's *tzu*; see "Tung-fang Shuo chuan," *Han shu*, 65.2841. On Tung-fang Shuo's habit of sending away his current wife and buying a new young woman each year with the wealth Han Wu-ti lavished on him, see "Hua-chi 滑稽 chuan," *Shih chi*, 126.3205.

28. On 衣囊, see "Wang Chi 王吉 chuan," *Han shu*, 72.3068. Wang, his son, and his grandson all maintained a reputation for being uncorrupted while they held high office. When they traveled, they took no more than one sack of clothes. But they lived so comfortably that it was commonly thought they had no need to be avaricious because they knew how to manufacture gold.

29. On 鴟夷, see "Yueh Wang Kou-chien 越王句踐 chuan," *Shih chi*, 41.1752. Fan Li 范蠡, after serving the King of Yueh, retired to devote himself to acquiring a vast fortune; he observed, "To accumulate a thousand in gold while living at home, to reach the rank of minister while serving in office—these are the most a commoner can attain," and he had done both. B. Watson, trans., *Records of the Grand Historian*, vol. 2, 481, renders the name Ch'ih-i Tzu-p'i as the "Adaptable Old Wineskin."

30. Reading 鐩 as 鐾. In Han, 赤仄 was a name for copper coins. Cf. Fang I-chih, *T'ung ya*, 27.2a.

31. To maintain the parallel between the two sentences, the *Ch'i tai i shu* text has a 終, which the *Fu-shan wen-chi* does not have, before 不爲.

at you, Hollow-Deceit] is able to create yellow gold and white silver, why,
rather than making himself the patriarch of a wealthy household, does he go
on drifting about in the world seeking to profit by giving advice to others?"

Old Hollow-Deceit: "That is only a petty skill anyway. If I may
speak of a superior one, there exists the Way of being pure and still.[32] One
who achieves it can turn his whole family into immortals in the full light of
day[33] and ascend to heaven mounted on a crane.[34] My young man, how
could you be without interest in such things?

"My master lives on the shady side of sacred Mt. Hua [in Shensi].
He is more than five hundred years old. He eats pine nuts and eschews
grain. He has the complexion of a virgin. He rides in Wei Shu-ch'ing's
white cloud carriage,[35] carries Li Ch'ung's diagram of the five sacred
mountains,[36] transforms Ch'in Kao's carp,[37] and plays Prince Chin's
pipes.[38] I will lead you to seek [instruction from] him."

Pao-shu Tzu: "I have observed that in this world those who speak of
immortals with supernatural powers all drift to the gates of the wealthy and
highly placed. How is it that only those who are wealthy and highly placed
can seek to be immortals with otherworldly powers? Since men as wealthy
and highly placed as the Ch'in Emperor and Han Wu-ti could not avoid
Sha-ch'iu and Mao-ling,[39] is there not even less reason for me to live in the
wilds wearing rags[40] to seek a drug of immortality?"[41]

---

32. On 清靜, see *Lao Tzu: Tao te ching*, 45. (Cf. D. C. Lau, trans., *Lao tzu*, 106: "Limpid
and still,/One can be a leader in the empire.")

33. Hsu Sun 許遜 is a famous example of an immortal who was able to *pa chai* 拔宅, "take
up his entire household" to the heavens and immortality. On the first day of the eighth
month of 377, at West Mountain in Hung-chou, Kiangsi, he "took up" 42 members of his
household. *T'ai-p'ing kuang chi*, 14.100.

34. Various immortals were able to ride about mounted on a white crane. E.g., Prince
Chin 晉; see Liu Hsiang, *Lieh hsien chuan*, A.12a–b.

35. Reading 卿, as in the *Fu-shan wen-chi* text. On 衛叔卿, see Ko Hung, *Shen hsien chuan*,
2.1a. Wei Shu-ch'ing was an immortal who, riding a cloud carriage drawn by white deer,
appeared before Han Wu-ti in 99 B.C.

36. Reading 克 as 充. See Kuo Hsien 郭憲, "Tung ming chi 洞冥記," in *Hsu t'an chu*, 1.17b.
Li Ch'ung, who claimed to be 300 years old, was famous for the diagram of the five sacred
mountains that he carried in a basket.

37. On 琴高, see Liu Hsiang, *Lieh hsien chuan*, A.11b. Ch'in Kao was able to live under
water and rode about on a red carp.

38. On 子晉, see Liu Hsiang, *Lieh hsien chuan*, A.12a–b. Prince Chin, heir apparent of King
Ling of Chou (r. 571–545), spent more than thirty years on top of a mountain and became an
immortal; as a young man he had liked to play the pipes.

39. Both the Ch'in emperor and Han Wu-ti avidly sought immortality, and yet both
proved quite mortal. The Ch'in emperor (r. 221–210 B.C.) died at Sha-ch'iu. Han Wu-ti
(r. 140–87 B.C.) was buried at Mao-ling.

40. On 藍縷, see "Ch'u shih chia 楚世家," *Shih chi*, 40.1705.

41. On 不死之藥, see Yü Ying-shih, "Life and Immortality in Han China," *Harvard
Journal of Asiatic Studies* 25 (1964–65), 90. The whole of Yü's incisive discussion provides
contextual material for the discussion between Pao-shu Tzu and Old Hollow-Deceit.

. . . *into Sensual Pleasures*

*Old Hollow-Deceit wanted to buttress his contention, but the words would
not come. Just at this juncture several carefree young men wearing short*   38b
robes[42] *of coarse white cloth and hair held in place by jade hairpins came
speeding along with some "record keepers"*[43] *in a luxurious carriage made
of the seven aromatic woods. The women, with bejeweled girdles*[44] *and
richly embroidered gowns, could be seen because the side curtains were
open. When the young men saw Pao-shu Tzu, they hailed him: "Why
are you sitting there, obscured by the dust [of the world]*[45] *and discomfited?"
When Pao-shu Tzu told them why, one young man said, "Enjoy yourself
when you can. Why wait for wealth and high standing? The men with the
most wealth and highest standing in the world begin by exerting all their
physical strength and use bribes to scheme. One day, when the metal seals
of high office are hanging behind their elbow, they make a move, transgress
the law, are put in prison; the basin is filled with water and the sword is
presented.*[46] *What joy do they then have? What is as good as having some
wine and singing? Scholars suffer so much. I shall wash your discontents
away for you."*[47]

    *Thereupon, taking leave of Elder Tough-Nut and Old Hollow-Deceit
on behalf of Pao-shu Tzu, the young man left with him. The other guests
wanted to follow Pao-shu Tzu to have a drink with the young men. Grasping each other's sleeves,*[48] *they went along. When they reached the [Ch'in-
huai] river's edge, they found a "green pelican" boat moored waiting for
them. The oarsmen's chant started up, and they went out into the middle of
the stream.*

    *Pao-shu Tzu noticed that there were many on board with whom he
was not acquainted. He did not inquire about who they were but took the*

---

42. Reading 襜 as 繬.

43. 錄事, a euphemism for prostitute.

44. Following the *Ch'i tai i shu* text, which has 袜, rather than the *Fu-shan wen-chi*, which
has 袾.

45. On 塵雝, see *Songs*, "Hsiao ya, Wu chiang ta ch'e." (Cf. Legge, trans., 2.6.2.3: "Do
not push forward a wagon;—The dust will only becloud you. Do not think of all your
anxieties;—You will only weigh yourself down.")

46. 盤水加劍, quoted from "Chia I chuan," *Han shu*, 48.2257. The basin with water symbolized the level impartiality of the law; the sword was to serve for the accused official's
suicide. (Some think the basin was intended to catch the blood.) At the beginning of Ming,
Liu Chi cited this phrase to the Hung-wu emperor in arguing that culpable officials should
not be humiliated by execution. *Ming shih*, 95.2329.

47. On 澆磊 (or 蠱) 塊, see "Jen tan 任誕," ts'e 23, *Shih shuo hsin yü*, 187: "Because Juan
Chi's breast harbored discontents, he had to wash them away with wine."

48. On 摻袪, see *Songs*, "Cheng feng, Tsun ta lu." (Cf. Legge, trans., 1.7.7.1: "Along the
highway, I hold you by the cuff. Do not hate me;—Old intercourse should not be suddenly
broken off.")

*seat of honor. [As they went up the river] the banks on both sides wound
ahead, long and twisty, like a mountain pass. By the rail repeatedly someone would bow in salute, but Pao-shu Tzu simply never noticed them. The
music of Mr. Drumming-and-Fifing Chang*[49] *flowed in the shallows. In
the deep water Mr. Mountain-shaped-Incense-Burner Tsai*[50] *burned in-
cense. Old Willow rose and danced for him. Good Breeze gave off her perfume for him.*

39a

    *Both boned meat and preserved meat were served. When the sauces
and kernels were laid out,*[51] *some seated guests resented his simple straight-
forwardness, but Pao-shu Tzu felt starved. He ate ravenously and, picking
up the wine pot, he drained it. His conduct made even those who were
perturbed at him smile. [The servant] passing the wine cup entered
again*[52] *and as of old they danced without stop.*[53] *Whereupon, wav-
ing*[54] *his circular fan and shouting as they were dicing, he motioned for some
men at the corner of the mat who could keep time to join him in singing and
others to play their flutes and pipes in accompaniment. Then he had someone strum a zither, and the ensemble of music caused everyone's heart to be
stirred. As the prostitutes and actors circulated in the company, every
form of dissolution was exhibited. [Men's and women's] shoes and
sandals became intermingled.*[55] *There was the subtle smell of hair perfume.*[56] *Though he could not drink a gallon,*[57] *he felt three quarts was not
enough. When drunk, he stood up and danced. Pao-shu Tzu tapped on an
oar and sang in a loud voice. He wanted to compose a poem, but there was
no one with whom to do it. He no longer knew why he had been depressed.*

    *He listened as the guests in parting called to each other about having
the gambling pieces ready again the next day at a certain place. He also saw
that when those who were ill-tempered from drink did not secure what they
desired from some of those in their company, they would drive them out
into the road. Increasingly, Pao-shu Tzu felt disconsolate.*

49. 張鼓吹 is a play on 鼓吹長, a name for frogs.

50. The allusion is to the river mists.

51. 殽核維旅, quoted from *Songs*, "Hsiao ya, Pin chih ch'u yen 賓之初筵." (Cf. Legge, trans., 2.7.6.1: "With the sauces and kernels displayed in them.")

52. On 入又, see *Songs*, "Hsiao ya, Pin chih ch'u yen." (Cf. Legge, 2.7.6.2: "An attendant enters again, with a cup. . . .")

53. On 侳侳, see *Songs*, "Hsiao ya, Pin chih ch'u yen." (Cf. Legge, 2.7.6.4: "They keep dancing and will not stop.")

54. Reading 揮, as in *Fu-shan wen-chi*, rather than 呼, as in *Ch'i tai i shu*.

55. 履舃交錯, quoted from "Hua-chi chuan," *Shih chi*, 126.3199: "Men and women were on the same mat, their shoes and sandals intermingled." (Cf. David Knechtges, "Wit, Humor, and Satire in Early Chinese Literature," *Monumenta Serica* 29 [1970–71], 84–85.)

56. 微聞薌澤, also quoted from *Shih chi*, 126.3199: "The subtle smell of hair perfume" was perceived when the host and his chief guest were relaxing after the other guests had departed.

57. As Chun-yü K'un 淳于髠 could do, when the setting was as informal as suggested above. See *Shih chi*, 126.3199.

Walking home alone, he went through the night without saying a word. A bitter wind struck him. He sat down in front of the door of his lodgings and only after a long while did the old servant get up and open the door. He went to his room and lay down, but he was unable to sleep. All night he tossed and turned. Sorrow arose from within him. What more can be said!

Man of the Mountains

The phrase "to enter the mountains" (*ju shan* 入山) served as a symbol of the syndrome of withdrawing from society.[1] The degree to which one cut himself off varied; although few men actually lived as hermits in the hills, usually something more than simply retiring from government was entailed. The motive for physically withdrawing also varied. Each man's personal predilections and particular circumstances must have played a part. The reclusive life was most appealing to religious men (*tao-shih* 道士) and would-be immortals (*hsien-jen* 仙人). In the third and fourth centuries the idea was attractive enough that Ko Hung devoted a chapter to the problem. He observed that "anyone who would live in retirement (*yin chü* 隱居) must enter the mountains, but if he does not know the right methods for 'entering the mountains,' he will likely meet with disaster."[2] Ko Hung gave all sorts of practical advice on what to do and what to avoid, as well as sets of talismans that would be useful when leaving society's dangers to confront those of the wilds.[3] The extreme of severing all ties with other men was seldom realized—or at least the successful cases were in effect dead men to society and history. Rather, when it was known, the *act* of "entering the mountains" was important primarily because of its political implications. That is, the man who willingly or not leaves society behind him is making a political decision regardless of how apolitical his motives may be. From society's perspective, the political content of entering the mountains can be perceived not

1. Cf. Li Chi, "The Changing Concept of the Recluse in Chinese Literature," *Harvard Journal of Asiatic Studies* 24 (1963), 234–47, for an attempt at a schematic survey of the ideal. Also see the general discussion of some types of eremitism in F. W. Mote, "Confucian Eremitism in the Yuan Period," *Confucian Persuasion*, 203–212. Nemoto Makoto 根本誠, *Sensei shakai ni okeru teikō seishin: Chūgoku teki in-itsu no kenkyū* 專制社會における抵抗精神: 中國的隱逸の研究 ("The Spirit of Resistance in an Authoritarian Society: A Study of Chinese Withdrawal"), discussed aspects of essentially elite retirement from society; to my mind, he overly stressed opposition to despotism as a motive and was too inclusive in his usage of "withdrawal" (*yin-i* 隱逸), but his book is still the fullest exploration of the problem.

2. Ko Hung, *Pao-p'u Tzu*, nei p'ien, 17.1a. I caution the reader against taking the *Pao-p'u tzu* literally; we might better read much of the book as a satire on contemporary beliefs and practices rather than as a serious representation of them.

3. Ibid., 17.8a–18b.

only as seeking refuge but also as an act of dissent which implies that the current state of human affairs is intolerable.

The well-known story of Chuang Tzu's continuing to fish rather than accept a summons to court suggests dissent at the same time that his reference to the unhappy tortoise sacrificed for its shell suggests that Chuang Tzu also was seeking refuge from a physical threat.[4] The figure of Lao Tzu, putative author of the *Tao te ching*, is another well-known example of a man giving up society to live in retirement because society was in decline.[5] The motive of evading the world's troubles on a group scale rather than as an individual was implicit in the story of the Peach Blossom Spring, where an entire community lived in contented plenty in an inaccessible mountain valley.[6] Their unwillingness to reestablish contact with the outer world represents a continuing negative judgment on the rest of society. The desirability of withdrawing from society to live in the mountains fluctuated with the times, but the idea was established, and it remained an important theme in poetry and painting.

Among historical examples, two modes of implementing the decision to "enter the mountains" might be distinguished; in the one, men sought an irrevocable break with society in its more elaborated and powerful aspects, and in the other they would desire a temporary departure from that society to await more propitious times. T'ao Ch'ien (365–427) preferred, and celebrated in his poetry, a simple, retiring life of relative poverty to suffering the harassments and self-degradation involved in holding office.[7] On the other hand, as a young man Chu-ko Liang lived in the mountains as a farmer, but his retirement was out of frustration at not being recognized for his true worth; he finally was visited by Liu Pei and became a motive force behind Liu's establishment of a revived state of Han in the early third century.[8] The man in retirement, of course, could adopt the one or the other attitude according to his perception of the times and his contemporaries' regard for him.

From the official point of view, there was no social reason to retreat to the mountains during a time of peace when the Way prevailed, and thus during such times retirement should be attributed to the man's own sense of his inadequacy.[9] In later dynasties entering the mountains attracted less notice in official

---

4. *Chuang Tzu*, "Autumn Floods" chapter; cf. B. Watson, trans., *Complete Works of Chuang Tzu*, 187–88.

5. See the biography of Lao Tzu in *Shih chi* 63; translated in D. C. Lau, *Tao te ching*, 8–10.

6. T'ao Yuan-ming, *T'ao Yuan-ming chi*, 92–94. Cf. J. R. Hightower, trans., *The Poetry of T'ao Ch'ien*, 254–56, and Ch'en Yin-k'o 陳寅恪, "T'ao hua yuan chi p'ang-cheng 桃花源記旁證," *Tsing-hua hsueh-pao* 11 (1936), 79–88.

7. Cf. J. R. Hightower, *T'ao Ch'ien*, 2–4, 268–70.

8. *San kuo chih*, Shu, 35.911–12. A comparable case, almost as famous, was Hsieh An 謝安 (or An-shih 安石), who hid out at East Mountain (Tung-shan 東山) in Kuei-chi 會稽 until he was given a post commensurate with his own estimation of his talents. (See *Shih shuo hsin yü*, "Erh Liang," 6.92, and *Chin shu*, 79.6a–b.)

9. See, for an example of this idea, the prefatory remarks to *Hsin T'ang shu*, 196.

histories, in part because to do so still implied a critical judgment of the times and thus the government, and in part because those in power were less inclined to honor the recluse with their attention. When noticed by his government, it was often the occasion to compel the recluse to recognize the sovereignty of the emperor by attending his court. To refuse was to risk being accused of sedition. Nevertheless, the ideal of isolated retirement continued to attract men, including some who put it into practice.

Although the term *man of the mountains* (*shan jen* 山人) in the sense of a recluse who lives away from society had some currency in T'ang and Sung times, from Yuan on, and especially from roughly the middle of Ming, it attained a sort of romanticized fashionableness as a label for a retired literatus (*yin shih* 隱士).[10] Poets and painters, the sort of men discussed above as "men of culture" (*wen jen*), provide many of the examples.[11] Early in the seventeenth century it was observed that in previous dynasties not one in a hundred men who were known for their painting or calligraphy had "lived in retirement in the mountains," but in Ming there had been many commoners and retired literati who became famous artists with no connections to the wealthy and powerful. They were literati of the "mountains and forests."[12] When Wang Yang-ming was twenty-seven, he became discontent with literary pursuits and gave thought to "entering the mountains."[13] Various city dwellers and even serving officials affected the style of "man of the mountains" to indicate their desire to be seen as men aloof from the world's business.[14]

An example of the ambiguities in such "withdrawal" is the case of Ch'en Chi-ju (1558–1639). He burned his scholar's gown and hat when, at the age of twenty-nine, he decided to abandon pursuit of success in the examinations and devote himself instead to a country life of painting, poetry, and good works. Although he earned his living by writing and remained involved with his friends and community, he gained a reputation as a retired gentleman who willingly had forgone an official career as well as the literary and social life of the city.[15] Ch'en set out what he called the "eight virtues" which made living in the mountains superior to living in society in the city: "One does not bear

10. See Suzuki Tadashi 鈴本正, "Mindai sanjin kō 明代山人考," ("The *Shan-jen* of the Ming Period"), in his *Mindaishi ronsō* 明代史論叢 ("Studies on the Ming Period"), 357–62. Suzuki tried to show quantitatively an increased incidence in the use of the term *shan jen* and its variants as an adopted name (*hao*) in Ming as compared to Sung.

11. Nemoto Makoto, *Sensei shakai ni okeru teikō seishin*, 108 and on subsequent pages gives lists of names of men of Ming times who lived in some degree of retirement.

12. Hsieh Chao-che, *Wu tsa tsu*, 7.29a–b (577–78).

13. Wang Yang-ming, *Wang Wen-ch'eng kung ch'üan shu*, 32.906. Cf. Julia Ching, "Wang Yang-ming (1472–1529): A Study in 'Mad Ardour,'" *Papers on Far Eastern History* 3 (1971), 104.

14. Suzuki Tadashi, 363–65; 370.

15. See Nelson I. Wu, "Apathy and Fervor," *Confucian Personalities*, 277–79. *Ming shih*, 298.7631–32.

vexatious ceremonial; one does not see strangers; one is not mixed up with banqueting; one is not engaged in contentions over real estate; one does not ask about changing political circumstances; one does not get into wrangles about what is right and wrong; one is not involved in debts; one does not discuss office-holding."[16] As an ideal, the man of the mountains represented untrammeled independence and freedom from society's demands; as a reality, he often sought to have contact with society on his own terms.

Recognition that actually withdrawing to mountain wilds had its short-comings led to arguments that the essential thing was not to "hide away," but to let one's mind be in the unencumbered state of the man of the mountains without physically removing oneself.[17] To live in the mountains could even be denounced because of the possibility one could become caught up in the sights and sounds, the beauty of the scenery, or the loneliness, at the expense of true tranquility.[18] The distinction thus came to be formulated between "lesser retirement" (*hsiao yin* 小隱), living in retirement in the mountains, and "greater retirement" (*ta yin* 大隱), living in town while maintaining the spirit of being a man of the mountains.[19] Such a distinction, however, also opened the way for pretense, and in the late sixteenth century there was criticism that certain men were feigning being men of the mountains as a cover for seeking fame, patronage, and personal profit.[20] Li Chih, in a characteristically acerbic tone, wrote in a letter,

> What in the present day is called a "sage" (*sheng-jen* 聖人) is identical with what is called a "man of the mountains," with good fortune being the noteworthy difference. If one has good fortune and is able to write poetry, then he calls himself a "man of the mountains." If he is not fortunate and is unable to write poetry, then he shirks being a "man of the mountains," but is known as a "sage." If one has good fortune and is able to discourse on "innate good knowledge," then he calls himself a "sage." If he is not fortunate and is unable to discourse on "innate good knowledge," then he declines to be a "sage," but is called a "man of the mountains." They turn things topsy-turvy in order to snatch some advantage for themselves. They may be known as "men of the mountains," but their mind is the same as a merchant's. They may speak of the Way and its virtue, but their aim is that [of a burglar who] bores a hole [in a wall].[21]

Li Chih's sarcasm, as much as any statistics, indicates the pervasive appropriation of the term *man of the mountains* in late Ming.

Men continued to play with the notion of entering the mountains. Fang I-

---

16. Ch'en Chi-ju, *Yen-lou yu-shih* 岩樓幽事, quoted in Suzuki, 373.

17. Suzuki, 373.

18. T'ang Chen, *Ch'ien Shu*, "Chü shan 居山," 92–93. T'ang (1630–1704) wrote his *Essays of a Recluse* late in the seventeenth century.

19. Suzuki, 377, 380.

20. Suzuki, 364, 381.

21. Li Chih, "Fu Chiao Jo-hou 復焦弱侯," *Fen shu* 焚書, 2, quoted in Suzuki, 379.

chih's paternal grandfather, leaving office in Peking in 1625 in protest against the current tenor of government, went to "live in obscure retirement at White Deer Mountain," but not in lonely isolation; there he ceaselessly discussed philosophy and morality with his followers.[22] Fang I-chih's maternal grandfather, old and nearly blind, announced in 1634 that henceforth there would be no peace in the empire, and he was going to live in the wilds away from T'ung-ch'eng.[23] The famous traveler Hsu Hsia-k'o (1586–1641) found as good a way to be a man of the mountains as any of his contemporaries. Although he did not cut himself off from family and friends, he declined to sit for the examinations and had no gainful employment. Most of his adult life was spent in a series of journeys to, and on, mountains. He visited famous peaks and unexplored ranges, tourist traps and remote temples. He had a taste for climbing higher, and for going on when the path failed. In 1624 Hsu met Ch'en Chi-ju, who sympathetically thought he looked and acted like some wizened old Taoist priest who lived in the mountain wilds.[24] Hsu's compulsion to travel culminated in a four-year trip in the mountains of Kweichow and Yunnan, from which he returned home to die. He was not a hermit, but whatever his motivation his sojourns in the mountains effectively removed him from society's entanglements. Like men who affected being men of the mountains, Hsu found something appealing in physically removing himself; he just went farther than most.

For most men, however, the act of retiring to the mountains was difficult if for no other reason than that it was not easy to know when to go, or if one could manage. In mid-1639, before the turmoil in his area had reached its worst, Fang I-chih wrote in a preface for a friend, "To enter the mountains and live in obscure retirement really is the foremost plan if we were to 'heedlessly preserve our lives.' Nevertheless, since we are already the way we are, it is difficult to avoid the encumbrances of the ordinary world. Even if we wore plain short work clothes [as opposed to the literati's long gowns], how would *we* be able to plow in the fields?"[25] The following year he still expressed his inability to withdraw from society as had the lofty men of the past.[26] But after 1644 Fang wrote of a friend who "understands that in disordered times one does not desire official honors but lives in obscure retirement deep in the mountains."[27] He

22. Ch'en Chi-sheng, "Fang Ta-li chuan," 1b, in *Ch'i tai i shu*.

23. Ma Ch'i-ch'ang, *T'ung-ch'eng ch'i chiu chuan*, 4.15b.

24. Quoted in Ting Wen-chiang, *Hsu Hsia-k'o yu-chi*, vol. 1, "Nien-p'u," 15. Cf. Li Chi, trans., *The Travel Diaries of Hsu Hsia-k'o*, 18. Li Chi denied (p. 25) that Hsu was a mountain recluse, but concluded (p. 28) that for ". . . men living in the oppressive atmosphere of late Ming, his importance lay chiefly in his freedom of spirit." Hsu's diaries seem to make no mention of current affairs.

25. Fang I-chih, "Sung Li Shu-chang hsu," *Fu-shan wen-chi*, 3.33a; also in *Ch'i tai i shu*, 2.18b. The allusion is to *San kuo chih*, Shu, 5.920.

26. Fang I-chih, "Sung Chou Nung-fu huan ku-hsiang hsu," *Fu-shan wen-chi*, 5.24a.

27. Fang I-chih, "Yu chi Erh-kung shu," *Fu-shan wen-chi*, 8.12a.

wistfully added that there must be somewhere a Peach Blossom Spring to escape the warfare.

In Fang I-chih's writings in the 1630s, personification of young, uncritical, engaged men of action, such as the young merchant and Master *Hsia*, are persuaded to follow the examples set by the old, reflective, retiring, wise Mr. Tranquility and Mr. Eastern Wall.[28] Their emphasis was on preserving one's moral integrity rather than physical self, but the means were similar—a lesser degree of withdrawal was acknowledged as a practicable course. Nevertheless, Pao-shu Tzu, and Fang I-chih, disparaged the extreme of literally entering the mountains as unfeasible for a man concerned both with his family and social responsibilities and with his own safety.[29] There is irony in Fang's circumstances. In the late 1630s in Nanking he could reject as foolish the recommendation that a man of integrity must remain aloof from social involvements as well as out of the government's service. A decade later, Fang lived for two years in a remote mountain village and among Miao tribesmen near the Kwangsi-Hukuang border when he repeatedly declined attempts to appoint him to office in the Southern Ming court.[30] The times had radically changed the attraction of being a man of the mountains.

A common gloss of "man of the mountains" (*shan jen* 山人) was "immortal" (*hsien* 仙),[31] which, as a still more extreme form of withdrawing from ordinary society, was the next proposal put to Pao-shu Tzu.

Immortals

Belief in what might be called Taoist practices and which we might consider superstitions enjoyed wide currency in Ming times, but so did a concurrent measure of scepticism. A story which appeared in a collection published in 1632 represents the tension between belief and disbelief. It relates the unhappy fate of Chen T'ing-chao, a wealthy literatus who squandered his resources on the Yellow and White art (*huang po chih shu* 黃白之術) of producing gold and silver from lesser ingredients[32] and, Chen's particular interest, making compounds which would aid in sexual endeavors.[33] Such pursuits were associated under the

28. In "Chieh k'o fu" and "Huo chih lun." Hou Wai-lu made a similar point in a different context; cf. *Chung-kuo ssu-hsiang t'ung shih*, vol. 4, 1148.

29. Hou Wai-lu, perhaps with guerrilla bands in mind, denigrated Fang I-chih's unwillingness to take the risk of establishing his independence of authority in the mountains, out of reach of the corrupt government. (*Chung-kuo ssu-hsiang t'ung shih*, vol. 4, 1149.)

30. Fang I-chih, *Fu-shan wen-chi*, 9.21a; 10.1a.

31. Suzuki, 375.

32. Ko Hung, *Pao-p'u Tzu nei-p'ien* 16; translated in James Ware, *Alchemy, Medicine, Religion*, 261–78.

33. Ling Meng-ch'u, eighteenth story in *Erh-k'o po-an ching-ch'i*, vol. 2, 399–400. (Cf. John Scott, trans., *The Lecherous Academician*, 106–7.)

rubric of the external elixir (*wai tan* 外丹), which supplemented inner elixir (*nei tan* 內丹) methods, including mental disciplines, breath control, and sexual practices. The primary intention behind the concern with the external and internal elixirs was to promote longevity.[34] The story depends both on the wealthy Chen's credulity in his ostensible search for longevity, but also on the presence of just about everyone else's suspicions of charlatans who would dupe others with promises of pills that provide fantastic sexual prowess and promises of the secret of manufacturing unlimited quantities of gold and silver in return for only a "small" investment in supplies. Chen expires when the pill he took to aid his efforts with his favorite concubine makes him more deeply involved with her than his strength can bear, but from the narrator's perspective he was clearly at fault. Rather than condemning all such Taoist practices as sham, however, the framework of the story suggests that longevity can be attained by those with fate and proper preparation on their side. The short story represents the ambiguity inherent in Ming attitudes toward Taoist techniques for achieving longevity and even immortality.

The most influential Ming patrons of purveyors of longevity and license, prognostications and pills were some of the emperors.[35] Although political considerations were a factor, the first and third emperors granted gifts and places at court to various experts in occult practices and acted as if they believed.[36] Several emperors apparently suffered from the ill effects of Taoist prescriptions. The Hung-hsi emperor (r. 1425), who died suddenly in his mid-forties, had been ingesting "longevity" elixirs in conjunction with sexual endeavors,[37] and interest in aphrodisiacs and other drugs may have also contributed to the demise of the Ch'eng-hua emperor (r. 1465–87).[38] The circumstances surrounding the death of the T'ai-ch'ang emperor (r. 1620) have led some to infer, without adequate evidence, that he, too, died because of "longevity" pills. Enthroned on the first day of the eighth month, he received eight beauties as a congratulatory present and shortly he felt indisposed. (The inference sometimes drawn from the juxtaposition of the two facts is that the emperor had overindulged himself with the new women.) After one remedy failed, he finally was able to prevail upon his ministers to allow a minor official to present

34. Liu Ts'un-yan, "Taoist Self-Cultivation in Ming Thought," in W. T. deBary, ed. *Self and Society*, 292–93.

35. See the survey of Ming emperors' involvement in such practices in Yang Ch'i-ch'iao, "Ming tai chu ti chih ch'ung-shang fang-shu chi ch'i ying-hsiang," in *Ming tai tsung-chiao*, 203–97, originally published in *Hsin-Ya shu-yuan hsueh-shu nien-k'an* 4 (1962). Yang points out that official historical compilations are generally reticent about such matters (pp. 204–5).

36. Yang Ch'i-ch'iao, 208–12, 217–24; Yang also quotes imperial as well as governmental expressions of doubt about, and even condemnation of, such beliefs and practices. Also see Anna Seidel, "A Taoist Immortal of the Ming Dynasty: Chang San-feng," in W. T. deBary, ed., *Self and Society*, 487–97.

37. Yang Ch'i-ch'iao, 228.

38. Yang, 242–43.

him with some "immortality" pills. The next morning he was dead, having reigned less than one month.[39] It seems impossible for us to know the contents of the pills, which one source identifies as "red lead" (*hung ch'ien* 紅鉛).[40] It is my supposition that the T'ai-ch'ang emperor may have been a habitual user of compounds containing arsenic (*p'i-shih* 砒石) before his enthronement and had been cut off from the pills. It is not impossible to come to a belief that arsenic provides healthier appearance, greater physical capacities and endurance, and even sexual excitability.[41] The emperor's desire for some "pills" and his sudden death might have been associated with the reported susceptibility of arsenic eaters " . . . to die suddenly from slight causes, especially after the rapid withdrawal of the drug. A sudden increase is also liable to cause a serious and even fatal intoxication in arsenicists."[42] Whatever the contents of the red pills, court officials debated among themselves whether they should be presented to the emperor and then, after the fatal result, whether they should have been allowed. The discussion indicates at least some degree of belief in pills and elixirs,[43] but it also reveals, on a small scale, that emperors sometimes had to contend with objections from their officials for indulging in esoteric practices.

During the long reign of the Chia-ching emperor (r. 1522–66), continual protests were directed at his patronage of adepts.[44] He had become involved in Taoist and Buddhist hygienic practices supposedly because of his poor health, and over his lifetime he increasingly tried medicinal and sexual methods of promoting longevity.[45] His impatience with the remonstrations against such endeavors led him repeatedly to order the punishment of those who even mentioned his interest in immortality.[46] The remonstrations might be taken to indicate a measure of scepticism,[47] but much of the protest seems to have been motivated less by disbelief than by opposition to the influence of men favored

---

39. Meng Sen, *Ming tai shih*, 304–6; Yang Ch'i-ch'ao, 278–79; C. O. Hucker, *Censorial System of Ming China*, 166–67.

40. *Ming shih-lu*, quoted in Yang Ch'i-ch'ao, 278. Yang (257) quoted from Li Shih-chen's *Pen-ts'ao kang-mu* (completed in the 1590s) which identifies the primary ingredient of "red lead" pills as the menses of young girls. (Cf. Li Shih-chen, *Pen-ts'ao kang-mu*, 52.1823.)

41. See Louis Lewin, *Phantastica: Narcotic and Stimulating Drugs: Their Use and Abuse*, 322–23. "Arsenic has recently found many defenders who had observed the good health, longevity and flourishing appearance of arsenic-eaters. . . ." (p. 326). Li Shih-chen, *Pen-ts'ao kang-mu*, 10.673–75, stressed the extreme toxicity of arsenic, but also recorded its use in certain medications. Fang I-chih, *Wu li hsiao chih*, 7, "Yü-p'i 礜砒," mentioned that in his time no one dared use it in compounds.

42. Lewin, 324.

43. Meng Sen, 305–6.

44. The most detailed account of the Chia-ching emperor's patronage of Taoism is in Ku Ying-t'ai, *Ming shih chi shih pen mo*, 52. Also see Meng Sen, 249–51.

45. Yang Ch'i-ch'iao, 254–56.

46. Yang, 272.

47. Scepticism about one's emperor engaging in esoteric practices was hardly an exclusively Ming phenomenon. An excellent T'ang example is Po Chü-i's poem against the em-

by the Chia-ching emperor because of their knowledge of esoteric techniques and his consequent neglect of court affairs. The adepts (*fang-shih* 方士) usually mentioned in this connection are Shao Yuan-chieh and T'ao Chung-wen.[48] Shao was a Taoist priest (*Tao-shih* 道士) who gained the emperor's trust early in the reign and accrued honors and influence over the next dozen years. The emperor was especially grateful to Shao when a series of imperial sons were born.[49] Before Shao died in 1539, he recommended another elderly adept, T'ao Chung-wen, to the emperor. T'ao had healing water (*fu-shui* 符水), prayers, and other esoteric means for curing illnesses. When these cures worked on the heir apparent and on the Chia-ching emperor himself, the emperor's confidence in T'ao developed to the point that he was a main channel of communication during the periods the emperor had withdrawn from court to devote himself to rituals for lengthening his life. For twenty years T'ao maintained his position. Some officials cultivated good relations with him as he continued to receive lavish gifts and unprecedented honors from the emperor, although repeatedly denunciations were sent in by others who sought to break T'ao's influence.[50] After the death of T'ao Chung-wen in 1560, the Chia-ching emperor's anxiety for secrets that would postpone his own death increased. He sent out agents to search the empire for adepts and esoteric techniques. They brought him thousands of writings and a collection of practitioners, but he died in 1566.[51]

Emperors and Taoist priests were not the only ones familiar with esoteric techniques. In the late fifteenth century, when the Ch'eng-hua emperor was patronizing a former subofficial named Li Tzu-hsing (d. 1488) and his friends with gifts and official appointments because of their knowledge of charms, talismans, prescriptions, and other such methods, including some that were regarded as lewd, regular officials used the same strategy to attract the emperor's attention. Even a Grand Secretary presented suggestions on sexual techniques.[52] In the sixteenth century, when the employment of Taoist terms and images in

peror's patronage of a Taoist who was to procure "herbs of longevity" for him. Translated in Arthur Waley, *Translations from the Chinese*, 179–81. It might be noted that Po Chü-i suggests that unless fate is on one's side, "immortality" is beyond "the striving of mortal men." There is also evidence that Po Chü-i, at least for a period in his life, believed in the possibility of immortality and tried his hand as well as his mind at some of the techniques. See Ho Peng Yoke, Goh Thean Chye, David Parker, "Po Chü-i's Poems on Immortality," *Harvard Journal of Asiatic Studies* 34 (1974), 163–91.

48. *Ming shih*, "Ning-hsing 佞倖 chuan," 307.7875. Lan Tao-hsing 藍道行 is also mentioned. Although he gained favor for his counsel on sexual matters, Lan did not have the pervasive and enduring influence of the other two men (307.7899).

49. *Ming shih*, 307.7894–96.

50. *Ming shih*, 307.7896–98.

51. *Ming shih*, 307.7903–4.

52. *Ming shih*, 307.7881–83. Most of those who gained positions by such means were dismissed after the accession of the Hung-chih emperor in 1487. Li Tzu-hsing died in prison in 1488 (307.7884).

the writings of officials and literati seems to have been at a peak,[53] there were any number of examples of literati acting on their interest in both the "inner" and "outer elixirs."[54] In the middle of the sixteenth century, Fang Yü-shih left home after passing the first degree in the examination system to devote himself to Taoist methods of mind control as well as the Yellow and White art of making gold and silver. He then began to travel, and wherever he went men of official rank as well as teachers welcomed him in awe. He met some of Wang Yang-ming's followers, including Wang Chi, who regarded him as a unique literatus. Keng Ting-li went to study with Fang for a while, but left once he realized Fang was a sham. By claiming that studying the way of the sages, i.e., Confucianism, was too easy, and that he was looking for someone to whom he could transmit the secrets of his Taoist learning, Fang enticed Lo Hung-hsien (1504–64) to go with him to a mountain retreat, but after a while Lo, too, felt he was not advancing and left.[55] There was interest, then, on the part of a number of serious-minded literati, in Fang's claims about his command of the "inner elixir," but he was not able, at least according to Huang Tsung-hsi, to fulfill their expectations. We might infer that the desire to believe did not result in the suspension of disbelief. To imply that Fang Yü-shih was indifferent to wealth because he could produce gold and silver nearly at will, the anecdote was related that once when at a banquet arranged by Ho Hsin-yin Fang arrived in a simple sedan chair, in contrast to the carriages and entourages of others, Ho took him by the arm and asked for a loan of a hundred taels. Fang not only assented, but willingly gave Ho a thousand. Later Fang went to Peking with his art of increasing silver nine-fold, but when the son of the powerful minister Yen Sung (1480–1565) became enticed by Fang's alchemy, Fang left the capital.[56] Again, there are indications of widespread acceptance of the possibility of the alchemist's making silver and gold.[57] My impression is that a general credence in the arts of immortality in the sixteenth century began to give way to a sceptical spirit from the Wan-li reign on, but a heritage of Taoist beliefs and practices remained as an area attractive to intellectual inquiry.

53. Cf. the discussion in Liu Ts'un-yan, "Taoist Self-Cultivation in Ming Thought," in W. T. deBary, *Self and Society*, especially 307–21, on the Taoistic interests of Wang Yang-ming and others. Liu Ts'un-yan notes in passing that there also was opposition to such interests. Also see his "Ming ju yü Tao-chiao," *Hsin Ya hsueh-pao* 8 (1967), 259–96.

54. Liu Ts'un-yan, "The Penetration of Taoism into the Ming Neo-Confucian Elite," *T'oung Pao* 57 (1971), 82, has gone so far as to assert that " . . . seven or eight out of ten of the Ming scholars believed in such things [as causing paper horses to come alive and producing a large number of fighting soldiers out of dry beans]. And if one believes in the possibility of these things, one believes in popular Taoism." Leaving aside the unfounded numerical estimate, the point remains that there was widespread belief among the educated stratum of Ming society in extraordinary phenomena.

55. Huang Tsung-hsi, introduction to *chüan* 32, *Ming ju hsueh an*.

56. Ibid.

57. Cf. the example in *The Scholars (Ju lin wai shih)*, chapter 15, for the mechanics of tricking the gullible into investing good silver to make alchemist gold.

Fang I-chih's attitude toward such beliefs and practices was one of critical interest.[58] He took notice of all sorts of magical arts and tricks,[59] but insisted that there is principle (*li*) behind the few that are not merely deceptions. He did not deny the existence of ghosts and spirits, but doubted claims that our minds can fully understand them.[60] As his son put it, "Such matters as life and death, ghosts and spirits, are in the realm of doubt."[61] Fang recorded traditional wisdom on the use of talismans,[62] and he included the comment by an adept that one might die from "outer elixirs" unless his "inner elixir" is first perfected.[63] But Fang also wrote that it was absurd that herbals had long passed on the tradition that ingesting gold which had been treated in certain ways could lengthen one's life. Fang suggested it merely acted the same way as mercury in preserving a corpse.[64] With regard to the desire for longevity, he observed, "Of course life encumbers a man, but how can he turn his back on life? Those who keep watch over it all end up ill. Those who use it well all end up happy."[65] Here we have a good clue to Fang I-chih's intentions in the "Seven Solutions" when he dismissed the gamut of outer and inner elixirs, from mind-expanding drugs to instruction in achieving immortality.

Fang was not concerned to refute the possibility of esoteric practices "working," and he was willing to assign reports of certain phenomena to the category of inexplicable events (*i shih* 異事) that we might not accept as veritable. Rather, Fang's aim was comparable to the aim of many of the high-minded men who protested their emperor's involvement in esoteric techniques. The protest was based not on a denial of the possibility of a given technique, but on the perception that such self-centered involvement distracted the would-be adept, whether the fictional Chen T'ing-chao or the Chia-ching emperor, from his larger responsibilities. Pursuit of immortality entailed escape from society's demands, and thus neglect of one's family and their interests.[66]

By 1637 Fang I-chih already had a family of his own. His eldest son was

58. I make this assertion primarily on the basis of Fang's writings dating from the 1640s rather than on what he wrote in the 1630s.

59. *Wu li hsiao chih, chüan* 12. For a description by a Korean traveler in Jehol in 1780 of magical performances by street "entertainers," see Eugen Feifel, "Pak Jiwon: Huan-hsi 幻戲, Magic Entertainment in Jehol," *Oriens Extremis* 19 (1972), 143–53.

60. E.g., *Wu li hsiao chih*, "Shen kuei pien-hua tsung-lun." Judging by the note his son appended, this discussion was completed in the late 1640s while Fang I-chih was in Kwangsi. Also *T'ung ya*, shou 2.4b–5a.

61. Fang Chung-t'ung, note appended to "Shen kuei pien-hua tsung-lun."

62. E.g., *Wu li hsiao chih*, 12, "P'ei yin 佩印," and various prescriptions calling for cinnabar and mercury, in *Wu li hsiao chih, chüan* 7.

63. *Wu li hsiao chih*, 7, "Yang sha 養砂."

64. *Wu li hsiao chih*, 7, "Chin 金."

65. Fang I-chih, "Yang sheng yüeh ch'ao hsu 養生約抄序," *Fu-shan wen-chi*, 6.46a.

66. Ku Ying-t'ai made a similar point in his final comment in *Ming shih chi shih pen mo*, 52.

born in 1632,[67] and his third son in 1638;[68] he also had at least two daughters.[69] Fang spent much of his time in the 1630s away from his wife and children, and after 1640 he apparently did not visit T'ung-ch'eng more than twice, before his final return in his coffin. Nevertheless, such "real world" entanglements as a family could not easily be put aside, and he remained in constant contact with them even after he became a Buddhist monk to save his life in 1650.[70] Before that, he was not willing to believe he should sever contact with them to devote himself to prolonging it.

Longevity, as well as chemical happiness, alchemical silver and gold, prodigious sexual capacities, and permanent avoidance of death were promised by purveyors of esoteric techniques. For the righteous man, however, they constituted enticements from his proper concerns—the larger social goods of morality and order.

Profligate

To escape is to be selfish. Entering the mountains in pursuit of independence entailed fleeing established society's entanglements. The esoteric techniques of Taoism for perpetuating one's self provided a way to avoid the flux of the ordinary world and its involvements with livelihood, family, and death. Pao-shu Tzu had rejected both modes of escape, only to be confronted with another possibility—losing himself in sensual pleasures. Compulsive devotion to drinking or sex perhaps was ultimately self-destructive, but along the way it was capable of blotting out responsibilities and doubts. Self-indulgence crossed into the realm of antisocial, escapist behavior when gratification became dominant in one's life. On the other hand, pleasure was sanctioned in Fang I-chih's time as a respite from daily cares and frustrations. It was a matter of degree.

Probably the best known drinker is T'ao Ch'ien, who made wine a major theme in his poetry and a major factor in his life. For T'ao, the connection between drinking and escape is apparent. To drink, for T'ao, was to avoid unsavory political involvement as well as unwanted thoughts.[71] Contributing to what became the stereotype view of T'ao, he wrote of himself, "He could not

---

67. Ma Ch'i-ch'ang, *T'ung-ch'eng ch'i chiu chuan*, 7.29b (p. 388), says Fang Chung-te was thirteen in 1644.

68. Yü Ying-shih, *Fang I-chih wan chieh k'ao*, 145–47, discussed the evidence that enabled him to determine Fang Chung-lü's dates were 1638–86.

69. Fang I-chih provided at least two of his father's three granddaughters. "Fang Chen-shu mu-chih-ming," in *Ch'i tai i shu*, 4b. Cf. Ma Ch'i-ch'ang, *T'ung-ch'eng ch'i chiu chuan*, 8.3b (416).

70. See chapter 8.

71. Wang Yao, introduction to *T'ao Yuan-ming chi*, 4–5. Also see J. R. Hightower, "T'ao Ch'ien's 'Drinking Wine' Poems," in Tse-tsung Chow, ed., *Wen-lin*, 3–44.

drink without emptying his cup, and always ended up drunk, after which he would retire, unconcerned about what might come."[72] And yet T'ao concluded his cycle of poems on "Drinking Wine" with a plea.

> Still I regret the stupid things I've said
> And hope you will forgive a man in his cups.[73]

A man who was always drunk had a "good excuse." Another famous drinker, Juan Chi (210–263), stayed drunk for sixty days in order to evade confronting a marriage negotiation that would have allied him to the most powerful, and dangerous, officer in the government.[74] Cultivating his reputation as a man who put drinking before his official responsibilities, Juan became known later as one of the Seven Sages of the Bamboo Grove. Many of the stories of their escapades include drunkenness,[75] and it remained a symbol as well as a means of escaping from the trammels of the world when one could not physically remove himself.

Later examples of drinkers, however, are mostly pale comparisons to the Seven Sages. In late Ming, a compilation of miscellaneous poems and prose, some whimsical and some historical items, relating to the *History of Wine* (*Chiu shih*) added a handful of anecdotes about drinkers who lived during the Ming dynasty.[76] The emphasis in the accounts about the more recent men was not on becoming a sot to escape from troubled times. Rather, the reader was to be impressed by one man's witty remark justifying his predilection for drink or another's capacity to consume huge quantities, "as much or more than the ancients," without showing any effect.[77] The reader is not given leave to infer that a political or philosophical or even a moral point is being made when someone devotes himself seriously to drinking.

For his part, Fang I-chih was not averse to drinking. As he wrote in 1639, "From time to time when there is someone to follow me and carry the food and wine, then with him I become carefree and indulge myself. Becoming drunk and crying out, I compel myself to feel consoled."[78] Recourse to alcohol as a temporary solace to his frustrations was tangled up with Fang's social drinking,

72. J. R. Hightower, trans., *The Poetry of T'ao Ch'ien*, 4. Cf. Wang Yao, ed., *T'ao Yuan-ming chi*, 123.

73. Hightower, trans., *The Poetry of T'ao Ch'ien*, 154. Cf. Wang Yao, 70.

74. *Chin shu*, 49.3a. Cf. E. Balazs, *Chinese Civilization and Bureaucracy*, 237.

75. *Shih shuo hsin yü*, "Jen tan" section.

76. The *Chiu shih* seems to be a product of the Wan-li reign and is attributed to the apparently pseudonymous Feng Ying-lung (Shih-hua) 馮應龍 (時化). For a list of titles, mostly from Sung through Ming, having to do with wine and drinking, see *Ku chin t'u shu chi ch'eng*, vol. 87, p. 12.

77. Feng, *Chiu shih*, A.41b–43b. For a similar emphasis on capacity rather than escape as the noteworthy element in drinking habits, see Hsieh Chao-che, *Wu tsa tsu*, 7.34a–35a (587–89).

78. Fang I-chih, *Fu-shan wen-chi*, 3.32b; also in *Ch'i tai i shu*, 2.18a.

which with its conventions and rituals was almost the antithesis of escape. Nevertheless, although his aunt had warned him against excessive drinking, and Fang later characterized his Nanking years as "given over to poetry and wine,"[79] drinking clearly never came to dominate Fang's life as a means of escape.

In Nanking, whoring was also an accepted part of the social life of wealthy young men, and Fang I-chih did his share, but his brother-in-law, Sun Lin, might serve as an example of the potential for involvement with prostitutes becoming a mode of escape. In 1630 or so Sun moved from T'ung-ch'eng to Nanking, where he was a neighbor of Fang's. (Sun had been orphaned when young and was married to Fang's eldest sister.)[80] At some point, Sun became friends with Yü Huai, who later wrote a reminiscence on denizens of the prostitution quarter he had known in the last decade of Ming. According to Yü, Sun liked to roam the quarter on the Ch'in-huai River while he was singing drunk.[81] Yü told the story of how late one night, when all the brothels and mansions in the quarter were shut up and quiet, Sun Lin and Fang I-chih were out on the prowl. For some reason they went to the residence of Tenth Maiden Li, a prostitute they knew, and got into her bedroom by climbing up on the roof. Brandishing swords, they acted like robbers, and a man from Shantung who was spending the night with Tenth Maiden Li went down on his knees before them to beg for his life. Sun and Fang then put aside their swords and had a great laugh. They shouted for drinks for everyone, and did not leave until they were drunk.[82] Another time, perhaps as late as the seventh month of 1639,[83] there was an assembly of more than twenty prostitutes at a mansion rented by Fang I-chih on the Ch'in-huai River. So many young men showed up that there was a traffic jam of carriages in the nearby lanes, and there was a wall of boats ringing the mansion on the water side. After each of the "flowers" was graded, the top-ranked woman, Wang Yüeh, was seated on a dais and presented with a gold drinking cup. The other prostitutes left in disappointment, but the party went on till dawn.[84]

On this level of involvement with prostitutes as part of an exuberant social scene, Fang I-chih was not unlike his brother-in-law. Sun Lin, however, was more deeply involved. Prior to the party he had already spent a month with

79. See above, chapter 2.
80. Ma Ch'i-ch'ang, *T'ung-ch'eng ch'i chiu chuan*, 6.5a (281).
81. Yü Huai, *Pan-ch'iao tsa chi*, 16, recorded that he was best of friends with Sun Lin. Cf. Howard Levy, trans., *A Feast of Mist and Flowers*, 54.
82. Yü Huai, 46–47. Cf. Levy, trans., *Feast*, 92.
83. Chin T'ien-ko, *Wan-chih lieh-chuan kao*, 1.25a (75), seems to have inferred from the accounts of Sun Lin in Ma Ch'i-ch'ang, *T'ung-ch'eng ch'i chiu chuan*, 6.5b–6a (282–83), and Yü Huai, *Pan-ch'iao tsa chi*, 35, that the talent contest occurred in the year *yi-mao* 乙卯 (1615), which I assume is a mistake for *chi-mao* 己卯 (1639).
84. Yü Huai, *Pan-ch'iao tsa chi*, 35. Cf. Levy, trans., *Feast*, 78. Yü Huai claimed to have been there, and presented the winner with a laudatory poem.

Wang Yueh away from Nanking,[85] and after the talent contest at Fang I-chih's place, Sun decided he would establish her as his concubine. Before he could act, however, Wang was taken by someone who paid her "father" three thousand taels of silver.[86] Sun was depressed at this turn of events, but one day he went with Yü Huai to pass some time at Tenth Maiden Li's. To change his mood and distract him from thoughts of Wang Yueh, Tenth Maiden Li told him about the unrivaled beauty and talents of a young woman called Tender Miss Ko. Sun's oaths of fidelity to Wang Yueh were forgotten and he went over to call on Ko. He found her combing her long hair in her room and was immediately smitten. Sun stayed with her continuously for a month, and later brought her into his household as a concubine.[87] Sun Lin was not included by Yü Huai among the examples of men whose conduct in the Ch'in-huai district was depicted by Yü ostensibly to serve as a warning for the rest of us.[88] Sun may not have ruined his family, fortune, or health, but he seems to have been more compulsive in his relations with prostitutes than Fang I-chih was. Sun was a small man who wanted to be known for his physical prowess in the martial arts,[89] and I am inclined to view his escapades as a way of working out his frustrations, for nearly everyone else expected him to cultivate his literary talents and leave military matters alone.

Sun's inclinations are similar to those of Mao Hsiang, who was another one of Fang's friends in Nanking in the 1630s. Much later Mao recalled, "When I was in Nanking at the beginning of the summer of 1639 for the provincial examinations [i.e., about the time, apparently, of the talent contest], Fang I-chih of Anhui told me that among the beauties in the Ch'in-huai quarter there recently was one comparable to the famous Shuang-ch'eng. She was very young, and unexcelled in both talent and beauty."[90] Obviously Fang was no novice in appraising the women who rented their various talents in Nanking. Mao Hsiang went on to have an enduring love affair with the young woman after her release from her profession had been purchased. Unlike Sun Lin, who, along with his concubine, Tender, was executed by a Ch'ing general in 1646,[91]

---

85. Chin T'ien-ko, *Wan-chih lieh-chuan kao*, 1.25a, wrote that Sun Chin went away with Wang Yueh in order to console himself after he had heard that his father-in-law was in prison and his elder brother was trying to resign from a frontier position. Fang K'ung-chao, however, had not yet been arrested. I suspect that the two later historians, Ma Ch'i-ch'ang and Chin T'ien-ko, were trying to provide a "good" explanation of Sun's devotion to prostitutes.

86. Yü Huai, *Pan-ch'iao tsa chi*, 35–36. Cf. Levy, trans., *Feast*, 78–79.

87. Yü Huai, 16. Cf. Levy, 54–55.

88. Yü Huai, 39. Cf. Levy, 83.

89. Yü Huai, 16. Cf. Levy, 54.

90. Mao Hsiang, emended from the translation in P'an Tze-yen, trans., *Reminiscences of Tung Hsiao-wan*, 7.

91. Yü Huai, *Pan-ch'iao tsa chi*, 17; Ma Ch'i-ch'ang, *T'ung-ch'eng ch'i chiu chuan*, 6.6a–b (283–84).

Mao Hsiang lived through the troubles of the dynastic changeover with his concubine at his side, and then lived on in retirement for many years as a man of culture (*wen jen*) after she died at the age of twenty-seven.[92] Mao Hsiang's relation with her became the subject of one of his most famous literary products, but we might view that romance as a manifestation of Mao's proclivities to escape from "more important" responsibilities just as much as Sun Lin's infatuations with Wang Yueh and Tender Miss Ko were. There is a continuum from prostitute as entertainer to prostitute as object of romantic love, but somewhere between them there is a fine line marking an established social institution off from self-indulgent escape. The possibility of crossing that line depended on one's character, for the attractions were unquestionably there.

In late Ming prostitution was flourishing. Writing early in the seventeenth century, Hsieh Chao-che observed:

> In recent times, prostitutes are everywhere in the empire. In places where they are most concentrated, there are hundreds and thousands, and even the most lowly districts have some. The whole day they sit at their door to offer smiles and sell sex for a living. . . . At the beginning of the Hsuan-te reign [1426–1435], [prostitutes in government employ] were for the first time prohibited, but officials living at home did not care. Because of this, although there are none at government offices, prostitutes are in every village. Moreover, since they are not attached to a government office and sell sex in homes, they are called "local prostitutes," and are popularly known as "private nestlings."[93]

In Peking, where the competition was keen, some brothels had two or three peepholes on the street side so that a passing young man might glimpse the women sitting naked while they made up their faces. When he went in, the nude women would parade before him, and for seven copper cash he could have his choice for an hour in bed.[94] Such reports of the lower end of the trade are relatively infrequent compared to the number of literary pieces celebrating the refinements and wonders of Nanking's pleasure quarter along the Ch'in-huai River.[95] The tendency in many writings was to romanticize the liaisons between

92. Mao Hsiang, P'an Tze-yen, trans., *Reminiscences of Tung Hsiao-wan.*

93. Hsieh Chao-che, *Wu tsa tsu*, 8.29b–30a (654–55). Also paraphrased in Wang Shu-nu, *Chung-kuo ch'ang-chi shih*, 198. Wang, 198–225, presented much evidence that private prostitution was flourishing in the last hundred years of Ming. For a fictional example of a "private nestling," see the third story in Feng Meng-lung, *Ku chin hsiao-shuo*, translated in John L. Bishop, *The Colloquial Short Story in China*, 65–86, as "Chin-nu Sells Love at New-bridge." Chin-nu ". . . was a prostitute in disguise or what is known as a 'private nester.'" (p. 70) She upset her neighbors when they realized what her occupation was.

94. Wang Shu-nu, 200. I hesitate to take this account too literally. Cf. the description of a flourishing brothel-resort at T'ai-an, Shantung, in Chang Tai, *T'ao an meng i*, 59–60.

95. See above, chapter 2. Cf. Wang Shu-nu, 200–202. Yü Huai's *Pan-ch'iao tsa chi* (H. Levy, trans., *A Feast of Mist and Flowers*) goes into loving detail on the personalities and practices in the Ch'in-huai quarter.

prostitutes and literati.[96] The marvelous talent and beauty of this or that woman, together with her sensitivity to higher moral values and to her paramour's dilemmas, were the subject matter of prose and poetry that played *tristesse* off against glamor, and lessons on fidelity off against titillation. In the 1630s entertainment by "singing girls" was well established for literati, especially in the cities, although it all seems more elegant than debauched.

There is some evidence that noncommercial sex was available in late Ming outside the institutions of marriage and concubinage. Love affairs (*ssu-ch'ing* 私情) were the subject of many of the songs of commoner origin which were collected in Kiangsu in the last decades of the dynasty.[97] One example, supposedly originating in Fang I-chih's home district of T'ung-ch'eng, illustrates both the possibility of such liaisons and the desirability of avoiding promiscuity.

> Playing guess-fingers last night with his girl,
> He wondered, "How many come out from your palm?"
> "There's only one, and he's you.
> "Were there another, you might open [more than one finger, too],
> "And from now on we aren't taking up with anyone else."[98]

For the perils of debauchery, we might look to the fiction of the seventeenth century.[99] A famous story, translated into English as "The Pearl Sewn Shirt," relates how a young merchant brought disaster onto himself with his single-minded devotion to seducing another man's wife.[100] The story's moralizing introductory remarks remind us that unchecked desire for sex is more ruinous than alcohol, avarice, or anger.[101] Carrying the point to an extreme, Li Yü (1611–c.1680) in his novel *Prayer Mat of Flesh* (Jou p'u t'uan) shows the havoc wreaked by a literatus who dedicated himself to being a compulsive womanizer. "Women and the pleasures of love are everything to me, they are my life," the young man affirms.[102] The novel may be read primarily for its prurient interest, but the message is clear—one can have too much of a good thing. "Losing"

96. This point has also been made in Robert van Gulik, *Sexual Life in Ancient China*, 308–13.

97. Preface by Kuan Te-tung 關德棟 to the 1962 edition of Feng Meng-lung's collection of *Shan ko* (Peking: Chung-hua, 1962), 2a–3a. Kuan discussed other late Ming collections of "folk" songs as well as Feng's earlier compilation of songs of popular (i.e., nonelite) origin (4a–b). Also see the preface written in 1934 by Ku Chieh-kang, reprinted in *Shan ko* (Taipei: Tung-fang, 1970).

98. "Guessing Fingers," in "T'ung-ch'eng shih-hsing ko," appended to Feng Meng-lung, *Shan ko* (Peking: Chung-hua, 1962), 10.85b.

99. The reader hardly needs to be reminded of the importance of physical pleasures in the two great novels that bracket the seventeenth century, *Chin p'ing mei* and *Hung lou meng*.

100. Feng Meng-lung, *Ku chin hsiao-shuo*, first story. Translated by Cyril Birch in *Stories from a Ming Collection*, 45–96.

101. Feng Meng-lung, *Ku chin hsiao-shuo*, 1.1a; Cyril Birch, 45.

102. Li Yü, *Jou p'u t'uan*, translated from Franz Kuhn's German version by Richard Martin, 101.

oneself in sexual adventures is, from the ostensible view of the novel, to be likened to withdrawing from social responsibilities to become a monk.

Fiction aside, in the writings of the time there is no pervasive sense conveyed that promiscuity was a threat to social mores or that a noticeable number of young men were losing themselves in sexual indulgence. The incidence of male homosexuality may have been on the rise,[103] but no one seemed especially concerned. Although opium addiction was almost unknown until the eighteenth century, tobacco smoking had spread from Fukien to the extent that there were repeated, but ineffective, attempts in the 1630s to suppress it.[104] In general, the last decades of Ming afforded a wealthy, gregarious young man such as Fang I-chih ample opportunity for self-indulgence in drinking, sex, gambling, and other endeavors sometimes considered vices. No doubt some men succumbed to temptations and lost their way. Fang, it seems, was in little danger. He recognized that such diversions, while attractive, were also potentially consuming. He pointed out to his friend Li Wen that the truly talented man should write a work which would "make clear the classics, discuss histories, and ascertain the causes for social change," and *only then* should he "drink some wine with old friends."[105]

103. Hsieh Chao-che, *Wu tsa tsu*, 8.5a–b (605–6). Chapter 30 of *The Scholars* (*Ju lin wai shih*) provides a good illustration of the place of male homosexuality in Nanking society.

104. Fang I-chih, "T'an-pa-ku yen-ts'ao," *Wu li hsiao chih*, 9.23b–24a. Cf. Jonathan Spence, "Opium Smoking in Ch'ing China," in Frederic Wakeman, Jr. and Carolyn Grant, eds., *Conflict and Control in Late Imperial China*, 146–58.

105. Fang I-chih, "Sung Li Shu-chang hsu," *Fu-shan wen-chi*, 3.33b.

8 Scholar

Pao-shu Tzu Is Recalled to the Right Way

The following day Pao-shu Tzu still had not left his bed when his old friend Right-Start[1] came to call. He struggled up, but felt sick again. When he came out with his hair in disarray, his old friend saw that he was hung over and chided him most gravely. "When you and I were younger, we looked to each other as 'men of antiquity.' If now your aims cannot be realized, let your model be what the men of antiquity did when they could not realize their aims. Why be so exasperated that you grow old before your time?

"You lament being poor as well as lowly. Others think little of your associations [with 'guests']. Your intention was to cut yourself off, yet you have not shut your door. You vacillate between declining and receiving guests. What is more, you force yourself to act mockingly contemptuous[2] with those drinkers in the marketplace so as to gloss over your noble character; but the nobility of your character ultimately cannot be hidden. Would you say that others consider you calm and levelheaded? Would you say that on this course you can cover yourself and escape the slander directed at those who do moral good?[3] Day by day we grow older. We cannot recover time past. Before one knows it, the bloom of youth turns to the white hair of old age. If the times are not right for you, both [examine] the very essence of and profoundly [think about][4] the classics and histories. You might learn of the course [of Po Yi][5] and have a transforming [influence like that of a timely] rain[6] to await later generations.[7] Then why wait?

1. 帥初 Shuai-ch'u's name connotes "to lead, to be led," and "start, beginning." It can be associated with the phrase "begin by being led (ch'u shuai 初帥 or 率) by the words" in *Changes*, "Hsi tz'u chuan," B8. He is called *ku-jen* 故人, "old friend." Old Friend Right-Start.

2. On 笑傲, see *Songs*, "P'i feng 邶風, Chung feng 終風." (Cf. Legge, trans., 1.3.5.1: "The wind blows and is fierce. /He looks at me and smiles, /With scornful words and dissolute,—the smile of pride. /To the center of my heart I am grieved.")

3. Cf. above, p. 20 of translation.

4. Reading 覃精 as 研精覃思.

5. On 聞風, see *Mencius*, 5B1. (Cf. D. C. Lau, trans., *Mencius*, 149: "Hence, hearing of the way of Po Yi, a covetous man will be purged of his covetousness and a weak man will become resolute.")

6. On 化雨, see *Mencius*, 7A40. (Cf. D. C. Lau, trans., 191: "Mencius said, 'A gentleman teaches in five ways. The first is by a transforming influence like that of a timely rain.'")

7. Cf. *Mencius*, 5B1. (D. C. Lau, trans., 149: Po Yi retired ". . . to wait for the troubled

Success has its own time. You ultimately will be ranked with those who are not consigned to obscurity. Further, you have unparalleled talent and a capacity for devotion to study; you have broad erudition and wide experience. Even in your occasional wanderings and pleasures[8] *you still have not lost your good breeding. If you cause young men in white hats and coarse black robes, who have not had the one success [in planning that accrues even to someone] with a stupidly narrow outlook,*[9] *to have stomachs so empty they are sipping ink because they followed in your steps and thereby laid waste their learning, then that would be an offense against Confucian teachings. We naturally avoid hastily picking up and dropping activities.*[10] *We do not want to be unique or go beyond what is fitting.*

40a

"For example, in being resolute in one's beliefs, why go so far as to tread the Eastern Sea and die?[11] *In being scrupulous, why go so far as to wear leather and coarse cloth until they are in tatters?*[12] *In having a lofty demeanor, why go so far as to place your foot on the emperor?*[13] *In being proud, why go so far as to be so arrogant as to keep working at your forge and not stand?*[14] *In being resolutely moral, why go so far as to rent a porch and hire out to hull rice for others?*[15] *In preserving one's integrity,*

---

waters of the Empire to return to limpidity.")

8. On 游衍, see *Songs*, "Ta ya, Pan 板." (Cf. Legge, 3.2.10.8: "Great Heaven is clear-seeing, /And is with you in your wanderings and indulgences.")

9. Cf. "Han Hsin 韓信 chuan," *Han shu*, 34.1870: The Lord of Kuang-wu 廣武君 said, "I have heard that a wise man inevitably has one failure in laying a thousand plans, and that a stupid man inevitably has one success in laying a thousand plans." Also see *Yen tzu ch'un ch'iu, chüan* 6, no. 18 (vol. 2, 411; "Duke Ching Thinks Yen tzu Does Not Have Enough Food.")

10. On 拔來報往, see *Li chi* 15, "Shao i 少儀." (Cf. Couvreur, trans., *Li Ki*, vol. 2, 11: "Ne soyes pas trop empressé à commencer ni à abandonner vos entreprises.")

11. On 蹈東海而死, see "Lu Chung-lien 魯仲連 chuan," *Shih chi*, 83.2461. When the state of Chao was being pressured to recognize the imperial majesty of the state of Ch'in, Lu Chung-lien disparaged Ch'in's barbaric practices and its oppression of peoples and threatened that if Ch'in came to rule the world, he would tread the Eastern Sea and die, for he could not bear to be a subject of Ch'in.

12. I have not identified the source of this allusion.

13. On 以足加帝, see "I-min 逸民 chuan," *Hou Han shu*, 83.2764. After having been a fellow student with the to be Kuang-wu emperor, Yen Kuang 嚴光 was sought out by the emperor. They talked of old times and stayed together for several days. The emperor, in an informal, relaxed manner, asked, "How do we compare to former times?" Yen Kuang, who was lying down with the emperor, replied, "Your Majesty has increased a bit over the past," and put his foot on the emperor's stomach.

14. Reading 鍛, as in *Ch'i tai i shu*, rather than 鋸, as in *Fu-shan wen-chi*. Once when Chi K'ang 嵇康 (223–62) was working at his forge and visitors arrived, Chi K'ang ignored them until the visitors stood up to leave. See *Shih shuo hsin yü*, 24.188. His insult was later avenged. See D. Holzman, *La Vie et la pensée de Hi K'ang*, 39–40.

15. On 僦廡爲人賃舂, see "Liang Hung 梁鴻 chuan," *Hou Han shu*, 83.2765 and 2768. Extremely poor when young, yet resolved not to compromise his morals (chieh chieh 節介), Liang Hung tended pigs as his living even after he became learned. Later when he had to

why go so far as to knock a hole in the back wall [to escape][16] *or climb over
a wall?*[17] *In being stupid, why go so far as to not know [the number of]
feet on a horse?*[18] *In being clever, why go so far as to understand 'chicken
ribs'*[19] *or explain 'yellow silk'?*[20] *In being quick-witted, why go so far as
to compose a piece of rhyme-prose on a parrot without so much as changing
a dot?*[21] *In being dilatory, why go so far as to take a dozen years to compose rhyme-prose] on three capital cities?*[22] *In being aloof, why go so far as
to make [a doorless] house with tamped earth and take in food and drink*

---

move, he changed his name and lived as a subordinate at a rich man's house, where he worked
hulling rice. On *chieh* 介, also cf. *Mencius*, 7A28.

16. On 鑿坏 (or 培), see "Ch'i su 齊俗 hsun," *Huai-nan Tzu*, 11.20b. When the Duke of
Lu sent an envoy with presents to try to persuade Yen Hui to become a minister of state,
Yen Hui, to escape seeing the envoy, knocked a hole in the back wall and left.

17. On 踰垣, see *Mencius*, 3B7. (Cf. D. C. Lau, trans., *Mencius*, 112: "Tuan-kan Mu
climbed over a wall to avoid a meeting" with a lord; Mencius thought he went too far.)

18. On 不知馬足, see "Chu Mu 朱穆 chuan," *Hou Han shu*, 43.1461–62. Chu Mu was so
intent on his studies that sometimes, deep in thought, he would not notice he had lost an
article of clothing, or he would fall into a hole. His father wondered if he were not so stupid
that he almost did not know how many feet a horse has.

19. On 雞肋, see note in "Wu-ti chi 武帝記," *San kuo chih*, Wei, 1.52. On a tour, Ts'ao
Ts'ao 曹操 issued a command, "Chicken ribs." None of his officials knew what to make of
the words, except Yang Hsiu 楊修, who began to pack. When the others asked him what he
understood by the words, he replied that chicken ribs are cast aside the way one says, "Too
bad," and one gets nothing from eating them. In both ways chicken ribs were like the place
where they were, that is, to leave would cause no regret and one gets nothing of substance
by staying. Thus Yang understood that the king wanted to return home.

20. See "Chieh wu 捷悟," *Shih shuo hsin yü*, 11.145. Once Ts'ao Ts'ao passed by a monumental tombstone on the back of which was an eight-character inscription: 黃絹幼婦外孫齏臼,
meaning roughly, "Yellow silk young wife daughter's son herbal-sauce mortar." The king
asked Yang Hsiu if he could explain the inscription, but then stopped Yang and said he would
think about it himself. They traveled on some thirty *li*, and finally Ts'ao said, "I've got it,"
and ordered Yang to write down Yang's explanation. Upon seeing it was the same as his,
Ts'ao said his wit was only thirty *li* behind Yang's. The explanation, for those who are still
further behind, was that "yellow silk" can be glossed as "colored silk" 色絲, which can be
combined to form the word 絕; "young wife" is glossed as "young girl" 少女, which combine to make 妙; "daughter's son" can also be written 女子, which combine to make 好; and
a mortar used to hold ingredients with a bitter taste can be said to "receive bitter" 受辛,
which combine to form 辤, or 辭. The meaning of the apparently meaningless inscription,
then, is "Most excellent, beautiful words," in praise of the quality of the tomb inscription on
the *face* of the monument.

21. On 賦鸚鵡文不加點, see "Ni Heng 禰衡 chuan," *Hou Han shu*, 80B.2657. At a banquet
during which a parrot was presented as a gift, Ni Heng was charged with composing a piece
of rhyme-prose on the parrot. He performed with such a facility that he did not have to add
or delete a character in his draft, so perfectly did it flow from his brush. Ni Heng, it may be
added, impressed his patron by being able to recall the "yellow silk" inscription after having
once glanced at it.

22. On 一紀三都, see "Tso Ssu 左思 chuan," *Chin shu*, 92.9a, 11a. The preface to Tso Ssu's
three *fu* is in *Wen hsuan* 4.15a ff.; the text of the three follow the preface. Tso wrote a *fu* on
the capitals of the three kingdoms. Before he had finished, they had all been conquered.

[through the window]?[23] *In being untrammeled, why go so far as to go in naked through the opening for the dogs?*[24] *In being valiant, why go so far as to throw away the linchpin [of your guests' carriages]*[25] *or compel others to drink?*[26] *In being extravagant, why go so far as to spend ten thousand cash [each day for food and still] not dip your chopsticks into it?*[27] *In being frugal, why go so far as to wear one fur coat for thirty years?*[28] *In writing, why go so far as to hang it up on the capital's gate [in the arrogance that] not one word can be added or deleted?*[29] *In having followers, why go so far as to cause them to call you 'the dragon who mounts to heaven'?*[30] *When you meet with what you ought to do, merely do it. Why think it can be done only after deciding what pleases the rest of the world, or what the rest of the world scoffs at?''*

23. See "Yuan Hung 袁閎 chuan," *Hou Han shu*, 45.1526. In about 165, before the punishments and proscriptions of large numbers of officials were implemented, Yuan Hung decided to cut himself off from the world. Because he had an elderly mother he felt he could not hide away deep in the mountains, so he built a house of tamped earth, but without a door, and had his food and drink passed in through a window. He spent the rest of his life ensconced there.

24. See "Kuang I 光逸 chuan," *Chin shu* 49.41b. Escaping from the troubled times, Kuang I went to Hu-mu Fu-chih's 胡母輔之 house, where Hu-mu and six friends were sitting around naked in a drinking bout that had been going on for several days. When Kuang I pushed on the door but got no response, he stripped off his clothes outside the door and unashamedly stuck his head in through the hole for the dogs. The others gave a shout of delight when they saw him, and Hu-mu exclaimed that only Kuang I would be able to do such a thing. Hu-mu, Kuang, and the six others were known to their contemporaries as "The Eight Untrammeled Ones" (*pa ta* 八達).

25. On 投轄, see "Yu hsia chuan," *Han shu*, 92.3710. Ch'en Tsun 陳遵 (d. A.D. 25) liked to drink, and when a large number of guests filled his hall for a banquet, he would suddenly close the doors and throw the linchpins from the wheels of his guests' carriages into the well, so they could not leave even if they wanted. (Cf. B. Watson, trans., *Courtier and Commoner in Ancient China*, 236.)

26. On 强灌, see "Yu hsia chuan," *Shih chi*, 124.3185. (Cf. B. Watson, trans., *Records of the Grand Historian*, vol. 2, 457–58.) A nephew of Kuo Hsieh 郭解, who had a reputation as a *hsia* for taking vengeance, once tried to force a drinking companion to drain a cup which was much more than his capacity. In anger the man killed the nephew, but Kuo Hsieh refused to seek vengeance for the death.

27. See "Ho Tseng 何曾 chuan," *Chin shu*, 31.17a. Ho Tseng was a most extravagant man as well as a fastidious eater. Each day his kitchen would prepare meals costing ten thousand cash, but he would still say there was no dish to put his chopsticks into.

28. See *Li chi*, "T'an Kung 檀弓," B.2.4. Yen Tzu 晏子 wore one fox coat for thirty years; in showing such frugality when the state was being prodigal, he demonstrated he perfectly understood the rites even though he was not being ritually perfect. (Cf. Couvreur, trans., *Li Ki*, vol. 1, 213.)

29. See "Lü Pu-wei 呂不韋 chuan," *Shih chi*, 85.2510. The wealthy Lü Pu-wei had his retainers compile the book known as the *Lü shih ch'un ch'iu* 呂氏春秋; he then hung it up with a thousand in gold on the city gate and issued the challenge that anyone who could change a single one of the more than 200,000 words would be given the gold.

30. See "Li Ying 李膺 chuan," *Hou Han shu*, 67.2195. Li Ying (d. 169) was so conceited

*Pao-shu Tzu in awe prostrated himself before his friend and said with
a sigh, "Those men of the world who exhort me to drink and those who
exhort me not to drink are men who do not understand me. Those men of
the world who exhort me to read books and those who exhort me not to
read books are men who do not understand me. Why should I have any
regrets, if I have one old friend in my lifetime who does understand me?
Let us [study with the same] ink slab and mat,[31] take some simple food
together, recall times past, and consider the present situation of the world.
In the evening we must examine that which we have understood [in our
deliberations]. Every few days we shall go out with some other young men
to seek a little pleasure[32] and then the next day again shut ourselves off
from everyone as our normal practice."*

*When his friend Right-Start acceded to this, Pao-shu Tzu was
depressed no longer.*

40b

At first sight, Pao-shu Tzu's relief may appear to be achieved merely by default.
When Literatus Expectation proposed to Pao-shu Tzu an easy way to the success the rest of society sought, he rejected it not only as unintellectual, but also
as too tainted by motives of personal gain. When he also dismissed making
money as corrupting, he was criticized by Clansman Grasper for being incapable of acting. When a way of acting effectively in society was proposed by Sir
Brazen, Pao-shu Tzu denounced attaching oneself to someone of influence as
demeaning and anachronistic. When a present-day means of being effective by
advising the government was proposed by Cunning-Courage, Pao-shu Tzu
dismissed it as dangerous and unrealizable. When a practicable way of detaching
oneself from the sullying world by retiring to the mountains was proposed by
Tough-Nut, Pao-shu Tzu spurned it as difficult and unsafe. When an easy, safe
way to realize all that a man could desire was proposed by Old Hollow-Deceit,
it was dismissed as a sham. And to drink and forget provided no real solution to

---

about his reputation that those gentlemen (*shih*) who were infected by his demeanor were
called "followers of the dragon who mounts to heaven" (*teng lung men* 登龍門), a play on the
name of the famous Dragon Gate (Lung-men) rapids in the upper reaches of the Yellow
River; any carp that could pass through the rapids was thought to turn into a dragon.

31. Reading 研 as 硯; reading 細 rather than 組, which is in the *Ch'i tai i shu* text. Both
研席 and 細席 refer to a mat on which one studies. There may be an allusion here to "Liu
Hung 劉弘, chuan," *Chin shu* 66.1b.

32. This part of Pao-shu Tzu's resolve brings to mind Tseng Hsi's response when Confucius asked him and three other disciples what they would like to do if their true worth were
recognized by their contemporaries. Tseng Hsi said his ambition would be ". . . to go with
five or six newly capped youths [boys who had just come of age] and six or seven uncapped
boys, perform the lustrations in the River Yi, take the air at the Rain Dance altars, and then
go home singing." Confucius gave a great sigh of sympathy for Tseng Hsi's wish. (*Lun yü*,
11.25; I have departed slightly from the translation in A. Waley, *Analects of Confucius*.)

Pao-shu Tzu's frustration, either. He did not want to incur personal risk or withdraw from society, nor did he want selfishly to pursue his own gain. What was left?, it might well be asked. To sit around with a friend, read books, and talk?

A hint about the significance that Fang I-chih might have intended to be read into the resolution of Pao-shu Tzu's dilemma is suggested to us in the *Book of Changes* under the hexagram *hsieh* 解. The hexagram's name is usually glossed as meaning "deliverance from difficulties," and is the same word Fang chose for the title I have translated as "Seven Solutions."[1] For the diviner who has derived a nine in the fourth place, the *Book of Changes* commentary which accompanies the hexagram *hsieh* says, "Deliverance (*hsieh*) from the big toe. The friend arrives and you trust."[2] For the instance when there is a six in the fifth place, the commentary says, "Good fortune only if there is deliverance (*hsieh*) for the gentleman. There is trust from lesser men." Pao-shu Tzu might explain these lines of commentary as showing that his newly formed resolve had to come from within himself (as Fang suggested in his preface to the "Seven Solutions"); the visit from his old friend and their immediate rapport are early indications that Pao-shu Tzu's decision will bring good fortune and must be respected by lesser men, who in their collective opinion represent the "big toe" which has been oppressing him and which he no longer needs to follow. In the context of hexagram *hsieh*, then, Pao-shu Tzu can be seen as a distressed gentleman who has sloughed off socially imposed impediments to his own capacity for achieving the Way.

The alleviation of Pao-shu Tzu's frustration should be seen as positive. It satisfied eight values or aims posited in the proposals and retorts in the "Seven Solutions." There were three core Confucian values, a continuum derived from the *Great Learning*: extending one's knowledge (*chih chih* 致知), cultivating oneself as an individual (*hsiu shen* 修身), and bringing order to the society at large (*chih kuo* 治國). Exactly what one must do to realize these values was a subject of continuing debate, but they can be taken roughly to refer to (1) the accumulation of knowledge through intellectual effort, (2) moral improvement through personal discipline, and (3) contributing to the well-being of society through government service. There are also other values which Confucius and Confucians acknowledged, but which cannot be taken as central. (4) Becoming cultured (*wen* 文) was a concomitant of acting as a gentleman (*chün-tzu*), and was sometimes regarded as more superficial, more a matter of the polite arts, than the accumulation of knowledge,[3] but partaking in the tradition of high

1. *I Ch'eng chuan*, 4.177. Cf. Richard Wilhelm, trans., *The I Ching*, vol. 1, 165. As the name of the hexagram, the word is usually pronounced *hsieh*; as a verb, or verbal noun, the same written word is pronounced *chieh*.

2. *I Ch'eng chuan*, 4.180. Cf. R. Wilhelm, trans., *The I Ching*, vol. 1, 167.

3. E.g., *Lun yü*, 1.6. Cf. Waley, trans., *Analects of Confucius*, 84: "If, when all that is done, he has any energy to spare, let him study the polite arts." I.e., *hsueh wen* 學文.

culture was generally esteemed. Reputation, or, more accurately, (5) good name (*ming* 名), was desired and cherished. (6) High social status (*kuei* 貴) and (7) wealth (*fu* 富) were not to be actively sought, although one need not refuse them either. Being cultured, reputation, high standing, and wealth were not solely within the preserve of Confucians, but were commonly held social values which in the seventeenth century could be acquired largely by one's own efforts, as the legal and social system tended to erode inherited wealth and status.[4] Finally, there is a rather hard to pin down value which is perhaps best represented by the phrase (8) being independent (*tzu-li* 自立), in the sense of being oneself, doing what one feels he must rather than doing what others think he should.[5] Pao-shu Tzu touched on this idea when he claimed that one can only do what by his nature (*hsing*) he is inclined to do. There is a Taoist tinge here, in that such independence might best be realized outside of society (*fang wai* 方外).[6] It was one of the aims of being a "man of the mountains,"[7] but being independent also was linked with the Neo-Confucian emphasis on integrity (*ch'eng* 誠), that is, being as one should be.[8] These eight values were always subject to varying interpretation. The weight each was accorded depended on the man and his assessment of his times. Pao-shu Tzu's problem was to discover a course which would best satisfy his scale of values and least involve him in unsavory compromises. As a record of an enlightening experience, Pao-shu Tzu's own resolution of his dilemma may not seem inspiring, yet it is a suitable symbol of the emerging evaluation of scholarship as a newfound "middle way."

In his own life, Fang appeared to have difficulty implementing the ideals he wrote about. In 1640 he passed the *chin-shih* examination and later accepted an appointment to office in Peking. He then wrote that he was unable to retire and try to have an effect at a remove, as had some high-minded men in antiquity, nor could he request leave to go out on campaign against bandits, nor disclose what was on his mind in an audience with the emperor, nor associate with powerful men in order to benefit himself[9]—all of which he had already disparaged anyway in the "Seven Solutions" in 1637. After 1644 Fang made money in commerce (by selling medicines in Fukien), again served his emperor in a

---

4. The eighteenth-century satire, *The Scholars* (*Ju lin wai shih*), leaves the impression that these four values were operative at all levels of society, with priority given to the acquisition of wealth and status.

5. Cf. the "Ju hsing" section, paragraph 4, of the *Li chi*, where *tzu-li* is the term which characterizes the conduct of a scholar (*ju*) as he waits for his prince to invite him to participate in government.

6. Huang Tsung-hsi, *Ming ju hsueh an*, 5.28, cited some of Ch'en Hsien-chang's followers as men who sought to be independent (*tzu-li*), and Huang added that from Wang Yang-ming's time on there were those, especially in the T'ai-chou school, who placed great emphasis on being "free-reined" (*k'uang*), which can be interpreted positively as acting out what was within.

7. Suzuki Tadashi, 371.

8. Cf. *Chung yung* (Legge, 418/4); A. C. Graham, *Two Chinese Philosophers*, 67.

9. Fang I-chih, "Sung Chou Nung-fu huan ku-hsiang hsu," *Fu-shan wen-chi*, 5.24b.

time of dire need and great risk, and finally lived in retirement in the mountains among less than civilized men—all acts he had previously said he could not bring himself to do. The press of events in the 1640s did not make it easy to reconcile one's conduct with his ideas, even when he knew what he should do. As Fang earlier had said with great accuracy of himself, "I live in these times, but I am unable to be resolute and I also am unable to flee."[10]

In spite of an undertone of withdrawal and escape in his writings of the 1630s, Fang then was not willing to forgo his sense of social responsibility. His sense of duty, in part, can be attributed to a two-fold inheritance which he bore. His father and grandfather had been high officials, serving their emperor in dangerous times. His famous great-grandfather, on the other hand, had never served, but had devoted his efforts to moral self-improvement and propagating his teachings as a means of bettering society. Fang I-chih had much to live up to, and yet, if for no other reason than his perception that times had changed, he could not simply follow the course of an official career or what had been an estimable alternative. Thus he was frustrated in his desire to be involved. In mid-1639 Fang wrote that his friend Li Wen " . . . asked what book I am writing, what extraordinary men I have met, what plans I have made for entering the mountains. On all three of these, I have no response. By nature rather stupid, I like to indulge myself in pleasure. I am already unsuccessful. 'Standing like a bird, not turning around,'[11] I am moved and want to do something. I feel for the age and want to help the times."[12] The implication of Fang's expression of concern for the world was that the Way did not prevail, that things were not quite right in the empire. He continued, "Those who do not understand think I am defaming the government. Those who do understand think our being restrained by material considerations is already too extreme. To like to be depressed and hateful without good cause is not what a true gentleman would like."[13] Fang then, too, had to bridge this conflict between being critical and being involved.

Scholarly Pursuits

Pao-shu Tzu's resolution to "recall times past, and consider the present situation of the world" implied the unambiguously Confucian aim of deriving guidance

10. Fang I-chih, "P'o-hsien chi," *Chi-ku-t'ang erh chi*, A, quoted in Hou Wai-lu, *Chung-kuo ssu-hsiang t'ung shih*, vol. 4, 1140.

11. *Ch'ueh li pu chuan* 雀立不轉, quoted from *Chan-kuo ts'e*, "Ch'u," 139. (Translated in Crump, *Chan-kuo Ts'e*, 234: He ". . . stood like a crane, never once lying down.") Fen-mei Po-su hastened to the Ch'in capital when his own state of Ch'u suffered severe defeats at the hands of Wu. He stood and cried out and starved until the King of Ch'in, impressed by his earnestness, sent his own forces to drive the Wu armies out of Ch'u.

12. Fang I-chih, "Sung Li Shu-chang hsu," *Fu-shan wen-chi*, 3.32a–b; also in *Ch'i tai i shu*, 2.17b–18a.

13. Ibid., 3.32b.

from history for moral conduct that has a social effect. More than that, it implied a life devoted to the scholarly pursuits that were to characterize the new orientation in thought in the seventeenth century.

Scholarship, as the accumulation of knowledge, was a form of intellectual effort that could be justified as a personal, moral discipline. It would contribute to the well-being of society by uncovering the Way—the tradition of high culture—without participating in government. It provided a means of being independent while remaining within the realm of Confucian concerns. Becoming cultured and establishing a good name for oneself were functions of one's scholarly achievements. High social status and wealth were not to be directly derived from scholarship, which reinforced its claim of not being self-aggrandizing, and which may have been one reason why the first generation of the new orientation—Huang Tsung-hsi, Fang I-chih, Ku Yen-wu—were sons of already prominent, wealthy families. Men of the second generation began to have access to some degree of wealth and status as they were patronized for their efforts, both by the imperial government, as reflected in the *po-hsueh hung-ju* examination of 1679, and by influential individuals, as at the villa near Soochow established by Ku Yen-wu's nephews.[14] Such patronage, especially in the eighteenth century, eroded "independence" (*tzu-li*), but for those men who sought a Confucian alternative to government service, scholarly pursuits were most attractive.

The first generation was concerned to distinguish the "new" orientation from conventional efforts at scholarship. Fang I-chih charged, "For their task the [so-called] scholars (*hsueh-che*) of the world want to gain riches and high status by mastering a single classic [for the examinations]. How are they able to search for the widest range [of relevant information] and do something about our situation?"[15] Ku Yen-wu later echoed this judgment. "The gentleman's pursuit of studies (*hsueh*) is not solely for his own advantage. If, having a mind set on making clear the Way and bringing out the virtue in others, and having an active involvement in dispelling disorder and reverting to what is correct, one understands why the condition of the empire has come to such an extreme, then he considers and seeks to do something about it."[16]

Fang's and Ku's insistence on contributing positively to the good of society in a troubled time may be distinguished from two alternatives to government service that had been pursued by high-minded men earlier—devoting oneself to moral self-cultivation (*hsiu shen*) and being a "man of culture" (*wen jen*). Fang

14. On the *Po-hsueh hung-ju* examination, see Hellmut Wilhelm, "The Po-hsüeh Hung-ju Examination of 1679," *Journal of the American Oriental Society* 71 (1951), 60–66. On Ku's nephews, see Hummel, *Eminent Chinese*, under Hsu Ch'ien-hsueh.

15. Fang I-chih, "Wen lun," *Fu-shan wen-chi*, 1.9a; also in *Ch'i tai i shu*, 1.4a.

16. Ku Yen-wu, letter to P'an Lei in *Ku T'ing-lin shih-wen-chi*, 173. Ku Yen-wu was alluding, at least in part, to the fall of the Ming dynasty. Fang had expressed his parallel sentiments before 1644.

agreed with Su Shih's complaint to the Emperor Shen-tsung (r. 1068–85) that scholars (*hsueh-che*) of the day were ashamed *not* to be talking of "human nature" and "destiny." Fang added that in this regard, Sung Confucians (*ju*) had gone to greater excess than the literati and officials of the third and fourth centuries who caused the downfall of the Chin dynasty with idle, speculative talk. In both cases, the fault was men's neglect of the everyday realities (*shih-wu* 實務).[17] Fang applied the same criticism to those of his contemporaries who were similarly disposed. "When literati of this age, chafing at the encumbrances of the world, are pleased to cultivate [their moral selves], then they hold to constant [i.e., nonphenomenal] principles."[18] They did so at the expense of a concern for the flux of the workaday world and helping to bring order to it. Like Fang, Ku Yen-wu chastised men in the recent past who had focused on irrelevant subtleties, such as questions of mind and human nature, to the neglect of more pressing social concerns.[19] Fang's and Ku's criticisms also were directed at those who turned to cultural pursuits. Ku wrote in 1646, "In the last twenty or thirty years those in the local districts who were known as 'men of culture' (*wen jen*) without exception devoted themselves to the attainment of empty reputation and unearned gain."[20] Years later he extended his condemnation. "The examinations are a case of the modern motive for pursuing studies solely being personal gain (*li* 利). Worse than that, the [so-called] 'men of culture' of all three hundred years of the Ming dynasty together are a case of creating literature, writing books, and engaging in the full panoply of activities producing [cultural] contributions merely for the sake of personal reputation."[21] Fang I-chih likewise complained of such men. "If they have literary talent, then they give themselves over to stylistic elegance. If they have wide-ranging intellect, then they take pleasure in being lazy. But who is willing to develop and extend to its essentials our knowledge so as to resolve what has been causing doubt?"[22] Perhaps Ku and Fang were more concerned to criticize the contemporary derogations rather than the original manifestations of Neo-Confucians' devotion to moral self-cultivation or men of culture's concern with maintaining the vitality of cultural forms, but they both also aimed to be doing something different. Theirs was to be a "new" approach to scholarly endeavor—wide-ranging, evidenced, original items of knowledge. Knowledge was to be accumulated not

---

17. Fang I-chih, "Lun hsu-t'an ta-tao pu chiang shih-wu chih ping 論虛談大道不講實務之病," *Fu-shan wen-chi*, 5.49a.

18. Fang I-chih, *T'ung ya*, shou 2.5a.

19. Cf. Edward Ch'ien, "Chiao Hung and the Revolt against Ch'eng-Chu Orthodoxy," *Unfolding of Neo-Confucianism*, 271–72, and W. T. deBary, "Introduction," *Self and Society in Ming Thought*, 1–2, for translated examples of a sentiment Ku reiterated a number of times.

20. Ku Yen-wu, *Ku T'ing-lin shih-wen-chi*, 5.119.

21. Ku Yen-wu, letter to P'an Lei, *Ku T'ing-lin shih-wen-chi*, 173.

22. Fang I-chih, *T'ung ya*, shou 2.5a.

for *its* own sake or *one's* own selfish purposes, but to fulfill a wider social responsibility. At the same time, their intentions represent a synthesis of the emphasis on self-cultivation and on culture as alternatives to government service. Part of the impulse of the one had been an assumption that true social order could only be effected on the foundation of individual morality rather than through institutional reforms, and, of the other, an assumption that one's responsibility to the culture could take precedence over assisting in the administration of the state. The new scholarly pursuits had a moral component—to help discover for the rest of society what was "good" and "right"—and made its own contributions to "our culture"—by writing books to persuade or enlighten others in the search for social order. This was the Confucian aim implied in Pao-shu Tzu's resolution to "recall times past, and consider the present situation of the world."

By 1640 Fang had begun working on evidenced scholarship. Early in his education Fang I-chih had acquired the habit of accumulating the notes he took as he read,[23] and he extended the practice in the late 1630s when he was in Nanking.

> While I have been living at the Study Antiquity Hall, if there is something I grasp, I make a note of it. If there is something which I doubt, I also make a note of it. I make a note when it is difficult to set down [a finished result] concerning any "thing" and which needs wait further revision. I make a note when the words of a friend please me. After a while, [as the accumulated notes have become sufficiently bulky,] I put book-wrappers around them. Chou Ch'i looked at them and said, "What joy! Without intending it, you have produced a work." I really do not understand how this is a joy. I really do not understand how this is even a work. I do not go beyond treating a "thing" (*wu*) or "affair" (*shih*) for what it is. I do not want to continue on with the pomposity and presumption [manifested in the so-called works of others]. Each person has his own temperament and "face." [For me], it is to be without that which is derived from others. It is enough that [compiling these notes] be regarded as a pastime. If someone who glances at them perceives the state [of the notes], he would not be moved to applause. When a cicada ensconced on a high branch drinks the dew and makes its humming sound, it has no intention that [the sound] should enter someone's ear. Its joy comes from being fully realized. Therefore, [if these notes induce joy,] it might be considered the joy of a cicada.[24]

By such comments Fang was maintaining that his note-taking was solely for his own self-satisfaction and was not intended for others. But within a few years after he claimed that his joy, and pride, was no more than the cicada's, an incident occurred which suggests that he regarded these notes as something more serious than an insect's hum.

He recorded that "All the work I did when I was young in making comparative notes on the classics and histories was previously lost when my boat sank at Ti-kang 荻港 [a port on the Yangtze in Anhwei]. I wanted to commis-

23. See above, chapter 1.
24. Fang I-chih, "Hsi yü hsin pi," 11b–12a.

sion a friend[25] to join in recompiling them, but he was even more reluctant than I. Therefore, I cut up some books and ordered a servant to paste them and to copy some [items] which were effaced."[26] One may wonder if notes that could be so reconstituted were much more than the juxtaposition of pieces of text which Fang found in one way or another to be mutually enlightening, but his concern suggests that such textual matters, even if at a low level of interpretation, were of some value to him. The sinking of the boat quite possibly made Fang realize that his accumulated notes might also represent something of interest and use to others.

It was, however, only from 1640, after he had left Nanking for Peking, that Fang began to rework his material and expand it into a manuscript which could with more justification be called a "work." Fang began to assemble his notes and thoughts and prepare sections of what eventually became two of his most important books, the *Comprehensive Refinement* (*T'ung ya*) and the *Notes on Principles of Things* (*Wu li hsiao chih*). It was asserted that the *Comprehensive Refinement* was drafted before 1639 in Fang's spare time while preparing for the examinations and that the material was revised while he was waiting for an appointment to office.[27] This should be taken to mean that the short, note-like entries which constitute the bulk of the *Comprehensive Refinement* had been largely accumulated by 1639 and were assembled and ordered in Peking. Most of the longer, discursive essays which appear in the introductory chapters, however, were dated as having been completed in 1641 and 1642. Fang's first preface was dated the summer of 1641, the second a year later, and his introductory comments (*fan-li*) were written in the summer of 1643. At about that time, Fang entitled a poem "On Taking the Miscellaneous Notes of Every Sort from the Study Antiquity Hall and Editing Them to Constitute the *Comprehensive Refinement*."[28] If the poem was composed in 1643, then Fang's reference in it to "three years of effort" could easily be taken to mean 1640–42, when he was in Peking aiding his father and then awaiting an appointment to office. Although some parts of the *Comprehensive Refinement* were dated after 1643, Fang had generally finished the manuscript " . . . before he became an official," probably early in 1643.[29]

The preface for the *Notes on Principles of Things*, written at the end of the last month of 1643, argued that comprehensive knowledge was possible, but Fang denied he had achieved such a state.

25. Fang may have been referring here to his friend Chou Ch'i; cf. Chou Ch'i's preface to Fang's "Chi-ku-t'ang erh-chi," *Fu-shan wen-chi* 2, where he refers to the sinking, and the loss of more than just Fang's notes. Chou's preface, dated the summer of 1639, reported that the loss of Fang's writings occurred "this year." It does not seem to be assuming too much to suppose that the incident Chou referred to is the same as the one Fang mentioned.

26. Fang I-chih, "Hsi yü hsin pi," 24b.

27. Fang I-chih, "Fan-li," *T'ung ya*, 1a.

28. In *T'ung-ch'eng Fang shih shih chi*, 26.8b.

29. Preface by Yao Wen-hsieh 姚文燮, 7a, in *T'ung ya*.

What sort of man am I that I dare speak of "comprehensively knowing"? Rather, it is simply that from when I was young I have liked this [sort of inquiry], pursued the ideas in the manuscript entitled "From Whence the Principles of Things" (*Wu li so*) by my teacher, [Wang] Hsu-chou, and over a time recorded what I have heard and what I have come to a judgement about, but I await some later day for comprehensive understanding. Meanwhile, I say this has been to please myself."[30]

Again Fang has referred to a long period of interest and note-taking which in 1643 came to fruition in the form of a book-like manuscript, but even at this late date he did not avow any more serious intent than to please himself. Why, when he had earlier argued for the importance of "study," was he unwilling to make that claim for the results of his labors? Not simply out of humility, although a ritual disclaimer of achievement would not have been out of place in his preface. More fundamental was his need not to appear to be self-seeking. His work could not be presented as a claim to fame or preferment any more than passing the examinations should be sought for reasons of the rewards that would come.

Fang's Fate

Although Fang made a commitment to scholarship by 1640, events outside of his control or influence prevented him from devoting his attention to intellectual matters. After his father was sent into exile instead of being beaten or executed, Fang remained in Peking in the hope of serving a government increasingly beset by economic and military difficulties. He received a junior appointment in the Hanlin Academy in 1642 or 1643,[31] and was still in Peking in the third month of 1644, when Li Tzu-ch'eng's army swept into the capital.[32] Ming officials who had not agreed to serve the newly proclaimed regime were rounded up and held at sword point before it was decided they could ransom themselves by payments on a scale commensurate with their former rank. A member of the Hanlin Academy was required to pay 10,000 taels of silver, and redemption of a Grand Secretary was set at 100,000 taels.[33] Fang was arrested, his life threatened, and his youngest son, only in his seventh year, was held hostage.[34] Released, Fang left his wife and children behind as he hurried south to his home in T'ung-ch'eng,[35] perhaps to raise the required sum.[36]

30. Fang I-chih, "Tzu hsu," *Wu li hsiao chih.*
31. Wang Fu-chih, "Fang I-chih chuan," in *Ch'i tai i shu,* said that Fang was made a Bachelor (*shu-chi-shih*) and then a Compiler (*pien-hsiu*) in the Hanlin Academy.
32. Fang I-chih, "Chi Chang Erh-kung shu," *Fu-shan wen-chi,* 8.9a.
33. Hsu Tzu, *Hsiao t'ien chi nien,* 127. Also, *P'ing k'ou chih,* 9.16a.
34. "Wen-i kung chia-chuan," in *Ch'i tai i shu.*
35. Fang I-chih, "Chi Chang Erh-kung shu," 8.9a. Wang Fu-chih, "Fang I-chih chuan," in *Ch'i tai i shu.*
36. Hsu Tzu, *Hsiao t'ien chi nien,* 131–32, recorded that Fang paid the ransom. Li Wen-

He was in Nanking by the fifth month of 1644,[37] when Peking had already been occupied by the Manchus with their newly enthroned Shun-chih emperor. The Ming government was reconstituted with its own new emperor in Nanking, but even in the face of the loss of the North, the Nanking court was bogged down in power struggles and the avenging of old political animosities. Fang I-chih and many of his friends found their lives were in jeopardy because Juan Ta-ch'eng had acquired influence in Nanking and wanted to settle his grudge against them for having attacked him in 1639. An acquaintance of Fang's was tortured in prison until both of his legs were broken in an attempt to force him to testify that Fang had committed treason in Peking. Fortunately for Fang, the man would not say that Fang had accepted an official appointment in Li Tzu-ch'eng's brief reign. Some charges were brought against Fang, and he escaped with a sentence of banishment, and then was pardoned, probably after someone had interceded on his behalf.[38] Fang realized he could not remain in Nanking.[39]

On his father's advice, he went south to Fukien to live in the district where his father had been magistrate twenty-five years before.[40] He did not become involved in the government of the Ming prince who was established as the new emperor at Foochow in mid-1645. Even before that emperor was captured by Ch'ing troops little more than a year later, Fang had fled on farther south. Dressed as a commoner and using his mother's surname as an alias,[41] he was joined in Canton by his wife and his youngest son.[42] Fang was trying to avoid any further involvement with the Ming cause by remaining unknown,[43] but one day he was recognized in a Canton bookstore by a Ming official out in his sedan chair with his full retinue. The meeting brought on tears, as the Ming official had known Fang in Peking in 1640, when they both passed the *chin-shih* examination. Fang was urged in the strongest terms to help the Ming in its troubles. Giving in, and again leaving his family behind, he went to Chao-ch'ing, in western Kwangtung, and joined with Ch'ü Shih-ssu (1590–1651), the civil official who was instrumental in having another Ming prince enthroned

---

chih, *Wan Ming min-pien*, 213, listed Fang I-chih as one of those who served Li Tzu-ch'eng's Peking government. Li Wen-chih's source probably was *P'ing k'ou chih*, 10.1b. Fang was adamant that he had not accepted an office in the new government. In a letter written in 1647 or so, he said, "Under extreme duress, I did not submit in the Northern Capital. . . . I was willing to face death rather than be sullied by accepting an illegitimate appointment." See "Chi Chang Erh-kung shu," 8.9a–b.

37. Ibid., 8.9a.

38. Ibid., 8.9a–b. Fang's friend Yang Wen-ts'ung was Juan Ta-ch'eng's brother-in-law.

39. Li Yao's biography of Fang, 2b, in *Ch'i tai i shu*.

40. Fang I-chih, "Chi Li Shu-chang shu," *Fu-shan wen-chi*, 7.1b. This letter was written in 1649.

41. Wang Fu-chih, "Fang I-chih chuan."

42. "Wen-i kung chia-chuan," in *Ch'i tai i shu*, and Fang I-chih, "Chi Chang Erh-kung shu," 8.10b.

43. Wang Fu-chih, "Fang I-chih chuan," said that after Nanking Fang lost his desire to be an official.

there late in 1646 as the Yung-li emperor.[44] Put to work in a secretarial post, Fang quickly became caught up in a court dispute. The chief eunuch suspected that Fang was behind a censor's memorial objecting to certain appointments proposed by the eunuch. Fang could not have been at court more than a few months when he quit, despite Ch'ü Shih-ssu's efforts to have him stay on.[45] As the Yung-li emperor's entourage, and government, retreated up the river from Chao-ch'ing to Wu-chou, in eastern Kwangsi, Fang went along, but he remained behind in the second month of 1647 as the imperial progress moved on to Kuei-lin.[46]

Fang I-chih's career as an official was over, but not his troubles. Suffering from illness, he lived for a while in the mountains on the border of Hu-kuang and Kwangsi provinces, near the court at Kuei-lin,[47] and then he took up residence for more than three years in a village farther south, in the vicinity of P'ing-lo.[48] He declined offers of appointment to nearby provincial governments controlled by generals, and in 1649 he refused to rejoin the Yung-li court with the lofty titles of Grand Secretary and Minister of Rites. Dressed in rough clothes, he rejected the blandishments of the imperial messenger.[49] At the beginning of 1650 he moved north into Hu-kuang province, perhaps because a Ming counter-offensive had just taken the city of Wu-kang, in southern Hu-kuang. Probably with his hair still not cut to conform to Ch'ing regulations, he lived incognito among the Miao people in the mountains west of Wu-kang. Almost immediately Wu-kang was recaptured by Ch'ing troops, and fearing arrest as a Ming collaborator, Fang fled back to the village forty *li* from P'ing-lo.[50]

In the winter of 1650 an acquaintance of Fang's from T'ung-ch'eng arrived in P'ing-lo and Fang went there to meet him. Just after they parted the next day, Ch'ing troops appeared in P'ing-lo. To escape the cavalrymen sent to search for him, Fang shaved his head in the style of a Buddhist monk and put on Buddhist robes.[51] Nevertheless, he was arrested and brought before a Ch'ing general, who threatened to execute Fang unless he would agree to serve the Manchus as an official. Fang adamantly refused, and finally was released to live as a monk.[52]

44. Wang Fu-chih, ibid.
45. Wang Fu-chih, ibid. Fang I-chih, "Chi Chang Erh-kung shu," 8.10a.
46. Fang I-chih, ibid. Hsu Tzu, *Hsiao t'ien chi nien*, 521–23. Huang Tsung-hsi, "Yung-li chi nien," *Li-chou i-chu hui-k'an*, 1b, recorded that in the second month of 1647 Fang was made a Grand Secretary; Fang almost certainly did not accept the appointment.
47. Fang I-chih, ibid.
48. Wang Fu-chih, "Fang I-chih chuan." Fang I-chih, "Liu Ta-ssu-ma chuan-lueh," *Fu-shan wen-chi*, 9.15a; "Chi Yao Tien-kuang wen," *Fu-shan wen-chi*, 8.37a. The man who recognized Fang in Canton in 1646 died in the village where Fang was in 1649.
49. Wang Fu-chih, "Fang I-chih chuan."
50. Fang I-chih, "Chi Chang Erh-kung shu," 8.10a–b.
51. Ch'ien Ch'eng-chih, "Yung-li chi nien," 62a–63a, in his *So chih lu*.
52. Wang Fu-chih, "Fang I-chih chuan." Li Yao's biography of Fang I-chih in *Ch'i tai i shu*, 2b. Hsu Tzu, *Hsiao t'ien chi-chuan*, 250. Cf. Willard J. Peterson, "Fang I-chih: Western Learning and the 'Investigation of Things,' " in W. T. deBary et al., *Unfolding of Neo-Confucianism*, 374 and n. 40.

During the troubled ten years after going to Peking to succor his father, Fang I-chih tried to pursue his scholarly endeavors. He continued to add to the manuscripts of the *Comprehensive Refinement* and *Notes on Principles of Things*. When he was briefly among the Miao early in 1650 he sent a box of manuscript material back to his family in T'ung-ch'eng.[53] But it was hardly a productive time for scholarship for Fang, any more than it was for Huang Tsung-hsi or Ku Yen-wu.

Although in the guise of a monk from 1651 on, Fang seems at first to have been ambivalent in his commitment to Buddhism. Late in 1652 he met with his father at, or near, the northern Kiangsi city of Chiu-chiang, on the Yangtze River.[54] Fang then stayed at a temple in the mountains near Chiu-chiang, for he dated a manuscript he completed in that year as done at the peaks known as the Five Old Men (*Wu lao feng*).[55] The manuscript, entitled *Tung-hsi chün*, cannot be called Buddhist any more than Confucian; it was a speculative amalgam of ideas growing out of more than twenty years of reading and thinking. In 1653 Fang went to Nanking to pursue his Buddhist studies under the eminent master Chueh-lang Tao-sheng (d. 1659) of the Ts'ao-tung sect of Ch'an (Zen),[56] and by the winter of 1654 he was resident at a temple near Hsin-ch'eng, in the mountains of northeastern Kiangsi.[57] It is not difficult to imagine that some of his friends and family were hostile to his being a monk. In 1653,[58] Hou Fang-yü, his friend from his Nanking days, sent him a letter that might have represented the attitude of many of Fang's old friends. Hou wrote of how pleased he was to hear that Fang had returned from the South and how he anticipated their seeing each other again after so many years apart. He said that their friend Ch'en Chen-hui had asked why Fang had returned, and Hou explained that it was because he had no brothers (Fang's younger brother had died in 1649), his father was old, and his sons were young. It was only fitting, Hou thought, for Fang to return to take care of his family. In the letter Hou recalled how in 1640 Fang had sent from Peking a robe made of "wild mulberry silk." Hou wore the robe often, and though it was darkened with dirt and grease, he had maintained that if it were washed it would no longer be the original from Fang I-chih. After 1646 or so, he felt it was so out of fashion he could not wear it. He packed it carefully

---

53. Fang Chung-t'ung, "Wu li hsiao chih pien-lu yuan-ch'i," 1b, in *Wu li hsiao chih*.

54. Shih Jun-chang, "Wu-k'o ta-shih liu-shih hsu," *Shih Yü-shan wen chi*, 9.2a. Cf. postface by editors of Fang I-chih, *Tung hsi chün*, 167, and Yü Ying-shih, *Fang I-chih wan chieh k'ao*, 8–9.

55. Fang I chih, *Tung hsi chün*, 10. Shih Jun-chang, 9.2a, recorded that he stayed for ten days with Fang between Wu lao and San tieh, the Three Cascades. I suspect that Fang was residing at the Fang-kuang ssu 方廣寺, which Hsu Hsia-k'o described in 1618 as "the new monastery of Five Old Men," and which was near the scenic Three Cascades. Hsu Hsia-k'o, *Hsu Hsia-k'o yu chi*, 1.23; cf. Li chi, trans., *The Travel Diaries of Hsu Hsia-k'o*, 114.

56. Yü Ying-shih, *Fang I-chih wan chieh k'ao*, 7, 15.

57. Ibid., 161.

58. The *Hou Fang-yü nien-p'u* assigned this letter to 1652, but since it refers to Fang's being at the Kao-tso temple in Nanking, 1653 seems the more likely date.

away, but he always thought about the robe. Hou told Fang that recently his wife had wanted to cut it down to make it more fashionable, but he had stopped her. "Other robes can be altered, but this robe is a kindness sent by Mi-chih and cannot be altered. If I am lucky, some day I shall be able to see Mi-chih. I shall appear to greet him wearing this wonderful, unchanged robe."[59] Hou Fang-yü was not being subtle in his symbolism. He depicted his wife as having given up, while he still had hopes for Fang. His imagined meeting with his old friend (whom he continued to refer to by his former, lay name rather than by his new Buddhist name) would be a confrontation between the past, with Hou dressed in the old soiled robe representing their friendship, and the unfortunate present, with Fang in a new monkish costume.[60] To show that he saw no necessity for Fang's remaining a monk, Hou wrote that if some day Fang would come to call, a room would be ready with a hanging scroll of rootless plums painted by Cheng Ssu-hsiao (1239–1316) after the fall of the Sung, and they would read some poems written by T'ao Ch'ien after the fall of the Chin dynasty in 419.[61] By citing two famous symbols of loyalty to a fallen dynasty, Hou made it clear that he thought Fang did not have to forgo his status as a literatus (*shih*) in order to be loyal to the Ming; he could change back into his old robe as easily as changing his clothes. I do not know whether Fang received this unsympathetic letter, but considerations of family responsibility and literati traditions must have militated against his being completely certain about remaining as a monk. Late in 1654, when he was in Kiangsi, he received a copy of a study that his father had written on the *Book of Changes*.[62] Fang's father had been living in retirement since the change of dynasties, and he was another example that one did not need to be a Buddhist monk in order to avoid serving the Ch'ing government. Whether or not these continuing entanglements affected him, Fang I-chih went into the prescribed three-year mourning period when he learned of his father's death in 1655. He returned to T'ung-ch'eng, where his wife and three sons were living, and resided at Ho-ming 合明 Mountain, in the eastern part of the district.[63] At that point he could have "changed clothes," as friends such as Hou Fang-yü might have hoped; after wearing mourning, Fang could have made the transition back into society as a literatus in retirement, which some other men who had sought temporary refuge as Buddhist monks did after the threat to them from Ch'ing military forces had passed.[64]

59. Hou Fang-yü, "Yü Fang Mi-chih shu," in "Chuang-hui t'ang i-kao," *Chuang-hui t'ang chi*, 1a–b.

60. Chin T'ien-ko, *Wan-chih lieh-chuan kao*, 1.23a–b (71–72), in his paraphrase of Hou Fang-yü's letter, also emphasized the imagined confrontation between the scholar's gown and the monk's robe.

61. Hou Fang-yü, ibid., 1b.

62. Fang I-chih, *Yao-ti p'ao Chuang*, 93; cf. Yü Ying-shih, *Fang I-chih wan chieh k'ao*, 127.

63. Chin T'ien-ko, *Wan-chih li h-chuan kao*, 2.12a (125).

64. Ch'en Yuan, *Ming chi Tien Ch'ien fo-chiao k'ao*, 200–61. In the 1660s Fang was friendly with Wu Yun 吳雲, who had been a monk for a period after the fall of the Ming.

For whatever reasons, Fang remained a Buddhist monk for the rest of his life. In 1658 he went back to the Hsin-ch'eng district in Kiangsi and stayed at several temples there for the next five years.[65] By 1660 he had begun his last, and his most Buddhist, book, called *Monk Yao-ti Roasts the Chuang Tzu* (*Yao-ti p'ao Chuang*). A compilation of comments on the *Chuang Tzu*, it included Fang's own views with those of Wang Hsuan, who had been his teacher thirty years earlier, and Chueh-lang Tao-sheng, who had been his master in Nanking, as well as a wide range of quotations from other sources.[66] In 1662 Fang was invited to take charge of a temple at Hsin-ch'eng.[67] The next year he went to the Ts'ao-tung temple complex at Ch'ing-yuan Mountain, which was ten *li* south of the town of Chi-an on the Kan River in central Kiangsi. At Ch'ing-yuan he participated in the ceremonies accompanying the internment of the former abbot, who had died in 1659. At the invitation of the Chi-an district magistrate, Fang returned in 1664 as the new abbot at Ch'ing-yuan.[68] He oversaw the construction of three new buildings,[69] and continued as abbot for eight years.

Fang did not live in isolation at Ch'ing-yuan. His two younger sons were with him for visits sometimes lasting more than a year,[70] and he received calls from a number of literati friends, most of whom had avoided serving the Ch'ing and who lived nearby or traveled to see him.[71] Fang also kept up a correspondence with Wang Fu-chih, who was living in retirement in Honan.[72] In the mid-1660s Fang had extensive contacts with Shih Jun-chang (1619–83), who was a 1649 *chin-shih* serving as a circuit intendant in Kiangsi.[73] They had met in 1652 in Kwangsi and traveled north together to Kiangsi.[74] After Fang moved to Ch'ing-yuan in 1664, Shih was a frequent visitor until he retired from office in 1667 to devote himself to writing the poetry which was bringing him fame among his contemporaries.[75] Shih praised the monk Fang I-chih, whom he knew as Master Wu-k'o 無可, for his literary abilities and his profundity, and especially for his detailed mastery and broad grasp of knowledge about " . . .

(Yü Ying-shih, 49–50) Ku Yen-wu's friend Kuei Chuang also had been a monk for a brief time.

65. Yü Ying-shih, *Fang I-chih wan chieh k'ao*, 24–26, 127.

66. Fang I-chih, *Yao-ti p'ao Chuang*. Cf. Yü Ying-shih, 16–17; 37.

67. Yü Ying-shih, 25.

68. Yü Ying-shih, 19–27. Cf. review by Willard J. Peterson, *Harvard Journal of Asiatic Studies* 34 (1974), 293–94, and Jung Chao-tsu, "Fang I-chih ho t'a te ssu-hsiang," *Ling-nan hsueh pao* 9.1 (1948), 99.

69. Fang Chung-t'ung, in *T'ung-ch'eng Fang shih shih chi*, 30.6a. Cf. Yü Ying-shih, 28–29.

70. Yü Ying-shih, 31–36, and Fang Chung-lü's biography in *Ch'i tai i shu*.

71. Yü Ying-shih, 47–51.

72. Ibid., 44, 47. Wang and Fang became acquainted in 1647 in Kwangsi. (Yü, 44)

73. Yü Ying-shih, 51. Hummel, *Eminent Chinese*, under Shih Jun-chang.

74. Shih Jun-chang, "Wu-k'o ta-shih liu-shih hsu," *Shih Yü-shan wen chi*, 9.2a. Cf. Yü Ying-shih, 52.

75. Teng Chih-ch'eng, *Ch'ing shih chi shih ch'u pien*, 580; Hummel, *Eminent Chinese*, under Shih Jun-chang.

heaven, earth, man, and things, images and numbers, calendrical astronomy and harmonics, medicine and divination."[76] According to Shih, although Fang had a great understanding of the *Book of Changes* and Ch'an (Zen), he did not talk about them.

> In his tireless efforts to instruct others, he cites the hundred schools of Chou times and the Three Vehicles of Buddhist teachings. When the discussion is flowing smoothly, he goes on without stop past midnight. Almost all of the literati (*shih*) and officials (*tai-fu*) who pass through Chi-an go to Ch'ing-yuan for instruction. When they hear what he has to say, they are all pleased and forget about leaving. Then they find they are suddenly losing their grip on what they had taken for granted.[77]

As a monk, then, Fang continued to display the brilliance of his Nanking years, and the messages of congratulations he received on the occasion of his sixtieth birthday in 1670 were an indication of his continued contacts with the outside world.[78]

During this decade, there were other reminders of his past. In 1664 part of his manuscript material from the 1640s was printed as *Notes on Principles of Things*, with a preface by Yü Tsao (d. 1676), who served as the district magistrate of Chi-an from 1662 to 1673.[79] The manuscript was recopied and prepared for the block carvers by Fang's three sons, with Chung-t'ung having done much of the work of sorting and arranging the notes.[80] Another bulky manuscript (52 *chüan*) of Fang's scholarship which he had completed before 1650 was printed in 1666 as the *Comprehensive Refinement*. These two books were to remain his two best known scholarly contributions. A short while later his sons and friends began editing his miscellaneous prose writings produced during the years before he became a monk. By 1671 the first collection, with the title *Fu-shan chi*, was printed at Shou-shan in T'ai-ho, the next district south of Chi-an.[81] Fang himself may have been involved in the publication process, for he sometimes stayed at a temple at Shou-shan.[82]

All of this publishing activity preserved Fang's work for us, but it may have been detrimental to him by attracting attention to the continued existence of a man who had been living under a series of Buddhist names for twenty years. As a monk, Fang I-chih had not been anonymous, but neither had he been ostentatious. With the publication of a collection of his prose, perhaps someone suspected that Fang's writings from the years when he was in touch

---

76. Shih Jun-chang, "Wu-k'o ta-shih liu-shih hsu," 9.1b. Cf. Yü Ying-shih, 52.

77. Ibid., 1b–2a. Shih Jun-chang wrote this in 1670.

78. Shih Jun-chang, 9.2a.

79. Yü Tsao, "Hsu," in *Wu li hsiao chih*. Cf. Yü Ying-shih, 55–56. As magistrate, Yü Tsao had the formal responsibility for inviting Fang to be the abbot at Ch'ing-yuan shan.

80. Yü Tsao, "Hsu," and Fang Chung-t'ung, "Wu li hsiao chih pien lu yuan-ch'i," in *Wu li hsiao chih*.

81. Fang Chung-t'ung, "Chi shih," in *T'ung-ch'eng Fang shih shih chi*, 28.8b.

82. Yü Ying-shih, 107–8.

with the Southern Ming court in Kwangsi might contain evidence to sustain an accusation that Fang had treasonably expressed anti-Ch'ing sentiments. In any case, in 1671 a legal proceeding was initiated against him in Kwangsi. His arrest was ordered. Not yet in custody, Fang was going south up the Kan River in a boat in the autumn of 1671 when he died, apparently by killing himself at the Fear and Trembling Rapids (Huang-k'ung t'an 惶恐灘) in Wan-an district.[83] His youngest son was with him, and his second son was soon on the scene. They both became implicated in the charges brought against their father.[84] Shortly after their father's death, Fang Chung-t'ung wrote two poems which hint at the sort of trouble they were in.

> Day after day yamen underlings
>   Are around in profusion.
> Governors-general, governors, circuit intendants,
>   And civil officials from the prefectures and districts
> In three provinces scrutinize
>   A huge number of papers.
> With brush and ink at the ready
>   They work with great diligence.
>
> My straw bed is at the side of the coffin;
>   The cloth for mourning tugs at me.
> Morning and evening are like before:
>   I serve him as his child.
> With his manuscripts crammed on the bed,
>   Leave-taking is over and done.
> The wick of the pottery lamp is used up
>   But I do not fall asleep.[85]

In a note to the poems, Fang Chung-t'ung explained what the "huge number of papers" were. "At this time at Shou-shan we printed the *Fu-shan chi*; we also had completed its continuation as well as the *Record of Winter Ashes* (*Tung hui lu* 冬灰錄)."[86] No action was taken against Fang's writings or his sons as a result of the investigation, but it was not until at least a year later that Fang Chung-lü was permitted to leave Wan-an and return home with his father's corpse for burial in T'ung-ch'eng, where Fang I-chih's widow lived in retirement.[87]

The tragic fall in Fang I-chih's life was captured in two lines by his son

---

83. Ibid., 95–106. Yü has uncovered a great deal of circumstantial evidence that Fang committed suicide. Cf. Teng Chih-ch'eng, *Ch'ing shih chi shih ch'u pien*, 130, and Jao Tsung-i, "Fang I-chih yü Ch'en Tzu-sheng," *Tsing Hua Journal of Chinese Studies* 10 (1974), 171.

84. Yü Ying-shih, 95, 110, 113.

85. Fang Chung-t'ung, "Chi shih," in *T'ung-ch'eng Fang shih shih chi*, 28.8b.

86. Ibid. Neither the *Fu-shan hou chi* nor the *Tung hui lu* has ever been published. Cf. Hou Wai-lu, *Chung-kuo ssu-hsiang t'ung shih*, vol. 4, 1123.

87. Fang Chung-lü's biography in *Ch'i tai i shu*, and Yü Ying-shih, 95.

Chung-t'ung. "How regrettable that in his lifetime my father was ensnared in fame. The difficulties and troubles after his death have been that much more difficult to endure."[88]

Following Some Threads

The emergence of a new orientation in intellectual endeavors in the seventeenth century meant several things which became apparent after the first generation's concerns began to be fashionable and after the flux of the transitional period had subsided.

The hegemony of Neo-Confucianism (*Tao-hsueh*) was broken. Though it remained the basis for the purposes of the examination system and continued to attract some men's minds through the eighteenth century,[89] the interests of most of the men usually regarded as leading thinkers went in other directions; they asked other questions and applied other methods. In particular, they pursued evidential studies (*k'ao-cheng hsueh*) at the expense of fathoming transcendent Principle.

The ideal of "scholar-official" was seldom realized. Among the important mid-Ching scholars who accepted posts, many did not hold substantive administrative, as distinguished from primarily scholarly, appointments.[90] By pursuing a policy of attracting scholars to the government with a series of imperially sponsored projects, the Ch'ing court aimed not only to garner prestige but also to obviate the tension between serving in office and pursuing a Confucian alternative, such as had occurred from the Sung dynasty on. It was pointed out to the K'ang-hsi emperor that orthodox teachings (*tao-t'ung* 道統) and legitimate government (*chih-t'ung* 治統) had stemmed from a single source in highest antiquity, but they had separated by the time of Confucius, and were separated during the five hundred years from Chu Hsi's time to the present; with a sage emperor on the throne, Heaven must be intending that teachings (*tao*) and government were to be again joined.[91] Whether this suggestion was mere rhetoric,[92] the K'ang-hsi and Ch'ien-lung emperors' extensive patronage of scholarship obfuscates any easy demarcation between serving in office and devoting oneself to evidential studies. Nevertheless, although there

88. Fang Chung-t'ung, quoted in Teng Chih-ch'eng, 132, and in Yü Ying-shih, 59.

89. Cf. Hellmut Wilhelm, "Confucianism on the Eve of the Great Encounter," in M. B. Jansen, ed., *Changing Japanese Attitudes toward Modernization*.

90. E.g., Ch'ien Ta-hsin (1728–1804), Hung Liang-chi (1746–1809).

91. Li Kuang-ti 李光地, "Chin tu-shu pi-lu chi lun, shuo, hsu, chi tsa-wen hsu," 進讀書筆錄 及論說序記雜文序; *Jung-ts'un ch'üan chi* 榕村全集 10, quoted in Hou Wai-lu, *Chung-kuo ssu-hsiang t'ung shih*, vol. 5, 412. Also cited in Nivison, *The Life and Thought of Chang Hsüeh-ch'eng*, 18.

92. The Southern Sung court, it will be remembered, had tried in its last years to capture Neo-Confucianism with imperial patronage. Cf. James T. C. Liu, "Orthodoxy."

are important exceptions,[93] most of the prominent thinkers and scholars through the eighteenth century were not in government service for a significant portion of their adult career.[94] As a sympathetic character in the mid-eighteenth-century novel *The Scholars* (*Ju lin wai shih*) observed, "As I see it, scholars should stick to scholarship without trying to become officials, and officials should stick to officialdom without trying to be scholars, too. A man who wants to be both will succeed in neither!"[95]

The vitality of artistic contributions generally waned in Ch'ing after a great burst of creative original work in the seventeenth century. This obviously was a complex phenomenon and there is no consensus on the reasons Ch'ing arts tend to appear to twentieth-century observers as dry and derivative. Nevertheless, any explanation must refer to the tenor of the times. As intellectual energies were channeled more into the scholarly products of "evidential studies," the efforts of the "man of culture" who devoted himself to poetry, *belles lettres*, calligraphy, or painting had come to be more lightly valued. Some men even adopted a certain *gaucherie* as if to demonstrate their integrity.[96]

The "new" orientation continues to attract men's efforts. Just as there are still, at the end of the twentieth century, adherents of the Neo-Confucianism formulated by Chu Hsi at the end of the twelfth century, one can view much of what is called "sinology" (in the narrow sense of evidenced studies focusing on texts and without larger explicit metaphysical assumptions or aims) as direct heir to the evidential studies that grew out of the new orientation in the seventeenth century. As it became fashionable and established, the original aim of joining moral significance with social relevance was eroded if not lost, and practitioners of evidential studies were subject to criticisms similar to those directed earlier at moral cultivation and a life devoted to culture. From the late eighteenth century,[97] but especially in the nineteenth century, concern with textual matters was perceived by some men as self-indulgent and irrelevant to solving society's problems. In the twentieth century, the Manchus were blamed for having coerced learned men into safe, innocuous scholarship, and having sidetracked the literati (*shih*) from both patriotism and science.

One of the central problems for twentieth-century Chinese intellectuals, and a problem which seems to me to remain unresolved, has been, and apparently is, the formulation of a "new" alternative to government service that will satisfy the requirements of being a morally justifiable endeavor which promotes

93. E.g., Chao I (1727–1814), Wang Nien-sun (1744–1832).

94. E.g., Hui Tung (1697–1758), Chiang Sheng (1721–99), Tai Chen (1724–77), Tuan Yü-ts'ai (1735–1815), Chang Hsueh-ch'eng (1738–1801), Chiao Hsun (1763–1820).

95. Wu Ching-tzu, *The Scholars*, 540.

96. Liang Ch'i-ch'ao, more dogmatically and just as simplistically, suggested concern with textual matters as a reason why Ch'ing arts and literature did not develop. Cf. Immanuel C. Y. Hsü, trans., Liang Ch'i-ch'ao, *Intellectual Trends in the Ch'ing Period*, 120.

97. E.g., Tai Chen.

and defends "our culture" as well as the general good of "our nation." This concern seems to lie behind the efforts of all the major thinkers of the twentieth century who are heir to the literati tradition, whether their aim has been to reinvigorate philosophically the Neo-Confucian teachings of Ch'eng-Chu and Wang Yang-ming, to transform historical understanding of the values manifest in the Chinese tradition, to incorporate Western ideas to effect a new synthesis, or to find refuge in cultural activities as an aesthete. Devoting one's efforts to science evades, rather than resolves, the problem, and government policy in the People's Republic, as in the K'ang-hsi and Ch'ien-lung reigns, seeks to deny the existence of any tension between intellectuals and the state.

Historians of China in the twentieth century generally grant the applicability of the term *intelligentsia*, that is, intellectuals in a narrow sense of comparatively small numbers of the educated elite who experience uncertainty, are critical of prevailing modes, dissent from conventions, and are somewhat negative in their assessment of current politics but mainly positive in their sense of responsibility to the public good—men who are "alienated" from government, but not, they hope, from society at large. This definition, and thus the terms *intelligentsia* and *intellectuals* (again, in a narrow sense), are also applicable to many of the men from the eleventh through the seventeenth centuries discussed in the preceding pages. To the extent the term *intelligentsia* connotes *revolutionary*, however, it is inappropriate, because the men who did grapple with the dilemma have seldom been perceived as advocates of radical change and usually portrayed themselves as preservers or recoverers. They were, by and large, literati (*shih*) rather than officials (*tai-fu*), and literati from the Sung dynasty on derived their social status as much from their relation to "our culture" (*wen*) as from government institutions or economic advantages. For them to have proposed a true "cultural revolution," rather than mere political reform, or even intellectual reorientation, would have been to put their place as the elite of the society into jeopardy.

Their collective strategy contrasts with a Western European parallel to the development in seventeenth-century China of a new alternative to government service. In the second half of the seventeenth century in England, the "new" scientific interests were found to satisfy commonly held social and religious values,[98] and attracted increasing attention from members of the intellectual elite, especially Puritans.[99] They were, in effect, an alienated minority who in the latter part of the century were, for personal as well as political reasons, turning away from the usually highly evaluated careers in government or clergy and who also were not content to devote themselves to commercial pursuits.[100] There was a need to be of use outside of the established channels. Ku Yen-wu·

98. Cf. Robert K. Merton, *Science, Technology and Society in Seventeenth Century England.*
99. Merton, 112–15.
100. Merton, 81, pointed out that one of the ways in which Puritans were reinforced in their favoring of science was " . . . their hostility toward the existing class structure which

and Fang I-chih were not scientists. My point is that, more than any similarity of method,[101] the motivations for their endeavors had similarities to those of the men involved in the "new" science of seventeenth-century Europe.

There was, then, a recurrent pattern of innovators effecting changes in intellectual outlook from the eleventh to twentieth century in China. The development of a new intellectual orientation in seventeenth-century China represents the temporarily successful working out of a morally justifiable, socially relevant alternative to government service when the available courses were perceived as corrupt. Huang and Ku and Fang, each in his own way, was unwilling to be a bitter gourd, fit only to hang up but not to be used. Francis Bacon, their near contemporary, who also was prominent in redirecting his society's intellectual outlook and endeavors, distinguished the intentions of such men well.

> For men have entered into a desire of learning and knowledge, sometimes upon a natural curiosity and inquisitive appetite; sometimes to entertain their minds with variety and delight; sometimes for ornament and reputation; and sometimes to enable them to victory of wit and contradiction; and most time for lucre and profession; and seldom sincerely to give a true account of their gift of reason, to the benefit and use of men.[102]

---

limited and hampered their participation in political control," before the Revolution. Merton did not explore the need to discover an "alternative" as a motive for the "shift" to science, although he passingly supplies data that support such an interpretation. Without, it seems to me, explaining why, he noticed that "many, who hitherto might have turned to theology or rhetoric or philology, were directed, through the subtle, largely unperceived and newly-arisen predisposition of society, into scientific channels." (p. 95)

101. Cf. Hu Shih, "The Scientific Spirit and Method in Chinese Philosophy," in Charles A. Moore, ed., *The Chinese Mind*.

102. Francis Bacon, *Advancement of Learning, Works* (Ellis, Heath, Spedding, eds.), vol. 6, 134.

Chinese Text of the "Seven Solutions"

也人生有一故人知我而我何憾乎請與子研絅席同食晈溫

古昔考當世暮必稽其所得間數日可出等少年一縱樂焉又

明日閉關以爲常帥初故人從之抱蜀子於是乎不悲矣

稽古堂文集卷上終

枵腹而啜墨則汝得罪于名教矣我等拔來報往自在所免獨毋好奇過當耳烈何必蹈東海而死廉何必韋褐至爛高何必以足加帝敖何必倨鍛不起介何必僦廡爲人賃舂節何必鑿坏踰垣曾何必不知馬足穎何必知雞肋解黃絹敏何必賦鸚鵡文不加點遲何必一紀三都遠何必築土室納飲食達何必裸裎入狗竇豪何必投轄强灌人侈何必費萬錢筯不下儉何必一裘三十年書何必縣國門一字不能增損門何必使人號爲登龍適至其所當爲則爲之而已豈定爲世人所喜與爲世人所笑而後可哉抱蜀子瞿然長跪而歎曰世之勸我飲酒與不飲酒者非知我者也世之勸我讀書與不讀書者非知我者

而抱蜀子何臥未起也强起復病披髮而出故人知其沉涸也

正色而譙讓之曰吾與汝少相期以古人今雖不得志則古人

不得志之所為可則也何必憤激以自老耶歎貧且賤結納不

為人所重意欲絕交而又不閉門處于謝客結客之間更與市

中酒徒作使笑傲以飾其慷慨而慷慨終不能隱也汝將謂人

以汝為和平平哉汝又謂此可以藏其身而免為善之訕乎哉

我日斯邁時不可追少壯忽忽即為白首不及此時覃精經史

聞風化雨以待後世將何待乎況遇合有時終非沒沒者比耶

且汝以絕世之材又能好學博雅多聞偶爾游衍尚不失其蘊

藉後生白袷烏衣無愚管之一得動欲頃步效之坐荒其學使

之發香脫之臘之殽核維旅座客或惡其淈厚而抱蜀子適饊
樂筋大嚼執辔畢之未嘗不使弊屑者笑也行酒入又卽巳故
僇僇矣于是呼團扇呼六赤指隅席能度曲者屬其歌吹笛或
笙或管者和之更使撥鵾絃繁聲促柱令人心動倡優迭進淫
嘗百狀履舄交錯微聞薌澤雖不能一石然亦不三升足也及
醉而起舞抱蜀子叩枻高歌欲賦詩而無與俱者又不自知其
何以悲矣聽客散相呼明日復治博具何所又見使酒者不得
意於座中則歐人于道抱蜀子益以黯然徒步而歸夜行無語
疾風中人返邸舍坐戶下老奴艮久乃起開門至庾而臥臥又
不能寐長夜展轉憂從中來謂之何哉翼日有帥初故人來訪

昔上立己文集

三七

少年襏衣白紈簪玉導與錄事七香車並驅焉寶袜文綦襪帷

可窺也見抱蜀子而招之曰何爲冒塵雌而儲與於此抱蜀于

語之故少年曰及時爲樂耳須富貴何時且世之極富貴者始

殫筋力肆苞苴以圖之一日縣金印肘後動卽犯法下獄盤水

加劍則又何樂焉孰如得酒且歌耶書生苦甚吾當爲若澆磊

塊也遂爲抱蜀子謝纜栗先生與老人而去諸客又欲因抱蜀

子以飲少年相與摻袪而行至河干則維青翰以俟久矣榜

歌發放乎中流顧舟中多不識者抱蜀子不問姓名而上坐其

兩厓陜而修曲倚檻與抱蜀子立拱者數數而抱蜀子未嘗見

也已而張鼓吹聲流瀨載博山爇沈水老柳爲之起舞好風爲

女子哉抱朴子曰古有黄白之術必仙人而後可得也世人好
此故求之而終不至仙人不必好此故可致而終不爲且果有
能得黄白者何不自作富家翁而尚出游于世以利告人也圖
寶老人曰此猶末技請言其上者則清靜之道存焉其至也可
以白日拔宅乘飛鶴而上天吾子豈無意乎吾有師在太華之
陰年五百有餘歲殂松絶粒顏若處子駕衞叔向之白雲車負
李克之五嶽圖化琴高之鯉吹子晉之笙當引子往求之抱朴
子曰吾見世之談神仙者皆游于富貴之門豈富貴乃可求神
仙乎富貴如秦皇漢武不能免于沙邱茂陵而況以蓬萊藍縷
求不死之藥耶圖寶老人又大欲扶其說說未出忽有數輕婿

天門呼長精吸玄泉正謂此也自此以後陽文南威列以百數
比御而無損則亦至適矣而即鑠以熄目鬢髮御病延年則人
間之藥莫加于此可隨吾壺中受之抱蜀子曰久已知世之有
此絕術也然家有細君善妒庸詎使綽約靡麗紛紛徘徊於左
右乎日摔胡而色于室耳且吾方謀饕殄之不暇又烏能效曼
倩日以上賜取少婦于長安中耶囷窶老人曰王陽徵名衣囊
鴟夷累致千金豈果拮据然乎古又有貧焉不移壘而石可爲
鉼鐐也赤仄可以爲鏐鐚也人亦患貧困耳故妻孥無所發憤
而嫉之亦其情也果金多而厚易珠玉之飾文綺錦毳丹珀異
珍粲然在前諒君家之詳語者亦必攺容焉況丈夫不難辭兒

居瑯瑯而不流寓也流寓之後始得南陽隆中一抱膝地知不

逯武侯尚未知抱膝何所也我瞻四方蹙蹙靡所騁先生雖有

薔蔡又烏能爲今日決與罔寢老人倨倨睤際我曰子誠長于計

人間事者亦能知世以外乎吾壺中有藥焉可以攄子之苑結

而開子之旦明也子庸服諸抱蜀子曰小子雖病不喜服藥以

世人之藥皆生病者也不如勿藥爲中醫今吾視公其飲上池

之水者乎必有禁方可得聞與罔寢老人曰人各睞睞自乖其

道箴縷縩之間攠捴呪齲之郄固不越其身而謀也深深旣

獲者欲可從玄牝之門豈浮琴無裏哉吾與子踽踽而坐不湙

旬黃庭紫闕可以豁焉周宣王郊聞採薪之歌所云巾金巾入

子太息曰過時艱難出既不若古人隱亦不能如古人也知幾
當斷我豈瞑瞑哉然業為世俗之人矣病且文弱不能躬耕婚
嫁未畢兒女沾沾似不能免又無同志入山者烟火不能相望
了然一廬吾雖大布藜藿土著之好能無疑焉曰好施以德之
則必一飯與之同飽而後可彼皆飽而我盡矣曰聲威以服之
則必多收武夫壯士以聚處是一日優游而行軍之費也且山
中之人盱目駴耳而有司文法又拘牽及之甯可以行軍法擅
殺人耶如此則有四塞之險而不能守猶之處康衢也今賊固
已巢穴於此矣往聞之曰小亂居城市大亂居山林天下其在
亂不亂之間乎苟全性命是必有道矣當以武侯之知亦不能

以仍仍書生外無所引重內無所援藉一痛哭而不見信則三

木瑱當足躓趑坍已耳又何如粃食糲衣之為消搖也纘粟先

生撻策跼跼諏然羞告曰古賢者進不足以得志則退而有以

自處今子負志偃蹇獨逢然于茲土非高士也聞子有山在濱

霍之隈其外達劇岐皆嶺谷嶄嶒絕壑懸度所謂一夫守之萬

夫莫當險阻四塞足以禦賊矣其中沃野數十里菽桑麻畜狗

彘如近郊然網野獸采野蔬足以供億此隆中高臥之地也子

既不合時而時又不用子山木膏火還自衒與何不避世長遯

入山而隱蟬蛻埃塩儻然攘木茹皮之萌相時而出無不可者

乃復樸遬市中將欲坐視江南之匈匈乎吾請為子占之抱蜀

嚳與鮑文長

三六

榮罰之故直陳極諫言人所不敢言者也乃一劇切及君身而
言者危矣一指陳及君之左右而言者更危矣其言者不過取
天下不甚切膚之利病掊撼論列若爲忠直然者庶幾得達黃
屋而柄者容之且自許伏闕上書以來而上書者無所不至矣
市井凸俚未嘗一誦詩書知咫尺之義苟得薄愚索息倏對則
即走長安而上書老吏熟習科條則上書腐儒擯困無所復之
亦上書董胥奸僧掉捎罔上以私陷人與大家悁忿而角不勝
則亦上書上書至今日而更迹是者君子恥之況乎朝奏暮召
非猶古之恨相見晚也彼固有其畜幸通呼吸完幕繫而後外
伏闕徼冗望之福焉一旦重礙爲嘗所輻若董亦未嘗逃也徒

某先生處何事我無此顏又安能巧言如簧動貴人聽邪吾甯

處陋巷安於無用耳程勇公橫肱奮然而腐聲曰於傺卑哉何

爲此浮沈流俗之語也方今聖明旴食求賢良方正以輔出治

力破文法與古盛舉匹夫之微可以進言草莽之謠直達大內

以于之明古今審成敗通達國體目天下內外攘攘如此何不

養爲一書極陳利病以効忠於國家而乃懷質确守木强撝擘

憂時以處不可謂傑也抱蜀子詻詻欲語曰悵悵曰今欲力破

文法而下奉行之仍爲故事耳今欲與古盛舉而下因循之止

成一弊端耳夯求進言雖得上進而下之情終不得上達也

夫踰分冒眛自扞殊死以上則必發憤於當世邪正是非名實

以知人愛才爲事哉抱蜀子曰我固知之熟矣輕診之未服霧
穀飾劍佩車澤可鑑從僮僕呼劇驂則與冠蓋爭馳四市皆避
之不知其所從來也賢者處湫隘門無車馬空蹻羸益出遊而
無招飲者則一壘之人始鄙之繼誶之親戚易而侮之嗟乎風
已如此雖欲不勢利何可得耶果其通三公交五侯寒暑請造
燕而狎之習遷除論朝事久而縉紳喜與之談又未嘗不驚于
他貴人之前也因人成事藉交報仇可以使富人供我可以使
鄉人畏我可以使不根浮慕之士影而附我雄乎哉然我見公
卿之門與閽者爭肉好而通一刺比比也不則坐廡下徘徊焉
此固難爲坐矣長裾盤辟動引所聞謂得之於某先生又嘗爲

橫世君變色而作誇嚴自詫曰丈夫生世上將以有用于斯世

也拘拘者何爲吾見有俄頃而散千金又俄頃而致千金者可

不畏哉古稱輕俠慷慨之士未有不廣結交者其結交未有不

先公卿者席戶而多長者車轍布衣而致結駟連騎甯戚揚于

齊桓洛陽顯于吳公食駃騠投夜光不以爲侈彈鋏掃相門

不以爲羞誠慨夫貧賤之不能自著而遊大人以成名也今挾

醫卜之常術焉三五之賤伎尚能讙於公卿以取厚利況能操

觚持長短者乎于何不少降其倨慢稍一委蛇上則可以廣令

聞下亦不失于餬口彼四方貧賤讀書之士不能爲人損益可

勿與也必欲抱膝嘯歌以待世有知已折節而好之今天下誰

矣卽欲五門讙譁但聞豚聲誰爲我埋此哉至若賈其所藏則

我生平無所玩好又嘗然于世人之徒以玩好爲好古也椎而

且簡居處麤具雖盡粥之不得鉤金若載書三十乘而舍之又

矣載爲且所爲彝鼎敦牟卮匜及他環玦璏珮之屬得之或不

數金可以稱數百金曰此秦漢三代器也果其藏之獨不十百

於魚鹽卽起而屏面笑曰魚鹽諸利而止如是則不若千澤黿

緣之爲得矣不若爲人處事受謝之爲得矣不若莫夜游手之

爲得矣又不若負大力者白晝攫之之爲得矣握轞氏竊聽之

曰子所言皆非子所能也此等智盡能索猶恐不足而于方咮

歌先王其不以子爲棄物者幾幾也吾且以子固無此肺腸耳

譽省而間中庸凸皆責子以好施親故自視不足則望子以緩

急往來聞子名而投刺者又期子以醉呼舟旋此不能不衣焦

不申者也子盍講計研之術乎出舉與生計與錢通近皆詭隨

徒為所軋耳逐什一徵貴賤盡賈其所藏圖書琴鐔玩好諸物

權會魚鹽其羡不爽更能家食約醬一切交遊皆謝之不數年

可以殖矣抱蜀子閔然吁曰治生之策儒者所急然其如儻惕

不備何旦起問困入若干蛛出若干已不憚煩不得不使藏獲

計之至乾沒十半而擿觸其償求數董廉如鮑叔亦已難矣當

吾與客噱談而使持其計出入之簿求求左驗批察米鹽靡密

能不厭而撝之及覺其雕悍則又濡忍始卜急怒甚少頃或怨

數千篇一踰年而又不適時用則又編新得第者之章句而誦
之我以爲莫苦若矣好古者計千秋逢時者計一日斯固迂談
不敢望人信而從之獨今天下童習白紛于此而不得售者尚
數百倍于好古之士彼一時高第享名者顧未必有一日揣摩
者也則又何居吾道其果非耶仇之罟之又妄辭即抑亦談此
可自贖邪握軹氏曰逢倍士不必爲子憂多盤也聰明過于人
者事一日即可當彌月安用朝夕苦此乎又安知其不一朝一
夕而畢此乎抱蜀子曰我實不能苦此而朝夕未嘗不苦也君
將何以免我苦握軹氏前撫几曰吾知于所愈愈者故鄉喪亂
田園荒蕪廉謹之家流寓困乏子又好函義遇人隱厚舒緩無

可趣而至號鍾之聲再鼓而得以子之材何此爲難乃復高務

經史追琢詞賦儷聲蔚氣發爲長篇雖千卷充棟無取于世人

之目也三冬篆刻餓於銖儒五經鑽厲不若牧豕人生因便以

取青紫其術甚易安用博洽苦難羈縻歲月聊且世之人羣以

便近爲業有好古者視之如仇賢子弟稍嚮風慕義而嚴父怒

兄卽詈而拘之塾中則子何取焉彼夫談制義以爲名者多矣

何必經史詞賦也吾願子貶其道閉門揣摩之何如抱蜀子逌

然曰我固然君之說也但性各有好斷不可强若以今人所爲

長業者則是鼓篋勿肆宵雅也諷籀勿九千字也霖雨勿假漢

書也刻燭叩鉢勿賦詩登高勿爲大夫也獨咕嗶一卷誦制義

令今之人一寓目乎時不遇矣求為上容即突涕滑稽庸詎與
人合與家貧不能好客有客至浮臾三豆好我者不罪其纖也
未嘗敢談先王尚古學況以此勸人耶意有所至則發嘯歌嘯
歌而悲人莫之知也間行市中遇逢偓士與握輒氏於道執手
未言望橫世君驅塵而來下車長揖時有繽栗先生垂簾於市
又假寓此分半席以賣藥者罔寶老人也程勇公來問卜見諸
子立日中呼延入坐坐定皆欲與抱蜀子言見抱蜀子顏色懲
墨心甚不懌或曰子何悲苦至于是吾黨欲有所勸子子能聽
乎抱蜀子曰唯唯否否敬將聞命逢偓士曰子豈非以不遇故
與子毋郵我之說也我以子為不攻苦逢時之業耳邯鄲之步

室周章不儔可歌可哭自得鼕如豈有所汲汲戚戚乎年二十

自以爲龍門此時周歷天下矣局促里巷老牖下胡爲者乃載

書籍遊江淮吳越間云自總角隨尊人經棧道見峨眉下三峽

又復過武夷太姥已北入京師馳驅齊魯之郊頗注意名山大

川有所興懷乃者東遊浩然不足當意矣處鄉曲時以天下必

有如古人者過古人者今見人物猶之山川也知已不過數人

斷斷名稱大畧材智相將耳於是歸擬入山大奮其力合古今

俯仰著爲一書而里中難作繼以寇賊往來殺掠兵火不絕流

離金陵豈得已哉家世好善而善不可爲家世好學而不學者

嫉之雖客居屑屑譏訐日至有所著作或傷時事則焚其草敢

漳浦黃先生文集

三三

之言人生重得故人也祖攝家故有七體而七發自仲
宜以下皆以繁華榮廬說高士此雖至愚亦知其不能
動矣又爲聲協比麗所掩使人誦之無所感發故變傳
記古文法別立一體以自解云
抱蜀子少倜儻有大志年九歲能賦詩屬文十二誦六經長益
博學徧覽史傳負笈從師下帷山中通陰陽筭數天官望氣之
學窮律呂之源講兵法之要意欲爲古之學者遇時以沛天下
而未之遘焉性疎達善得大意而彌記爲難久之署總篇自恨
甚恨材知不及古人而復身弱多病也又善臨池取二王之法
好圍棋舞劍少知彈琴吳歌雜技之末有所見輒欲爲之居一

七解丁丑答客作

七解者為七客以解其悲也悲不可解而終解于故人

曾与堂文集　卷

三尸

A Genealogical Chart for FANG I-CHIH

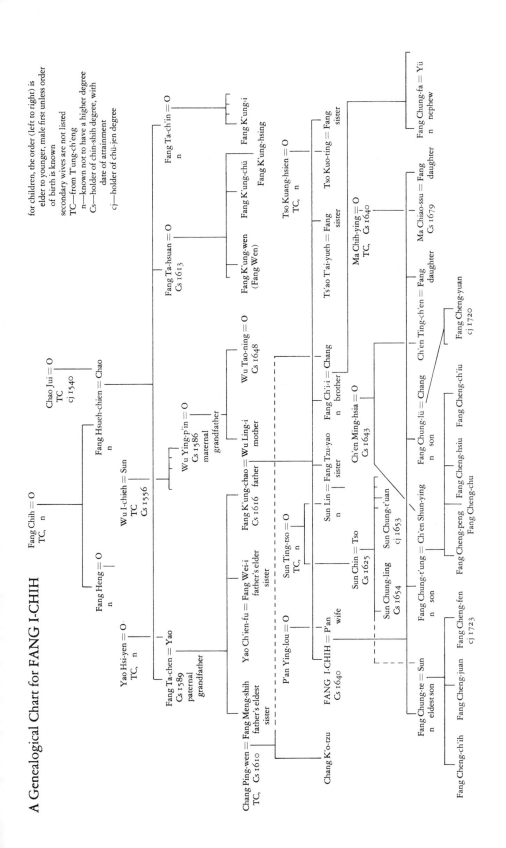

for children, the order (left to right) is
elder to younger, male first unless order
of birth is known
secondary wives are not listed
TC—from T'ung-ch'eng
n—known not to have a higher degree
Cs—holder of chin-shih degree, with
date of attainment
cj—holder of chü-jen degree

A Chronology of Events
Related to the Life of Fang I-chih

		before taking up appointment		
1626	in T'ung-ch'eng		Huang Tsung-hsi's father and others put to death in Peking	6
1627	in T'ung-ch'eng		T'ien-ch'i T'ien-ch'i emperor dies and Wei Chung-hsien commits suicide	7
1628	founds literary society with friends in T'ung-ch'eng	father appointed to Ministry of War	Ch'ung-chen Fu-she begins to be organized	1
1629		father in office at Peking	Manchu raiding force approaches Peking	2
1630	lives in Nanking	father in office great-grandmother Chao dies(?)	great meeting of Fu-she at Nanking	3
1631	meets Ch'en Tzu-lung	grandfather dies father retires to enter mourning		4
1632	visits Hang-chou returns to T'ung-ch'eng	first son, Fang Chung-te, is born	great meeting of Fu-she near Soochow	5
1633	lives in Nanking fails provincial examination (?)			6
1634	lives in T'ung-ch'eng returns to Nanking in autumn	women and children of Fang family move to Nanking	uprising in T'ung-ch'eng in eighth month	7
1635	lives in Nanking		fighting near T'ung-ch'eng ends	8
1636	fails provincial examination (?)		Manchus proclaim Ch'ing dynasty	9
1637	writes "Seven Solutions"			10
1638	goes to Hu-kuang	father appointed governor of Hu-kuang third son, Fang Chung-lü, is born nephew, Fang Chung-fa, is born in Hu-kuang		11
1639	in Hu-kuang returns to Nanking and passes provincial examination in autumn	as governor, father campaigns against bandit armies father impeached, arrested, and imprisoned in Peking	men associated with Fu-she publish Manifesto against Juan Ta-ch'eng in Nanking Manchus raid into Chihli	12

1640	in Peking to aid his father in spring passes metropolitan examination and becomes a *chin-shih*	father in prison		13
1641	in Peking works on manuscript for *Comprehensive Refinement* and *Notes on Principles of Things*	father banished to Shaohsing, Chekiang	T'ung-ch'eng attacked by Chang Hsienchung's army	14
1642	in Peking works on manuscript		T'ung-ch'eng surrounded by Chang Hsienchung's army	15
1643	serves in Hanlin Academy edits his *Comprehensive Refinement* in twelfth month writes preface to *Notes on Principles of Things*	in third month, released from banishment, father returns to Peking and has audience with emperor	Ming Ch'ung-chen	16
1644	serves in Hanlin Academy captured by Li Tzu-ch'eng's troops released and goes home to T'ung-ch'eng reaches Nanking in fifth month	father appointed censor	Ch'ing Shun-chih Peking captured by Li Tzu-ch'eng in third month Peking occupied by Ch'ing armies and new Ch'ing emperor enthroned	1
1645	goes to Fukien		Nanking taken by Ch'ing troops	2
1646	in Canton goes to western Kwangtung to participate in new Yung-li court	brother-in-law, Sun Lin, executed by Ch'ing troops in Fukien		3
1647	declines further appointment to Yung-li court lives in mountains near Kuei-lin takes up residence in village near P'ing-lo, Kwangsi		first year of Ming Yung-li reign period	4
1648	in village near P'ing-lo			5
1649	in village near P'ing-lo	brother, Fang Ch'i-i, dies	.	6
1650	goes north and lives among Miao in southern Hu-kuang		Kuei-lin captured by Ch'ing troops Ch'ü Shih-ssu executed	7

	near P'ing-lo in winter, tonsures himself to escape Ch'ing troops arrested, released as a monk by Ch'ing general		Ku Yen-wu adopts Manchu hair style (?)
1651	at Yun-kai temple at Wu-chou, Kwangsi		8
1652	goes north to Chiu-chiang, northern Kiangsi, and meets with father writes preface to *Tung-hsi chün* at Wu-lao feng, Kiangsi		9
1653	goes to Nanking, takes Chueh-lang Tao-sheng as his master, and lives in retirement at Kao-tso temple, Nanking		10
1654.	at Chü-kuan temple near Hsin-ch'eng, Kiangsi, by winter		11
1655	at a temple near Hsin-ch'eng enters mourning for father	father dies	12
1656	in mourning near T'ung-ch'eng		13
1657	in mourning near T'ung-ch'eng		14
1658	goes to a temple near Hsin-ch'eng		15
1659	at Ta-han shan temple, Hsin-ch'eng	Chueh-lang Tao-sheng dies	16
1660	at Lin-shan temple, Hsin-ch'eng works on compiling *Yao-ti Roasts Chuang Tzu*		17
1661	at Lin-shan temple		Shun-chih 18
1662	takes charge of Nan-ku temple at Hsin-ch'eng		K'ang-hsi 1 Yung-li emperor executed in Yunnan
1663	visits Ch'ing-yuan temple at Chi-an, Kiangsi, for internment ceremony for former abbot		2
1664	becomes abbot at Ch'ing-yuan completes *Yao-ti Roasts Chuang Tzu*	*Notes on Principles of Things* printed	3

1665	at Ch'ing-yuan temple		4
1666	at Ch'ing-yuan temple	*Comprehensive Refinement* printed	5
1667	travels to Hsin-ch'eng and Fukien		6
1668	at Ch'ing-yuan		7
1669	at Ch'ing-yuan visits Shou-shan temple at T'ai-ho, Kiangsi		8
1670	sixtieth birthday, at Ch'ing-yuan (?)		9
1671	leaves Ch'ing-yuan in summer dies (suicide?) in boat near Wan-an, Kiangsi	*Fu-shan wen-chi* printed	10

Bibliography

The two most important published collections of Fang I-chih's miscellaneous prose writings are the *Fu-shan wen-chi ch'ien pien* and the section devoted to him in the *T'ung-ch'eng Fang shih ch'i tai i shu*.

The compilation and printing of the *Fu-shan wen-chi ch'ien pien* (Earlier Part of the Prose Collection of Fu-shan) was completed in 1671 or so, just prior to Fang's death, and seems never to have been republished.[1] Sometimes referred to as the *Fu-shan chi* and the *Fu-shan ch'ien chi*, it is in ten *chüan*, which are divided as follows: the first is called "Chi-ku t'ang ch'u chi" 稽古堂初集 ("Initial Collection from Study Antiquity Hall"); the second and third are "Chi-ku t'ang erh chi" 二集 ("Second Collection from Study Antiquity Hall"); these first three *chüan* contain writings from his Nanking years, through 1639; the fourth, fifth, and sixth are called "Man-yü ts'ao" 曼寓草 ("Drafts from the Handsome Dwelling") and were written when Fang was in Peking from 1640 to 1644; *chüan* 7–9 are "Ling wai kao" 嶺外稿 ("Drafts Written beyond the Mountains") and include material written in Kwangtung and Kwangsi between 1646 and 1650; the tenth *chüan* is "Yao-t'ung fei kao" 猺峝廢稿 ("Drafts Written while out of Office in Yao-t'ung"), that is, among the Miao tribesmen on the Hunan-Kwangsi border, and contains writings from 1648–50. There apparently is a copy of the *Fu-shan wen-chi ch'ien pien* in the National Library in Peking. A blueprint of that copy is held in the Academia Sinica Library in Taiwan, and it is that imperfect blueprint copy which I have consulted and to which reference is made.

The *T'ung-ch'eng Fang shih ch'i tai i shu* (Literary Inheritance from Seven Generations of the Fang Family of T'ung-ch'eng) was compiled in the nineteenth century by Fang Ch'ang-han (1827–97) and printed in 1888, probably in T'ung-ch'eng. As the title suggests, it is a collection of selected writings by seven members of the Fang family: Fang I-chih's great-grandfather, Fang Hsueh-chien; grandfather Fang Ta-chen; father, Fang K'ung-chao; Fang I-chih; his son Fang Chung-lü; grandson Fang Cheng-yuan; and great-grandson Fang Chang-teng. Fang I-chih's writings are presented under three titles. The first is "Chi-ku t'ang wen-chi" ("Collected Prose from Study Antiquity Hall"), which is two *chüan* of pieces selected from all ten *chüan* of the *Fu-shan wen-chi ch'ien pien*. The second title is "Hsiang yen" 嚮言, and is not by Fang I-chih but

---

1. The *Fu-shan wen-chi hou pien* (Later Part of the Prose Collection of Fu-shan) has never been published.

by his older contemporary, Ch'ien Ch'ien-i (1582–1664), who published it in 1643 in *chüan* 23–24 of his *Mu-chai ch'u-hsueh chi*.[2] The third title attributed to Fang I-chih in the *Ch'i tai i shu* is "Hsi yü hsin pi" 膝寓信筆 ("Veritable Jottings from Room for My Kness"), a series of informal notes written during his Nanking years and not available anywhere else. The *T'ung-ch'eng Fang shih ch'i tai i shu* is relatively rare; I have consulted the copy in the Harvard-Yenching Library in Cambridge.

The text of the "Seven Solutions" ("Ch'i chieh") is printed in the third *chüan* of the *Fu-shan wen-chi ch'ien pien* and at the end of the first *chüan* of the "Chi-ku t'ang wen-chi" in the *Ch'i tai i shu*. There are some orthographic and other differences between the two texts, as indicated in the annotation accompanying the "Seven Solutions" translation. The text that is reproduced here is that found in the *Ch'i tai i shu*.

The only significant collection of Fang I-chih's poems is in *T'ung-ch'eng Fang shih shih chi* (Edited Poems by the Fang Family of T'ung-ch'eng), which was compiled late in the Chia-ch'ing reign (1797–1820) and printed in 1821. It includes six *chüan* of Fang I-chih's poetry written before 1650. I have consulted the copy in the Bibliothèque Nationale, Paris.

In addition to the *Fu-shan wen-chi ch'ien pien*, four other manuscripts by Fang I-chih have been printed as books. The *Wu li hsiao chih* (Notes on Principles of Things) was first printed in twelve *chüan* in 1664 and has been republished several times, including an 1884 edition as well as twentieth-century typeset editions. The *Wu li hsiao chih* was written as part of the *T'ung ya* (Comprehensive Refinement), which was printed separately in 1666 in 52 *chüan*. There was also a 1666 printing of the *Yao-ti p'ao Chuang* (Monk Yao-ti Roasts Chuang Tzu), which I have not seen, but which is held at the library of the Academia Sinica in Taiwan. The *Yao-ti p'ao Chuang* appeared in a new edition published in 1932 in Ch'eng-tu by Mei-tzu-lin 美子林. The 1932 edition, according to Hou Wai-lu,[3] is not complete (it lacks the preface, introduction, and the three general discussions), but the reduced version was made more widely available when it was reprinted by the I-wen yin-shu-kuan, Taipei, in 1975. Finally, one of Fang I-chih's previously unpublished manuscripts, the *Tung hsi chün*, was printed for the first time in 1962 in Peking.

An extensive, and presumably exhaustive, list of Fang I-chih's extant manuscripts, unpublished as well as published, twenty-four titles in all, is given in Hou Wai-lu, *Chung-kuo ssu-hsiang t'ung shih*, vol. 4, pp. 1123–24. Hou also mentioned some titles by Fang which are thought to be lost.

Listed below are the titles, with bibliographical details, of the books and articles cited in the notes. I have inserted the word "reprint" before the place of publication for books which were first published earlier than the date of the

2. Cf. Jung Chao-tsu, "Fang I-chih ho t'a te ssu-hsiang," 99.
3. Hou Wai-lu, *Chung-kuo ssu-hsiang t'ung shih*, vol. 4, 1123.

edition I cite; in some instances I have made a judgment that the edition I have cited is original in a significant sense and thus I have omitted denoting it as a "reprint." There are two abbreviations used in the Bibliography: SPPY indicates a book published in the *Ssu pu pei yao* 四部備要 series by Chung-hua in Shanghai in 1927–35; SPTK indicates a book published by the Commercial Press (Shang-wu) in Shanghai in three series from 1919 to 1936 under the general title of *Ssu pu ts'ung k'an* 四部叢刊. Both series have been republished in Taipei.

Araki, Kengo. "Confucianism and Buddhism in the Late Ming." In *The Unfolding of Neo-Confucianism*, 39–66, edited by W. T. deBary. New York: Columbia University Press, 1975.

Atwell, William S. "Ch'en Tzu-lung (1608–1647): A Scholar-Official of the Late Ming Dynasty." Ph.D. dissertation, Princeton University, 1974.

———. "From Education to Politics: The Fu She." In *The Unfolding of Neo-Confucianism*, 333–67, edited by W. T. deBary. New York: Columbia University Press, 1975.

Bacon, Francis. *The Works of Francis Bacon*. Collected and edited by James Spedding, Robert Leslie Ellis, and Douglas Denon Heath. 15 vols. Boston: Brown and Taggard, 1860–65.

Balazs, Etienne. *Chinese Civilization and Bureaucracy*. New Haven: Yale University Press, 1964.

———. *Political Theory and Administrative Reality in Traditional China*. London: School of Oriental and African Studies, 1965.

Beattie, Hilary J. "Land and Lineage in China: A Study of T'ung-ch'eng County, Anhwei, in the Ming and Ch'ing Dynasties." Ph.D. dissertation, Cambridge University, 1973.

Birch, Cyril, trans. *Stories from a Ming Collection: Translations of Chinese Short Stories Published in the Seventeenth Century*. Bloomington: Indiana University Press, 1959.

Bishop, John L. *The Colloquial Short Story in China: A Study of the San-Yen Collections*. Cambridge: Harvard University Press, 1965.

Burtt, E. A. *The Metaphysical Foundations of Modern Physical Science*. 1924, 1932; New York: Doubleday, 1954.

Busch, Heinrich. "The Tung-lin shu-yüan and Its Political and Philosophical Significance." *Monumenta Serica* 14 (1949–1955): 1–163.

Bush, Susan. *The Chinese Literati on Painting: Su Shih (1037–1101) to Tung Ch'i-ch'ang (1555–1636)*. Cambridge: Harvard University Press, 1971.

Cahill, James, ed. *The Restless Landscape*. Berkeley: University Art Museum, 1971.

Chan, Albert. "Peking at the Time of the Wan-li Emperor." *Second Biennial*

Conference Proceedings, *International Association of Historians of Asia*, Taipei, 1962: 119–147.

Chan kuo ts'e 戰國策. Reprint, Hong Kong: Shang-wu, 1963.

Chan, Wing-tsit, trans. *Instructions for Practical Living and Other Neo-Confucian Writings by Wang Yang-ming*. New York: Columbia University Press, 1963.

———. *Reflections on Things at Hand: The Neo-Confucian Anthology Compiled by Chu Hsi and Lü Tsu-ch'ien*. New York: Columbia University Press, 1967.

———. *The Way of Lao Tzu*. Indianapolis: Bobbs-Merrill, 1963.

———. "The Ch'eng-Chu School of Early Ming." In *Self and Society in Ming Thought*, 29–51, edited by W. T. deBary. New York: Columbia University Press, 1970.

Chang Chun-shu and Chang Hsueh-lun. "The World of P'u Sung-ling's *Liao-chai chih-i*: Literature and the Intelligentsia during the Ming-Ch'ing Dynastic Transition." *Journal of the Institute of Chinese Studies of the Chinese University of Hong Kong* 6:2 (1973): 401–23.

Chang Tai 張岱. *T'ao an meng i* 陶庵夢憶. Reprint, Taipei: K'ai-ming, 1957.

Chang Te-chün 張德鈞. "Fang I-chih 'Wu li hsiao chih' te che-hsueh ssu-hsiang" 方以智物理小識的哲學思想. *Che-hsueh yen-chiu* 1962, no. 3: 60–71.

Chang Tsai 張載. *Chang Heng-ch'ü wen-chi* 張橫渠文集. Reprint, Taipei: Shang-wu, 1965.

Chao Ch'i 趙岐. *San fu chueh lu* 三輔決錄, in *Shih chung ku i shu* 十種古逸書. Mei-jui-hsien, 1834.

Chao I 趙翼. *Nien-erh shih cha-chi* 廿二史劄記. Reprint, Taipei: Shih-chieh, 1971.

Ch'en Chen-hui 陳貞慧. *Shu shih ch'i tse* 書事七則, in *Chao-tai ts'ung-shu hsu-pien* 昭代叢書續編. Shih-k'ai t'ang, 1833.

Ch'en Shih-hsiang and Acton, Harold, trans. K'ung Shang-jen, *The Peach Blossom Fan*. Berkeley: University of California Press, 1976.

Ch'en T'ien 陳田. *Ming shih chi shih* 明詩紀事. Reprint, Taipei: Shang-wu, 1968.

Ch'en Yin-k'o 陳寅恪. "T'ao hua yuan chi p'ang-cheng" 桃花源記旁證. *Tsing-hua hsueh-pao* 11 (1936): 79–88.

Ch'en Yuan 陳垣. *Ch'ing ch'u seng cheng chi* 清初僧諍記. Peking: Chung-hua, 1962.

———. *Ming chi Tien Ch'ien fo-chiao k'ao* 明季滇黔佛教考. Peking: Chung-hua, 1962.

Ch'eng Hsi 程曦. *Mu-fei ts'ang hua k'ao p'ing* 木扉藏畫考評. Hong Kong: Lung-men, 1966.

Cheng Te-k'un. "Paintings as a Recreation in China: Some Hsi-pi Paintings in the Mu-fei Collection." *Journal of the Institute of Chinese Studies of the Chinese University of Hong Kong* 6:2 (1973): 357–400 and 50 plates.

Chi Liu-ch'i 計六奇. *Ming chi nan lueh* 明季南略. Reprinted in *Ming Ch'ing shih-liao hui-pien* 明清史料彙編. Taipei: Wen-hai, 1968.

———. *Ming chi pei lueh* 明季北略. Reprinted in *Ming Ch'ing shih-liao hui-pien* 明清史料彙編. Taipei: Wen-hai, 1968.

Chi Wen-fu 嵇文甫. *Wan Ming ssu-hsiang shih lun* 晚明思想史論. Chungking: Shang-wu, 1944.

Chiang Fan 江藩. *Kuo-ch'ao Han-hsueh shih-ch'eng chi* 國朝漢學師承記. SPPY.

Chiang Liang-fu 姜亮夫, ed. *Ch'ü Yuan fu chiao-chu* 屈原賦校註. Reprint, Hong Kong: Chung-hua, 1972.

Ch'ien Ch'eng-chih 錢澄之. *So chih lu* 所知錄. Reprint, Taipei: Shih-chieh, 1971.

———. *T'ien-chien chi* 田間集. Ch'ien shih hsueh-she, 1909.

Ch'ien Chi-po 錢基博. *Ming tai wen hsueh* 明代文學. Hong Kong: Shang-wu, 1964.

Ch'ien, Edward. "Chiao Hung and the Revolt against Ch'eng-Chu Orthodoxy." In *The Unfolding of Neo-Confucianism*, 271–303, edited by W. T. deBary. New York: Columbia University Press, 1975.

Ch'ien Mu 錢穆. *Chung-kuo chin san-pai nien hsueh-shu shih* 中國近三百年學術史. Reprint, Taipei: Shang-wu, 1966.

———. *Sung Ming li-hsueh kai-shu* 宋明理學概述. 2 vols. Reprint, Taipei: Chung-hua, 1962.

Chin shu 晉書. Compiled by Fang Hsuan-ling 房玄齡. 2 vols. In *Erh-shih-wu shih* 二十五史, Wu-ying tien 武英殿 edition, 1739. Reprint, Taipei: I-wen, 1956.

Chin T'ien-ko 金天翮. *Wan-chih lieh-chuan kao* 皖志列傳稿, in *Chung-kuo fang-chih ts'ung-shu* 239. Reprint, Taipei: Ch'eng-wen, 1974.

Ching, Julia. *To Acquire Wisdom: The Way of Wang Yang-ming*. New York: Columbia University Press, 1976.

———, trans. *The Philosophical Letters of Wang Yang-ming*. Columbia, South Carolina: University of South Carolina Press, 1973.

———. "Wang Yang-ming (1472–1529): A Study in 'Mad Ardour.'" *Papers on Far Eastern History* 3 (1971): 85–130.

Chou Liang-kung 周亮工. *Tu hua lu* 讀畫錄, in *Tu hua chai ts'ung-shu*. Reprint, Taipei: I-wen, 1968.

Chu Chi 朱偰. *Chin-ling ku-chi ming-sheng ying-chi* 金陵古蹟名勝影集. Shanghai: Shang-wu, 1936.

———. *Chin-ling ku-chi t'u k'ao* 金陵古蹟圖考. Shanghai: Shang-wu, 1936.

Chü Ch'ing-yuan 鞠清遠. "San kuo shih-tai te k'o" 三國時代的客. *Shih huo* 3 (1936): 161–65.

Chu Hsi 朱熹. *Chu Tzu ch'üan shu* 朱子全書. 1714 edition.

Chu Kuo-chen 朱國楨. *Huang Ming ta hsun chi* 皇明大訓記. Late Ming edition.

Chu Yen 朱偰. "Ming chi T'ung-ch'eng Chung-chiang she k'ao" 明季桐城中江杜考. *Kuo-li chung-yang yen-chiu yuan li-shih yü-yen so chi-kan* 1 (1930): 251–65.

Ch'ü T'ung-tsu. *Han Social Structure*. Seattle: University of Washington Press, 1972.

Ch'ü Yuan 屈原. *Ch'u Tz'u* 楚辭, in *Kuo-hsueh chi-pen ts'ung-shu* 國學基本叢書. Reprint, Taipei: Shang-wu, 1968.

Ch'üan Han-sheng 全漢昇. "Ming-Ch'ing chien Mei-chou pai-yin te shu-ju

Chung-kuo" 明清間美洲白銀的輸入中國. *Journal of the Institute of Chinese Studies of the Chinese University of Hong Kong* 2.1 (1969): 59–79.

Chuang Tzu tsuan chien 莊子纂箋. Reprint, Hong Kong: Tung-nan, 1963.

Ch'ung-chen ch'ang pien 崇禎長編. Shanghai, 1917.

Chung-kuo jen-min ta-hsueh Chung-kuo li-shih chiao yen-chiu shih 中國人民大學中國历史教研究室. *Chung-kuo tzu-pen chu-i meng-ya wen-t'i t'ao-lun chi* 中國資本主義萌芽問題討論集. 2 vols. Peking: San-lien, 1957.

Confucius (K'ung Tzu). *Lun yü*, in *Lun yü yin te* 論語引得. Peking: Harvard-Yenching Institute, 1940.

Couvreur, S., trans. *Li Ki, ou Mémoires sur les bienséances et les cérémonies*. Shanghai: Imprimerie de la Mission Catholique, 1913.

Crawford, Robert B. "The Biography of Juan Ta-ch'eng." *Chinese Culture* 6.2 (1965): 22–105.

——, Lamley, Harry M., and Mann, Albert B. "Fang Hsiao-ju in the Light of Early Ming Society." *Monumenta Serica* 15 (1956): 303–27.

Crump, J. I., Jr. *Intrigues: Studies of the Chan-kuo Ts'e*. Ann Arbor: University of Michigan Press, 1964.

——, trans. *Chan-Kuo Ts'e*. Oxford: Clarendon Press, 1970.

deBary, Wm. Theodore, et al. *The Unfolding of Neo-Confucianism*. New York: Columbia University Press, 1975.

——. "Chinese Despotism and the Confucian Ideal: A Seventeenth-Century View." In *Chinese Thought and Institutions*, 163–203, edited by John K. Fairbank. Chicago: University of Chicago Press, 1957.

——. "Individualism and Humanitarianism in Late Ming Thought." In *Self and Society in Ming Thought*, 145–247, edited by W. T. deBary. New York: Columbia University Press, 1970.

Dimberg, Ronald G. *The Sage and Society: The Life and Thought of Ho Hsin-yin*. Honolulu: University Press of Hawaii, 1974.

Dolby, William, trans. *The Perfect Lady by Mistake*. London: Elek, 1976.

Fang Hao 方豪. "Fang I-chih ho T'ao-shih shou-chüan chi ch'üan-wen" 方以智和陶詩手卷及全文. *Tung-fang tsa-chih* 7.7 (Jan. 1974), 26–29.

Fang Hung 方竑. "Fang Mi-chih hsien-sheng chih k'o-hsueh ching-shen chi ch'i Wu li hsiao chih" 方密之先生之科學精神及其物理小識. *Wen i ts'ung k'an* 文藝叢刊 1 (1934): 179–99.

Fang I-chih 方以智. *Fu-shan wen-chi ch'ien pien* 浮山文集前編. Probably 1671.

——. *Tung hsi chün* 東西均. Shanghai: Chung-hua, 1962.

——. *T'ung ya* 通雅. 1666.

——. *Wen chang hsin huo* 文章薪火, in *Chao tai ts'ung shu* 昭代叢書. Tao-kuang edition.

——. *Wu li hsiao chih* 物理小識. Kiangsi, 1664.

——. *Yao-ti p'ao Chuang* 藥地炮莊, in *Chuang-tzu chi-ch'eng ch'u-pien* 莊子集成初編. Reprint, Taipei: I-wen, 1975.

Feifel, Eugen, trans. "Pak Jiwon: Huan-hsi, Magic Entertainment in Jehol." *Oriens Extremis* 19 (1972): 143–53.

Feng Meng-lung 馮夢龍. *Ching-shih t'ung-yen* 驚世通言. Reprint, Hong Kong: Chung-hua, 1965.

———. *Hsing-shih heng-yen* 醒世恒言. 2 vols. Reprint, Hong Kong: Chung-hua, 1965.

———. *Ku chin hsiao-shuo* 古今小說. 6 vols. Reprint, Peking: Hsin Hua, 1955.

———. *Shan ko* 山歌, in *Ming Ch'ing min ko shih t'iao ts'ung-shu* 明清民歌時調叢書. Reprint, Peking Chung-hua, 1962.

———. *Shan ko* 山歌. Reprint, Taipei: Tung-fang, 1970.

Feng Shih-hua 馮時化. *Chiu shih* 酒史. Reprint, Taipei: I-wen, 1965.

Franke, Wolfgang. *The Reform and Abolition of the Traditional Chinese Examination System.* Cambridge, Mass.: East Asian Research Center, 1960.

Fu I-ling 傅衣凌. *Ming Ch'ing nung-ts'un she-hui ching-chi* 明清農村社會經濟. Peking: San-lien, 1961; Reprint, Kowloon: Shih-yung, 1972.

———. *Ming tai Chiang-nan shih-min ching-chi shih t'an* 明代江南市民經濟試探. Shanghai: Jen-min, 1957.

Gaillard, Louis, *Nankin d'alors et d'aujourd'hui: aperçu historique et géographique. Variétés Sinologiques* 23. Shanghai: La Mission Catholique, 1903.

Goodrich, L. Carrington, and Fang, Chao-ying, eds. *Dictionary of Ming Biography.* 2 vols. New York: Columbia University Press, 1976.

Graham, A. C. *Two Chinese Philosophers: Ch'eng Ming-tao and Ch'eng Yi-ch'uan.* London: Lund Humphries, 1958.

Greenblatt, Kristin Yü. "Chu-hung and Lay Buddhism in the Late Ming." In *The Unfolding of Neo-Confucianism*, 93–140, edited by W. T. deBary. New York: Columbia University Press, 1975.

Grieder, Jerome B. *Hu Shih and the Chinese Renaissance: Liberalism and the Chinese Revolution, 1917–1937.* Cambridge: Harvard University Press, 1970.

Grimm, Tilemann. "Ming Educational Intendants." In *Chinese Government in Ming Times*, 129–47, edited by Charles O. Hucker. New York: Columbia University Press, 1969.

Gulik, Robert H. van. *Sexual Life in Ancient China.* Leiden: Brill, 1961.

Han shu 漢書. Compiled by Pan Ku 班固. 12 vols. Reprint, Peking: Chung-hua, 1962.

Han Ta-ch'eng 韓大成. "Ming tai shang-p'in ching-chi te fa-chan yü tzu-pen chu-i te meng-ya" 明代商品經濟的發展與資本主義的萌芽. In *Ming Ch'ing she-hui ching-chi hsing-t'ai te yen-chiu* 明清社會經濟形態的研究, 1–102. Shanghai: Jen-min, 1957.

Hawkes, David, trans. *Ch'u Tz'u: The Songs of the South.* Boston: Beacon Press, 1962.

Henke, Frederick Goodrich. *The Philosophy of Wang Yang-ming.* Chicago: Open Court, 1916.

Hightower, J. R., trans. *The Poetry of T'ao Ch'ien*. Oxford: Clarendon Press, 1970.

———. "T'ao Ch'ien's 'Drinking Wine' Poems." In *Wen-lin: Studies in the Chinese Humanities*, 3–44, edited by Tse-tsung Chow. Madison: University of Wisconsin Press, 1968.

Ho Hsin-yin 何心隱. *Ho Hsin-yin chi* 何心隱集. Peking: Chung-hua, 1960.

Ho Liang-chün 何良俊. *Ssu-yu-chai ts'ung shuo che ch'ao* 四友齋叢說摘抄. Reprint, Ch'ang-sha: Shang-wu, 1937.

Ho Peng Yoke, Goh Thean Chye, David Parker. "Po Chü-i's Poems on Immortality." *Harvard Journal of Asiatic Studies* 34 (1974): 163–91.

Ho Ping-ti. *The Ladder of Success in Imperial China: Aspects of Social Mobility, 1368–1911*. Reprint, New York: John Wiley, 1964.

———. "Salt Merchants of Yang-chou." *Harvard Journal of Asiatic Studies* 17 (1954): 130–68.

Holzman, Donald. *La Vie et la pensée de Hi K'ang*. Leiden: Brill, 1957.

Hou Fang-yü 侯方域. *Chuang-hui t'ang chi* 壯悔堂集. *SPPY*.

Hou Han shu 後漢書. Compiled by Fan Ye 范曄. 12 vols. Reprint, Peking: Chung-hua, 1965.

Hou Wai-lu 侯外廬, et al. *Chung-kuo ssu-hsiang t'ung shih* 中國思想通史. vol. 4, parts 1 and 2. Peking: Jen-min, 1959–1960; and vol. 5. Peking: Jen-min, 1956.

———. "Fang I-chih—Chung-kuo te pai-k'o ch'üan-shu-p'ai ta che-hsueh-chia" 方以智—中國的百科全書派大哲學家. *Li-shih yen-chiu* (1957) no. 6, 1–21, and no. 7, 1–25.

Hsieh Chao-che 謝肇淛. *Wu tsa tsu* 五雜組. Reprint, Taipei: Hsin-hsing, 1971.

Hsieh Kuo-chen 謝國楨. *Huang Li-chou hsueh-p'u* 黃梨洲學譜. Reprint, Taipei: Shang-wu, 1967.

———. *Ku T'ing-lin hsueh-p'u* 顧亭林學譜. Shanghai: Shang-wu, 1957.

———. *Ming Ch'ing chih chi tang-she yun-tung k'ao* 明清之際黨社運動考. Reprint, Taipei: Shang-wu, 1967.

Hsin T'ang shu 新唐書. Compiled by Ou-yang Hsiu 歐陽修. 20 vols. Reprint, Peking: Chung-hua, 1975.

Hsu Dau-lin 徐道鄰. "Ming T'ai-tsu yü Chung-kuo chuan-chih cheng-ch'üan" 明太祖與中國專制政權 ("The First Ming Emperor and Chinese Despotism"). *Tsing Hua Journal of Chinese Studies* 8 (1970): 350–72.

Hsü, Immanuel C. Y., trans. Liang Ch'i-ch'ao, *Intellectual Trends in the Ch'ing Period*. Cambridge: Harvard University Press, 1959.

Hsu t'an chu 續談助, compiled by Chao Tsai-chih 晁載之, in *Shih-wan chüan lou ts'ung-shu*. Reprint, Taipei: I-wen, 1968.

Hsu Tzu 徐鼐. *Hsiao t'ien chi-chuan* 小腆紀傳. 2 vols. Reprint, Peking: Chung-hua, 1958.

———. *Hsiao t'ien chi nien fu k'ao* 小腆紀年附考. 2 vols. Reprint, Peking: Chung-hua, 1957.

Hsu wen-hsien t'ung k'ao 續文獻通考. Chekiang shu-chü, 1887.

Hu Shih. "The Scientific Spirit and Method in Chinese Philosophy." In *The Chinese Mind*, 104–31, edited by Charles A. Moore. Honolulu: University of Hawaii Press, 1967.

Hu Wei-tsung 胡維宗. *Shu yen ku shih ta ch'üan* 書言古事大全. Wan-li edition.

Huai-nan Hung-lieh chi chieh 淮南鴻烈集解. 2 vols. Reprint, Taipei: Shang-wu, 1969.

Huang Hsing-tseng 黃省曾. *Wu feng lu* 吳風錄, in *Po-ling hsueh shan* 百陵學山. Ch'ang-sha: Shang-wu, 1938.

Huang Jen-yü (Ray Huang) 黃仁宇. "Ts'ung 'San-yen' k'an wan Ming shang-jen" 從三言看晚明商人. *Journal of the Institute of Chinese Studies of the Chinese University of Hong Kong* 7.1 (1974): 133–54.

Huang, Ray. *Taxation and Government Finance in 16th Century Ming China*. Cambridge: Cambridge University Press, 1974.

———. "Fiscal Administration during the Ming Dynasty." In *Chinese Government in Ming Times*, 73–128, edited by Charles O. Hucker. New York: Columbia University Press, 1969.

———. "Ni Yuan-lu: 'Realism' in a Neo-Confucian Scholar-Statesman." In *Self and Society in Ming Thought*, 415–49, edited by W. T. deBary. New York: Columbia University Press, 1970.

Huang Tsung-hsi 黃宗羲. *Li-chou i-chu hui-k'an* 梨洲遺著彙刊. 2 vols. Taipei: Lung-yen, 1969.

———. *Ming ju hsueh an* 明儒學案. Reprint, Taipei: Shih-chieh, 1965.

———, Ch'üan Tsu-wang 全祖望, et al., *Sung Yuan hsueh an* 宋元學案. SPPY.

Hucker, Charles O. *The Censorial System of Ming China*. Stanford: Stanford University Press, 1966.

———, ed. *Chinese Government in Ming Times*. New York: Columbia University Press, 1969.

———. "Governmental Organization of the Ming Dynasty." *Harvard Journal of Asiatic Studies* 21 (1958): 1–66.

———. "The Tung-lin Movement of the Late Ming Period." In *Chinese Thought and Institutions*, 132–62, edited by John K. Fairbank. Chicago: University of Chicago Press, 1957.

Hummel, Arthur W., ed. *Eminent Chinese of the Ch'ing Period*. 2 vols. Washington, D.C.: United States Government Printing Office, 1943–1944.

I Ch'eng chuan 易程傳. Reprint, Taipei: Shih-chieh, 1962.

Jao Tsung-i 饒宗頤. "Fang I-chih chih hua lun" 方以智之畫論. *Journal of the Institute of Chinese Studies* 7 (1974): 113–31.

———. "Fang I-chih yü Ch'en Tzu-sheng" 方以智與陳子升. *Tsing Hua Journal of Chinese Studies* 10 (1974): 170–75.

———. "Painting and the Literati in the Late Ming." Translated by James C. Y. Watt. *Renditions* 6 (1976): 138–43.

Jen Yu-wen. "Ch'en Hsien-chang's Philosophy of the Natural." In *Self and*

Society in Ming Thought, 53–92, edited by W. T. deBary. New York: Columbia University Press, 1970.

Jung Chao-tsu 容肇祖. *Li Chih nien-p'u* 李贄年譜. Peking: San-lien, 1957.

———. *Ming tai ssu-hsiang shih* 明代思想史. Reprint, Taipei: K'ai-ming, 1962.

———. "Fang I-chih ho t'a te ssu-hsiang" 方以智和他的思想. *Ling-nan hsueh pao* 9 (1948): 97–104.

Kessler, Lawrence D. "Chinese Scholars and the Early Manchu State." *Harvard Journal of Asiatic Studies* 31 (1971): 179–200.

Knechtges, David R. "Wit, Humor, and Satire in Early Chinese Literature." *Monumenta Serica* 29 (1970–71): 79–98.

———, and Swanson, Jerry. "Seven Stimuli for the Prince: The *Ch'i-fa* of Mei Ch'eng." *Monumenta Serica* 29 (1970–71): 99–116.

Ko Hung 葛洪. *Pao-p'u Tzu* 抱朴子. SPPY.

———. *Shen hsien chuan* 神仙傳. Reprint, *Po pu ts'ung-shu*, 1966.

Ku Chieh-kang. "A Study of Literary Persecution during the Ming." *Harvard Journal of Asiatic Studies* 3 (1938): 254–311.

Ku Yen-wu 顧炎武. *Jih chih lu chi shih* 日知錄集釋. SPPY.

——— *Ku T'ing-lin shih-wen-chi* 顧亭林詩文集. Peking: Chung-hua, 1959.

———. *T'ien-hsia chün-kuo li-ping shu* 天下郡國利病書. SPTK.

Ku Ying-t'ai 谷應泰. *Ming shih chi shih pen mo* 明史紀事本末. 2 vols. Reprint, Taipei: San-min, 1968.

Kuan tzu 管子. SPTK.

Kuei Yu-kuang 歸有光. *Kuei Yu-kuang ch'üan chi* 歸有光全集. Reprint, Hong Kong: Kuang-chih, 195-.

K'ung Shang-jen 孔尚任. *T'ao hua shan* 桃花扇. Reprint, Peking: Jen-min wen-hsueh, 1959.

Kuo-ch'ao ch'i-hsien lei-cheng ch'u pien 國朝耆獻類徵初編. Compiled by Li Huan 李桓. Reprint, Taipei: Wen-hai, 1966.

Kuo-li chung-yang t'u-shu-kuan 國立中央圖書館. *Ming jen ch'uan-chi tzu-liao su-yin* 明人傳記資料索引. 2 vols. Taipei: Kuo-li chung-yang t'u-shu-kuan, 1965.

Lang Ying 郎瑛. *Ch'i hsiu lei kao* 七修類稿. Reprint, Peking: Chung-hua, 1961.

Lao Kan 勞幹. "Lun Han tai te yu-hsia" 論漢代的游俠. *Wen shih che hsueh-pao* 文史哲學報 1 (1950): 237–52.

Lau, D. C., trans. *Lao tzu: Tao te ching*. Harmondsworth, England: Penguin, 1963.

———, trans. *Mencius*. Harmondsworth, England: Penguin, 1970.

Legge, James, trans. *The Chinese Classics*. 5 vols. Reprint, Hong Kong: Hong Kong University Press, 1960.

Levenson, Joseph R. *Confucian China and Its Modern Fate*. Berkeley: University of California Press, 1968.

Levy, Howard, trans. *A Feast of Mist and Flowers: The Gay Quarters of Nanking at the End of the Ming*. Yokohama: privately published, second printing, 1967.

Lewin, Louis. *Phantastica: Narcotic and Stimulating Drugs: Their Use and Abuse.* London: Kegan Paul, 1931.

Li Chi, trans. *The Travel Diaries of Hsü Hsia-k'o.* Hong Kong: Chinese University of Hong Kong, 1974.

———. "The Changing Concept of the Recluse in Chinese Literature." *Harvard Journal of Asiatic Studies* 24 (1963): 234–47.

Li chi cheng i 禮記正義. SPTK.

Li Shen-i 李愼儀. "'Tung hsi chün' chung 'ho erh erh i' te yuan-i ho shih-chih" '東西均' 中 '合二而一' 的原意和實質. *Che-hsueh yen-chiu* 哲學研究 (1965) no. 3:53–58.

Li Shih-chen 李時珍. *Pen-ts'ao kang-mu* 本草綱目. 2 vols. Reprint, Peking: Jen-min wei-sheng, 1957.

Li Wen-chih 李文治. *Wan Ming min-pien* 晚明民變. Hong Kong: Yuan-tung, 1966.

Li Yü. *Jou Pu Tuan.* Translated by Richard Martin from the German version by Franz Kuhn. New York: Grove Press, 1963.

Liang Ch'i-ch'ao 梁啓超. *Chung-kuo chin san-pai nien hsueh-shu shih* 中國近三百年學術史. Reprint, Taipei: Chung-hua, 1966.

Liang Fang-chung. *The Single-Whip Method of Taxation in China.* Cambridge, Mass.: East Asia Research Center, 1956.

——— 梁方仲. "Ming tai kuo-chi mao-i yü yin te shu-ch'u-ju" 明代國際貿易與銀的輸出入. *Chung-kuo she-hui ching-chi shih chi-k'an* 中國社會經濟史集刊 6 (1939): 266–324.

Liao Ta-wen 廖大聞, et al. *T'ung-ch'eng hsu-hsiu hsien-chih* 桐城續修縣志. 1826; reprint, Taipei: Ch'eng-wen, 1975.

Ling Meng-ch'u 凌濛初. *Erh-k'o po-an ching-ch'i* 二刻拍案驚奇. 2 vols. Reprint, Shanghai: Ku-tien, 1957.

Liu Hsiang 劉向. *Lieh hsien chuan* 列仙傳. Reprint, Taipei: I-wen, 1967.

Liu, James J. Y. *The Chinese Knight-Errant.* London: Routledge and Kegan Paul, 1967.

Liu, James T. C. *Reform in Sung China: Wang An-shih and His New Policies.* Cambridge: Harvard University Press, 1959.

———. "How Did a Neo-Confucian School Become the State Orthodoxy?" *Philosophy East and West* 23 (1973): 483–505.

Liu Lin-sheng 劉麟生. *Chung-kuo p'ien-wen shih* 中國駢文史. Hong Kong: Shang-wu, 1962.

Liu Ts'un-yan 柳存仁. "Ming ju yü Tao-chiao" 明儒與道敎 ("Taoism and Neo-Confucianists in Ming Times"). *Hsin Ya hsueh-pao* 8 (1967): 259–96.

———. "The Penetration of Taoism into the Ming Neo-Confucian Elite." *T'oung Pao* 57 (1971): 31–102.

———. "Taoist Self-Cultivation in Ming Thought." In *Self and Society in Ming Thought,* 291–330, edited by W. T. deBary. New York: Columbia University Press, 1970.

Lo Ch'ang-p'ei 羅常培. "Yeh-su hui-shih tsai yin-yun-hsueh-shang te kung-hsien" 耶穌會士在音韻學上的貢獻. *Kuo-li chung-yang yen-chiu-yuan li-shih yü-yen yen-chiu so chi-k'an* I (1930): 267–338.

Ma Ch'i-ch'ang 馬其昶. *T'ung-ch'eng ch'i chiu chuan* 桐城耆舊傳. Reprint, Taipei: Wen-hai, 1969.

Ma, Y. W. "The Knight-Errant in *Hua-pen* Stories." *T'oung Pao* 61 (1975): 266–300.

Mannheim, Karl. *Essays on the Sociology of Knowledge.* London: Routledge & Kegan Paul, 1952.

Marías, Julián. *Generations: A Historical Method.* Translated by Harold C. Raley. University, Alabama: University of Alabama Press, 1970.

Maspero, Henri. "Le Roman de Sou Ts'in." *Etudes Asiatiques* 2 (1925): 127–41.

McMorran, Ian. "Late Ming Criticism of Wang Yang-ming: The Case of Wang Fu-chih." *Philosophy East and West* 23 (1973): 91–102.

———. "Wang Fu-chih and Neo-Confucian Tradition." In *The Unfolding of Neo-Confucianism,* 413–67, edited by W. T. deBary. New York: Columbia University Press, 1975.

Mencius. *Meng Tzu i chu* 孟子譯註. 2 vols. Peking: Chung-hua, 1960.

Meng Sen 孟森. *Ming tai shih* 明代史. Reprint, Taipei: Chung-hua, 1957.

Merton, Robert K. *Science, Technology and Society in Seventeenth Century England.* Burges, Belgium: Saint Catherine Press, 1938.

Meskill, John. "Academies and Politics During the Ming Dynasty." In *Chinese Government in Ming Times,* 149–74, edited by Charles O. Hucker. New York: Columbia University Press, 1969.

———. "A Conferral of the Degree of *Chin-shih.*" *Monumenta Serica* 23 (1964): 351–71.

Metzger, Thomas A. "The Organizational Capabilities of the Ch'ing State in the Field of Commerce: The Liang-huai Salt Monopoly, 1740–1840." In *Economic Organization in Chinese Society,* 9–45, edited by W. E. Willmott. Stanford: Stanford University Press, 1972.

———. "The State and Commerce in Imperial China." *Asian and African Studies* 6 (1970): 23–46.

Ming Ch'ing li-k'o chin-shih t'i-ming pei-lu 明清歷科進士題名碑錄. 4 vols. Taipei: Hua-wen, 1969.

Ming hui-yao 明會要. Compiled by Lung Wen-pin 龍文彬. 2 vols. Reprint, Shanghai: Chung-hua, 1957.

Ming shih 明史. Compiled by Chang T'ing-yü 張廷玉 and others. 28 vols. Reprint, Peking: Chung-hua, 1974.

Morgan, Evan, trans. *Tao, the Great Luminant: Essays from the Huai Nan Tzu.* Reprint, New York: Paragon, 1969.

Mote, F. W. *The Poet Kao Ch'i, 1336–1374.* Princeton: Princeton University Press, 1962.

———. "Confucian Eremetism in the Yuan Period." In *The Confucian Persua-*

sion, 202–40, edited by A. F. Wright. Stanford: Stanford University Press, 1960.

———. "A Fourteenth-Century Poet: Kao Ch'i." In *Confucian Personalities*, 235–59, edited by A. F. Wright and D. C. Twitchett. Stanford: Stanford University Press, 1962.

Nan-ching ta-hsueh li-shih hsi Chung-kuo ku-tai shih chiao yen-shih 南京大學歷史系中國古代史教研室. *Chung-kuo tzu-pen chu-i meng-ya wen-t'i t'ao-lun chi* 中國資本主義萌芽問題討論集. Peking: San-lien, 1960.

Nan-shih 南史. Compiled by Li Yen-shou 李延壽. 6 vols. Reprint, Peking: Chung-hua, 1975.

Needham, Joseph, et al. *Science and Civilisation in China.* 7 vols. projected. Cambridge: The University Press, 1954–.

Nemoto Makoto 根本誠. *Sensei shakai ni okeru teikō seishin: Chūgoku teki in-itsu no kenkyū* 專制社會における抵抗精神―中國的隱逸の研究. Tokyo: Sōgen, 1952.

Nivison, David S. *The Life and Thought of Chang Hsüeh-ch'eng (1738–1801).* Stanford: Stanford University Press, 1966.

———. "Protest against Conventions and Conventions of Protest." In *The Confucian Persuasion*, 177–201, edited by A. F. Wright. Stanford: Stanford University Press, 1960.

P'an Tze-yen, trans. Mao Hsiang, *Reminiscences of Tung Hsiao-wan.* Shanghai: Commercial Press, 1931.

Parsons, James B. "The Ming Dynasty Bureaucracy: Aspects of Background Forces." In *Chinese Government in Ming Times*, 175–231, edited by Charles O. Hucker, New York: Columbia University Press, 1969.

Pei-ching ta-hsueh wen-k'o yen-chiu so 北京大學文科研究所. *Ming mo nung-min ch'i-i shih-liao* 明末農民起義史料. Peking: K'ai-ming, 1952.

Pei shih 北史. Compiled by Li Yen-shou 李延壽. 10 vols. Reprint, Peking: Chung-hua, 1974.

P'eng Sun-i 彭孫貽. *P'ing k'ou chih* 平寇志. Peiping: Kuo-li Pei-p'ing t'u-shu kuan, 1931.

Peterson, Willard J. "Fang I-chih: Western Learning and the 'Investigation of Things.'" In *The Unfolding of Neo-Confucianism*, 369–411, edited by W. T. deBary. New York: Columbia University Press, 1975.

———. "The Life of Ku Yen-wu (1613–1682)." *Harvard Journal of Asiatic Studies* 28 (1968): 114–56, and 29 (1969): 201–47.

P'u Sung-ling 蒲松齡. *Hsing-shih yin-yuan chuan* 醒世姻緣傳. 2 vols. Reprint, Hong Kong: Chung-hua, 1959.

Ruhlmann, Robert. "Traditional Heroes in Chinese Popular Fiction." In *The Confucian Persuasion*, 141–76, edited by A. F. Wright. Stanford: Stanford University Press, 1960.

Sakade Yoshinobu 坂出祥伸. "Hō I-chi no shisō" 方以智の思想. In *Min-Shin jidai no kagaku gijutsu shi* 明清時代の科學技術史, 93–134, edited by Yabuuchi

Kiyoshi 藪內清 and Yoshida Mitsukuni 吉田光邦. Kyōto: Kyōto daigaku jinbun kagaku kenkyūjo, 1970.

Sakai Tadao. "Confucianism and Popular Educational Works." In *Self and Society in Ming Thought*, 331–66, edited by W. T. deBary. New York: Columbia University Press, 1970.

San kuo chih 三國志. Compiled by Ch'en Shou 陳壽. 5 vols. Reprint, Peking: Chung-hua, 1959.

Schirokauer, Conrad M. "Chu Hsi's Political Career: A Study in Ambivalence." In *Confucian Personalities*, 162–88, edited by A. F. Wright and D. C. Twitchett. Stanford: Stanford University Press, 1962.

Schneider, Laurence A. *Ku Chieh-kang and China's New History: Nationalism and the Quest for Alternative Traditions*. Berkeley: University of California Press, 1971.

Scott, John, trans. *The Lecherous Academician*. London: Rapp and Whiting, 1973.

Seidel, Anna. "A Taoist Immortal of the Ming Dynasty: Chang San-feng." In *Self and Society in Ming Thought*, 483–531, edited by W. T. deBary. New York: Columbia University Press, 1970.

Shang Yen-liu 商衍鎏. *Ch'ing tai k'o-chü k'ao-shih shu lu* 清代科舉考試述錄. Peking: San-lien, 1958.

Shang Yueh 尙鉞. *Chung-kuo tzu-pen chu-i kuan-hsi fa-sheng chi yen-pien te ch'u-pu yen-chiu* 中國資本主义關係發生及演變的初步研究. Peking: San-lien, 1956.

Shih chi 史記. Compiled by Ssu-ma Ch'ien 司馬遷. 10 vols. Reprint, Peking: Chung-hua, 1959.

Shih Jun-chang 施閏章. *Shih Yü-shan ch'üan chi* 施愚山全集. 1747 edition.

Shih shuo hsin yü 世說新語. Reprint, Hong Kong: Chung-hua, 1973.

Shimada Kenji 島田虔次. *Chūgoku ni okeru kindai shii no zazetsu* 中國における近代思惟の挫折. Tokyo: Chikuma, 1949.

Siren, Osvald. *Chinese Painting: Leading Masters and Principles*. 7 vols. London: Percy Lund, Humphries, 1956–58.

———. *A History of Later Chinese Painting*. London: Medici Society, 1938.

Spence, Jonathan. "Opium Smoking in Ch'ing China." In *Conflict and Control in Late Imperial China*, 143–73, edited by Frederic Wakeman, Jr. and Carolyn Grant. Berkeley: University of California Press, 1975.

Strassberg, Richard E. "The Peach Blossom Fan: Personal Cultivation in a Chinese Drama." Ph.D. dissertation, Princeton University, 1975.

Suzuki Tadashi 鈴木正. "Mindai sanjin kō" 明代山人考. In *Shimizu Hakushi Tsuitō Kinen Mindaishi ronsō* 清水博士追悼記念明代史論叢 ("Studies on the Late Ming Period presented to the Late Taiji Shimizu"), 357–88. Tokyo: Daian, 1962.

Ta-jan 大然 and Shih Jun-chang 施閏章. *Ch'ing-yuan shan chih shu* 青原山志書. Fang chang lou 方丈樓, 1669.

Ta Ming hui tien 大明會典. Reprint, Taipei: Tung-nan, 1963.

Tai Ming-shih 戴名世. *Chieh i lu* 孑遺錄. Reprinted in *Ming Ch'ing shih-liao hui pien* 明清史料彙編. Taipei: Wen-hai, 1968.

T'ai-p'ing ching ho-chiao 太平經合校, edited by Wang Ming 王明. Peking: Chung-hua, 1960.

T'ai-p'ing kuang-chi 太平廣記. Reprint, Peking: Jen-min, 1959.

T'an Ch'ien 談遷. *Kuo chueh* 國榷. 6 vols. Peking: Ku-chi, 1958.

T'ang Chen 唐甄. *Ch'ien-shu* 潛書. Peking: Hsin Hua, 1955.

T'ao Hsi-sheng 陶希聖. *Pien-shih yü yu-hsia* 辯士與游俠. Shanghai: Shang-wu, 1931.

T'ao Yuan-ming 陶淵明. *T'ao Yuan-ming chi.* Reprint, Peking: Tso-chia, 1956.

Teng Chih-ch'eng 鄧之誠. *Ch'ing shih chi shih ch'u pien* 清詩紀事初編. 2 vols. Peking: Chung-hua, 1965.

Ting Wen-chiang 丁文江, ed. *Hsu Hsia-k'o yu-chi* 徐霞客遊記. 2 vols. Reprint, Taipei: Ting-wen, 1972.

Tso Yun-p'eng 左云鵬 and Liu Ch'ung-jih 刘重日. "Ming tai Tung-lin tang cheng te she-hui pei-ching chi ch'i yü shih-min yun-tung te kuan-hsi" 明代東林黨爭的社會背景及其與市民運動的關係. *Hsin chien-she* 新建設. 1957 (10): 33–38.

Tu, Wei-ming. *Neo-Confucian Thought in Action: Wang Yang-ming's Youth (1472–1509).* Berkeley: University of California Press, 1976.

Tullock, Gordon. "Paper Money—A Cycle in Cathay." *Economic History Review* 9 (1956–57): 393–407.

T'ung-ch'eng Fang shih ch'i tai i shu 桐城方氏七代遺書. Compiled by Fang Ch'ang-han 方昌翰. 1888.

T'ung-ch'eng Fang shih shih chi 桐城方氏詩輯. 1821.

Wakeman, Frederic, Jr. *History and Will: Philosophical Perspectives of Mao Tse-tung's Thought.* Berkeley: University of California Press, 1973.

———. "The Price of Autonomy: Intellectuals in Ming and Ch'ing Politics." *Daedalus* (Spring 1972): 35–70.

Waley, Arthur, trans. *Analects of Confucius.* London: Allen & Unwin, 1938.

———. *The Life and Times of Po Chü-i.* London: Allen & Unwin, 1949.

———. *Translations from the Chinese.* New York: Knopf, 1941.

Wang Fu-chih 王夫之. *Ch'uan-shan ch'üan chi* 船山全集. Reprint, Taipei: Ta-yuan, 1965.

Wang Shu-nu 王書奴. *Chung-kuo ch'ang-chi shih* 中國娼妓史. Shanghai: Sheng-huo, 1935.

Wang, Tch'ang-tche. *La Philosophie Morale de Wang Yang-ming.* Paris: Geuthner, 1936.

Wang Yang-ming 王陽明. *Wang Wen-ch'eng kung ch'üan shu* 王文成公全書. SPTK.

Wang Yao 王瑤, ed. *T'ao Yuan-ming chi* 陶淵明集. Peking: Tso-chia, 1956.

Ware, James R., trans. *Alchemy, Medicine, Religion in the China of A.D. 320: The Nei P'ien of Ko Hung*. Cambridge: M.I.T. Press, 1966.

Watson, Burton. *Ssu-ma Ch'ien, Grand Historian of China*. New York: Columbia University Press, 1958.

———, trans. *Chinese Rhyme-Prose; poems in the fu form from the Han and Six Dynasties Periods*. New York: Columbia University Press, 1971.

———, trans. *Complete Works of Chuang Tzu*. New York: Columbia University Press, 1968.

———, trans. *Courtier and Commoner in Ancient China: Selections from the History of the Former Han by Pan Ku*. New York: Columbia University Press, 1974.

———, trans. *Records of the Grand Historian of China*. 2 vols. New York: Columbia University Press, 1961.

Wen Chü-min 溫聚民. *Wei Shu-tzu nien-p'u* 魏叔子年譜. Shanghai: Shang-wu, 1936.

Wen hsuan 文選. Compiled by Hsiao T'ung 蕭統. SPTK.

Wiens, Mi Chü. "Cotton Textile Production and Rural Social Transformation in Early Modern China." *Journal of the Institute of Chinese Studies of the Chinese University of Hong Kong* 7 (1974): 515–34.

———. "The Origins of Modern Chinese Landlordism." In *Shen Kang-po pa chih jung-ch'ing lun-wen-chi* 沈剛伯八秩榮慶論文集 ("Festschrift in Honor of the Eightieth Birthday of Professor Shen Kang-po"), 285–344. Taipei: Lien-ching, 1976.

Wilhelm, Hellmut. "Chinese Confucianism on the Eve of the Great Encounter." In *Changing Japanese Attitudes toward Modernization*, 283–310, edited by M. B. Jansen. Princeton: Princeton University Press, 1965.

———. "On Ming Orthodoxy." *Monumenta Serica* 29 (1970–71): 1–26.

———. "The Po-hsüeh Hung-ju Examination of 1679." *Journal of the American Oriental Society* 71 (1951): 60–66.

Wilhelm, Richard, trans. *The I Ching, or Book of Changes*. Rendered into English by Cary F. Baynes. 2 vols. New York: Bollingen, Pantheon, 1950.

Williamson, H. R. *Wang An-shih, A Chinese Statesman and Educationalist of the Sung Dynasty*. 2 vols. London: Probsthain, 1935.

Wu Ching-tzu 吳敬梓. *Ju lin wai shih* 儒林外史. Reprint, Hong Kong: Yu-lien, 1963(?).

———. *The Scholars (Ju lin wai shih)*. Peking: Foreign Languages Press, 1973.

Wu, K. T. "Ming Printing and Printers." *Harvard Journal of Asiatic Studies* 7 (1942–43): 203–60.

Wu, Nelson I. "Tung Ch'i-ch'ang (1555–1636): Apathy in Government and Fervor in Art." In *Confucian Personalities*, 260–93, edited by A. F. Wright and D. C. Twitchett. Stanford: Stanford University Press, 1962.

Wu Ying-chi 吳應箕. *Ch'i-Chen liang ch'ao po fu lu* 啓禎兩朝剝復錄. 1900 edition.

———. *Liu-tu wen chien lu* 留都聞見錄. 1900 edition.

Yang Ch'i-ch'iao 楊啓樵. "Ming tai chu ti chih ch'ung-shang fang-shu chi ch'i ying-hsiang" 明代諸帝之崇尚方術及其影響. In *Ming tai tsung-chiao* 明代宗教, 203–97. Taipei: Hsueh-sheng, 1968.

Yang Hsiung 揚雄. *Fa yen* 法言, in *Han Wei ts'ung-shu* 漢魏叢書. Reprint, Taipei: I-wen, 1967.

Yang, Lien-sheng. "Historical Notes on the Chinese World Order." In *The Chinese World Order: Traditional China's Foreign Relations*, 20–33, edited by John K. Fairbank. Cambridge: Harvard University Press, 1968.

———. "Ming Local Administration." In *Chinese Government in Ming Times*, 1–21, edited by Charles O. Hucker. New York: Columbia University Press, 1969.

Yang T'ing-fu 楊廷福. *Ming mo san ta ssu-hsiang-chia* 明末三大思想家. Shang-hai: Ssu-lien, 1955.

Yen tzu ch'un ch'iu chi shih 晏子春秋集釋. 2 vols. Reprint, Peking: Chung-hua, 1962.

Yoshikawa Kojirō 吉川幸次郎. *Gen Min shi gaisetsu* 元明詩概說. In *Chūgoku shijin senshū* 中國詩人選集, part 2, vol. 2. Tokyo: Iwanami, 1963.

Yü Che 余哲. "Fang I-chih te chu-shu chi ch'i sheng-p'ing" 方以智的著述及其生平. In *I lin ts'ung lu* 藝林叢錄, vol. 6. 319–22. Hong Kong: Shang-wu, 1966.

Yü Huai 余懷. *Pan-ch'iao tsa chi* 板橋雜記. Collated edition privately published by Howard S. Levy: Yokohama, 1966.

Yü Teng 于登. "Ming tai chien-ch'a chih-tu kai-shu" 明代監察制度概述. *Chin-ling hsueh-pao* 金陵學報 6 (1936): 213–29.

Yü Ying-shih 余英時. *Fang I-chih wan chieh k'ao* 方以智晚節考. Hong Kong: Hsin Ya yen-chiu so, 1972.

———. "Life and Immortality in Han China." *Harvard Journal of Asiatic Studies* 25 (1964–65): 80–122.

———. "Some Preliminary Observations on the Rise of Ch'ing Confucian Intellectualism." *Tsing Hua Journal of Chinese Studies* 11 (Dec. 1975): 105–46.

———. "Ts'ung Sung Ming ju-hsueh te fa-chan lun Ch'ing tai ssu-hsiang shih" 從宋明儒學的發展論清代思想史. *Chung-kuo hsueh-jen* 2 (1970): 19–41.

Yueh-jen 越人. "Kuan yü Fang I-chih te sheng-p'ing ho nien-shou" 關於方以智的生平和年壽. In *I lin ts'ung lu*, vol. 6. 322–23. Hong Kong: Shang-wu, 1966.

Index